The Blood of The Covenant

Andy J N McRae

Hope you enjoy
Andy's

Published through AJNMBOOKS
Andy McRae / AJNMBooks
Unit 149425
PO Box 7169,
Poole,
BH15 9EL
United Kingdom
© Copyright 2025 Andy J N McRae
Andy J N McRae possess all legal and moral rights to be recognised as the creator of this work
Paperback ISBN: 978-1-0369-1612-1

This novel is entirely a work of fiction. The names, characters, and events described are all works of the authors imagination. Any resemblance of actual persons, living or dead, is purely coincidental.

All rights reserved.

No AI has been used in the production of this work. The author is vehemently against the use of AI to create art, and deeply concerned as to its environmental impact. As such this work should not be used in part or in whole to train or create with generative AI.

Praise

for The Blood of The Covenant

McRae is the master of suspense, red herrings and surprises and a true magic wielder of unique character voice. Prepare yourselves for a thrilling page-turner full of darkness and joy in equal measure, exquisite handling of the queer experience and characters you will never forget. Andy J N McRae is here to leave his mark on the reading world and his moon is about to rise.

— J. M. Rose, author of *Usurper*

A love-letter to queer youth and found families.

— Jake Vanguard, author of *First Snow, First Rose* and *Higanbana*

*This book is for my **mates**. For late night buses, trains and training sessions. For hair-dye. For handwritten notes. For blanket forts and video games. For running through the rain.*

This book is also dedicated to people like Mitch, Oscar, Lolly, Radwa, and Wren. This novel is for us because we deserve to see ourselves as something more.

Trigger Warnings

The Blood of The Covenant acts in part as an extended criticism of the challenges the patriarchy presents for queer and trans people. As such there is a notable critique of rape culture. The novel contains references to this theme as well as homophobia, transphobia, poor mental health, and abuse received as a result of coming out.

The novel does not intend to use these for shock factor but to make a social critique on some of the *real* challenges faced by queer and trans youth.

This book comes with the following specific trigger warnings.

Brief or coded mention:

War, Childhood Sexual Assault, Suicide Attempt, Transphobia, Homophobia, Deadnaming

(All characters who have changed their names have their deadnames redacted and represented with '____'.)

Multiple or moderate mentions, and mentions of previous experiences without detail on what, where and how:

Spiking, Rape (previous or implied), **Self Harm** (either previous or vague), **Eating Disorder Recovery** (no numbers or methods), **Dermatillomania, Torture, Physical Abuse**

Graphic descriptions, sensitive but detailed:

BPD, Autistic Meltdowns, PTSD, OCD, Coming Out, Homelessness, Neglect, Physical Fights Werewolf transformation, Cannibalism

The Blood of The Covenant is a novel intended for older Young Adult audiences and New Adult audiences, and as such contains explicit swearing and fade-to-black sexual content.

Prologue

Mitch

I remember the night the wolf came. It doesn't feel like nearly three years have passed. Every time I recall that night I shift back to being that scared, scrawny, seventeen-year-old boy.

I was with my sister, Mel, and her friend, Val. Mel was going through a breakup. The guy had cheated on her. He threatened to hurt himself if she broke up with him, and, while I'm not sure it was on purpose, he did end up getting jumped one night shortly after she called it off. She was convinced this was her fault and was really cut up about it.

So, I decided to take her and Val out for ice cream. I decided we should walk by the river afterwards. I decided to take the route home that passed through the woods near the school.

The wolf met us on that path, and for the next two years, Val and I walked along it every single day. Mel didn't. Each thing I *decided* led my sister to her death.

The path where my little sister bled out is now bordered with fucking flower boxes. To 'honour' her. That's what we do when people die – we have to make it somehow beautiful, instead of acknowledging the fact it's a fucking tragedy.

Well, there was nothing beautiful about the way our blood crusted our clothes to our skin. There was nothing romantic about Val pulling me away from the body of my sister to stop me from bleeding out through the slash across my throat. No one will write poetry about the 'mats of blood in Val's bubblegum pink hair' and how it 'represented the loss of innocence'.

No one should. If you ask me, anyone who tries to make the murder and mutilation of a fifteen-year-old poetic is a fucking dickhead.

To honour her. What does that even really mean in terms of death? Christians, like me, believe if you live an honourable life you'll get sent to Heaven. The Norse believed if you die an honourable death you'd go to Valhalla.

Mel's death wasn't honourable, and her life had barely begun.

To me, honour is a term associated with martial arts. It's one of our tenets. 'In fighting, choose with sense and honour.' It means don't showboat by choosing the hardest battle, but don't pick on the little guy either. That's why I say Mel's death had no honour, because whoever killed her was a fucking coward.

Val

Things started to change a week later, just after Mel's funeral. She had been buried quickly and the community rallied around her family.

All that week I felt ill. I assumed it was grief. After all, my best friend, the girl I'd imagined as the maid of honour on my wedding day, was gone.

I had this headache I couldn't shake, like when you have the flu and your nose gets blocked up to the point where you can feel the pressure behind your eyes. Everything was too bright.

It was odd, though. Usually when I'm ill, everything looks fuzzy, as if seen through someone else's glasses. Now, everything was in ultra-high-definition, like I'd never seen clearly before. When our eyes changed colour they expected the opposite to be true. They thought maybe we'd been scratched there and the tissue was damaged. But no. We were acutely aware of our surroundings: sights, sounds and most especially scents.

Everything smelled like Mel, even days after she passed. The heavy air carried our longing for her in fresh notes of her citrus perfume. I'd later find out this was just how grief smelt.

Mitch experienced changes too. First it was the eyes, his green and brown heterochromia which changed to silver and gold. But that wasn't all. His body ran warmer, and it ached like he had a fever, too. But then, he had just started new medication, and he was still recovering from the attack. We chalked it up to that. We thought that nothing would come of it. We hoped.

I was staying over at Mitch's when we realised something was truly wrong. It was early, maybe eight or nine. I always wake up before Mitch. Him and Mel were so bad for sleeping in I started bringing books to sleepovers.

Propping myself up on the pillows, I sat up to read an Ian Rankin novel. In those days I found comfort in crime novels: bad guys getting caught and explanations of why bad things happened to innocent victims.

Mitch's soundly sleeping form sprawled across three quarters of the bed next to me, the silver cross he wore around his neck glinting in the sun. His skin burned red, hot to the touch, wherever the metal had been. He had not yet replaced it with a titanium one.

Mel's death brought her family closer to God. They find comfort in the idea that she is in a better place. If anything, it's what made me leave the church. The idea that good people go to Heaven and bad people go to Hell became too simple for me. I'd much prefer it if the bastard got their come-uppance here – where someone who loved her can ensure it's justly delivered.

I cracked the book open. That was when a sharp pain stung my thigh.

I pulled back the covers, thinking I'd been bitten by something. I was bleeding. Worried that I might've popped some stitches, I turned to shake Mitch awake, only to find he wasn't there next to me.

It was then I realised that my skin was a shade or two darker than normal. A cooler, more olive tone compared to my usual warmth inherited from my dad's Dominican genes.

My hands were more slender, fingers willowy. There was a cloth pressed against my leg I didn't remember picking up. I had been transported into someone else's reality. Radwa's reality.

I remember knowing exactly what she was thinking. Like I was her and she was me.

Three things became clear immediately.

The reality I was seeing was that of a girl not far off my own age. There was nothing about her thoughts that made this clear. It was more that she knew this instinctively so in turn I did as well.

The next thing I realised was that she was trans. This information didn't just sit there on the surface; it was weighing on her mind. She hadn't told anyone yet.

Finally I realised, from the desperation of her thoughts and the heavy burden of guilt and shame, that the wound was intentional and self-inflicted.

She knew what had happened but she couldn't remember doing it. She had blacked out in a fit of emotion so strong that it felt like anger but it wasn't nearly as simple as that.

She had wanted the emotions to shut up for a second but

they hadn't really. They'd just been replaced with regret, fear, and utter disgust with herself.

Shit, I thought, looking down at the scene through her eyes.

She jumped. Her heart hammered as she pulled the cloth tighter to her thigh, trying to hide the fresh wounds. The scent of blood and silver sliced through the air like sharpened scissors through silk.

Hello? she called out, internal voice angry. It always was with her back then.

Hi, I tried.

Who's there? How are you there? Get out of my head! She felt violated.

Wish I could, I admitted. *Don't know how I got here. My name's Valeria, but I'd say you've earned the right to call me Val right now. What about you?*

She tried to tell me her deadname, voice small, lacking all personality.

I stopped her. That's not the kind of information I wanted to know about her. I wanted to know who she was, not what other people called her.

I'm in your head, I told her. *I know, and it's okay. I'm bi, and I have friends who are trans. You're safe with me.*

Relief had washed over her thoughts. It smelt warm and sweet like cardamom. *…Radwa.*

I knew from the way she said it that this was the name that belonged to her. The sound captured her spirit.

Okay, Radwa, I started, *any idea how I can hear you right now?*

I dunno, everything's been weird since the night we were attacked. Her thoughts immediately became defensive. *Was it you?*

That attacked you? I asked.

Yes, she demanded.

No! I was appalled at the thought.

She settled. *Then, was it you who was screaming? The night that the wolf came?*

It was my turn to feel exposed as my mind rushed: Mel's body, her dead stare looking up at us. Mitch's warm sticky blood under my finger as I clamped my hand over his throat hoping against hope I wouldn't lose him too. I was definitely screaming, screaming for all three of us, because neither he nor Mel could.

Can you meet me? she asked upon seeing this. *I'll introduce you to my friend who was with me.*

Leaving her mind was almost as jarring as entering it, like when you're video calling someone and you're able to see them, hear their voice, and then your phone dies mid-conversation and you're left sitting in silence with nothing but the four walls around you.

I got up and pulled on one of Mitch's hoodies before dragging him out of bed. We weren't dating then but we were close enough that he let me do it anyway.

'What's up?' he mumbled groggily.

I tossed him his binder. 'I think I've found someone else who was attacked.'

Lolly

Radwa and I met on the night of the attack. She had been battering a stick off a tree. I shouted at her to stop.

Before that, I was just watching from my little corner of the forest floor, surrounded by mushrooms, picking at the ladders in my tights. I don't think she realised that I was watching her. We were quiet until then, both clearly not in the mood to talk, both hiding from something or someone.

Then we heard the screams and went to investigate. Fight, flight or freeze right? I've never been the kind of person who knows when to run. Before they took him away, dad used to warn me it was the kind of thing that would get me in shit one day. Maybe he's right. I mean, he would know.

And you're not really meant to run towards screams and jump in front of danger but I've fucking never learnt. Without thinking about how 'ladylike' it was, I had gathered my overly long school skirt in one hand and knotted it so I could run freely.

'Wait!' Radwa yelled, frozen momentarily, bouncing on her feet, before eventually giving up on stopping me and deciding instead to follow after. She likes to think things through a lot more than I do.

We were both bitten. Mine was around the bottom of my leg. She helped me hobble home, giving me her hoodie to keep me warm when the heavens opened up.

We only learned later about the girl that had died; we never did reach Mitch and Val. I didn't really know Mel. I mean, we went to school together, but she was popular and I was sort of one of the weird in-between kids.

Honestly? My immediate thought when hearing about her death was absolute horror that it could've been me or Radwa. Once I got to know Mitch I grieved for the person he lost, for a person I never knew, but I didn't really feel it so heavily at the time.

Radwa thought we should've reached out, but it seemed insensitive – like we were trying to make their grief about us. I'd be pretty pissed off if some randomers showed up on my doorstep after I had been through something that massive.

We got off lucky with a bite. Or at least, we thought we did. That was before we knew it wasn't just a regular wolf.

She called me a week later, her voice frantic on the phone. 'Lolly? Hello? Lolly!'

'Hey! Hold your horses, I'm right here, what's up?' My alarm clock read *8:45 am*. Fucking really? I only got to sleep three hours ago.

Unravelling myself from the covers, I gagged at the sour

smell seeping through the curtain that hung where I once had a door. Mam's vomit had missed the toilet the night before and was now drying in the hallway. Just another wine red stain on the carpet.

'You said to call you if I needed anything after' – she paused as if imploring me to understand – 'that night.'

'Okay, so what do you need?' I pushed myself up out of bed and put my glasses on.

'So I was in my room alone, right, and I heard this voice. This girl – Val – her name is Val. She started talking to me in my head, and – she's the same Val from the report, okay? She was attacked the same night as us, so anyway, I need you to meet me at mine in fifteen minutes, okay?'

'Okay, so you're hearing voices?'

'I know how it sounds but—'

I laid back down and started fidgeting with my duvet cover. 'Okay, okay, it's totally chill, don't panic. Did I mention when we first met that I hallucinate? It's perfectly okay, we just need to find someone for you to talk through things with. Maybe it's a trauma response, maybe—'

Lolly, I need you to meet me at mine in fifteen minutes okay? her voice echoed in my mind.

Of course then I had to meet her, and I was glad I did, because that was the day I met some of my best friends.

Radwa

The one thing I remember the most about the year that followed the attack was feeling on edge all the time. The sensation was ever present and red hot. People tiptoed around waiting for me to combust.

I regret snapping at my younger brothers when they snuck up on me researching 'how to come out as trans' on our shared laptop. They didn't understand and I knew I couldn't tell them yet. My parents had to be the first to know after Val.

The closer I got to fifteen the more desperate I became to come out while I was still 'young enough'. The pressure was mostly from myself; if I came out before anything permanent happened, maybe it would be easier for me. Maybe I could stop everything from changing. I was also afraid that my self-destructive urges would get the better of me and that something even more permanent would happen.

But every time I tried to tell my mum, either my nerves got the better of me or her temper did. I'd approach her in the kitchen, flicking the kettle on in the hopes we could have a heart-to-heart, only to be greeted with the heavy sound of porcelain banging against the metal draining board – an immediate indication of her mood.

Back then the pack saw me cranky quite often. Lolly affectionately nicknamed these episodes my 'storms', because initially I seemed very calm, then everything poured down at once. The weather forecast was always cloudy back then, between turning and coming out. No one does 'emotional' quite like a freshly turned, pubescent werewolf.

My post-moon fights with my parents, when they found out I'd snuck out, didn't help.

The pack quickly discovered that turning at home was much too dangerous. Lolly and I managed to lock ourselves in our respective houses because our families were both out. That's how we learnt that when enclosed the wolf form became more agitated. Many pillows were sacrificed to that discovery. I hurt myself quite badly too.

Val and Mitch went camping, anticipating that something might be on the horizon. They seemed to get on slightly better. It became apparent we needed space to run and play and… hunt.

The others sometimes chase after small animals because of the prey drive. Fortunately, I seem to remember my vegetarian diet. We're still *there* when we turn, just more energetic and impulsive. But we still hold onto our human conscience.

Lolly and Mitch found an old derelict house when out walking together before the next moon. It was covered in graffiti, broken glass and all sorts when we first got there, but we managed to make it cosy enough. We slowly moved in sleeping bags, blow-up mattresses and garden chairs. The best thing we ever found was a second hand couch Mitch made us carry for like a mile and a half.

We started staying there which meant I had to start sneaking out, and that was where the issue began.

My parents weren't extremely strict, but they were strict enough to keep me out of the trouble that usually accompanies that sort of behaviour. Of course, they assumed it was linked to drinking, or girls – the truth lay far outside their imagination.

Me being me back then I didn't see them as protective. I just saw myself being stuck in a cycle of these emotional hurricanes with Mum.

That first year, Mum and I fought a lot. The silent lead ups to the storms would hold the house in suspense for days before it all kicked off again.

That's why I left after I eventually came out. My friend Aadilla and her parents found out first. Luckily they took it well and gave me some hope for my own family. But my parents, like many parents, didn't quite know what to think. My big gender reveal literally stunned the whole house into silence.

I waited for a day, then three more, then a week, then a month. Then, after that month, I exploded. I was so scared for the storm to start that I started it myself.

I remember them constantly saying, 'We're not kicking you out, we would never do that.'

And I bitterly thought, *Wow, thanks for doing the bare minimum.*

Harsh as that reaction may be, it felt justified for how raw my pain was. I don't think I can even begin to explain the pain and frustration that comes with being a trans teenager. The road to becoming yourself can often be paved with sharp and jagged stones, and while the journey can be beautiful, that initial stretch is always the hardest. First there is coming out to ourselves, which is a battle that can last years. I was confused for so long before I found the word for how I felt: 'transgender'. It felt as warm and welcoming as it did terrifying. It took even longer to figure out how to say it aloud. When I finally did I didn't want to give anyone 'more time'. I just wanted to be seen.

So I packed my bags and went to the only place I could. I went to Val's. Ever since the first day she heard me, Val has acted as my best friend, my sister, my rock. I got over my storms by learning how to communicate my needs better. There aren't really words to describe how thankful I am to her family for taking me in and letting me grow how I wanted to.

My Dad eventually did see me for who I am. He even uses my name and – more than once – he's begged me to move back home. I never have. It's partly my pride. I'm embarrassed to have been so moody back then. It's partly my mum, who hasn't quite come around to using my name yet and has the final say on everything in the household. It's partly because being here makes it less complicated on the full moon.

I think it's also because, after two and a bit years, I've grown to like it here. And while I love my family, that initial blow when I first came out has left our relationship fragmented. There are wounds I've not quite stitched closed yet. Besides, I'm going to university soon anyway.

And, after everything I've been through, everything *we've* been through, we seem to have gotten through it. Other than our monthly transformations and a lifetime of trauma, life is finally back to normal.

Chapter One

Mitch

The static from the clingy blue hair net makes my hair stand up straight as I tug it off, making my way out the door. Today is the first day of the summer holidays, or it would be if I was still in school. Instead it's just another Friday that sees me home from work at twelve after a seven hour shift, stinking of fucking fish.

It's been years since the incident – two years and nine months, to be exact.

I've been working overtime the entire week so I'm well and truly in need of a joint. I'll settle for a cuppa while it's still sunny outside, before the burning heat and smell of barbeques start to intrude on my every sense.

On paper, I have the next couple of days off so I can get a break and help out with my church's summer camp. But it's the full moon tomorrow so it's not half as relaxing as it sounds.

Fortunately the walk back from work isn't very long. It's honestly easier to walk than it is to fight for my parking space when I get back.

This appears to be especially true today because there's a van parked behind the resident cars. It looks like someone's moving into the house next door. The council really wasted no time on getting someone else moved in, did they? Fuck me. The last tenant is barely in his grave.

Life just goes on I guess.

He was a younger guy, lived with his brother. They were one of those families everyone knows, you know? I think he had a kid and all.

His was just one more body to show up recently. Animal attacks, they say.

Then again I don't know any animal that hunts once monthly for human flesh. Your man went missing for quite a bit before he showed up, and the state his body was in – I didn't see, but from what I've heard they couldn't have a viewing.

Well, what Mum's heard. She's a gossip, I swear. She prides herself in knowing what's going on around here. The attacks especially are kind of an obsession. It didn't used to be so bad, only once or twice a year. Then it became every second month. In the past three months it's multiple, and Mum is almost as hooked as we've been.

As soon as she hears anything, it's relayed to me, Dad and Lolly over dinner – usually with the tag lines 'now you didn't hear this from me' or 'now this goes no further' as if any of us are in communication with anyone who would give a single fuck – except maybe the girls, but they have usually already found out over the radio system Lolly hacked for Radwa a couple months back.

Right now, Mum's conveniently decided that it is the best time to put her washing away so that she can peer over the mossy fence to see what's going on.

'You're terrible,' I mouth to her as I walk in. She waves me away with a flick of the towel.

Dad's in the kitchen making tea when I get in and start

taking my lunchbox out of my bag.

People always say I look like my dad. He leans over the kitchen counter. He's taller, not exactly clean-shaven, and yet I still see it. I look like him when he was younger: we're both covered in freckles, we both have the same bump in our nose, we both have big front teeth and full cheeks. I like looking like him. Through him I've got a vision for what I might look like after some time on T.

The concept makes me kind of giddy. I wonder how long it'll take to notice that my face is shifting into something more like his, where my hair will grow first, what I'll be doing when my voice first breaks.

I suppress my beam, looking down at the floor as I place mine and Lolly's mugs next to his, trying to act natural. 'You're not planning on being a one cup wonder are you?'

He chuckles, taking the teabags back out.

'New neighbours,' I add, nodding to the side as I bin the apple core and take the tupperware over to the sink.

'Aye, your mum and Lin next door have been conspiring on how they got the house.' He chuckles fondly, putting the sugar back in the cupboard. 'I helped them move a couple of heavier boxes. It was taking the dad and the two older kids to move just one.'

'Did you find out what was in them?' I ask, my mum's curiosity bleeding through into me.

Dad shrugs. 'Seemed nice though.'

Just then, Mum comes bustling through the door with the washing. 'I've not had the chance to talk to them yet. Here Mitch, go water my hanging baskets, see if you can find anything out.' She hands me a half full jug.

The soil is already damp when I get there. Great. That doesn't look suspicious at all.

'I think your mum already got that one,' one of the older kids, who looks about my age, says conversationally through the slats of the fence. They're holding a tall cage, covered with a light blanket, in their arms. Resting it on the old coal bunker in the corner, they turn back to look at a little kid toddling around the garden with a husky, holding a chewy dog toy.

'That,' I laugh, tapping the slat on the fence between us, 'is becoming very apparent.'

They smile, collecting their thin brown braids up into a ponytail and rolling up their sleeves. 'You're Mitch, right?'

'How did you—?' I start to ask, confused.

'The patches on your vest.' They point to the patches embroidered on the battle vest by the kids at church camp when I helped them learn how to sew last year.

Usually I wear a leather jacket. The kids have sewn the arms shut a few too many times. But summer has called for a transition to the vest. Five little letters across the top spell out my name.

'Sorry, does reading it off of there give a kind of stalker vibe?' They laugh awkwardly.

Because bringing up the idea of stalking someone is really chill the first time you meet them.

I scrunch my nose up with a grimace. 'It's kinda why I wear this. So that people know who I am. That I'm not a prick.'

They laugh a little too hard at that. Then they pause, scanning over the badges on my chest with their eyes. I know I said I wear them to be read, but when people bend over like this to read them it makes my skin crawl. I hold it away from my body purposefully while they read. 'Well, let's see: Mitch, he/him, not a prick.'

I scoff. 'Yup, that about covers it. And you?' I ask, gesturing towards them.

'Oh, Wren, they/them. Also not a prick.' They hold their hand to their chest. My lips pull up into a smile despite myself. New people moving in is chaotic but the possibility of new trans friends is always pretty fucking cool

The covered cage next to them squawks which in turn sets

their husky yelping. They rest the cage on their hip and turn to look at the dog pointedly. It tilts its head to the side before giving a final disgruntled whine and sulking off to the corner.

In the near distance, a younger teenage boy emerges from the van. He's wearing all black and carrying the back end of a couch in one hand. The other hand is on his phone, texting. I squint at him. His long, lanky limbs do not look strong enough to hold that amount of weight. He catches my gaze mid-thought and jumps a little, then as if on cue puts both hands on the couch. The tall bald man on the other end gives Wren an upwards nod.

'Being summoned.' They laugh. 'Catch you around I guess.'

I set the jug down and hurry back inside to get a quick shower before church, just managing to feed the rats all while dodging Mum's tirade of questions.

By the time I've cleaned up we have to get in the car. Dad passes me a travel mug of tea on the way out. So much for time to chill.

Oh well. Seeing Val tonight is my real chance to switch off.

I still have a day before the moon, I tell myself. One more day to chill. And, if the pharmacy finally has it in, I'm starting testosterone today. Today doesn't have to be a write-off. So many were when we first turned, and so many seem futile even now. But it's just one day a month, twelve days in a year. If I think any further it starts to get depressing. First today, then tomorrow.

My phone buzzes loudly in my back pocket. It's Val.

We can talk to each other in our heads but texting is just more polite. Sometimes you don't want your best mates perving around in your mind, like when you're showering and don't want a live studio audience. Val often needs a reminder of this. Admittedly we all accidentally hear random shit like, *I need to pee,* or, *should I make coffee?* but generally, you get the hang of drowning people out at inappropriate times. Although Lolly is the worst for accidentally letting people hear shit.

Val's asking about plans for later. I text her back.

> MITCH
> I'll drive over after the
> pharmacy and church. Mine is a
> bit loud cause we have new
> neighbours moving in :/ xx

She takes a second to reply. She's probably crafting. Without even hopping into her head I can picture her sitting on the couch with her knitting, in her pyjamas, hair tied up in a bun so it doesn't get tangled in the wool. She looks so serious when she's doing that. The effect is counteracted by the fact she sticks her tongue out while she concentrates.

> VAL
> You excited? Moved them in quick
> didn't they? Xx

Her and my mum could go for hours over a cuppa I swear.

I start to reply to her text, trying to find a way to explain that I'm equally excited and nervous. I've spent enough years thinking it over to come to the conclusion that starting T is right for me, but I've heard it can make people more anxious, which wouldn't be great for my PTSD. Plus I didn't have any acne during my first puberty, so I figure I can only be that lucky once.

A new text buzzes onto the top of my screen as I'm replying.

> LOLLY
> You still cool to give me and
> Radwa a lift to the party
> tonight?

Shit, I completely forgot about that. Anyone else I would

tell to fuck off. Not Lolly though.

I look out for all my friends but especially Lolly. My family is all the support they've really got. They've been living with us on and off since the attack. I don't quite remember how it started; I think they just showed up and refused to leave. That, or mum refused to let them.

Either way, I'd rather give up some of my time to drop them off somewhere than see them in the state they are in after visiting their mum any day. I guess I'll just have to wait a little longer for that joint.

Lolly

The shop door bell jingles when I walk in, signalling my arrival to Iain who's sitting with his head sticking out the door at the back of the shop while he smokes.

Usually I don't come into work on my days off, but I keep seeing this one crystal online and I feel like it's a sign I need it. Malachite. It's supposed to be good for courage and luck, and I'm going to a party with Radwa tonight so I could use some of that.

The shop smells like incense – it always does, but it's 'Dragon's Blood' specifically today. I'm a fan of sage or lavender, personally. The stronger smells are bad for wolf senses, and this one gives me a headache pretty quickly. It used to be one of my favourites as well.

There are new books on the shelf by the tarot cards. I pick up one on the *Sidhe* written in *Gàidhlig* and another one on The Morrigan when the door opens again and the wind-chimes hanging above the mirror in the corner start to clunk off of one another.

Someone walks in carrying a tote bag sporting the non-binary flag. Their bare arms show a mass of black ink tattoos. They're so impossibly pretty. How is it fair that people like that exist – blessed with the height and grace of a ballet dancer, capable of drawing eyeliner sharp enough to cut someone – when I'm lucky if I can reach the kitchen cupboard without climbing, and luckier if I can get there without falling or pulling something? The Gods must have favourites.

I ding the bell repeatedly for Iain.

'Alright, I'm coming,' Iain groans from the corner, stubbing his joint out against the door frame and rattling his way through the beaded curtain to the back room.

Iain is the manager/owner of the shop. He's always high, and I don't think I've ever seen him wear anything other than his one green-and-brown Baja hoodie and patchwork tribal pants that *stink* of weed so badly that it chokes you. You get high just standing next to him – and if I'm saying that, you know something is wrong.

Most people around here call him Jesus. I don't know who started it but it's probably to do with the long hair and goatee combination. In a small town like this, if you've got something noticeable you're getting a nickname. And if you're as much of a character as Jesus is you're *definitely* getting a nickname. It's usually a sign of affection, believe it or not.

'Oh, Kearney, it's you!' he says with a smile. 'I was going to text you. We got tapestries that your goth friend might like.'

My nickname is just my surname. The most notable thing about me is my dad. I can't move in this place without someone recognising me as his kid. It's sweet. I like it.

'Val,' I return, rolling my eyes. 'She has a name, you know, and I'm pretty sure we rely on her purchases to pay rent so you should probably learn it.'

He chuckles at this, pointing at me with a crisp packet in one hand that he's just retrieved from behind the counter. Then he looks at me, confused. 'Are you supposed to be working today?'

I shake my head. 'Nah, I'm just looking for a crystal. We got any malachite?'

'Nah. It's hard to store because of the toxicity,' he says. 'Reacts to water and skin.'

Maybe I should've researched more. I just heard it would help and decided to go for it no matter what.

'What do you need it for?' he asks, walking around the counter, bare feet slapping off the lino. Jesus doesn't believe in shoes.

'Courage and good luck,' I confess.

'Exams again?' he asks, peering over the shelf to look at what he's got.

'Nah, they're done. I have a party,' I tell him. Jesus is honestly more like a friend than a manager. He knows a shit ton about my life so I don't mind telling him the truth.

'Ah, your girlfriend's gonna be there, huh?' he asks.

'Shut up.' I shove his arm.

Everyone knows I like Radwa. Or at least, everyone except her.

We're not dating, but we do treat each other differently from our other friends: we message every night, and sometimes we fall asleep calling each other. I've never tried to push it further. The last thing I want to do is make her uncomfortable.

So we're in this weird space where we're not just friends but she doesn't even know I like her. I guess from her perspective we actually might just be friends… But me? Fuck. I've been in love with her for years now.

I turn to the person stood behind me, eyeing up the jewellery on the shelf next to the clothing rails. I know that shelf like the back of my hand. I got Mitch some red jasper pendants that he wears on a trouser chain. 'Can I help you while he does that? I actually work here, just not today.' I laugh.

Iain says, 'You two actually always miss each other. Wren's a regular. Their package is in the box behind the counter.'

'You must work weekends. I'm usually busy then,' the stranger says, shaking their hand out as if getting rid of a bad sensation – sometimes the lady who makes the nickel rings misses a sharp bit – before coming up to the desk.

I put my book down on the counter to ring them up.

They look down at it. '*A bheil Gàidhlig agad?*'

I feel my face twist up into a grin. '*Tha. Is mise* Lolly. *Math coinneachadh ruit.*'

'*Tapadh leat.*' They take the package from me with a smile, then turn to leave. 'Amazonite, by the way – you have that. It's good for luck in relationships and – bonus – it helps with emotional regulation,' they say as they push against the door.

Funnily enough that might be my best option. I can be a little… sensitive.

'What did they order in, anyway?' I ask, walking behind the counter to steal from the stash of snacks Jesus keeps there for when he gets the munchies.

'Weird one,' Jesus says, letting me out and then swinging back into his stool. I pick my books up from the desk. 'Aconite seeds.'

Aconite. As in wolfsbane.

My heart starts pounding in my ears, my stomach tying itself in knots.

What the hell would anyone want with that? That's sketchy as fuck. Not to mention toxic – to humans as well, not even just wolves.

If Iain can't find malachite how the fuck is he gonna get aconite? Maybe Wren just gave him more notice.

But that still doesn't answer what they needed with it—

'Kearney?' Jesus asks, leaning forward. 'Are your eyes glowing?'

Shit. That happens. It turns out the attack left us with a little more than just telepathy and a monthly ritual. We have claws now, and teeth and shit. Takes a lot of focus to keep that shit in, and to stop our eyes from looking all glowy silver and stuff. Mitch's are silver and gold but mine are normally just this dull kinda grey colour. And when I get emotional – which I do a lot – or lose focus – which I also do a lot – little things can slip through the cracks.

Sure enough when I look down at the book, my nails have elongated, thicker and darker. I take a deep breath and retract them. They catch on the cover of the book as they do. Guess I'm buying that now.

'No man, they're just sparkly. The smell of that shit makes my eyes water.' I nod towards the incense burner. That's not technically a lie. He purposely doesn't burn it when I'm due in. 'Lay off the psychedelics maybe,' I laugh, trying to add depth to the excuse.

He scratches his head for a minute then gives himself a shake. I almost feel bad for lying to him. Even if he did grass us in, it's not like anyone would believe him anyway.

'Let me get a picture of that tapestry for Val and then I'll buy these,' I tell him, setting the book down, scratches facing the counter.

When he returns from the back he's carrying a black canvas tapestry and a small package that's clearly been hand wrapped. It's an OXO cube box, with a plastic glove wrapped around it and a rubber band securing it in place. It sort of looks like a turtle. He always wraps our weed like that.

'Give that to Fish when you see him, will you?' he asks, tossing it on the counter as he kneels down on the floor to spread out the tapestry for me. When he does I feel myself start to grin. Oh Val *is* going to love that. I snap a picture quickly and hit send before ringing up my stuff.

Val

Before Lolly messaged me about the tapestry I *was* doing uni work outside at the garden table. My assignment's due soon so I had been sketching up some pieces to bulk up the design portfolio. The assignment was on 'environmentalism in fashion'. I went all in on an oil-spill style dress because I liked being able to add a gothic aspect, but I'm starting to wonder if I should've done something on fast fashion.

Lolly's text broke me out of the cycle of second guessing myself and gave me an excuse to take a step away.

So now I'm in my bedroom, trying to visually measure the space above my desk. Dad comes in to hand me a measuring tape that he just spent ten minutes raking through the kitchen drawers to find.

'Papi to the rescue.' He grins, placing it on the top shelf of my desk triumphantly.

I thank him as I sweep stray false nails and kirby grips into my hand so I can put them somewhere safe while I climb up onto the desk. The jars of bleach and hair dye he got me from work have already been pushed aside on the floor. My laptop, sewing machine and reading glasses have been more delicately placed on the bed, along with the little Post-it notes Mitch wrote and hid around the desk to encourage me to do my college work.

Dad starts to grumble concerns at me in Spanish as I ungraciously haul my ass up onto the desk to measure, keeping his arm out and prepared to catch me if he has to.

'Are you really going to replace your flag for another gothy tapestry?' he asks, dismayed. 'Valeria, please. It's the only colour you have in here. It's not good for your brain. I'm worried you are going to start seeing in monochrome like a dog.'

I roll my eyes at him, taking his hand to steady myself as I get down.

Technically, dogs don't have monochromatic vision, it's dichromatic like a wolf – and I only see like that once a month when I'm fully transformed. Of course I don't say this to him.

'Papi, where else do you suggest I put it?' I ask, gesturing around at the walls which are completely and entirely covered in random shit.

The one behind my bed already has a tapestry and two shelves – one in the shape of the moon and one in the shape of a coffin. Any more there and the ivy leaf fairy lights would just get drowned out. He doesn't want me to cover the window. And the corner between it and the chair that is perpetually covered in clothes is where I hang the net that holds all my teddies. They stay put. My wardrobe is built into the other wall and neither of us would even think about suggesting moving the pictures of Mel beside it. So this is the only option.

'You don't need two shelves,' he suggests, pointing to the coffin shaped one that he has a vendetta against.

I give him a look. He knows fine well that I need two shelves for my bone collection. It's already spewing out along the windowsill, the desk and my bedside cabinets.

'Valeria, it's spooky. It gives me the heebie jeebies.' He shakes his hands in response to my glare, stamping his feet like a disgruntled toddler. 'I'm starting to believe you really are becoming a dog. You need the colour. Do you want me to get you a little smaller version like the one I stick to my mirror at work?'

God love him, my dad tries his best.

After I reassure him that I'll rehang the flag lengthways behind the teddies, and let him rant about how Tía Marianna – my favourite of his sisters, definitely a witch – is a terrible influence on me, he lets me show him the tapestry.

Fortunately, he seems to be taken by the bat it features, and says that he can stay because 'he looks polite'. I text Lolly to say that I'll take it, before letting Dad help me carry the massive overlocking sewing machine from the bed back to the desk, refraining from mentioning that I managed to carry it there myself. I'm pretty capable of carrying most things. It's one of my better enhanced abilities.

Lots of weird little things like that improved when we were turned: smell, taste, hearing, speed, strength, healing. The latter is probably the most useful but strength is where I'm most improved.

After setting the machine down, Dad wipes sweat from his shiny bald head, then leaves to go and make us both some coffee.

My laptop chimes loudly as I'm adjusting one of the Post-it notes so it covers my webcam. It's an Etsy order for some of the thread Pride bracelets I sell. Making them forces me to slow down and be in the moment when I'm panicking.

I stop in my tracks, leaning over the computer to check what they wanted. Trans, non-binary, and bi. I think I have some pre-made for those colours actually. I slide the mirrored door of my wardrobe open and grab my box of jewellery-making stuff from inside, taking it back to the desk so I can properly untangle the bracelets from some stray embroidery floss.

When I sit down I notice the address. *Kirkside*. Oh, that's Mitch's street. Actually, it's right next door to Mitch. Huh, that must be his new neighbour.

Wren Blackburn. What a weird coincidence.

Maybe I could drop it off by hand... No, that's weird. Still, maybe I could message them and let them know... No, still creepy.

I shoot Mitch a text showing a picture of the order and then continue digging in the box. After a couple minutes I've found a trans bracelet and a non-binary one, but the bisexual one is proving harder to find. My new purple thread hasn't been delivered either – there is some here but it doesn't look like it's the right shade. I check my wrist so I can compare it to my own.

Radwa made this one for me just after she started living with us. It twists a little and the ends are fraying but it's fine. She had more to worry about back then and it's still enough to convince me that she's safe so long as I'm wearing it.

The only issue is that when I look at my wrist it's missing.

I pause momentarily, feeling my chest go tight, before pushing the box from my lap. Then I dive onto my bed, frantically tapping at the duvet, hoping I dropped it earlier. Nope. Not there. It's not there. Where is it? Is she okay? I grab my phone to send her a text before getting back to searching.

My brain starts cycling through St. Anthony's prayer, not that I actually believe in all of that anymore. It's more a habit, like if I *don't* say it then I won't find it. And if I don't find it... I glance over to the corner of the room where Mel stares back at me, freckled cheeks full of laughter, in a picture of the three of us bunking off of Sports Day together because Mitch didn't want to use the girls changing room.

By the time I've cycled through it in English and Spanish, I decide that Radwa's lack of reply warrants more drastic measures.

When I get into her head I can barely understand a word of what is being thought.

That's because you don't speak Bengali! she hisses in her mind as I desperately try to find my bearings and see through her eyes.

We've been over this, Val, she sighs, putting her pen down on her exam paper. *You've got to stop just jumping in when you're worried.*

Busted. I feel my stomach tie in a guilty knot. It didn't even occur to me that she had her exam today. She took Bengali because her parents used to speak it at home and she thought it would be an easy pass. That explains the lack of response.

Sorry, I whisper in my thoughts, overtly aware of how busy she is.

It's fine, I'm just finished. She rolls her eyes. *Your bracelet is on the shower shelf, by the way. Saw it this morning,* she adds. I hear the warmth and understanding coming back into her thoughts as she closes the test paper over.

Radwa

I gather up my stuff from the desk after handing my paper to the invigilator. Since I was the only one taking this exam I didn't do it in the main hall, so I can pack up as loud as I like.

That's one of those things that actually makes me nearly as anxious as the exam itself. People always say I'm too quiet and I sneak up on them accidentally, but when I'm actually trying to be quiet I might as well be screaming and throwing things for all the difference it makes. I pick up my pencil case from the desk, making sure the good luck charm Lolly made me is still firmly attached to the zip. They're so sweet.

I pause for a moment looking down at it, running my finger over the yellow wax on the top of the bottle cork. They gave it to me before my exams started, after spending nights on end trying to help me understand maths. A feat that was admittedly harder than it needed to be because I kept getting so distracted by the dimples that their excited smile carved out in their face that I completely forgot to listen to what they said about the quadratic formula.

Fortunately, my Bengali studying went a little better.

I give the charm a little rub before tucking it back inside my bag. The invigilator gives me a big smile and starts packing her own stuff away as I head out the door, turning my phone back on to check my messages.

Sure enough, Val has tried checking in. Lolly has asked what I'm wearing to the party. Mitch wished me good luck. I'm typing out my replies to them when Aadilla texts me to ask how it went. She did this exam last year when she was in school – she's two years older than me so she helped me study.

It probably went fine, right? I answered all the questions – not like my maths one. That one I definitely failed.

I round the corner turning away from the classroom to walk down the long corridor to the closest exit. These corridors are always so nauseating and anxiety-inducing. Or maybe exams just make it feel that way. The breeze let in by the flimsy plastic windows always makes my tremor feel worse, like my bones themselves are shaking inside of me.

When I get into the main part of the school building I decide to use the toilets really quickly. Normally I avoid them. No one has been weird about it for a while, but I still get kind of anxious using the girls' room just in case. Since I'm the only one here, I know it'll be fine. I'm adjusting my hijab pin and have some of my makeup out on the sink when the door opens.

'Shit, sorry,' they say.

'No it's fine I'm sorry I –' I say, tucking my lipgloss back into my bag without even using it, 'I'm just leaving.' I turn to the door, finally looking up to see who it is.

Oh. New person. That's a new person. I don't know them.

'Sorry,' they say again, pulling their tote bag back onto their shoulder. 'I was just looking for reception and I needed to use the loo.' They turn their head to look behind them at the door.

I slow down, taking my lipgloss back out and eyeing them carefully. Maybe they don't know, or they don't realise. There's no reason for them to be weird right?

My heart hammers more in my chest now than it was in the exam hall. It's as though I'm a little figurine in a music box and someone keeps winding up a key attached to my heartstrings. I figure I'll just wait for them to go into a cubicle to make my exit.

Then I see the Pride flag printed on their bag as they turn. The winding stops, and slow and hopeful music takes its place.

When they come back out I'm blotting the gloss, taking my time with each action in the hopes that one of us will say something. With Lolly leaving school after this year I'm kind of short on friends for the next one. Honestly, I'm a bit worried the bullying will start again. People weren't the nicest when I first came out. There was a blog set up and some nasty posts. There were other things, too, but healing took care of those. The blog was the only one that had a really lasting impact.

'Did you have an exam today?' they ask, fishing a small tub of gel and an edge comb out their bag to fix some baby hairs that have come loose with the humidity.

'Yeah. Bengali,' I say with a smile. 'Last one.' *Alhamdulillah*, I add mentally as I tuck the lipgloss back into my bag, hesitant to make my way out but not really knowing what else to say.

They nod, checking their reflection once more before following me out the door.

'Reception that way?' they ask, pointing in the totally wrong direction.

I shake my head and try pointing them in the right direction before deciding to just walk them there.

The first few steps pass in silence. I should say something. I should really say something. But what should I say? Literally all I know how to talk about is werewolf stuff and videogames and I do not want to infodump on a potential new friend this early into meeting them. People don't like that in conversations. What do they like? What do they talk about? The weather? No, that seems too cliché.

'So, wee brother is making me pick up his new timetable for him,' they start. I hope they didn't sense my awkwardness.

Okay that's something to work with, cool. Good, okay. Make friends, take an interest. 'Oh, are you guys moving school?'

They shake their head. 'Nah, I'm finished as of this year.'

Urgh, there goes that idea. Okay. That was so awkward. Okay and we're walking in silence again.

This is… so awkward.

'Phelan's moving though. He was being bullied at his old one.'

Oh! Yes! Finally! Something I can relate to. 'That's awesome!' I say, a little too excitedly. Their eyebrows shoot up their forehead. 'Not that he got bullied, no I –' My face feels hot. 'That he's moving, I mean. The bullying. That sounds rough. What happened?'

Smooth. Really smooth Radwa, good recovery. I tap my fingertips against my leg wishing I was even half as smooth as Lolly when it comes to these kinds of things. They're such a smooth-talker they could make anyone like them. My parents even met them one time and Dad still goes on about how well mannered and polite they were.

'He's gay so…' My potential new friend trails off. Then they roll their eyes. 'He doesn't exactly do himself any favours. He's a bit weird.'

My shoulders tense. I hate when people push the whole 'some people need to be bullied' thing. Bullying doesn't build character, it destroys you. Nothing that has that much of a kill rate among queer teenagers could ever be *needed*.

They must catch my eye because they add, 'In a good way, don't get me wrong. I love that little freak.' Their smile when they speak about him is so warm that my muscles relax again, tension melting away. 'He's nearly sixteen. And he's a bit of an emo… and all he does is hide in quiet classrooms to play his Switch or call his boyfriend… *and* he wears cat ear headphones to school.' They crinkle their nose, continuing to talk, as we walk through the doors to reception. 'I dunno. He's kinda cool. I think at his age it takes courage to be yourself. But himself is … soft … and – in my experience – that's not a good trait for a teenage boy to have.'

'No.' I take a second to adjust my hijab so it's sitting right under the straps of my backpack, trying to decide how to phrase the next part. 'That wasn't my experience of it either.'

Their narrow grey eyes widen slightly as they find mine. A knowing smile spreads across their face and we spend the rest of our walk in a comfortable and familiar silence.

I go with them to the office to grab my own timetable, hoping we can walk back onto the high street together at least.

'So, it's Radwa, right?' they ask as we walk down the steps to the main exit.

How did they know that? I feel my eyebrows knit together.

They must sense my confusion because they add, 'I heard you asking for your timetable. You're going into S6 right? Year above Phelan?'

Oh. That makes sense. I thought I was really quiet asking for it. Once again, no volume control for the win.

'Yeah.' I nod in answer to the question. 'Radwa Hashmi, and your brother's name is Phelan…?' I add, hoping that if I can't make friends with one of the only other transfemme people my age I have ever met in this town I can, at least, look after their brother when he gets here.

'Blackburn.' They smile. 'You'll recognise him. I'm Wren by the way.' They give me a smile.

They pause at the bit in the road halfway between Val and Mitch's houses. 'Would it be weird if I asked for your number before we went our separate ways? I don't have a lot of friends, especially not ones who – well—'

'I get it.' I nod, with a smile, taking their phone from them to punch it in.

Then they ping my phone with a text so I can add them to my contacts: *Wren Blackburn.*

Chapter Two

Mitch

Mum flicks on the radio only to be accosted by Green Day's 'Basket Case' at full volume. Our car is too old to have Bluetooth or even a working aux cable. I was the last one to drive it so it's playing one of the CDs I've burnt.

'Mitchell!' she tuts loudly, turning it down.

'Sorry.' I hold my hands up. Green Day have to be listened to at full volume. Me and Mel used to listen to them together. They were one of the only one of *my* bands she could actually stand. 'Not convinced I left it on that loud though, I'm just saying.'

I see Dad roll his eyes in the rearview mirror.

We have this running joke that Mel got one of their concerts cancelled from up in Heaven because me and Val were going to go to it without her.

'Are you trying to blame your sister *again*?' he asks, an eyebrow raised.

I shrug. 'I'm not saying she did, I'm just stating the facts.'

Mum scoffs, a gentle smile in her eye, and turns it back up so it's to Mel's liking.

When we get to the church, the kids seem delighted that I'm the one to take them today. Hannah and Phoebe high-five and Issac clings to my leg as I try to walk through the sanctuary. I grin, ruffling his hair as the girls engage me in conversation about the new crafts they've been working on. Between these guys and the younger class at martial arts, I'm starting to think I might actually stand a chance at being a good dad.

I take them into the small room next to the sanctuary. It's an older part of the building. There are peeling vinyl details with the animals from Noah's Ark parading down the yellowing cream-coloured walls in sets of two. The rest of the church is like that too. It boasts just one modest and dusty stained-glass window. I think that's how a church should be. It shows it cares more about its community than appearances. There's no real Christianity in a church of lavish gold when children all over the country go to bed without dinner, or sleep in shelters and on streets.

We watch *Voyage of the Dawn Treader* for the third time this month. They got sick of *The Lion, The Witch and The Wardrobe* around March this year. The younger ones seem bored after a while but some of the older girls – and boys – are transfixed everytime Caspian appears.

By the time the Bible study group the adults were having has finished, the movie is halfway done, and Hannah and Phoebe have added four more badges to my vest.

When I leave the hall I catch a glimpse of my Dad looking at the notice board that sits on the front wall overflowing with flyers for charity events, funeral notices, and most recently missing person reports.

His eyebrows pull together slightly and he looks at the ground with a grimace before walking away. The radio stays shut off on the journey back to ours.

Once we get there I'm straight out the door again, first to the pharmacy and then Val's.

She lives on a council estate, same as I do, but on the opposite side of town. Her mum and dad are sitting on their garden step together when I get to theirs. Most families seem to be outside today. It's probably the first hot day of the year. The next door neighbours are all sitting in a kiddy pool holding tins of Tennent's. Mateo's chihuahua yaps away at the staffies next door who look at him with comical disinterest.

I bend down to pet him while Mateo shouts upstairs to Val to let her know I'm here. He says it in Spanish so the only word I actually recognise is '*Bobo*' – the nickname I was lovingly assigned when I started dating his daughter. Val shouts back down and he nods me up.

When I get up she's sitting at her desk in a little black sundress with her head in her hands. Cluttered around her are a few last minute sketches on an assignment she's changed her mind about right at the last hurdle. She studies fashion at the local uni. Specifically, she's interested in making a size inclusive goth clothing brand since she got really tired of goth fashion being so inaccessible for her.

A cup of, now cold, coffee sits beside her. Picking it up, she takes a sip before grimacing at the temperature as I bend over to kiss her head. She drinks so much coffee that the smell has started to remind me of her.

'How's it going?' I ask, laying back on her bed.

'Well, it fell to pieces,' she says, crawling up onto the bed next to me and laying between my legs with her head on my chest so she can look up at me. 'But I think I have a plan now.'

I look at her, concerned. 'Not literally fell to pieces right?'

'No!' she laughs, hitting me with one of the main decorative pillows on her bed. This one is shaped like a spider. 'My stitching is better than that!' she adds defensively, pushing herself up.

Then she looks down at me in a way that makes me feel as though she is falling in love with me again. Her eyes widen, tiny smile lines pressing their way into the corners of her eyes where I know they will one day find a more permanent home as we grow old together.

I tilt my head up and she reaches down to kiss me.

There are moments when I suddenly realise that Val is the one I want to be with forever. These moments get closer and closer together as of late.

The next occurs slightly later in the day when we're chilling wrapped in her duvet, both shirtless. The cover comes over my chest and Val's arm falls down the middle of it to rest on the flat bit. Looking down I can't see anything that makes me dysphoric but my arms look strong and I can see *her*.

I follow the little stitches and embroidered flowers covering the scars on her chest from the attack with my eyes. My breathing is slow. God knows we need this time to exhale together before the moon.

You know that one person who you're not afraid to show any side of you, who sees whatever invisible weight you're carrying and ducks underneath it with you to grab a handle? Yeah, for me that's Val. I think I'm that for her too. That's why I feel comfortable laying like this with her. That's why I want to marry her.

I'm saving for a ring I found that just seems so perfectly her. Mateo knows. I told him I wanted to last week. He understands it might take me a while to save, but I wanted to ask his permission before I started. For all his silly nicknames, he was practically dancing when I asked him, and pulled me into a strong, rib crushing hug. I think I saw him *actually* dancing through the blinds on my way out, a slow waltz with the dog clutched to his chest.

Val pauses the TV show we were watching and pushes

herself up with the hand that lays on my chest. Her hair falls down like a waterfall.

'Are you okay?' She smiles softly. Her nose crinkles when she smiles. 'You're blocking me. You only do that because of dysphoria or Mel.'

I feel the blush rising to my cheeks. 'No you're fine, it's nothing really.'

She eyes me suspiciously before lying back down. I rub her ribs gently as she settles, pressing play.

There's a knock at the door. Radwa shouts, 'Can I come in?'

'Gimme a second!' Val shouts, pulling on a hair dye-covered cropped top and shorts set from the floor, throwing me my hoodie.

She pulls at the edges of her top, checking herself out in the mirror. Her stomach peeps out the bottom of her shirt, and her stretch marks glitter in the sun.

I grab her around the hips and pull her down with me to kiss her cheeks. 'You look pretty.'

'I know.'

God, I love her.

Radwa walks in and throws herself into Val's desk chair. The strings of the hoodie she's wearing are pulled tight to cover her hair. She often walks around the house like this.

Tucking her feet up under her, she starts spinning herself like she does when she's waiting for gaming lobbies to load. 'Can you help me with my makeup?' she asks Val, continuing to spin so fast I feel sick just watching her.

Val untangles herself from me to get up.

'Are you sure you don't wanna come?' Radwa asks, stopping as she approaches. 'Someone has to stop me from making a fool of myself in front of them.'

I scoff. Her and Lolly are both as ridiculous as each other when it comes to their crushes.

'I'm sure I don't want my boyfriend getting a criminal record,' Val laughs.

We agreed to skip this one on account of Mel's ex Tyler being there. I know I'll lose my temper if I see him again. He's the reason she was even out that night. Without him—

'But speaking of Lolly,' Val continues, turning to look at me, 'would you mind picking them up while I do this?'

'Sure.' I smile, reaching over the bed to give her a final kiss.

When I stand up I'm eye level with some pictures of Mel. I wonder how she would feel about all of this – about me dating her best friend. As I leave Val's house I swear I can hear her, cursing us out from the afterlife.

Lolly

This must be where I die.

I stare at the growing sea of clothes flooding infinitely towards the doorway, barricading me in. T-shirt after t-shirt after t-shirt lies rejected on the floor in front of me. A truly insurmountable amount of clothes separate me from my exit.

My only source of water is Monster, and my only available food? Space Raiders. I'll starve to death in hours. Let my tombstone read:

HERE LIES
LOLLY KEARNEY.

RAGING FUCKING LESBIAN.

DIED AS THEY LIVED –
DESPERATELY TRYING TO
FIND A WAY TO
IMPRESS A PRETTY GIRL.

Seriously though, how is it possible to have this many clothes and still have *nothing* to wear? I'm not going – that settles it – I can't.

Radwa is bound to look absolutely gorgeous and I'm just – urgh.

Mitch knocks on the door as I'm sitting, arms crossed, on the floor with my back against my bed frame.

'First of all,' he says, muscling his way into the room laughing, 'you're not gonna starve to death.'

Fuck. I must've thought that too loudly. I have got to be careful of that tonight.

'Second of all,' he continues, 'Radwa's already ready and you're not standing her up.'

Shit! *Now*, I have to be careful *now*! We need to go *now*!

Okay, maybe I'm a wee bit disorganised.

'Do I look okay?' I turn frantically on Mitch as he walks in.

He rolls his eyes, throwing me my The Damned t-shirt and a pair of Converse. 'It'll look better if you open the shirt and wear it with those.'

I start unbuttoning my shirt.

'Are you wearing my old binder?' he asks, seeing a glimpse of red peeking out under the plaid.

When I came out to him, he said I could try it on if I wanted to. So, when I got a chance to try it out when no one else was home, I jumped on it. 'I was curious! I was having a minute, okay?' I wave him away, grinning.

He grabs my hand. 'Did you do something to your nails that isn't biting them?'

'Shut up.' I snatch it back. I just wanted to paint them because it looks cute, not because I wanted to kill time before I saw Radwa. The varnish is also his.

'And you're wearing makeup?'

That is *mostly* not his. I roll my eyes, pulling on the shirt I was originally wearing and running downstairs after him.

He pauses in the garden listening for something as we pass the house next door. It's quiet. No one is talking.

'New neighbours?' I ask, walking past him to open the gate.

'Yeah,' he says, following me. 'Someone called Wren. And their family.'

I grin in memory of the ethereal being that graced the shop today. 'I think I actually might've met them'

Mitch looks at me confused as he throws himself back into his shitty car. 'That's weird. Me too, and they also ordered from Val's Etsy. Don't you think the silence is kinda spooky?'

'They just moved in, probably just decompressing.' I shrug.

'Maybe,' he says thoughtfully, placing a CD into the player – Against Me! – one of my favourite bands.

Some people always know what to say. Mitch is not one of those people. But I'll be damned if he doesn't always know what to play.

We pull into Val's estate with his shitty car speakers still butchering Laura Jane Grace's musical genius. Mitch turns the speakers down ever so slightly as Radwa gets into the car. Back when we first turned, she really struggled with the whole enhanced hearing thing. While she's better at regulating now, there's no reason to make it unnecessarily hard for her.

She ducks into the back seat next to me, stooping slightly so she doesn't hit her head.

Wow.

That's all that really comes to mind when I see her smile. It just has a way of making you feel warm, like your insides are made of... soup.

No wait, that sounds weird.

My granny makes this tattie soup whenever I'm ill and it's the only thing that makes me feel better.

And that's what Radwa's smile does. It brings me that kind of comfort you know?

Then I notice the cute little love hearts drawn on her cheeks in white eyeliner. I feel my dimple crease into my cheek despite my effort not to smile.

'What?' she whispers in a half-laugh as she catches me looking.

I shake my head in a small way that I hope seems nonchalant. 'Nothing.'

At the party, we get split up pretty quickly. She needs to use the toilet and – while I'm completely okay with waiting around for her – she tells me to go in and enjoy myself.

To be fair, the *noble* offer was partly because the hallway you go down to get there is already full of people, and I want them to know that *I'm* with her. I know she's not *mine* but I want her to be.

And I want people to know that.

Which I know is rich considering the fact I only know about this party because the host is a guy who was friends with the brother of a girl I used to – well not date exactly, but…

Anyway, as per her wishes, I make my way out to the garden for a joint.

I find a boy from my year in school outside. He's a pretty sound dude who was in the pipe band and Musical Theatre Society. Not my vibe, but okay for conversation while I have a joint on the doorstep.

I'm chatting to Jack or John or whatever his name is when I hear someone ranting to their mates. A boy, whose name I only know because I've seen how Mitch tenses upon seeing him, places himself in the centre of the conversation.

'Nah. Right, listen to me, *listen*, okay? We were mates but like…' Tyler sways to the side drunkenly as he talks. '*Never* like *that*.'

His heart rate increases rapidly. I can smell the sweat

pooling on his brow. Spotting a liar has always been a strong point of mine but it got easier when my senses got more keen.

'See, this is why you can't cater to their delusions. But I tried to be nice, didn't I? And this is the thanks I get,' he continues.

Even from here I can smell the cheap vodka on his breath as he glances over to where we sit on the step. It makes my nose wrinkle. There's a reason I smoke more than drink.

'I'm sorry, what was that?' I ask John/Jack, looking back to my hands and rolling the joint between my fingers.

I really try to listen to what Jack/John is saying about a character called Angel – who his friend is playing in a musical – but I keep tuning into the conversation in the background.

Tyler has turned back to his group, lowering his tone. 'I mean, if you can just *decide* to be a girl or a boy or a *thing*,' – he chuckles at his own joke – 'what's stopping them from deciding one day they identify as a seven year old? It's ridiculous. Of course, we can't say that without hurting their precious little feelings.'

Ah, cool, some casual transphobia. That's fun.

People calling me sensitive isn't new to me. I've spent years trying to bully my feelings into being small and digestible for other people.

Being called a nonce, on the other hand, strikes a slightly different chord. I feel my claws press into my palms. The smell of rust trickles into the cool night air as I approach the group without really knowing what I'm going to do…

…until my fist connects hard with someone's face.

Radwa

The bathroom door barely blocks out the noise from the party outside. I needed to step out for a few seconds when we arrived. The lights and music were too much to be immediately thrown into. A techno song was playing, with a heavy bass line that jolted my heart into a new and uneasy beat.

Upon exiting, I spot a few girls from the year below me sitting on the floor outside, gossiping about something. I notice one of them, fairly new to school, is chatting in an easy and friendly tone to someone I recognise.

'Thanks so much, Emma,' Wren says, attempting to straighten up to their full – though admittedly not very tall – height.

Emma shakes her head, long shimmery brown hair dancing gently as she does. 'No,' she hiccups. 'No, babes, it's okay. That school was toxic! I'll keep an eye out for him, promise!'

Emma offers Wren her pinky finger. They hesitantly link their own through it. Upon seeing me, Wren makes an excuse to hurry to my side.

'Friend of yours?' I ask, walking down the stairs with them, feeling socially emboldened just knowing Lolly is here to fall back on if I totally fail at making any friends.

'Not until now.' Wren laughs. 'I gave her eyelash glue and I think she's decided we're bonded for life,' they admit, in a voice so hushed it would be undetectable without my enhanced senses.

An awkward beat of silence passes where I'm not really sure if I'm supposed to keep moving through the party with them or if that'll make me look like a lost puppy.

Then they turn back to me. 'What about you? You here with friends?'

'Lolly.' I nod, struggling to listen to them over the music. 'But they're not just – I mean they're not not but… There's feelings, it's complicated.'

Wren nods. 'Been there.' They sway slightly and smile understandingly.

Then they catch the eye of someone in the crowd and roll

their own far enough back to see their brain before declaring, 'I need a drink. Do you want anything?'

I shake my head. 'I don't drink,' I shout over the noise.

Actually, I could use some water. The music has started to mix with the deafening sound of my own heart racing in my chest. There's no evident reason for this anxiety but still I'm choking just to breathe.

'It's okay, I have mixers! Come on! Do you do hand holding? Is that okay?' They give me a reassuring smile, managing to look radiant as the blue and purple lights dance off their dark skin.

I nod, taking their hand as they lead me through the crowd to the drink table.

They look out the window, confused. 'Isn't that your *not, not just friend*?'

I turn around to see Lolly through the window with their hands balled up, claws slightly elongated but not enough that anyone would notice. Their bottom lip is split and bloody, and their teeth are bared in a manic smile.

I *hate* fighting. The main reason being I'm terrible at it. At least if I was good I could claim that I avoided it for a noble reason. I really don't like hurting other people, but when I'm in a fight it never really gets that far. Right from the get go I get overwhelmed; it's too hot, it hurts, people are all around me at every angle and it's humiliating. I *always* lose and even if I did get a hit in I'd feel horrible about it for days.

Lolly, on the other hand, seems addicted to it. They used to get into fights like these all the time when we were in school together. More than half of them were unnecessary attempts to defend my honour. All of them made my heart race like this, sometimes before I even knew what was happening.

I wipe my sweaty hands on my skirt, preparing myself for the inevitable as I walk past James from the Musical Theatre Society who has been stuck with their weed.

He shouts something at me but I'm too concentrated on the glint of silver I've just seen glaring in the dusky sunlight.

One of the guys is wearing a ring.

I'm about to jump in and warn Lolly when a hand appears seemingly out of nowhere, blocking the attack just before it makes contact with the side of their head.

It's Wren.

Wren is quick to switch from countering the attack to putting the boy on his back, moving as they throw him so they land back to back with Lolly. The rest of the boy's friends move back, seeing that the fight has somewhat evened.

I push my way through the crowd to get to Lolly.

'Fucking Tyler, man!' they rage under their breath, kicking a tuft out of the grass and sounding remarkably like Mitch. Then they turn to me and say defensively, 'He started it but then he sulked away like a *fucking coward!*' they yell towards the house, blood spraying from their mouth as they speak.

I put a hand on their shoulder, pushing them towards the back of the garden so that no one notices that some of their injuries have started to heal.

'Thank you!' Lolly shouts over the noise, blowing a kiss to Wren as I push them back further. 'Can you get my weed from whatshisface?'

Wren shoots them a quick thumbs-up, leaving us alone in the garden.

'Who threw the first punch then?' I ask as I turn my torch on on my phone to check out their injuries.

They turn away letting out a non-distinct grumble.

'Thought so.' I pull them back.

'I'm already healing,' they mumble, noncommittally, as they let me examine their injuries.

The top of their cheekbone just under their eye is bruised, and there is a slight burn from the ring.

'You can't fight everyone who has something bad to say about me.' I sigh pointedly, turning my torch off again.

It frustrates me how willing they are to throw and take punches in a futile attempt to defend me. It's just like Val's protection rituals. Aside from patronising it feels... useless. I'm not helpless or incapable. I'm sure if I put my mind to it, I could learn to fight just like I learnt to argue in Debate Club. But winning one fight doesn't change how society views people like me.

Even if fighting gained me respect, what about every other trans person after me? Mitch had no bother winning fights when he was in school, and they left him alone after that, sure. But then I came along and proved their attitude wasn't changed at all.

There will always be an underdog, someone who's less socially acceptable. Winning one physical battle just seems redundant when the war rages on regardless.

Lolly shrugs me off, tapping the burn with the corner of their flannel. 'Who says it was to do with you?'

'Lolly.' I look at them softly.

They meet my eyes; then their face turns hot and they look away. 'It wasn't about you.'

I raise an eyebrow in disbelief. While Lolly will take any excuse to get in a fight, righteous anger on my account is their favourite.

'It wasn't *just* about you. They were being generally transphobic, and I just got so angry that I had to – I just sort of blacked out.' Then they scoff, shaking their head. 'Must be genetic, I guess.'

Lolly doesn't speak about their dad often. Even my knowledge on Aengus Kearney is limited. I usually only learn tidbits when Lolly is starting to get sleepy on our late night FaceTimes. The extent of what I know is that he is Irish, he is a massive Celtic fan, and he is where Lolly gets their passion. Other than that, the only thing worth noting is that he's been in prison for murder for eleven years.

They look up at me with a small smile to see if their joke

helped ease my racing heart, hoping to be back in my good graces again. Not that they ever were in the bad books, but I would rather they just rose above it all. There's no winning with those kinds of people and they *know* it makes me uneasy. My nerves must amplify my thoughts because they swallow and look down at their scuffed high tops.

'I know. I'm sorry. I'll text Mitch to come get us,' they add bashfully.

Then there's a beat of silence where, though I know we can both hear hundreds of other noises around us, the tapping of their fingers on the keyboard seems loudest.

'I don't know that Val will approve when he tells her,' I say finally, wiping some still-wet blood off their face. Their lip is now healed, by the looks of it.

'Looking after me and mine.' They shrug defensively. It was their Dad's excuse as well.

The person he killed messed with Lolly. They don't talk about that much either.

I know that when they say I'm one of *theirs* they mean it in a friendly way but I can't help but wish their protection had a slightly different intent.

'Next time pick a fight you can win without Wren having to bail you out.' I shove them with my shoulder.

'Oh you met them? They're great right?' They grin.

'Do you just know every queer person in the Highlands?'

Of course they know Wren. They're beautiful. Why *wouldn't* Lolly know them? That's great, that's totally fine, absolutely peachy. I don't even care. I'm *so* relaxed about that.

'I work in a crystal shop.' They laugh as if this explains everything. 'I actually just met them today though.'

'Me too!' I exclaim. 'At school, picking up their brother's timetable! How weird is that?'

They shrug. 'They just moved next to Mitch, must just be getting used to the place.'

I nod in agreement. That does actually make sense. I

wonder how bad Phelan's bullying was that they had to move house. Bless him, poor thing.

Then a thought occurs to me.

'Why were you at work on a Friday?' I ask.

'Buying a good luck charm for tonight,' they say, looking down at the weeds poking through the cracks of the slabs.

'Hoping to meet a pretty girl?' I ask.

They let out an abrupt, barking laugh at that. 'Something like that, sure.' They look at me thoughtfully and open their mouth to say something, but they're interrupted when their phone starts ringing loudly.

Val

I sit on the bathroom floor with a mug of coffee on my lap and my laptop in front of me playing Netflix. Both me and Mitch have an earphone each connected. He kneels behind me, drying my hair. We just spent hours re-bleaching, toning and dyeing it. The entire room smells like ammonia and hair products.

Dyeing our hair together has always been a bonding activity for the two of us. It started a couple of days before my *quinceañera*. He'd gotten a suit to be in my party and he tried it on but something was still off. Something felt wrong. *He* felt wrong. Then, when we were alone together, the truth finally came out. I'd already put two and two together: the suit, all the books he used to read back then. But I was the first person he said it to out loud.

That night we dyed his hair black and red, and cropped it up above his ears. It was so messy but the joy that radiated across his face told me that wasn't really what mattered in that moment.

Since then, he's had black hair and red hair but never at the same time again. I've only gotten lighter. Back then I was bubblegum pink. Then I went lavender. Right now, I'm platinum silver, a colour that requires vigilant protection from the red dye clinging to gloves and towels surrounding us.

'I look ridiculous,' he laughs, catching himself in the mirror as he gathers my curls up with the diffuser trying to make sure they're evenly dried.

I made him cover the wet dye on his head with a plastic bag so there was no chance of it dripping.

'It's like a nurse's shoe.' He pokes it experimentally.

I spit my coffee, choking. 'A nurse's shoe?'

'You know, with the plastic wrap,' he says, defensively.

I shake my head, turning back to my show. His phone chimes on the ridge of the bath behind us. He wipes it on the towel on his lap making sure there's no dye on it. He pauses for a second too long.

'Who is it?' I ask, taking out my earphone.

'Listen.' He slumps on the floor, fishing his out of the bag too. 'I don't want you to freak out. There's been a fight—' Shit shit shit shit shit shit shit.

'Is Radwa okay?' I spring up, feeling my heart hammering. I know Lolly can look after themself, but Radwa… She's been my responsibility from the second she came through my door that night, soaking wet and shivering. My hand snaps to my wrist to fiddle with the bracelet.

'She's okay, it was just some transphobic dickheads that Lolly got a temper with,' Mitch assures me.

Of course, it was. My throat starts to close.

I can see *her* so clearly again, as if she's sprawled on the stairs in front of us like she was that first night we did this. Thick ginger hair pulled over one shoulder. Mismatched eyes full of warmth.

She looked at me when I had to pull Mitch away from her. Those colourful eyes were set with utter betrayal.

Mitch makes a point of breathing slowly and loudly. He knows who I'm thinking about now.

I was protective of her, too. Maybe subconsciously I knew she wouldn't have long.

'You okay?' Mitch asks gently, rubbing his thumb along my hand. I nod. 'You're not responsible for everyone, you know? Not for Mel, not for me, not for Radwa.'

I should've gone with her, I'm a bad person.

I should've gone with her, I'm a bad friend.

I should've gone with her, I'm a bad sister.

The tiles plastered to the wall crash to the floor and break in fragments around me.

Hey, one thing that's red? Mitch's voice calls out in my mind.

Your hair. I can hear my breathing loud and heavy, my chest heaving up and down with each exhale.

One thing that's orange?

My pumpkin. I gesture to where it sits on the cabinet. It's an oil burner shaped like a jack-o'-lantern and currently holds a pine scented melt. I breathe it in deeply focusing the smell, letting it transport me.

One thing that's yellow?

I point to the warning label on the pot that the bleach is in.

Green?

I feel myself crack a smile and nod towards his makeshift hair protection.

Blue?

I point to the bleach still sitting in the mixing bowl across the room.

Purple—

My toner. It's sitting on its side, leaking slightly into the bath. Noticing this, he springs forward to catch it. Then he sits back on his heels placing a comforting arm on my shoulder. The tiles return to the walls.

Water?

I nod and take a big sip of the drink he passes me. The burning in my lungs subsides.

I don't feel the need to apologise. We both still have some triggers relating to the attack. He doesn't make me feel like a burden.

Reaching for my hands, he smiles softly then pulls me up. When we are standing he wraps his arms around me. They feel grounding. He rests his chin on my shoulder, giving me a kiss on the cheek. He must be only a couple of inches taller than me without his platforms but it feels like his arms engulf me. He has very tall energy.

'You're here with me. You're okay,' he murmurs softly into my hair. I turn my head and place my forehead on his lips. It's a request he happily fulfils, pressing two swift kisses between my eyebrows.

He laces his fingers through mine, bringing my hand up to touch the pale jagged line across his throat, then the one on his face.

'You are a wonderful person,' he whispers, 'who has always done the best she can for those around her,' he promises me, giving me another two kisses, this time to the side of my head. Then he pulls back. 'I need to rinse this out. Are you gonna be okay for five minutes?'

I wipe my eyes, trying to be brave despite still feeling like my heart is in my throat.

He must hear it because he lifts his phone again, bringing it to his ear. 'Hey Lol… Yeah, no, I know, I saw. Are you guys okay? … Okay, that's good… Yeah, I'm just coming. Do I have time to rinse my hair dye out, the timer is about to go off… Okay, awesome, just stay out there…' Then he glances at me softly and says more quietly, 'Can Val speak to Radwa?'

Mitch drives us to the party. It's on the other side of town from mine but it doesn't take long.

Something in me still feels on edge as we pull up. I feel sick, as though something bad is going to happen. Mitch hasn't even put the handbrake on before I wrench the door open and launch myself out the car.

I walk into the house with – what should be – a very simple mission: find my sister and her ... whatever Lolly is to her ... and then leave. Only, the walk through the door already has me met with sticky floors and boys touching my waist to get past.

Then I see a face. It's not one I recognise consciously, but it somehow makes everything stop rushing around me.

My heartbeat stabilises immediately, calming, as though it had been a dog frantically barking to alert its owner of something then settling once it was followed.

They're tall. Taller than me, and strong. Lean, but their muscles are defined where their sleeves and bra strap fall from their shoulder. They stagger behind someone who clutches their wrist tightly, leading them upstairs.

The gaunt look on their face tells me whatever strength they have is irrelevant. It often is when a person is afraid.

Something comes over me and I act almost on instinct.

'There you are!' I smile, linking my arm through the person's arm and pulling them away. 'I've been looking everywhere.'

I make eye contact with the boy who was dragging them as he drops their wrist. It's only then he even registers properly in my mind, only then I see who it is. *Tyler.*

My jaw sets, determined not to let him see me cry. Images of blood spatters through freckles flood my mind. If it wasn't for the person on my arm, a new soul to protect, I think I'd deck him myself. Instead I just turn away, steering my new friend towards the hall.

'Mmm ... I don't know you, do I?' they half whisper, half slur, as he walks away. Their skin feels hot against mine, the little metal clasps in their braids click together as they stumble clumsily into the wall. 'I would remember someone as pretty as you,' they hiccup, pushing themself back and swaying again. 'I'm Wren, by the way.'

I laugh, catching them and feeling my face grow hot. 'Not

yet. I'm Val. Are you okay?' I ask, steadying their shoulders trying to look at them.

Their eyes fail to focus on me, fluttering open and shut as they tuck a single braid behind their ear. I can't quite catch their colour, but they're so bright that the lights in this place seem to make them shine silver. Purple eyeliner runs down their face and their dark lip gloss is half-smudged off their soft round lips.

They nod, then lurch like they're going to be sick, but manage to keep their composure. 'Mm, Wren … I'm not usually this drunk. Mmm … sleepy … Can you take me home?' they ask earnestly, before staggering a little where they stand.

'Yeah, you said that.' I catch their arm landing where Tyler's were moments ago. I scan over them. Their confusion, their dizziness, the situation I found them in. 'Are you *only* drunk? You can tell me. I can help.'

I only catch a few words of the mumbles that come next. 'Mmm not sure … I've not taken anything. But … Tyler, wouldn't be the first time. Mouth … salty … mmm tired … you take me home?' Then they fold like a house of cards down the wall.

My blood flows cold through my veins as I realise what they're saying. Tyler spiked them. It wouldn't be the first time? I knew Tyler was a dickhead and a cheater but I didn't think he was this low.

I crouch next to them. 'My boyfriend Mitch is outside. I swear he wont do anything to harm you. He's in the red car just right up front. I just need to find my sister Radwa and our friend Lolly.'

'Mmm … in the living room dancing I think … they're really nice…' They look around then stage-whisper, 'I think they like each other.' They throw their head back, letting it thud against the wall behind them and then they start laughing.

Just then Radwa comes towards us. Lolly's smiling behind her in a dumb kind of tipsy way. 'There you are, Wren. I was worried, you've been gone for like half an hour or so.' She pauses, looking at them. 'Woah you look—'

'A lot drunker than when you last saw them? I think they've been spiked.'

'I feel sick,' the pile of limbs on the floor mumbles.

Radwa looks stormy – her hand clenches around the bottle of water she grabbed on her way out. It crinkles slightly under her strength. She passes it to Wren.

Are you alright Lolly? I ask them, eyeing the dark smudge of dried blood on their chin.

A'okay-a Valeria. They giggle, snuggling into Radwa's arm while holding her hand. They seem to be the happy kind of high tonight. Which is good because it can sometimes make them quite sad.

When I get in the car Mitch rolls his eyes at me picking up a stray – yes, this is a completely normal occurrence. You're talking to the girl who brought the entire pack together! He looks like he wants to say something but thinks better of it.

'Oh – 'syou,' Wren says as they throw themself into the car. 'Thanks for the lift … gotta get away from Tyler.' Radwa climbs in after them, pulling their seatbelt on for them.

Even though only those nine words of what they were trying to say were somewhat discernible, they seem to be the only ones that Mitch needed to hear. His eyes soften as he readjusts his mirror, glancing back at them as if he's expecting to see someone else in their place.

We drop Lolly and Radwa off at mine. I'm staying with Mitch tonight as it's a full moon tomorrow and we both need a distraction the night before. Besides, he keeps working overtime lately and I've missed him.

Lolly cheerfully wishes everyone a good night while Radwa makes sure Wren's okay and asks them to text her when they're home safe.

When we get there, I open Wren's door and grab them under their arm, to stop them falling out the car.

'Thank you,' they mumble. 'You're so nice, so nice and so pretty.'

I laugh. 'Come on, let me help you to the door.'

They shake their head quickly, putting their hands out so they don't fall. Holding their shoes in one hand, they manage to stumble with a little more stability as they reach their house – which is shrouded in darkness with all the blinds closed. As they open their gate and wave to us, I hear footsteps coming down the stairs, and, when the light turns on, I see the silhouette of a man meeting them in the kitchen.

Radwa

We sit on the steps outside my front door. It's cold, so I pull my jacket tighter. Lolly's arms are covered in goosebumps but their face is flushed red with the warmth of alcohol. They look like a Polaroid picture right now – sharp and alive. Their silver eyes are bloodshot red, and filled with adventure and adrenaline. They're not sober at all, but it's more than that… they seem high on life. They get like that sometimes, passionate, excited, driven, and happy. Yeah… happy. They get like that sometimes, and it's relieving.

I take a moment to steal a glance at them now as they're looking away, to capture that bright smile and those dimples in my mind's eye. I take a deep breath of night air. Right now, they smell like love. Which, for them, smells like weed, Mitch's mum's baking, his cheap cologne, wax crayons and coconut oil.

Lolly was the reason we figured out emotions have scents. They feel each one more intensely than anyone else I've ever known. It's to the point that when they are happy the room stinks of sun cream for hours until something changes it. I've grown to love the smell.

All of their moods are overpowering like that. I know it's probably related to their borderline personality disorder, but I'm not sure exactly how it works. All I know is that it's Lolly. They're passionate about everything you could imagine. They cried with joy at their first pride, and when Mitch's mum Anna last baked brownies. They sob when they watch old gay movies, and when they burn their porridge. And when they found out Natasha Lyonne was straight they completely refused to leave their room. To be loved by them is a blessing, to be on their bad side a curse, but once they love you, really truly love you, there's no getting on their bad side because no matter what that love overshadows it all.

They look at me, then look down. Their face is flushed red from whatever they were drinking. Sometimes I think Mitch and Val could be right. Maybe they do like me.

I like them. I think if we do like each other, we need to talk about it, to know where we stand and talk about boundaries, but I can never figure out if they do. They're affectionate with everyone. Just yesterday they were cuddling Mitch on the couch in the pack's clubhouse. The day before, they were wearing one of Val's jumpers. Friendships with Lolly are just like that. Like I said, they love with their whole heart.

They look at me again – their heart is racing, I think it's because they're high – and rustle their hair at the back. It's currently styled in an overgrown brown mullet. A tad cliché. They look at me with those eyes that seem to hold life by the reins.

'You look pretty tonight.' They smile.

'I know.' I glance down, smoothing the wrinkles in my skirt. 'Thank you.'

'It's like… the stars you know? You're like the stars.'

They're definitely high.

'Yup.' They smirk. 'A whole five-foot-three-and-a-half. But that's not why I'm calling you pretty.'

I roll my eyes and gently shove them away.

I think for a moment, looking up at the stars. Lolly is holding my hand. It started off as a joke to annoy Val and Mitch with their incessant shipping. Only, they're gone now. It's just us, and we still haven't let go.

I don't know where the line is on this, given that I have feelings for them. I don't touch or show my hair to men, and that's supposed to cover any romantic prospects. But I don't know how it translates to me being queer. I've never really had to address it.

How would a relationship between us actually look? Would it mean no touching? No more hand holding and late night conversations on the step, sitting so close our legs press against each other? No more sleepovers?

Would that change things? Would it mess with our friendship? Is it even worth it?

We've been physically affectionate the whole time we've known each other. This came before the feelings. The feelings have just complicated things a little.

They rest their head on my shoulder. 'I love you.'

'I love you too,' I say, leaning my head on top of theirs. I wish they understood just how much I meant it, but this also came before the feelings so its meaning has been complicated, too.

They look up at me through the thick frame of their glasses, and for a second I believe that they want to kiss me. The moment hangs in silent anticipation.

Then they drop their gaze. It's better this way. Even if Val and Mitch were right and they did feel that way, I wouldn't want it to happen like this.

Scanning the garden, I search aimlessly for something to distract us with. The small wooden table on the uneven grassy floor in front of us captures my attention. I can't help but laugh as I remember opening the door to see Mitch standing in the garden not long ago in a crisp white shirt, his hair combed and flat instead of the usual glued up look, asking to speak to Val's dad.

'We have something to discuss,' I announce to Lolly, who looks at me nervously. I decide to put them out of their misery. 'Do you know why Mitch showed up at my house looking like he was going to a job interview last week?'

They sit back, pulling their hand away at last and looking at me suspiciously. 'I might know something, but if you don't know something then I don't know shit and I'm not telling you shit.'

There's that undying loyalty I mentioned.

'Does what you know involve Val? Perhaps something her sister might have been told so that she can sneakily acquire sizing information?' I feel my excitement rise from my stomach to turn up the corners of my mouth.

Their eyes sparkle. 'You do know.'

'I know! And you know!'

'I know!' They flap their hands excitedly in front of them. 'I don't know why he fucking told me. I can't keep secrets from you guys. My brain is loud!'

'You are his best friend, you realise? You live together. Of course he told you! Forget all your other secrets, this is the only one that matters until he asks her!'

They drape themself over the step and me. 'I'm so glad you know because I couldn't not tell you. I'd explode. Keeping secrets from you is hard!'

I tilt my head and look at them. 'Secrets, plural? You have other secrets from me, of all people?'

They sit up straight and take my hands in theirs. The way they look at me straight on is enough to make my heart flutter. 'I'm secretly not a dog person. I'm sorry I had to tell you like this.'

I mock-gasp, dropping their hands and clutching at my chest.

'I'm a reptile person Radwa. My dream pet is a skink.'

I look up, pretending to cry. 'I just don't know how you could keep this from me.'

They laugh and then shrug. 'Nah, but you'd know what I meant if you heard.'

There they go again giving me false hope. 'Lolly Kearney!' I nearly full-name them. Nearly. But they prefer to keep their middle name private. 'What secrets are you keeping from me?'

Their med alarm goes off on their phone. 'Oh, look at that. I think that means it's bed time.' They pull me up. 'Hey, would you be offended if I said I wanted to sleep in the living room tonight? It's just figuring out gender stuff... I don't know if I should see you without your hijab or not. Feels a bit more serious than just dancing together.'

It's sweet that they're trying to respect those boundaries. It feels right considering how I feel about them. If they do feel the same way, this simple act means so much to me.

'Yeah, no, that's totally fine. I will sleep much better without your sleep talking, anyway.'

They frown. 'Hey!'

They walk over to give me a cuddle before going to sleep. As their arms come over my shoulders I feel them come onto their tiptoes. That's even with me ducking. They're pretty short.

'*Tha mo ghion ort,*' they whisper quietly, face nestled into the crook of my neck. I feel my face go hot against them without really understanding why. They make Gaelic sound so beautiful. '*Oidhche mhath mo leannan.*' They smile.

I don't speak Gaelic, but I assume they said 'goodnight, sweet dreams' or something. I don't really have time to consider it as they saunter into the living room with a smirk.

I don't know why it feels like a moment but it does, and the moment hangs in the air as I stand there at the bottom of the stairs hand resting over my heart. It feels like it's doing cartwheels. My smile is so wide it hurts.

I can't sleep at all.

    RADWA & VALERIA

                            RADWA, 12.21 AM
                    Do you know any Gaelic?

Sometimes being loved by Lolly Kearney, when you love them differently, is complicated.

Chapter Three

Val

It doesn't take long for Mitch to fall asleep after finally getting the joint he had been craving all day. I lie anxiously awake in his room, listening for Wren's movement through the walls – something to prove they're safe and sound in bed. This would be an easier task if it wasn't for the sound of my own breathing and heart rate filling my eardrums. God, enhanced hearing would be so much more useful if I could actually hone in on the noise I'm looking for.

Eventually I hear them clatter up the stairs accompanied by the sound of heavy footsteps and gentle murmurs from a man telling them to be careful. The care in his voice relaxes me, allowing just enough reprise from the anxiety for me to think about falling asleep.

Then a door in their house shuts, and so does another, and suddenly I can't hear anything coming from it at all.

As I stare up at the glow in the dark stars peeling off Mitch's ceiling, listening out for any sign of life, I don't really know how much time is passing me by. Seconds? Minutes, maybe? It feels like I'm awake for hours. Maybe if I could just hear them breathe or snore or mumble once, I'd be content to settle. But there's nothing, so I can't help but keep listening, praying that the next noise I hear isn't the sound of them choking on their own vomit. I don't sleep.

By the time the morning light comes, my eyes are burning like I haven't slept in days. I pull out the uni work I stashed under Mitch's bed and prop myself up with my laptop, trying to focus on something, anything other than worrying about the person on the other side of the wall, who until yesterday was a total stranger to me.

Staying up all night wasn't a great choice the night before the full moon.

But then again, it didn't feel like much of a choice at all. I don't know why, but I can't get the image of them walking into that hall out of my head.

When bad things like that happen, my mind can't help but fill in the blanks with the worst-case scenario. I've always been like that, but it got worse after Mel, and it's especially bad on the full moon.

What would've happened if I hadn't been there? He probably would've led them across that sticky floor, up the dark staircase while their timidness went unnoticed, his cowardice unchecked.

It doesn't bear thinking about. Mitch's thin, grey and smoke-stained pillows do very little to cushion my back as I push it against the slats of his headboard, willing myself into the house behind me so I can check on Wren.

I thought about adding them on Facebook. My phone has been stuck on their profile for hours now. Their face looks back at me like it knows it's being watched. The picture does them no justice. It looks like it's been posed for the sole purpose of updating their profile a few weeks ago. It shows them just sort of standing in a garden, arms crossed over their chest, shoulders rounded forward with a tight sort of smile on their face. There's a year between that and the previous one.

In that one they smile naturally. Their body seems a lot more relaxed, in a languidly beautiful way. It's the same in their cover picture, which looks more recent but seems to be at some sort of martial arts camp. I flick between the two profile pictures opening the comments of each. As expected, one commenter on the previous seems missing from the current: *Tyler*.

Every time I close my eyes, I see the marks his fingers left on their wrist. I wonder if he is to blame for the change in their expression.

What if it had been me? How would I react?

I wonder if the drugs he slipped them had the same kind of sluggish effect that weed does. Maybe stronger. I've smoked with Mitch before and just that made me feel so strangely vulnerable. It made me feel slow and fuzzy. Anything more would be enough to make my hands droop by my sides like pinned organza. Too light, too fragile. Fit to do nothing but hang there.

My stomach lurches as my imagination sets in. I cover my ears, screwing my eyes shut. It does little to stop me from envisioning my limbs as weak and malleable as stray threads; primed and ready to be pulled and plucked at, capable of making the whole project unravel.

Jesus Christ Val, it's first thing in the morning. There is humour in Lolly's tone.

They are the last person who would judge me for these intrusive thoughts. They're also probably the last person who should see them, but it's not like we have total control of it.

Sorry! I cringe, trying to push them back a little.

It's chill. Are you okay? they ask.

I will be.

After tapping my arms four times to protect myself and

my pack – and then another four because the first time didn't take – I resolve to add Wren. Checking in is the only way I can make the thoughts stop racing.

Mitch stirs next to me right as I'm about to do it. I look down to see him squinting at me through the sunlight that's flooding his room by now.

'Are you awake?' I whisper.

He pulls the cover over his eyes.

'Mitchell! I saw you!'

He pulls the cover back down. 'Only just.'

'Good, because I'm nearly finished up here.' I yawn and stretch, cracking my neck as I do.

The sound of static electricity clinging to his hair crackles through the air as he turns over on his thin polyester pillowcases. I jump, giving him a careful glance. I know they give him a weird sense of euphoria but it's getting beyond a joke.

'By the way, Radwa's having a freak out. Lolly was talking to her in Gaelic again,' I tell him, cracking my back so loudly that he has to scoff at the noise.

Maybe that's indication enough of how dire his pillow situation is.

He rolls his eyes hearing me thinking that, and hands me a Squishmallow to lean back on. 'Again?'

'Bet Lolly's already messaged you about it. Let's find out the translation.'

Reaching back down the side of his bed, he grabs his phone from the floor.

'Oh my God! Look at this shit.' He shows me his phone. He has a *few* messages from Lolly.

```
LOLLY, 1.12 AM
Well, I told Radwa I loved her
with my entire heart last night
so you can get off my case now.
```

    LOLLY, 1.15 AM
    Ok it was in Gàidhlig but I
    still did it.

    LOLLY, 2.45 AM
    I relly wanted it to be a moment
    but obviously it was just like
    awkward and dumb.

    LOLLY, 2.46 AM
    I've been drinking and smoking
    the hole night I probably smelt
    like grass and alcohol fml

    LOLLY, 3.01 AM
    I also called her my sweetheart.
    You know what this isn't on me I
    speak enough Gàidhlig you guys
    just need to learn it.
    She is so OBLIVIOUS!

    LOLLY, 3.21 AM
    Mitchhhhhhh
    I compared her to the stars. I
    compared her to the stars in the
    night sky like a Goddamn
    Jesus song

    LOLLY, 3.29 AM
    Sorry for taking the piss out
    off Jesus songs

    LOLLY, 9.30 AM
    So we woke up and made pancakes.
    She's been showing me some
    singer she likes all day but I
    can't focus cause she's to
    pretty and my brains going fast.
    Then we cuddled on the couch.
    She's at the loo rn. I think
    were good.

'We were never that bad, were we?' I ask, looking at him incredulously.

He shrugs as he turns his phone off and lays on his side to look at me, tucking his hands under the sorry excuse for upholstery. 'I feel like Mel probably knew we liked each other,' he finally admits.

He's right about that. She asked me about it at my *quince*.

We'd been in the toilet together. I needed her help to hold my dress so I could pee because there were so many damn layers.

He'd just saved me from embarrassment. I'd been trying to cut across the room unnoticed so I could step out for air but I'd been intercepted by some cousin or auntie or something. So, Mitch cut in to dance with me all the way to the other edge of the dance floor, so that I could sneak off while he distracted my *abuelita* with his good-natured charm.

I hadn't been stealthy enough for Mel to miss the look I gave him though. She *cornered* me when she knew I needed her so I couldn't avoid the question.

'But,' Mitch continues, 'everyone within a fifteen mile radius knows that Radwa and Lolly like each other.'

I groan and roll my eyes. 'Radwa's still gonna think that was a platonic "I love you with all my heart" even if we translate for her.'

We both laugh. He looks at me, squinting through the small lines of sunlight that his shutters let in. One corner of his mouth turns up into a smirk, and a light red blush creeps between his freckles as we make eye contact.

'Wait, did you just say Mel knew *you* liked *me*?' I ask. She definitely knew I liked him, but I can only imagine the bollocking he got for crushing on her best mate.

He shrugs, pulling the cover up over his chest and leaning forward. 'Mel knew everything. Even if I didn't tell her, she just knew me.'

She was like that, especially with him. Until I was literally in his head, Mitch's thoughts seemed impenetrable, but not to Mel. She always knew how to read him before even he did. I think that's why she was one of the first people he came out to. Being social came easy to her and it never did with him, but she helped him find where he fit in social situations without ever trying to change or quiet him.

I don't ask Mitch if he wants to go and see her, or anything corny like that.

Visiting her grave doesn't feel like visiting her. It doesn't feel like she's there. Maybe it would be different if we'd been allowed to see her body to say goodbye. I don't think so though. She could never lay buried in the dirt.

No, her spirit is in sunflowers looking at each other in the middle of the field. Her spirit is in dandelion clocks, blown in the wind and granting wishes. Mel could never be anything other than free. I think that's why her absence makes us feel so stuck.

I twirl the charm of my necklace around the chain. Mitch got it for me. It's got a bumblebee pendant on it. They're kind of our thing.

It's hard to know how to comfort Mitch on moons. I wish I could ask Mel. He doesn't like being touched when he's sad unless he starts it, but sometimes he just wants a hug and doesn't know how to ask. I settle for putting my laptop to the side and making room for him to cuddle me if he wants, which proves to be a good decision given that he promptly plonks his head into my lap, and lifts my hand to put it in his hair before tracing his own over my thighs, drawing hearts subconsciously in his wake. I lean back against his head board, and the very moment I do, as if granting me permission to relax, a door opens in the house on the other side of the wall and I hear Wren's groggy voice as they greet their husky.

Lolly

My phone lights up on the table across from us. I really don't want to disturb this moment. Radwa's head rests on my shoulder while a movie plays on the TV as background noise. I wonder how many more moments like this we have. If they will ever become something she's uncomfortable with.

I can feel her looking at me. At least, I think she is. Every time I look at her she looks down at her lap, twirling the bottom of her scarf between her fingers and her thumb. But I can feel something. Something has changed between us lately, but it doesn't feel wrong, or bad. It feels kind of exciting. I just worry that it means change.

My phone flashes on the table again.

I gently get up and reach for it. Mitch *always* comes first on moons.

```
MITCH
Well, that was a fucking
rollercoaster. Val suggests
flirting in a language Radwa
actually understands. She speaks
6. Pick one!
You guys coming over today?
```

He has got to stop showing Val my texts I swear to fuck.

```
                                LOLLY
        STOP SHOWING VAL MY TEXTS
        DICKHEAD
        Aye were just watching Steven
        Universe rn heading in ten. Are
        you ok?
```

I ask this even though I know he's not. He never is on a moon. Even if he doesn't say anything, his thoughts are more… foggy and… fragmented. Like he doesn't know where he is.

>MITCH
>She was next to me! That sounds
>nice, and yeah I'm fine.
>Hey! I start T today. That's
>pretty cool right?

I know what he's doing. Three years of being his best mate has taught me that. He's distracting himself with something good to convince both me and himself that it's not gonna be so bad.

But he doesn't want to talk. It's Mitch. He never wants to fucking talk because he doesn't want to feel like a burden. Usually, Val and I are pretty good at making him talk anyway. But it's better not to push him on a day like today so I leave it and send him a congratulations text.

'Is everything alright?' Radwa asks, pausing the TV.

Radwa knows. It's one of the things I love most about her. She reads our faces like she reads a book: rapidly, but with care and attention to detail. Translating every eye roll, every grimace, and every sigh. She knows that Mitch is bad with moons and she knows that I will jump to help him. Honestly, she is probably one of the most emotionally intelligent people I have ever met. Which makes sense because, excluding myself, she's also one of the most emotional people I know. Though, that sounds insulting. Maybe passionate is the right word.

Yeah, she's passionate. About everything, and you can tell just by looking at her. When she's really excited to talk about something she flaps her hands up and down as if she can't contain the feeling. When we went to school together she was in the Debate Club and you could always tell the other team had said something really stupid when Radwa started flapping her hands and bouncing in her seat. Overflowing with excitement, at the chance to educate? To win? I'm not quite sure, but anyone could see she was excited. She looks at me softly and expectantly through silver eyes.

Shit, what did she say again?

'I'm sorry my mind left for a second there. What did you say?'

'You're so cute.' She laughs. 'I asked if everything was okay?'

I'm cute? Cute like a puppy or cute like *cute*?

Wait, what did she say? Oh right yeah. 'Oh, same old, same old. You know Mitch, he says he's fine but we all know he's not. He asked if we'd go over.'

'Okay, let's go.' She hops up ready to go, ready to be there for her friends.

She looks so beautiful today. Every day. Last night, sitting in the garden while the moon illuminated her dark skin. Today, sitting next to me on the couch close enough to see the sparkles in her rose-gold eyeshadow.

I look a state the day of the moon but she still makes an effort. Her makeup shade matches both her hijab and her pink tartan trousers perfectly.

'Habibi.' She's looking at me expectantly again.

Fuck I've got to stop doing that! I'm not just ignoring her. I can't help it. My concentration levels are either at maximum power or turned off completely, and today it's the latter.

She rolls her eyes and places her hand in mine. 'You're so silly.' Then she pulls me up. She's standing so close to me that our noses almost touch and I can feel her breath on my cheek.

She turns red then drops my hands and steps out into the hall to grab our shoes. We tie them in silence and I feel the tips of my ears turn red. I've never been embarrassed around girls I like and not to sound like a slag but I've liked a *lot* of girls. Radwa isn't just any other girl though.

She stands and makes for the door before walking backwards a little and sheepishly holding out her hand for me to take. 'Wanna annoy Mitch and Val?'

I look at my skateboard. I'd been planning to take it to Mitch's. It's perched against the hallway wall. Looking at it, I can't help but feel that I don't mind walking if it means I get to hold her hand. Maybe this isn't just to annoy Mitch and Val. Maybe it's for us.

We get to Mitch's about an hour later. The gate squeaks as it's pushed open and clicks as the lock slides back into place. I can smell his mam's brownies already. It's kind of fucking hilarious how often she makes us brownies considering that we've not really been able to eat chocolate since the attack. We just have to pretend to take it 'camping' tonight.

'Hey Anna. How are you?' I ask as I walk in.

'Oh Lolly, Radwa, it's yourselves. Did you have fun at your wee party? Not too hungover to eat your favourite food I hope.' She gives each of us a squeeze in turn.

They say you can't choose your family, and while I don't know who the fuck 'they' are, I've got to admit they're right. If I could I wouldn't have chosen an alcoholic mam. And, while I love my dad, and he's sound and all, I would rather that if mam had to be an alcoholic he wasn't in prison. I mean don't get me wrong, what he did was justified, but I'd rather have someone around to care for me and Lotta.

I'd choose Mitch's family, Charlie and Anna Reid. They've definitely cared for me more than my own mam. My dad in fairness did care about me enough to land himself in prison so I can't fault the man too much. Then, for siblings, I'd choose to have both Lotta and Mitch, and Mel of course. Not that I knew her all that well in her lifetime, but I feel like I know her through Mitch by now.

I shake myself awake. 'Is Mitch upstairs?'

Anna confirms before going to talk to Radwa.

I run upstairs and pound on Mitch's door. 'Get up, dickhead, it's me!'

He grunts and I walk in. Val's sitting on his bed. He has

his head in her lap and she's fidgeting absentmindedly with his hair.

'We good?' I ask him and he gives me a small smile that fails to reach his eyes.

Mitch

The heat radiating from the flames of the campfire mixes with the ash and sparks that flicker from it and makes my eyes sting. When I blink, water streams down my face in a way that's not quite like crying but it feels close enough.

We're sitting in the garden of an old rundown house in the woods that we stay at on moons. It's the den we all dreamed of as kids: our clubhouse. It's miles away from – well – anything really, and that's for a reason. While we can mostly control our wolf forms, we don't want to fucking risk it. We refuse to be monsters. I think I'd rather off myself than hurt someone like that, especially someone I care about.

Lolly and I found this spot while we were out 'walking' – smoking a joint – one Easter Sunday early into our friendship. I was originally trying to show them the old town that lays underneath ours. There's a tunnel entrance right on the outskirts of town. Mel and I used to try and navigate it all the time.

We actually thought about using the tunnel for full moons, but it was too cramped to walk through as a human, let alone a wolf. The clubhouse is old but somewhat more stable. It *is* supposedly haunted, and covered in graffiti, with creaky stairs and no window left whole. But it's not *quite* falling apart, and it's home during the moon.

Honestly, I'm surprised the cops haven't scrapped the place yet. Guess they don't really care to get off their asses unless they're arresting people for defending their kids – yes, I think Lolly's dad should've got to walk free.

The crackles coming from the fire licking at the dry

brachan and wood are just enough to drown out whatever the others are talking, and thinking, about.

I'm grateful for that.

It's hard not to think about Mel on full moons. It's weird though. I'm strange with grief. I never feel it in the way I'm supposed to or when I'm supposed to. And yes I know there's no 'right way to grieve' – I've been to therapy too. I get it, okay? But everyone else seems to know what to say and how to act, how to feel, and I just don't. I'll be sitting there just fine and then all of a sudden my stupid ass brain conjures up a slideshow of memories and I'll be greeting my eyes out.

But then in the same breath, I can talk about her for hours with people who *are* crying and not feel a goddamn thing. Even worse is when I can feel the same sadness but my body switches off on how to show it, and people get angry with me for not talking, but I don't think I know how to.

Don't get me wrong, I'm not some hard man who's allergic to talking about his feelings. I always check in on my friends and have conversations with them about their shit. I just struggle to understand what emotion I'm feeling and how to make it come out of my mouth.

Especially on moons. I'm kind of out of it today... or I want to be.

I turn to Lolly. *Wanna go on a 'walk'?*

Listen, you can judge me all you want for smoking the devil's lettuce, but you have your wee sister bleed to death in your arms and then you can tell me how to fucking deal with it.

Nah, man. They're lining bottles along the back wall to catch rainwater, hair tucked up into a beanie. At least someone uses these nights to their advantage. *I said I'd start lessening how much I did it and I was already on at that party. My psych is always on my ass about it,* they add, squinting through the sunlight to look at me.

Fair enough. I step back a little out of the breeze so that the smoke doesn't blow over to Val and Radwa.

Transformations hurt less the less you fight them. We don't have long. My skin has already started to crawl, microscopic itchy bumps rising in preparation for hundreds of coarse hairs to poke their way through. I can see them along my hands and through the holes in my jeans.

I pick at the glue spilling out from the patches that have been ironed onto them. The stitch work feels rough under my fingers and is fraying where my rats have been nibbling at it. Those feeble stitches are all that holds these bad boys together and even then I have to admit they're still falling the fuck apart.

Val fans herself from across the fire, pulling at her top. Radwa itches her arm. They can feel it too. We've left it as long as we can.

'C'mon.' I pull myself up and nudge Lolly with my foot. 'Trust me, you don't wanna know what happens if you transform with a binder on. Let's go get ready.'

We're going to be okay. We've got each other.

I keep telling myself that.

As I hop up and down trying to unlace my boots before my claws come in.

We're going to be okay. We've got each other.

Standing naked with Val around one side of the house while the others hide out individually in their own respective corners.

We're going to be okay. We've got each other.

Of course, even then I'm fighting it. Jaw clenched, as if holding my mouth shut will keep my teeth clamped – small and human.

It doesn't stop anything. My mouth still fills with blood as the canines come through, same as it always does. My tongue still becomes so long and wide that keeping my mouth shut would only choke me. Then my jaw gives out, snapping out of place, dislocating and elongating.

It becomes harder to believe it'll be okay, harder to believe I even have myself let alone anyone else.

I try to hold onto whatever shred is still left, crouching into a ball curled protectively around what is still mine in some way or form. But eventually, no matter what way I try to force them, my shoulders hunch over, my knees snap backwards and I stop being able to fight it.

Chapter Four

Radwa

When I wake up, I can't find my hijab anywhere. After turning the room upside down, the closest thing I can find is Lolly's hoodie hanging over their skateboard. I slip it on and lift it to my face. The smell of smoke sticks to it, along with Lynx body spray and their handmade lavender perfume. I breathe in. It feels like a warm hug from them. That soft sage green colour I associate with them curls around me gently.

There is a soft knock on the door. 'Hey, I left my meds up here yesterday, can I come in?' It's Lolly.

I straighten out their hoodie bashfully, pulling the strings tight. 'Yeah, yeah here they are!' I open the door slightly for them and hand their meds out.

They raise an eyebrow. 'Are you okay?'

'I can't find my hijab.'

They bring a hand up to cover their eyes. 'Oh I – sorry. Can I help you look?'

'I'm covered, it's fine I've got a hoodie on.' I open the door and tug at their hand.

They instantly turn pink, their blush creeping between their freckles and over their nose. 'Is that mine?'

It's my turn to blush. 'It was just the first thing I found,' I mumble.

They smirk and nod. 'Cute. You can borrow it. I'd like that.'

Why are they so infuriating!? What is that supposed to mean? Is this flirting? It feels like flirting but – ARGH!

They look at me, confused. Before giving their shoulders a shake. 'Sorry, I – I'll help you look, have we checked outside?'

When we get out of the clubhouse we can all smell it. Another wolf has been here, and they've left their clothes behind. As the scent hits my nose I see blue and purple lights glinting and glistening in my head. It's bright, it bounces and dances. I recognise it. It smells like vanilla, and something strong, almost like what Lolly and Mitch smoke but it doesn't burn your nose as much. It's more subtle. Sage?

No one recognises who it is. But something in me feels connected to them.

Mitch goes to pick the clothes up, but I get a weirdly protective urge and stop him. *Leave it. You wouldn't want someone to take your clothes, would you?*

He scoffs. 'Another wolf has been here and you're worried about what they would *want*?'

My cheeks burn with embarrassment as he says it. Mitch and I don't disagree often but this appears to be something he feels strongly about.

He turns back to the pile and lifts a jumper to his face, sniffing it gingerly. 'This scent feels almost familiar but not – like it's missing something.'

He tosses Val the jumper so that she can check it out. She lifts the purple fabric to her face and inhales deeply. Then her expression softens, a small smile toys with the corners of her mouth. Something in her recognises it too.

Then she frowns, crouching next to him to examine the

pile. 'Whoever it is, I don't think they're dangerous.' She riffles through, looking for more evidence. 'I mean, they would've hurt us last night if they were, right?'

Mitch looks at his girlfriend incredulously.

'Could be reconnaissance.' Lolly shrugs, putting their hand out for the hoodie.

'Exactly!' Mitch points at them. 'What if they're watching to see what we do?' He's getting louder as he talks.

Val looks irritated, I can tell from the way her jaw tenses and her mouth and eyebrows set in a scowl. The tension makes me freeze. I half expect one of them to commit to a steady silence which will haunt the car on the ride home. That's what would happen with my parents. But they don't, because they've never really been like that.

Instead Val tries again. 'We have no evidence to suggest—'

'Babe!' Mitch cuts her off. 'People are going missing every month *on the full moon.* And now there's a new wolf for the first time since –' He tails off. The words don't need to come out to reveal the weight behind his panic.

Val's expression softens. 'I know,' she whispers very gently, looking at him as if they are the only two here, as though he is all that matters to her for a moment. 'I just don't think taking their stuff is a good idea either way. I mean, if they're a friend, it looks rude at best. But what if it *is* a trap and they're *expecting* us to take it so they can use it to track us?'

Mitch stops, straightening up and raking a muddy hand through his matted red hair.

For a second, we all just stand staring at this discarded pile of clothes sitting in a little rabbit hole, clumsily buried with twigs and branches. Val has placed the hoodie back down on top. It's not torn, so whoever left it knew they were turning and took it off in a hurry. The labels flap and rustle in the breeze, carrying the scent through the air to us once more. I still can't place it.

'So what do we—' Mitch starts again more defeatedly.

'The tags.' I nod, reaching for Val's bag.

She beams proudly, fishing out her travel sized sewing kit then cutting a tag from the middle of a set so that no one will be able to tell it's missing.

'You're a genius.' Lolly grins, passing me one of the many small cork bottles they keep about their person at any given time.

My cheeks flush warm as I look down at my hands, hoping they don't notice the change in my expression.

Evidence secured, we wander back to Mitch's car, having agreed that we will go home, shower, eat and then reconvene to discuss what to do next.

I swear I see a face watching us, but as soon as I look around they're gone.

Val

My dad's cooking is everything I need after a full moon. It feels like a warm hug, like nothing else matters. So, once Mitch drops me and Radwa at mine, it takes about nought-point-five seconds for me to get into some joggers, a Goosebumps top, and tie my hair back so that it doesn't get in the way of his *yaniqueques*.

I pass Radwa's plate to her as I walk into the living room. Mitch and Lolly have gone home to shower and change before we reconvene back here. Radwa is also in her pyjamas, but has conveniently decided to put Lolly's hoodie back on.

'What's our movie today?' I ask, taking a seat on the couch next to her.

Full moons are knackering, so we have a tradition of slobbing out a bit together. I love how much Radwa likes movies that are a little more macabre. She does with games as well. That's why she's my favourite movie partner.

'Is it too early for *Sweeney Todd*?' she asks.

It's one of our more tame movies admittedly, but I turn it on and pull my craft box into my lap.

I don't ask about her wearing Lolly's hoodie because I can tell she doesn't want to be asked. She's already set up in her usual post-moon station in front of her laptop with alerts set for any information on new attacks, the hacked communication system quietly feeding through a transcript of anything it picks up.

I've taken on the far more relaxing task of making Pride bracelets for my Etsy. They're a simple pattern, just a series of knots, almost like knitting with your fingers. It's something that comes to me easily, an absentminded fidget to comfort me after moons.

Turning is kind of like being drunk. You don't really remember everything that happened. Both activities play on my OCD a bit too much, weaving false memories into my mind of coming across people, of hurting them, or turning them or worse. But all of that drifts when my hands move over the threads.

I only notice it's started to twist when I look down to check how long it's gotten. I can't help but smile.

Mel taught me how to make these bracelets. I remember she kept tying her knots wrong and eventually, her entire bracelet would curl backwards on itself. It was a work in progress until we perfected it together. We used to hold the cords down for each other or safety pin them in. I smile softly to myself as I take it back to the problematic knot. Annoying as it is to undo everything after getting lost, it's still better and far more sanitary than when I used to pick at my skin instead.

'I feel like some of these people were better off as pies.' Radwa breaks me out of a trance. 'Like yeah, murder is bad, but the character played by Alan Rickman, deffo better off as a pie.'

'Radwa what? You're vegetarian.' I laugh, releasing a row of pink knots.

'Better him than the cats.' She stares ahead, her eyes flicking between screens.

I shake my head, laughing at her. 'Anything interesting?' I ask, nodding over to her computer.

She's sat across from me, transfixed as she watches the auto-transcript for the hacked radio appear and disappear from the screen. 'Nah,' she sighs, 'probably too early yet.'

She looks back at the movie, pulling on the hoodie sleeves which ride up her arms, slightly too short to reach her wrists. The hood's down now since we're home alone. It's evidently no longer *just* being worn to cover up. I decide to bite the bullet and ask her.

'Are we gonna talk about that whole situation?' I gesture to her outfit.

'Don't think I'm ready yet.' She smiles back at me, only briefly chancing a glance away from her screen.

She might not want to talk, but I know what she's doing, why she's still wearing it. In all my years of studying fashion – both academically and in my free time – this is the one topic I love examining the most.

Clothes mean more than people think. The wrong length skirt can imply immodesty, or disrespect – you wouldn't wear a cocktail dress to a black tie event. Celebrities can make a political statement just through their choice in jewellery. Certain thread colours were deemed unlucky for long enough. The wrong colour can imply the wrong intention – wearing red to a wedding would be absurd in the eyes of some people, though it would play a key part in Radwa's, for example.

The one thing I've noticed that remains consistent through decades and cultures is the implication of wearing your loved ones clothes. Maybe it's universal. Human nature. The longing for their scent, to be wrapped up in their embrace.

And I *know* this is what Radwa's doing because I keep catching her smiling to herself and looking down every so often when she breathes in. Honestly, it's so glaringly obvious. I was the same when I fancied Mitch. I was wearing his jacket when we first kissed, sans all the patches and additional badges.

It's funny how it happened. He showed up at my house that day reeking of aftershave in a fucking shirt-and-tie combo with flowers and all, asking if I wanted to go see a movie. He paid for dinner before the movie and even bought tickets and snacks at the theatre. This was a big deal because the cinemas here are extortionate, and the whole night I could tell all he wanted was for us to have a nice time together.

It happened at the end of the night. We were waiting for our bus home in the freezing cold shelter. His jacket was wrapped around my shoulders while he shivered in his thin shirt. I could see the goosebumps forming on his arms.

He never was very good at blocking me out, so I could tell how much he wanted to kiss me, and I decided to make the first move for him.

As we came apart, he confessed to having been thinking about that all night, resting his forehead on mine. I knew this, of course I knew this; I was in his head.

It might've been telepathy back then but that ease has followed us into our day to day life without either of us having to say or think a word. We find the comfort that we used to find in each other's hoodies in our relationship.

I want that for Radwa. I know where she is right now with Lolly is uncharted territory, but I really hope they work it out. I've watched them go from cautious acquaintances, to friends united against the world, to something that might blossom into love. Both of them deserve it, whatever that will mean for them. But I don't want to push Radwa for any information that she's not ready to figure out herself.

We go back to quietly existing together while she tries to convince me that a far more interesting conversation would be to debate which of us could get away with murder.

'I don't think I could,' she says thoughtfully, looking up from her bracelet for a second, 'morally I mean.'

I laugh. 'But physically, no problem.'

'Oh for sure,' she scoffs. 'We watch *so* much true crime and I've been to, like, ten of Mitch's classes over the years, so I'm basically a ninja. And I'm a *werewolf*. Not only could I do it, I could get away with it. I just can't imagine anything that would justify it,' she rationalises.

'Not even –' I tail off, about to ask about Lolly and their dad.

She blinks. 'I guess, but everything has a consequence. Doing that is what meant they were left alone to look after themself.'

I think for a moment. Knowing what it's like to watch someone die in front of me, to hold someone I love as they bleed out, I've thought a lot about how far I'd go to protect someone. I reckon I'd go as far as I needed to. For Mitch, or her, or Lolly. For anyone in my family. If anyone threatened their lives…

'Well' – I smile, finally – 'as long as you help me hide the body, I guess I can cover our backs.'

Lolly

Being stuck in the car with Mitch's nervous energy on the way home makes me a little tense. He doesn't even put on any music when we get in, he just drives in silence. At first I thought about saying something to him, but approaching the topic of Mel always makes me feel a bit uneasy. I know it's when he's at his most volatile and I don't want to put my foot in it.

So instead I just kind of stare out the window imagining skating along the road next to us. The council have recently redone the road between the girls' house and the high street, and I like how it feels to skate on. The board glides easily over the smooth black surface. It feels so clean. So easy. There's no resistance. It's peaceful.

I think Radwa would like skating; it clears your head. Sometimes, I think she needs time for things that calm her down because she's good at bottling up everything that stresses her out. I'm like that, but that's why I skate. It's also why I smoke but she doesn't ever want to do that.

Maybe I should take her on a skate date. I could help her learn. But I don't know exactly where the line for us lies anymore. She seemed surprised at the party when I wanted to dance with her. We're gonna need safety pads if she doesn't want me to touch her anymore.

'What's the craic with you guys, anyway?' Mitch eventually grumbles beside me as we pull into the highstreet, halfway done our two mile drive back to his.

Oh. Yeah. Something happened with Radwa.

'I don't know?' I blush. 'I told her I'd like it if she borrowed my jumper, and she kinda froze? She's definitely got to know I like her now right?'

'Babe.' Mitch calls me 'Babe' all the time. Especially when he's being serious about something. The nickname almost punctuates the tone of his voice. It's an indication that I need to be fucking real about something and is usually followed with something like 'I'm telling you this because I love you'. 'I'm pretty sure half of my outfit is yours right now. My socks definitely are.'

That was a confession I definitely didn't want to know. 'Gross!' I reach out to shove him.

He dodges. 'And you tell me and Val we look hot all the time.'

It's true, I like complimenting and low-key flirting with my friends. 'Well I'm not gonna outright kiss her without talking to her about stuff, am I? I don't know where the line is, religiously.'

It's hard to try and talk to Radwa about religion too. Not

because she's not open to it or that I'm not open to learning, but more because talking about it makes me feel flighty and uneasy. My family don't really talk about it, and not in a 'it's not something that comes up' way. They *won't* talk about it. Perks of being Scots-Irish with a half-Catholic half-Protestant family who were married in the eighties. And no one really seems to get what I believe in. Well, except for Jesus, ironically.

I shrug, looking at Mitch. 'I don't want to overstep it or disrespect her boundaries.'

He looks done with my shit. 'Babe.' He *is* done with my shit. 'If you don't know where the line is? Maybe... fucking ask her.'

'Why is that my job?' I ask as we pull into our street. 'She knows I like her now she's got my hoodie.'

He parks the car, slowly and deliberately pulling the handbrake on as if giving me time to think about something. Then he looks down at his outfit. He is *also* wearing my jumper, but that's different and he knows it.

'You know that Radwa can be a bit oblivious,' he finally says. 'You really need to spell things out for her.'

'Well that's great because I'm dyslexic.'

Mitch does not find me funny. Radwa would've laughed at that. 'Ask her on a date. You can talk about it there and figure out what you want,' Mitch suggests. He's a bit of a dick sometimes but he's good at relationships.

'Okay! Okay!' I roll my eyes, taking my phone out of the butt pocket on my left side. It's smashed to shit because I keep it in there when I'm skating.

'Remember to specify it's a date,' he insists.

'I will!' Pushing him away, I pull my phone closer to my face to type, adjusting my glasses and hoping my screen can still register what I'm typing.

                                          Hiya!

Yikes, too eager, and too '90s mum.

>   Sup

Too casual and who the fuck do I think I am.

>   LOLLY
>   Hey mo leannan you doing okay?

Mitch scowls at me, gesturing for me to get to the point.

'Fuck off, I'm working on it,' I whine, biting the inside of my cheek. I always do that shit when I'm nervous. Granny said she did it when she was my age too. Sometimes I still catch her doing it and I wonder what she looked like at eighteen. Grandad tells me about when they were young and full of teenage rebellion every time he's got a shot in him. Then he starts playing The Cranberries.

'*Mo leannan*?' Mitch asks, looking over my shoulder at the sent text awaiting Radwa's response.

'It's a Gaelic term of endearment, like saying "my sweetheart".' If my friends don't start learning Gaelic, I am going to start throwing hands. Genuinely, I don't think they understand how important keeping it alive is to me.

'Does Radwa actually know that one?' Mitch raises his eyebrow and I glare back at him turning my phone so he can't see.

>   RADWA
>   Yeah I'm starving but all good!
>   No nicks or scratches this time!
>   Wby? How was the drive home w
>   Mitch?

The text smiles up at me while I bite my cheek again.

>   RADWA HASHMI HAS CHANGED YOUR
>   NICKNAME TO HABIBI <3
>
>   RADWA
>   Hehe ;) x

This girl has my whole heart in her hand.

```
YOU CHANGED RADWA HASHMI'S
NICKNAME TO MO LEANNAN X
```

Okay cool. This is cool. This is fine.

```
                          HABIBI <3
      Quiet… think I'd rather have
      skated XD
```

I text back as Mitch pops his door open, grabbing his keys and his juice from the cup holder. Oh shit wait—

```
                          HABIBI <3
                                Xx
```

Nailed it.

```
MO LEANNAN X
I feel for him this must be hard
:((
If you do go skating at some
point send me videos of your
tricks I was talking about them
to Aadilla the other day :3
```

Oh so she just casually talks about me to her other friends. That's *cool*. That's *fun*.

```
                          HABIBI <3
      Was thinking that may be you
      might like to try skating w/ me
      sometime? I could teach
      you :) xx
      After we stop hurting from the
      moon obvs xx
```

Are the kisses excessive now? Why has she stopped doing them? My heart hammers so hard against my chest I feel sick.

```
MO LEANNAN X
Sure thing! Maybe Friday?
```

> Aw no, are you hurt? Sending
> kisses to make it better! xxxx

Oh my God. OH MY GOD.

I muffle a little scream into my t-shirt and yank the door open to go and show Mitch before he hops in the shower.

By the time we've both cleaned up and eaten we feel a lot more ready to address the pressing issue of the clothes we found.

Honestly, I reckon I'm more nervous to see Radwa again after that wee text flirt than I am to deal with a potentially psychopathic killer werewolf. Mitch actually has to remind me to grab the little bottle with the scent in it as we're heading out the door because I'm too busy checking my septum ring is sitting right in my phone camera so I don't look a state when I see her.

I almost miss the purple hoodie hanging on the line in the garden next door. But as I lock the door behind us I notice Mitch's eyes narrowed and fixed on it.

It's inside out, tags showing, and flapping in the breeze. The scent of sage and vanilla no longer clings to it, but it clings to other things around the garden: the dog sitting in the sun nibbling at its paws, the punching bag, the shed in the corner.

I think I know why that scent was so familiar. Mitch's thoughts come out as though he's speaking through gritted teeth. *Those clothes are the exact same ones we found near the clubhouse.*

Chapter Five

Mitch

Somehow, Lolly manages to persuade me that I have to pick up Val and Radwa before I try to break down Wren's door. So now, we all sit parked outside my house, just watching the heavy purple fabric flapping gently in the wind.

I'm just saying, I think, rather than say it out loud so that we're not overheard, *it's weird that they happened to move next door to us, show up at Lolly's work and Radwa's school, and order from your shop all on the same day.*

I thought that was strange too! Radwa chimes in.

Val's brow furrows as she fidgets cautiously with her necklace. For some godforsaken reason, she has been apprehensive to admit what we all already know. She kept insisting that lots of people could have that hoodie when we first told her what we saw, and even now when the scent is undeniable she's *still* looking for some kind of innocent explanation to all of this.

Honestly it makes me kind of mad. Why is she of all people so defensive of them? Does she not remember that night? Was the weight of my sister's fucking corpse, as she pulled me out from underneath her, not heavy enough to leave a lasting impression?

Mitch! She looks at me, hurt, letting the necklace drop on her chest again.

I press my hands into my eyes for a second before letting them drop down my face to come together on my lips. *I'm sorry. I'm just saying they're literally a werewolf. And they clearly made a conscious effort to seek us all out the night before the moon.*

Okay, but, Lolly starts, leaning forward on their seat and crinkling the empty cans of Monster that they've collected there this week, *being a werewolf doesn't necessarily make you evil. None of us are exactly monsters. If they wanted us hurt they could've just let Tyler's mates beat the shit out of me.*

Val turns in her seat so that she's looking back at them instead of looking forward with me. I know I've hurt her feelings and the guilt from it sits heavy in my stomach. But I can't understand why they're all so fucking quick to trust this.

Exactly, she thinks, winding a silvery strand of hair around her finger. *Maybe they just recognised what we were and wanted to make friends so they wouldn't have to spend the moon alone.*

Okay, but why are they so desperate to make friends that they moved in next door? I turn around in my seat and look at Lolly, refusing to be locked out of this conversation. *And you said they bought wolfsbane from Jesus. That's weird.*

Their little brother was being bullied, Radwa chimes in helpfully from behind me. *His name's Phelan.*

I imagine she's referring to the elder of their two brothers, the lanky emo kid I saw glued to his phone when they were moving in. He does seem like he'd be kind of an easy target for that shit unfortunately.

The wolfsbane thing is still sketchy as fuck, Lolly admits. *That shit's even poisonous to humans.*

Radwa nods in agreement.

But, Val starts, as my hairs stand up on end, jaw tensing, *it doesn't necessarily mean they're after us specifically, and it can be—*

Why are you being so defensive of them!? I finally snap. My thoughts unintentionally cut her off, loudly enough for everyone to hear. *They have been nothing but suspicious and, even if they have nothing to do with him now, they* did *know Tyler.*

Val turns back to look at me with an expression I've not been on the receiving side of for quite some time. It's one I've often seen her give to Lolly when they switch on me or Radwa. Her stunned silence is not for lack of argument. She's just appalled that I'd dare to say what I'm saying. The guilty knot twists further.

The icy silence between us is interrupted when Lolly butts in. *Having bad taste does not make you a serial killer.*

Val cracks a smile. *Exactly, just ask Lolly's ex-girlfriends.*

They kick her seat with a chuckle, but I can't find the humour. Before I know it I clamber out of the car and march up Wren's front path.

'Mitch, calm down, it might not be what you think!' Lolly lets themself into the garden, leaving the gate swinging open for Val and Radwa to follow.

I pound on the front door with both fists.

Moments later, Phelan opens it, eyes glued on his Switch. Between the big black fringe, the insane amount of wristbands covering his right arm, and the My Chemical Romance t-shirt, looking at him is like staring into a mirror of my past.

He pauses the game and looks up. His *silver* eyes grow wide.

'Wren!' he immediately shouts. 'Someone is here for you!' There is caution in his voice. He picks up the TV controller to turn the music down.

Wren rushes in, nearly being taken out by a gigantic husky as they do. 'Phelan, can you give us some space please?'

He looks at them apprehensively and then leaves.

Wren backs off into the house, nodding us in with a slight

tilt of their head. It's almost surreal to see my house but reversed as we enter, just missing the collection of clutter my parents have accumulated over the years. I never thought it would be so disconcerting to see the old lino on the floor, scratched up by dog claws. Nor did I ever think I'd actively seek out my mum's collection of magnets in the fridge filled with cheesy quotes that Lolly and I have started getting her for Mothers' Day. But, staring at this blank canvas, I can't help myself.

Wren slides into a chair beside the dining table in the corner which is cluttered with hair supplies. They are wearing silk pyjamas and novelty slippers, and are pleating synthetic purple hair into their own tight coils.

'Sit,' they say, nodding to the chairs in front of them.

Radwa and Val take a seat each. Lolly lowers themself onto the edge of one, keeping a careful eye on me as I stay standing. Wren keeps braiding. They don't look like they've been caught withholding a grave secret.

'Ask, then,' they prompt.

'Are you – you're—' I start spluttering.

'You're a werewolf,' Radwa butts in, as if simply stating a fact.

They nod, fastening an elastic band around a braid. 'Born that way, so are my entire family.' They're not denying it. I find it strange how calm they are acting. They turn to me. 'We didn't attack you though. If that's what you're wondering.'

Val gives me a look as if to indicate that she told me there would be another explanation.

I'm not sure I'm convinced until I actually hear one.

'We didn't move here until about a year ago for a start. You guys turned three years ago, right?'

I nod. They continue to braid, their fingers effortlessly weaving three sections around each other. It's mesmerising to watch, but not quite distracting enough to take away from the fact that they've yet to prove anything to us.

It feels like an eternity before they start speaking. In what should be a very loud house, the only sound worth noting is the drumming of Lolly's fingers on the table.

'We heard about it happening.' They rock back in their seat, reaching over to the counter to grab another tiny elastic band. After securing it tight, they continue. 'But initially we weren't too worried.'

Even Val's head snaps up at that. She leans back from the table into her chair. My claws start to dig into the palm of my hand as I ball my fists tight. I only realise I've been pacing when I stop dead in my tracks. How the fuck does someone dying not warrant concern? Not *someone*, my sister. A kid. She was a *kid*.

Wren's face flushes and their hands fall from where they were separating their hair into sections. 'Sorry, that was insensitive, wasn't it? I didn't mean… We figured whoever turned you was dead. Wolves don't normally turn people unless it's life or death. If they do, they get sick, like rabid and dying levels of sick. We call them rogues.'

Rogues. Rogue wolves. As opposed to… normal wolves, I guess.

But that still doesn't answer why no one came. Clearly, a sick rogue is still dangerous. And what if there were multiple of these rogues?

The drumming of Lolly's fingers finally stops. 'So why not check in?' they ask the question everyone else is thinking.

A dark cloud crosses Wren's expression, turning the room unseasonably cold. 'We couldn't spare the resources.' Their voice is a whisper. Their eyes are cast down. They start fidgeting with the purple hair in front of them again, sectioning it out. I never noticed before how scarred their hands are. 'My pack were at war. Had been since before I was born. A lot of people died. Then, when things calmed down and we realised the rogue was still active, my Uncle Cygnus –

our alpha – sent me to find it.' They give an awkward grimacing smile and lift a hand in a wave.

That… makes some amount of sense. If they have a mission to find this rogue wolf that would explain the wolfsbane. And it also explains getting close to us, but then—

'You said you've been here a year, so why only reach out now?' I ask, unsure why I'm starting to believe them, to trust them even.

They glance around, then lean forward across the table and whisper so quietly they're basically just mouthing the words. 'Dad figured you'd be wary of other wolves. And the frequency of the attacks means the rogue is close to dying, so he thought it was better to watch from afar. To just try and keep everyone alive until it died naturally. I disagree.' Their eyes twinkle. 'But I suppose it doesn't really matter. Now that you've found us, the cat's out the bag.'

They side-eye the clothes in the garden. A tiny smile toying with the corners of their mouth tells me they wanted to be found. They nod.

'Back home, I was training to become a soldier. That's why they sent my family on this mission. Dad thinks it's too dangerous, but…' They scrunch their nose, lifting the hair to their own again and leaving the sentence hanging.

I feel that hot bubbly feeling trickling away slowly. In a way, the lack of answers is more frustrating. At least, if they were the one who killed her, I'd know, you know? Instead I'm left with an open wound on my heart, the kind you get from picking at a scab.

'So what?' I ask, interrupting them. 'Your family just so happens to be the good guys sent here to investigate the bad guy and I'm just supposed to believe that?'

'No.' They shake their head, standing up and approaching me tentatively. 'I can show you. You just have to let me in. It's harder, when I'm not in your pack. But you can still hear if you're receptive to it.'

I side-eye Lolly. I don't know why I want to trust Wren, but I do. They remind me of Mel. They seem so genuinely friendly, trusting, and even a little naive.

You've done it before, or you wanted to, when you took me home. I hear a new voice echoing in my head. They smile. *Gotcha.*

They show me all of it through their eyes.

Wolves like us, half-turned, running through the woods, leather armour covering their vitals, silver weapons in gloved hands.

I'd never seen a dead body before Mel, but Wren's memories have shown me a dozen in the first few snippets of their life. It all comes back to this same room: a bunker, a training centre with armoured walls. A man, their dad – no – Magnus doesn't use that word but he *is* her parent, and her instructor, a valued soldier turned teacher in the war.

Their mum is next, staggering home in front of them and Phelan after she was nearly fatally injured. Phelan's dismay and sense of betrayal when they announced their decision to follow in her footsteps. His howls of anguish into a tear streaked pillow when the boy across their street did. A man who looks like he could be their older brother – no, cousin – and his friends who they spent their childhood running after.

Then I see a man who looks almost exactly like my memory of their dad, but not quite the same. Nearly a foot taller than me and twice as wide and muscular. He sits next to them, manner friendly but golden eyes solemn.

Wren knew they would be given a mission. It was expected from them being one of the first in line for alpha. After the war it was only a matter of time before they'd have to prove themself. They just thought they would have longer.

'Find the rogue. Then you know what to do. Dead dogs don't bite,' he says with a wink, handing them something before their memories whisk him away.

Wren is left holding a silver dog tag with an aconite flower stamped on the front. They add it to their chain along with their ID number. It's a special rank among their soldiers, a hunter among wolves. Someone who's sent to handle the rogues.

Their mum paces frantically, yelling at the friendly man who is now looming over her as their dad tries to reason with him. Magnus's hand on their shoulder gives it a reassuring squeeze.

They were excited when they got here but that quickly faded to hurt.

'I'll call Cygnus,' their dad says, standing, agitated, in a cramped living room. I can tell the difference between him and his brother, Wren's uncle, just by how they handle themselves. 'You don't have to stay here. If any of them think *any* less of you, they can answer to me. If *he* says anything, I'll challenge him myself. Do you hear me?' His voice wavers as if he's swallowing tears.

Magnus places a gentle hand on his partner's chest, gathering his long cardigan around himself and approaching them with more tact. 'Do you want to report him?' he asks, sitting next to them on the couch where Phelan has his arm wrapped around their shoulders, holding them in a tight embrace.

They knew in their gut they would never win any court case. Their family would support any decision they made, but dragging them through all of that felt unnecessary. No one would believe someone like them. And besides, *he* had the money to get away with it.

I catch a glimpse of a familiar face, teeth bared in an ugly knowing smile.

Tyler. The guilty knot from earlier creeps back in. I hope they can't hear me thinking about what I said.

The image is shooed away as quickly as it comes in.

He is why their dad was worried about them getting hurt again, why he wants them to stand down and try to keep people safe instead of hunting the rogue.

As they think of the rogue, I see exactly what they mean by that word.

A wolf whose body seems to give in when they turn. It decays as time goes on. I see images of wolves in pain, and anguish, failing to heal, and injuries turned gangrenous.

I feel a strange kind of pity for the wolves in the images. I know what it's like for your body to fail you.

Why does this happen to them? I ask, watching them screaming in pain.

It happens when they turn and choose *to feed off of people after being attacked. When presented with the choice they choose to be monstrous. Some human beings will take any excuse to act like an animal.*

The command they have over their thoughts is incredible. They only show us what's relevant to what they're telling us, guiding us through their memories precisely with no random interruptions from unconscious thoughts. I've never known anyone who could control their internal voice that well.

Consuming human blood aggravates the lycanthrope gene. They stop healing and start dying. The only way to stop it is for them to consume the blood of freshly turned werewolves.

They pause for a moment, choosing their next words, while still letting us see the images.

The more time goes on the more they need to turn and kill, they finally add, mental voice a little constrained.

Somehow Val still catches what they're thinking. 'You think Mel's blood turned it rogue, don't you?'

Wren shuts the image down. It's like a screen going black in the cinema. We're all thrown out of their head. In the present, they stare at Val, perplexed.

'How – did you—' they start, breathing heavily, chest rising and falling as though they've just ran a marathon.

'You think *that* is what turned us? What *killed* my sister?' I interrupt, feeling the red hot feeling bubbling up in my chest again.

What does that mean? Was that awful night a targeted attack from someone *willing* to become a monster? Someone who *wanted* to become a monster?

It's too much to hear all of this. I pat my pockets down for my lighter and tobacco, making for the door.

When I open it, one of the tall bald men from their memories is standing there, coarse and coily beard cutting sharp lines across his features. He stoops as he walks through the door frame.

Wren looks up, fingers pausing in their hair, biting their lip.

'Wren,' he says, reprimanding, 'care to explain what's going on?'

Chapter Six

Val

Wren's internal voice is so *loud* in my head. Almost as loud as Mitch and Radwa, and swimming with random little thoughts and bids for safety. What would they do if someone attacked the house right now? Where are their main exits? How close are Phelan and Conan?

All hidden behind their calm exterior.

That's how I know that they're not scared of their dad when he walks in. He cocks an eyebrow at them, folding his arms over his wide chest and leaning back on the counter when he asks what's going on.

There is some worry in the back of their mind, but it's about disappointing him. They've never genuinely been scared of him. There's a real and clear difference between that and how Lolly and Radwa fear their parents.

'They found out?' they say, by means of an answer, but their voice makes it sound like more of a question.

Their Dad's silver eyes glance from the garden back to where they sit. 'I wonder how that happened.' He doesn't look disappointed. If anything he looks sort of impressed. His face contorts slightly as he fights the smile threatening to break through his expression.

'It's lovely to meet you all,' he says kindly, addressing us. 'My name is Art. I imagine you're all understandably overwhelmed right now. So I suggest we continue this little *lesson* my daughter has *taken it upon themself to teach* shortly.' He gives a curt nod to the door filled with the same sort of blunt awkwardness Wren has in their speech but lacks in their internal voice.

Once outside, Mitch makes for his at a pace. Lolly looks after him with some concern.

I've got it. Give us a second, I tell them carefully, before running in after him.

When I find him he's sitting on the edge of his bed, hands shaking as he fumbles with his grinder, the bitter scent of weed and metal filling the air. He looks like a shell of himself. He stares forward with eyes not really seeing, like he did the first few months after Mel.

I knock on the bookshelf by the door. Its shelves are buckled slightly and it blocks off half of the built-in-wardrobe covering the hole where his door should be.

Sweetheart? I ask softly, trying to draw his attention back to the present.

They don't get it. His thoughts are coming fragmented and fast. Images of Mel, happy and in our lives, intertwined with images of her laying on that path, lifeless. *None of them fucking get it. It's like she's just a corner piece of their fucking puzzle. She was a person. She was* my *person,* our *person.* He looks up at me, hair messy from running his hands furiously through it.

His eyes are dry, and he's furious at that fact – a red hot bubbling fury he can't put into words.

I understand, I promise him, sitting down next to him and placing a hand over his knee, giving it a little squeeze.

He places his hand over mine and for a moment we just sit

there, neither of us really okay but content in the fact that that *is* okay.

I wait for him to pull back first. When he does he shuffles over to the other side of his bed gingerly, expression slightly pained as he pulls his knees to his chest and leans against the wall behind him.

'Are you okay?' I whisper.

He nods. 'Just stressed and sore,' he admits, freeing one arm from the cocoon he's wrapped himself in and signalling for me to join him.

I tuck myself under it sitting just under his window.

'I'm sorry about earlier,' he whispers into my hair, pressing two kisses onto my head. 'I know I was out of line I was just – thinking about that night triggers something in me and—'

'None of us were really listening to your concerns,' I admit, my stomach twisting. Trusting Wren so automatically over him feels like some kind of betrayal. 'I'm sorry for that too. I don't know what came over me I just – feel connected to them, I guess. Like maybe they're the key to unravelling all of this. Maybe they're how we get closure and get our old memories of Mel back instead of…'

That night. Instead of the spatterings of that night that have interrupted any thought or fond memory of her for years.

'It's okay,' he says sincerely, thumb rubbing the back of my hand. 'We both have our shit from that night.'

I reach to kiss him but he pulls back.

'It is *genuinely* okay, but I feel kinda sick right now. I wouldn't.' He grimaces.

I study him: he hunches over his legs; his usually pale skin looks grey. Maybe it's the lack of smudged black eyeliner but I can't help but feel his water line is a little pale too.

'You don't look very well.' I push myself up to take him

in, concerned, placing a hand to his forehead. He feels clammy.

The grip on my shoulder gets slightly tighter as a spike of pain shoots through him. I know what this is. I've had to hold him through this before, his hand clutching desperately at the back of my shirt willing me never to let go.

Mitch has endometriosis. Very few people are allowed to go near him with a ten foot barge pole when he's going through this. Fewer still are allowed to touch him at all. He is on medication to hold it off, but starting T must've put everything out of whack, hormonally.

'Could this day get any fucking worse?' he groans, throwing his head back and letting it hit off the wall. Which is apparently a very stupid idea because the next second he shoots up, letting his grinder drop on the duvet beside me.

The sound of him being sick in the bathroom across the hall confirms my suspicions. It's going be a long week.

My phone buzzes twice in my pocket as I lean back against the windowsill. He gets weird about people seeing him like this so I don't follow.

```
WREN BLACKBURN HAS ACCEPTED YOUR
FRIEND REQUEST.
```

The other notification is a message.

```
WREN, 4.08 PM
Hey, sorry about all of that!
Dad said you can come over for
dinner in a couple of days so
that we can talk it all over if
you want. Let me know!
```

It buzzes again as I'm reading it.

```
WREN
Is Mitch okay? I think I heard
him being sick.
```

I don't realise I'm smiling until my cheeks start to hurt. It's the sincere punctuation that gets me. I wonder if texting, like speaking verbally, is something they don't take to quite as naturally as telepathy. They could've just jumped into my head to say hi, but I kinda respect that they didn't. The OCD would probably be off-putting to people who don't know me. I wouldn't want them to think I *enjoy* half of what's going on in there right now with Mitch being ill. I touch my tongue to my bottom lip, toying with the piercing there, while I debate how to reply.

> VAL
> Hey!!! Sounds good. Yeah he's fine he's just got a health thing :)

I stare at it for five full minutes debating whether or not it needs the smiley face at the end.

Mitch comes back in right as I press send. I show him it and he nods before burying himself in the crook of my neck for a desperate and exhausted cuddle.

Radwa

I'm sitting at my computer desk a few days later with Val, feet tucked under me and my orange weighted blanket on my lap. Val's on my right side, legs curled on her own chair, clicking the screen to make a runway look for the next category. She leans forward, pushing her glasses up. Her eyes are locked intently on the screen as she pops another Magic Star into her mouth.

I'm pretty sure this game was made for seven-year-olds, not actual fashion students who need a distraction from course work and worrying about their boyfriend.

Mitch goes radio silent for a week or so whenever all this happens.

It really takes it out of him, especially after the moon. By the end of it, he is very weak and tired. Usually, the vomiting lasts for about two days. He loses a lot of muscle weight during these episodes and a lot of nutrition. He's already quite naturally slim, but this makes him skinny, and people notice. They compliment him. He gets quite irate at this. As if he's willing them to see that he just had to battle for his life for two whole days, minimum. The whole thing makes him dysphoric, too.

Not that he tells us.

I stare at the message I sent him last.

RADWA

```
hey! you doing okay? let me know
if you need to scream xx
```

There's no reply. Instead, he's heart-reacted to the message. That's fine. It's our way of talking when it all gets too much, which is actually kind of nice. Lolly and Val need so much reassurance on these things that it's comforting to have someone I can just shut-down on without it being an issue. Reacting to it means we've seen it, we appreciate it, but don't have the social battery to respond right now. We've agreed on this meaning, so it works.

I just worry because I can hear him bullying himself every time he looks at his wrists or his shoulders and sees sharp bone poking at the skin, feeling feeble and useless – half the man he *thinks* he should be. He's usually better at blocking us out when he's dysphoric but he doesn't have the energy to think or even move right now. At least this time it wasn't on the full moon. That is always hellish.

Lolly lights up my phone providing an actually useful update.

> LOLLY
> He stopped being sick yesterday
> touch wood. Witch usually means
> hes on the mend! How's Val? Xx

I smile, looking over at her as she savagely rates some random kid's outfit two out of five stars.

> Radwa
> she's been quieter than usual …
> worried about him I think but
> maybe also sad about the Mel
> stuff?? Think she's kinda
> excited to make a new friend.
> She KEEPS talking about Wren! Xx

They text me back as quickly as always. Val glances over at me, rolling her eyes with an affectionate smile.

> LOLLY
> Should I tell Mitch to be
> jealous lmao

Then they continue.

> LOLLY
> If you need some air I thought
> maybe we could go skating
> together now we're healed up
> a bit?
> Just the two of us?
> Xx

What is *that* supposed to mean? My cheeks burn hot as my smile rises. I pause for a second debating what to say next.

Val exits the game, then turns to me swinging her legs around over one of the chairs arm rests.

'What's Lolly saying?' she asks, crossing her arms over one of the plushies she brought from her room that sits in her lap. She has so many it's ridiculous.

I only have one teddy, a bunny called Bonnie. She is also

sitting on my lap right now. Lolly got her for me when they found out I hadn't gotten any teddies growing up. I don't know why. It's not that my parents were neglectful. I had plenty of other toys. A bike, train sets, a Wii. But now I have Bonnie. She smells like lavender, and she has a little red heart somewhere deep within her stuffing.

I tuck her under my arm as I spin my seat to look at Val. 'They're asking how you are and also maybe thought that we could go out together today just the two of us.'

There's that phrase again. Specifically *just* the two of us. I know they *probably* don't mean it how I'm taking it, but the fact it could be mildly dubious is enough to make my heart skip a beat.

'Like a date?' Val asks.

I slide my eyes off into the corner of the room. 'They didn't phrase it like that.'

Val grabs my hands, shaking them. 'They obviously mean it like that. Have you not been flirting ever since the jumper thing? And you said the thing about kis—' she starts.

'I know what I said!' I butt in immediately, sinking into my chair and feeling a little guilty.

'Okay,' – she holds her hands up – 'I'm gonna go make us breakfast so you have space to get dressed for your date.' She laughs.

I throw a pillow at her and she leaves.

It's not like I *don't* want to kiss Lolly. Actually it's the opposite. I think about it all the time. I even dream about it. But I don't know if I'm okay with the idea of doing it – with anyone – if I'm not married.

That was always my expectation growing up. It's how my parents did it, and I always thought they were pretty romantic and loving when it came to each other. Not great parents, admittedly, but a great couple, you know?

Anyway, the way they taught it, the way it was always taught to me, is that you don't touch any romantic prospects before marriage. So generally, before marriage, men don't touch women and vice versa unless it's life or death, they're family, or if one of the people in question is a very young child.

Which worked for a time. Until I realised I was trans, and a lesbian, and then the person I actually fancied turned out to be non-binary, so all of those guidelines got muddied.

I roll Bonnie's long ears with my thumb and forefinger and I glance at my phone trying to decide how I want to reply. Things have been kind of flirty lately and I like that. It's just, even though some other queer Muslims I've seen online seem okay with more physical stuff before marriage, I don't know if I am. I mean, kissing leads to other things and, while *they* have experience there which I am completely okay with, I *definitely* don't want to give myself that completely to someone unless I know it's going to be forever, unless I'm certain Allah set them on my path for *me*.

Not that any of that even matters right now. I don't even know if Lolly likes me or if they're just jokingly flirting like they do with everyone. At the party I thought there was maybe a vibe, but I'm terrible at interpersonal stuff as a whole.

Actually, I think I might be autistic, and given that *Lolly* is the one who was helping me try to sort out the diagnostic papers, you'd think they'd know to be a little more direct if they are trying to flirt.

I pull the blanket up so it's covering me better, in an attempt to pull myself back into the moment and convince myself to stop over-thinking it and focus on the here-and-now.

RADWA
Sounds good! Meet at mine? xx

I text them back, pressing my mouth into the top of Bonnie's fluffy little head.

In the back of my mind I *know* Lolly wouldn't be the kind of person to push me into doing anything I didn't want to do. I just don't want to lead them on, and it's pretty hard to avoid that when I've not decided what *I* want from a relationship yet.

But whatever it is I want, I know I can't rush myself into deciding. My religion means a great deal to me. Afterall, it helped me get clean from self harm *and* it motivated my Dad's acceptance of my identity.

I waited seven months before my dad spoke about me being trans. It wasn't even him I heard it from. I was at my friend Aadilla's house and had gone downstairs for a glass of water. Her father, Nazim, was talking to her mother about how my dad had come to him for guidance. Nazim was the first person from my community who accepted me. It meant a lot.

When my dad finally came around and spoke to me, he spoke to me about something in Sûrah At-Taghâbun.

He said that having children is equal parts challenge and reward. As his child, I was never intended to be his carbon copy. I was always supposed to challenge him. Sure, he would never have predicted it, but he had ultimately decided that challenging ignorance made him a better man.

'And that,' he said softly, 'is my reward for having such a brilliant child.' He met my eyes. 'The greatest gift Allah has ever given me.'

On that visit, Dad used my name for the first time. He smiled softly and told me that Mount Radwa had been one of the highlights of his first holiday with my mother.

'It's very tall' – he smiled – 'and one of the most beautiful things I've ever witnessed.'

The crows feet on the side of his dark eyes had crinkled when he looked at me, corners of his mouth turning up.

From then on I was his daughter. I was Radwa. My father saw my happiness and decided there was no way that Allah would favour how I had been before. And that was that. It was inspiring to see him pair Islam and my queer identity with such unapologetic harmony.

I could use some guidance on that ground now. Though I worry that asking him about Lolly might confuse him entirely. I'm not sure he even realises you can be trans *and* gay yet. We're taking baby steps together.

My phone buzzing pulls me out of my memory. Lolly has just let me know Mitch is driving them up in ten minutes because he wants to see Val.

I launch myself up and trip across the room trying to unwind from my blanket so that I can get dressed.

After clattering my way into several objects and managing to poke a hole in one of my tops, I manage to make my way down the stairs clinging onto a shred of poise.

Val's sitting in her kitchen with her parents when I get down. This room is definitely not intended for four people but we somehow make it work. The shelves overflow with ingredients and planters of herbs hang over the edge of the windowsills and the fridge.

They greet me with a chorus of good mornings as I grab a waffle from the bread bin and sit down on the floor next to the fridge with Tato – their dog – as the kettle brews. This is one teaching I'm dead set on my feelings about. I'm literally a wolf so I'm pretty sure petting dogs is a-okay.

'You look very nice today,' Val's mum, Karen, comments. She's sitting at the little wooden bar in the corner under a little cabinet by some hanging garlic.

'It's because she has a date.' Val smirks at me over the rim of her coffee cup, sitting on the other side of the bar, still in her pyjamas. Her silvery grey hair is tied in a ponytail.

I reach up to kick her, which makes Tato start yapping and Mateo tells us off for upsetting his favourite little princess. He lifts her from the floor, and lets her lick his beard, laughing heartily as she does.

'Okay, sorry, not a date. Radwa just really *really* likes Lolly and has slept in their hoodie every night this week despite it being the height of summer but it's "not a date *gawd*",' Val mocks, giving her mother a meaningful look over the bar.

'Karen, my love,' Mateo says dreamily, his accent making the pet name somehow cuter. 'I feel another nickname brewing.'

Karen chuckles, leaning her head against her husband's stomach. 'You two leave Radwa alone,' she chastises them, despite her grin.

Then a car door closing outside makes Tato jump up and yap again. I glare at Val. Lolly could've totally heard that.

Seconds later, there's a knock at the door.

'Come in, Bobo!' Mateo shouts with a smile as he lays out two more cups for tea. I hear him murmuring to himself in Spanish. With my limited ability I manage to discern him wondering whether 'Bobo One and Two' is too unimaginative on his part.

Mitch comes in and gives Val a big cuddle which lifts her onto her tiptoes. It's obvious he needed that. He's in joggers and a t-shirt with a zippy hoodie on top, which is markedly unusual for him.

'Sexy jammies Val,' Lolly chuckles as they walk in.

Val tells them that she and Mitch are having a 'shitty horror movie and blanket fort' date. I envy the ease they have in their relationship. There's no second-guessing. Mitch is as bad at figuring out what's happening as I am so it works for him.

Lolly and I take a bus into the next town over to go skating. They have a skatepark there. As we leave, Lolly takes my hand in theirs. Just to annoy Mitch and Val of course.

They let go as we get on the bus. It takes forever to get into even the next town when you take a bus in the Highlands, because the driver *kindly* goes down *every single* street picking up old ladies to take them to the shops.

Lolly hates public transport. Which is unfortunate since they would have to fill out a huge amount of paperwork if they wanted to learn to drive, on account of them having BPD. They keep saying they want to try because buses are so overwhelming but then putting it off because of their ADHD.

The passengers are loud and often overbearing. That's why we listen to music together on journeys like this instead of talking. Lolly lays their head on my shoulder. They turn their hand on their knee so their palm faces upward. Then they shrug. I take it. It's just for comfort. They hate buses.

The skatepark is a little crowded when we get there so they take me to a path next to it instead. It's mostly away from everyone else, and the sound of wheels thundering and clattering against tarmac is a little less obnoxious here. The ramps definitely seem daunting. There appears to be some kind of code of etiquette as to who can drop in when, and a spatial awareness between skaters to know how to just nearly miss each other. Two things I'm profoundly bad at.

This was a horrible idea. I'm so clumsy. I almost want to back out until Lolly looks back at me, eyes shining in the sun, lips pulled into a soft kind of smile.

'We can go here 'til you find your feet,' they tell me. 'I've got kneepads and shit, but I don't think you need them for just gliding on the path.' They put their bag down next to us.

I stand on the board, already feeling like my feet are going to fly out from underneath me. I flail my arms out aimlessly. Lolly grabs my hands in theirs to steady me. They hold me upright at first then start to walk along next to me as I helplessly scoot along the path.

It feels like learning to ride a bike. I remember my dad taught me. He held onto the back of my seat while I screamed at him not to let go. 'Beta I won't,' I remember him laughing in my ear.

'Are you ready to try by yourself?' Lolly asks. I feel my hands close tighter around theirs. 'Maybe?'

I feel them open their hands but I'm still holding on. 'You're gonna have to let go eventually.' They laugh, gently pulling their hands away.

I let go and glide about two centimetres on my own before grinding to a halt.

I hop off the board and scoot it towards them. 'That was *so* scary.'

They grin, looking over to the ramps which are now clearing up. I encourage them to go and have a shot after firmly telling them that neither love nor money could convince me to try them myself.

They attempt to take a turn and showboat but, apparently, my very presence interferes with their skating ability and they 'can't do it the same' when I'm watching.

After attempting a few more tricks and landing most of them on their butt they decide it's time to teach me one.

I stare at them wide-eyed when they suggest this. They must be joking.

'I could literally teach a two year old this trick. Come on! If you can jump you can do it.' They bait me over to a mossier area, promising me the board won't slip as much there.

They show it to me first. Placing the board upside down atop their feet, they jump and then land with the board the right way around.

I try it, but the wheels slide out from underneath me and I land on the floor.

'I thought it was easy?' I say from my heap on the floor.

'It is!' they reply, rushing down to me.

I scowl at them. They hold their hands up. Then they grab my arm. I've scuffed my hand on the grip tape and there's a small graze. They take a plaster out of their pocket and cover it, then give my arm a gentle squeeze.

I stare at the small patch on my hand where a tiny picture of Sylveon now looks back at me. 'Pokémon plasters?'

'Got them for you. Just in case.' They shrug.

They look at me softly for perhaps a second too long. I catch their gaze and then blush, looking down.

They turn scarlet. 'It's coming up to time for your afternoon prayer,' they say, not making eye contact.

That's funny – between their blush, and the fact that they constantly remember my prayer times when I've seen them forget everything from homework to their own birthday before, I almost dare to think for a second that they actually do like me back.

'We should head back to the clubhouse,' they say, still looking at the floor.

I nod. I need to pee anyway.

'Oh, there are toilets over by the ramps,' they offer. I grimace. They shake their head and shrug. 'I wonder if Mitch would feel up to picking us up?'

We start walking to the bus stop in case he isn't. Lolly has kicked up their board and is holding it in one hand. When we walk together we always zig zag along the pavement in opposite directions and bang into each other in the middle but this time they lace their fingers through mine and we zig-zag together.

I don't know when we started holding hands without needing an excuse or an audience. But I do know that I like it, and that makes me nervous. I also know that because I am nervous my hand is sweaty and clammy and I feel terrible. But I also feel happy.

They look up at me out of the corner of their eye, smile, and then blush at being caught. *I hope people see us like this and think she's my girlfriend. I'd be the luckiest fucker alive.*

What?

Wait.

What?

Do they – ? They actually –

I stare at them in wonder for a second as they walk,

bobbing side to side in time with the music they're listening to, completely unaware I've heard them.

Lolly. *Lolly*. That Lolly. *My* Lolly. Lolly Ann Kearney… likes *me*.

And their thoughts weren't about kissing me or anything like that. They were just about being seen with me, belonging to each other.

My heartbeat thunders in my ears as we come to a shop on the high street. It has a tall wall in front of it. They let go of my hand to climb on top.

My chest starts to feel heavy as they do. Part of me knows that it was different when I didn't know we both felt this way. Dancing, hugging, and hand-holding was okay then. But I'm not sure if it's okay now. I've not decided if it's okay. This complicates everything and I am *terrified* of hurting them or letting them down.

'Mitch says they're on the road right now and will be with us in just a second.'

'Oh… okay.' I nod, fidgeting with the bottom of my hijab. My hands are shaking. I take a sharp breath in, stuffing them in the pockets of my dungarees.

'You okay?' they ask, looking down from where they sit.

'Definitely.' I smile, leaning back against the wall. I look at the plaster on my hand again. I pause for a moment. 'Lolly—'

'There's Mitch.' They hop down from the wall as a red car approaches. 'Were you gonna say something?'

'Just…' I blink, holding up my shaky hand. 'Thanks again for this.' I point to the plaster.

Mitch is, surprisingly, riding shotgun when we get in the car, with his feet on the dash and knees pushed into his chest. Val is in the driver's seat.

She *does* know how to drive and she *is* insured on his car. She just likes to be driven about way more.

'Did you guys have fun then?' she asks, glancing back at me in the mirror.

'Yeah, Lolly taught me a trick.'

'Let me guess. Kickflip, first try?' Mitch jokes, turning back in his seat to look at us. Despite looking frailer than before the moon, he looks better today. He has more colour in his face.

Lolly tells him what trick it was. I feel the butterflies in my stomach settle as we sit in the back seats together, seatbelts clicking into place.

They offer me their hand and I wipe mine dramatically on my skirt indicating I'm too sweaty. They laugh.

I can't help but think that I would quite like for people to have seen us like that earlier and assume I was their girlfriend. I'd quite like to be their girlfriend. But I think I need to figure out what both of us expect from that first. I think I need to talk to them.

Chapter Seven

Wren

The sensation of the cold gravel pushing into the knuckles of my middle and pointer fingers makes me feel proud. My triceps burn as I push up for one final rep before jumping back to my feet. I glance down at my hands to confirm that the skin hasn't broken yet – looks like I'm all good to continue.

When we moved here, I knew the tree in the corner of the garden was going to be perfect for shin conditioning. I ready myself in a fighting stance in front of it, sticking my front leg out carefully to measure the distance so I don't accidentally catch it with my instep instead of my shin. Then I pull back, bouncing up and down on my feet, preparing to kick.

You know, the school guidance team recommends a warm bath and a cup of tea when you feel compelled to engage with unhelpful coping mechanisms, Phelan jibes as he comes outside to sit on the doorstep. *Or, alternatively, we could go on a walk together.*

I roll my eyes. He's been on my case about my training recently. Ever since we were younger he's wanted to be a healer, but recently he's been looking into studying psychology while we're here, too. A lot of the pack back home have obvious signs of PTSD from the war, so it makes sense, and it's really helpful to know, but it's a little irritating how dead set he is on the idea that bone conditioning is just a form of self harm. It's purely to help with your endurance in hitting things. When you have to fight, as a soldier, tooth and nail to survive attack after attack after attack, your training is going to look unpleasant to those outside of that sphere. And Phelan has never been a soldier.

Another person went missing after the last moon. To be honest, considering the recent pattern, it wasn't shocking, exactly, but I didn't expect it to be someone I *knew*. I was literally just talking to Emma a couple of days ago.

That's what Phelan doesn't seem to grasp. Not taking my training seriously on this mission would be way more suicidal than some routine bone conditioning. Something – worse, *someone* – is taking a victim every full moon. Mutilating them, turning them, then murdering them.

What time is it? I ask, going over to him to get some water.

Today is set to be pretty full. Val and the others are coming over for dinner and I want to make sure everything is somewhat tidy and sorted for them coming.

Phelan groans. *Half eight.* I hear the hiss of a can opening and the sound of his Switch booting up.

Fuck, this was only supposed to take two hours and it's already been an hour and a half!

I pace back and slam my shin hard into the tree trunk, again, attempting to ignore the delightful sting it brings. It'll be worth it in the end.

My next kick is a lot lighter. God, when did I become so timid? This cannot be the same version of me that was chosen to be an aconite.

There is no suppressing the growl of disappointment that hums in my throat as I readjust my stance, tucking my dog tags back into my sports bra. This is what I get for sleeping in and missing training after that stupid fucking party. For letting my guard down and letting him get to me *again*.

Bark blisters off the tree with the next kick.

Thank God Val was there. If she wasn't, the same thing would've happened again, and I don't think there is any way in hell I could blame anyone other than myself for ending up there.

I don't think I could've lived with myself.

I give a final hard kick before changing my stance, breathing heavily in through my nose and out through my mouth as I imagine the first moment I saw her, silver ringlets framing her face like a fucking halo. I've never had another wolf save my life like that before.

That, coupled with the fact she could hear what was underneath the deliberate arrangement of my thoughts when I was telling them about the rogues is… odd. I know what that usually adds up to for us but I'm not – I've never – I don't have anyone like that. It's always just been me.

It's not normal.

Every other wolf has a mate – usually several of varying relationship styles. Someone whose fate is tied to theirs, who saves them, who's drawn to their side in a time of need. Someone who can hear and understand them in a way few other people ever will. Mates can be human, too, but it's rarer, and they usually don't stay that way for very long.

Do you know how lonely it is to know soulmates are real and never have one?

When we first got here I was wrapped up in this romantic notion that I'd find mine here, in a human I'd fall head over heels for, like how Mum and Dad found Magnus.

But that desperation did nothing but make me vulnerable.

I pull back from the tree with another aggravated snarl through my teeth. The bark has cut through my skin. It heals just as easily as it forms. It's not the pain that gets to me, it's the fact that I'm not putting my all into it. Something is holding me back, stopping me from being the soldier I used to be.

Putting my head in my hands, I sit next to Phelan on the step.

Do you think that girl is your mate? Or one of them? he asks, pausing his game to look at me.

Maybe. I dunno. I wrinkle my nose, feeling my face go hot as I remember the warmth of her hand around my waist holding me steady.

Admitting to a sliver of hope that I might even have one is mortifying, even one that would likely be platonic given that she's clearly very settled with Mitch. Humans, and wolves who grow up human, usually have a weird thing about monogamy, as if soulmates are something singular and finite.

I know I want to be friends with them, figure it out. Beats having to read through Dad's library of leaflets, I say, picking a pile up off the counter. He collects flyers for social clubs for teenagers in the area for us.

Dad has some weird obsession about getting us to socialise with the humans. I get that Magnus was a human when they met and they're not all bad but I'm really not interested in making friends with them anymore. Look, I tried, but I can't help but think Phelan has the right idea. I mean, they bully people for the gender they're attracted to, as if soulmates don't exist.

I mean, I get that they don't know that, but still. How are you going to bully someone for who they are attracted to when they have literally no choice in the matter?

And they don't give a shit about each other. They don't care what anyone else has going on mentally. Sure, they can't read each other's thoughts, but they don't even think to ask each other, and if they do they don't really want to know.

There's a queer one there which doesn't look so bad. Phelan gestures to the flyers.

Ugh, I know, he's making me go to it as punishment for talking to the newbies. I roll my eyes at him and he laughs. *He's framing it as me being too obsessed with the mission and needing to spend some time out in the human world doing something else, but I know it's just a punishment.*

I'll come with you if you want, he offers, looking at his phone to message Harley.

The two have been inseparable since they were babies. We don't know for sure they're mates yet, but we're pretty positive. It makes me kind of mad. I mean he had this guy who was perfect for him, with Harley's sunshiny disposition the perfect contrast for Phelan's 'grumpy' one, right across the road from him from the moment he was born, yet I've never had anyone? It doesn't seem fair.

Nah, you're fine. I know you'd rather stay at home and message Harley, I tell him, partly because I want to spare him the hell that is navigating human interactions.

He's not great with people. All he ever wants to do is play games or talk about Harley or Spiderman. I love him, I just think that his kind offer would overcomplicate things for me. I want to get out of there as soon as I can, come Saturday night.

Do you want help tidying up for the others coming over? he offers, putting his phone down in his lap. His lock screen is a picture of him and Harley dressed up to go to a comics convention the last time he visited. He was leaning over to take the picture, but the angle it's been taken at looks like they're doing the upside down Spiderman kiss.

Sure. I smile, lifting my bottle up off the step. *I'll do the dishes to start?*

He nods. *Did you want that cup of tea?* he asks, standing up to flick the kettle on.

Between the two of us and Dad, we manage to get the house looking ready for visitors before dinner time. We make a good team, us three. It's usually just us. Mum has her own mission from Uncle Cygnus, and Magnus is back home training new soldiers. He's in touch with us a lot more than Mum. We get to call her and her mate Ailsa once a month if we're lucky, and even then we've been ordered not to give them any bad news.

Our younger brother, Conan, does make tidying a little harder. He's three, and constantly leaves his toys everywhere with help from his best friend – Luna, our husky.

They play tug of war together in the living room behind me as I finish my makeup, finally getting a chance to focus on myself. I stretch up on my tiptoes, trying to see my full face in the mirror, as I dust highlighter over my nose and my Cupid's bow.

There's a hard knock at the door as I pack the brushes up. Conan jumps back in surprise, letting out a soft 'offt' as he closely misses falling through my drum kit.

I hear Mitch chuckle through the door as I approach. 'Right, calm down, they can hear you. No need to knock like a cop.'

He's standing back from the rest of the group when I answer the door, hands in his pockets, and watching the others, Val especially, with a gentle fondness. I can tell he hasn't come around to me yet. That's okay though. The past couple of days must've been quite triggering for him, trauma-wise. I wouldn't much like someone falling into my life and dragging up the war or Tyler, even if they were only trying to help.

For the most part, dinner goes smoothly. Dad managed to figure out something that everyone would be okay with. After a week or so of thinking long and hard he landed on… pasta. We eat a lot of pasta as a family of seven who spent years under war-induced food scarcity.

Dad has dragged the collapsible table from the hall through and pressed it side to side with the one that's usually in here. It makes me miss the old kitchen back home where houses were built for more than tiny families of four. We all sit crammed together knee to knee eating in a pregnant silence.

Lolly is the first to break it. If you count all noises, they actually break it at least twelve times in five minutes: jiggling their leg, shifting position, popping their lips repeatedly, shifting position again, cracking their neck, cracking their ankle, shifting another time, popping again, and so on. But they are also the first to speak.

'So, is the silver eyes thing like an *us* thing, or?' they ask, gesturing around the table.

I nod with what I hope is a friendly smile as I reach for the garlic bread.

'So,' Radwa starts, sitting across from me, 'we've actually been talking about this. Why can't we just look for people with silver eyes?'

Well not everyone has silver eyes for one. They're supposed to indicate— Phelan starts.

Dad gives him a careful look then shakes his head and claps his hands together. Then starts to speak out loud. We discussed how this might make them more comfortable to start with rather than Dad or Phelan trying to reach them when they haven't before. 'The rogue wolves have normal eyes.'

Mitch nods, thoughtfully, bringing his hands up to his lips like he's praying. 'So – what's, like, the difference between us and them? What makes them so different? What does human blood do? Why do they have to replenish it?' I see Val examining him carefully as he speaks, looking between my Dad and him, eyes narrowed.

Phelan drops his fork, head snapping up, eyes sparkling. 'Okay so,' he starts, and I swear when he talks about medical shit he starts vibrating at a frequency that *I* can barely understand, bouncing up and down in his seat like a kid talking about going to Disneyland, 'most people think of lycanthropy as a disease, and it is, sort of, in that it can be spread through spit or blood, or passed down genetically. But it's more like a mutation.' He continues, waving his hands quickly in front of himself as he speaks, 'Lycanthropy actually changes how our very cells appear. So, normally, wolves like us would have an excess of mutated platelets, neutrophils, things like that to help us heal faster.'

'Pup.' I give him a nudge with my knee, examining the faces around the table.

Lolly's brows are furrowed as they turn to the side, biting their cheek from the inside and pulling an odd sort of face towards Mitch who sits next to them, head tilted, watching Phelan like a confused puppy.

Phelan doesn't seem to notice either of them. '…As well as this, we have lycanthropic cells in our blood and spit which carry the "disease" and cause transformation, enhanced strength and things like that. When rogues consume human blood, this aggravates those cells. They become malignant and attack the "friendly" healing cells. Luckily, for the rogue that is, the blood of freshly turned werewolves has extra "friendly" cells to make up for the initial transformation, so drinking it pulls their levels up a bit.'

'Pause,' Val tries, putting her head in her hands and rubbing her temples.

Phelan cuts himself off, halfway through his next sentence, tucking his hands underneath his legs on the computer desk chair he's dragged down from his room.

'When you say "freshly turned"?'

'Wolves who haven't had their first moon yet,' I add helpfully.

She nods, sitting back in her seat.

Lolly is tapping the table again now, agitated. 'So how does that relate to the eye thing?'

Dad sighs, reaching over to try and encourage Conan to eat his food. It's funny that he's such a fussy eater. Phelan and I never really had the option. 'The lowered healing cells mean that rogues don't usually live long enough to need a rank. They don't have any place in the pack that's why you usually can't hear them unless they're consciously trying to make commands.' He grimaces, his warm and kind face twisting into one of discomfort.

This is a topic we have to be careful with. Mitch *already* doesn't like us.

'So, betas are the only wolves with silver eyes. It makes sense you all might be. There are really only three things that can make someone a beta.' He pauses again, eyeing them carefully as he turns back around. 'The first being a willingness to stand beside or serve their alpha unquestioningly. Which is extremely unique unless they are one of the alpha's mates.'

He brushes over the concept of mates quickly. We don't need to get into that right now.

'The second is if they themselves are in line to become alpha. If no one kills the current alpha of a pack it's passed down genetically when they die. That's why myself and my children are betas to my brother.' Uncle Cygnus only has one kid himself and no living mates, so during the war all that responsibility could have been thrust onto our shoulders at any given time. 'The third kind of beta is more common than some people would have you think. They are those who are willing and able to challenge or kill their own alpha — or in your case, the rogue wolf that turned you.'

I glance over to where Mitch and Val sit together. Val is looking at her boyfriend with some concern, wrapping one springy curl around her finger. Mitch is looking at his hands and picking the skin around his fingers.

Lolly, sitting on his other side with their back pushed against the handle of a cabinet, is looking at him too. 'What about *other* wolves who *don't* have silver eyes?' they ask, without ever taking their eyes off of him.

'The omegas have bronze eyes,' Dad adds, helpfully.

'That's everyone who's not an alpha or a beta. A lot of healers are omegas if they don't have any relationship with the alpha. Then there's the alpha, one per pack, the head wolf responsible for protecting everyone. Their orders are impossible to disobey.' Dad's face twists into an ugly expression as though there is a bad taste in his mouth.

For us that's Uncle Cygnus. Typically, civil alphas don't throw their weight around all that much, but I have seen him give orders before – to my parents. They don't get on the greatest.

Dad continues, 'Alphas have golden eyes.'

All at once the four new wolves turn from Mitch to him sharply. Four heartbeats raise beating in unison.

Mitch scratches his face and down his neck, fingers lingering on the jagged scratch across it. Then he takes a deep breath in. 'And one silver and one gold?'

Dad puts his cutlery down, folding the napkin on his lap up tightly. 'Well, it's a special type of beta. Rogue wolves can't be alphas because they can't have a pack, but they can give orders to those they sire. And in most cases, one wolf out of the many they turn will possess an inordinate aptitude for rebellion. This wolf has both *reason* and *will* to challenge the rogue. They're usually the one that has lost the most to their attack.'

Mitch is staring at the table, unblinking, as if he's not really there. His thoughts are quiet but his hands are shaking.

'Not only will this wolf be able to challenge the alpha, they will usually be able to disregard orders from the rogue, so long as they can remain in control of their thoughts. As well as this, they can issue their own orders to the others in the pack. For this reason we call them the acting alpha.' Dad looks over to Mitch carefully, his kind silver eyes washing over him, eyebrows bunched together in his distress. 'They're usually responsible for killing the rogue, and once that's been done they will become the alpha.'

I can hear Mitch's heartbeat hammering in his ears, his finger picking at the tape holding his tobacco shut in his pocket, the shaking of his leg up and down under the table. But he doesn't say anything. He just swallows hard. 'Guess we all need a couple of pointers on how to fight this thing then,' he murmurs, taking a sip of his water.

The rest of the night is spent on more mundane things. No one brings up the rankings until a little later. Mitch and Lolly are out smoking in the garden while Dad helps cut the cake that Conan insisted they make this morning so that he could be involved. Radwa is sitting at the table talking to Phelan about the game he's playing on his Switch. Honestly, the past few months made me forget that he could smile as wide as he is now.

Val approaches me as I'm washing up. She glances up at me with a gentle smile and picks up a dish towel from the counter to start helping me.

We've been talking a lot since the group found out about me. She's the one who started our first long conversation.

It was that same night. She had some free time since Mitch was ill, so she messaged me about the bracelets I ordered from her store. Honestly, until then I forgot I ordered them. She wanted to double check if there was a different Pride flag I wanted that wasn't in her store because I just asked for the generic non-binary and trans pride ones. So I showed her some of my badges on my tote bag and explained that I actually do prefer that one because I feel more femme than not. We just kept talking from there. She's probably the only cis person I've ever spoken to that actually makes an effort to *get* it – except maybe Lycaon. He was the first person I came out to so he did some pretty serious research on it.

Val looks up at me again out of the corner of her eye, fidgeting with the bottom labret of her lip piercing.

So the acting alpha thing, she asks, glancing to the side where Mitch is walking down the path chatting to Lolly. The delicate chain around her neck has been twisted around her fingers, holding her hand close to her chest as she picks at a healing scab there. *He's gonna be okay – right? I know he seems fine but – he's been through so much and I – I just – I don't want to find out where his breaking point is—*

That's why I'm here. I cut her off, swaying to the side and giving her a gentle nudge with my elbow. *To make sure he gets through it,* I promise.

She gives me a gentle smile, meeting my eyes and releasing her piercing from between her teeth. Then she looks back down to the cup she's drying.

They leave not long after we've finished with dessert – each with an extra slice of cake for the road. Mitch and Lolly walk out together first. Mitch fiddles with his lighter while Lolly tries to lick melting – dog safe – chocolate from their fingers. Radwa gives me a quick smile and awkward wave on the way out, wrapping her own cake in some kitchen roll.

Val hangs back. She leans her head against the door frame. She holds her hands up by her chest hesitantly. *Do you do –?*

I've never really understood why people need to hug their friends whenever they see them. I'm not like that. I usually only do it to be polite. But she makes it make sense.

Thank you, she thinks quietly as she rubs my back, embracing me, *for being here, and for earlier.*

It seems silly that she's the one thanking *me* for being there for *her* all things considered but I just smile, give her shoulders a squeeze, and tell her that she's welcome.

She finally lets me go, holding my arm for a second after she does and insisting I need to come and hang out with them soon, before walking back to her car with Radwa.

I don't see any of them again until a few mornings later when I'm training in the garden.

I'm doing weapons on a FaceTime call with Magnus. Training with him has always been fun. There's pictures of us together in the dojang when I was only about three or four. It's always been our thing.

My weapon of choice is a silver bo staff with a black rubber hand grip in the middle. After a warm up I sit down to strap my armour on so that the silver doesn't burn my hips, ribs or shoulders. The main pieces are leather panels on each side, shaped to my body, and some smaller shoulder pads. My gloves are the final piece. By the time I pull them on, their black fabric has absorbed enough of the sun's harsh summer rays to make my hands instantly clammy. Training in this weather never gets easier. I pick up the staff, giving it a twirl in each hand to warm my wrists up before tossing it experimentally above my head and then catching it. Then I make a start on my forms – sequences of moves we use to practise combat techniques.

I'm on my final one when Lolly comes out into the garden to water some of the many plants littering the garden. They're bending over some lavender by the front door when they notice what I'm doing. They walk up to the fence as I finish.

'That was sick.' They grin as I walk over to the fence to get my water from the step. 'With the—' They try to imitate the jumping turning axe kick and manage to somehow slosh nearly a full jug of water down their front. 'Okay, so maybe not – you get what I mean.' They flap their hands in exasperation.

'Elegant.' I laugh.

They seem to take the sarcasm well because it earns me a chuckle. 'We were actually gonna go train in our clubhouse today. You should come join us,' they offer with a smile. 'I'll drop you the location.'

I think for a second, resting my staff under my arm. I was a little rigid today and I should probably train a little more to make up for it. But helping them train and getting in some training of my own is a different thing entirely. 'I'll have to see when I finish up.'

Lolly nods understandingly. 'Well, here.' They lift their phone and tap out a message that makes my own buzz where it sits over on the step. They were the second out of all the new wolves to add me as a friend online. 'Just let me know,' they say, then they peel their t-shirt away from their skin with a grimace and retreat back into the house to change it.

You should do it, Magnus thinks as I approach my phone again. *Go make friends.*

I roll my eyes, picking up my staff again. *You sound like dad.*

Magnus scoffs. *Well, considering he is my husband, we are bound to agree occasionally.*

I kick the stones away from the fading tile in front of the bunker my phone is balanced on before planting my feet in place ready to start again. He of all people should understand how seriously I have to take training. He's never trained me to pull back or take a break before.

His face twists mournfully on my screen, eyebrows knitting together forming creases just above his nose. *Before was about training for survival, sweetheart. Now I just want you to live.*

I can feel his careful eyes watching me as I run my forms with the same rigidness as before. He crosses his arms when he's thinking, standing with his arms crossed and biting his lip.

I know! I say as I finish, feeling the frustration bubble in me like an overflowing pot. The urge to take my position by the tree and start knocking the rigidity from my joints is overwhelming. *See, this is why I can't just skive for an afternoon, because that was shit.* Everything's going shit right now. Maybe I'm just shit at this.

Magnus takes a slow and deliberate deep breath, picking up the phone and sitting down on the floor of the training centre as I throw myself on the cold faded red slate beneath me.

Your performance is suffering because you're putting too much pressure on yourself. Take a breather and go out with your friends, he tells me pointedly. *Go on. Have fun. Mess around. Try and come up with your own sequence!*

I pick at the weeds between the slates, refusing to look up at the phone.

Wren, Magnus says reproachfully.

Fine, I grumble, pushing myself up and snatching my bo staff from the floor. The thing is, when it comes to training, even if Magnus is telling me to do something I don't like, I'll still do it because I trust him as an instructor.

Lolly's rambled instructions via text somehow, miraculously, lead me to the new wolves' den – or clubhouse, as they call it. It's a shambles, quite possibly the most run down building I've ever seen in my entire life. I dismount my motorbike next to Mitch's car. I feel sort of weird about leaving it here, but it is tucked in the corner so hopefully no one will see it. Is that judgemental of me? Or just self preservation?

The house itself seems to be caught in a constant custody battle between humanity and nature. The ivy and graffiti climbing the walls intertwine with each other. Four sets of shoes sit on the front doorstep: a pillarbox red pair of combat boots; black platforms; torn up Vans with doodles and writing all over them; and some muted orange Converse hightops with cartoon leaves painted across the sides.

The pack is here.

I can smell them out in the back garden. The bitter smell of sweat counteracted by the individual scents that each person's depiction of joy and love brings to the air. Suncream. Pine. Hair dye. Leather.

Mitch is holding some pads for Lolly to kick at when I come around the corner. Apparently inspired by our conversation earlier, they're attempting to learn some jumping turning kicks. Their clothes are covered in dirt and pine needles and their arms in bruises which – thankfully – disappear before my eyes as I approach.

'Wren!' they whine dramatically, walking away from Mitch as they spot me. 'How did you make it look so easy?'

I grin. At least *someone* thinks that shit show looked good. 'Here, let me show you.' I put my helmet down on a tree stump, pulling off my leathers so that I can come and join them.

Mitch takes a seat by the back wall of the house as I approach, drumming the floppy bat up and down on his knee. I wish I could get him to come over and hang out with us. Maybe it's just me being anxious, but I get the vibe that he straight up doesn't like me, and it's kind of important to me that he does. Partly because I want to be closer with Val, but also partly because, well, we need to get on if he's the acting alpha.

As I'm trying to show Lolly a drill to lead with their hips, and one to *actually* get their feet off the ground *while* they kick, Val and Radwa emerge from the clubhouse. Both of them are also dressed ready to train. Val's hair is tied back off of her face in a high ponytail. Two little twists fall out the sides, framing her face, and her baby hairs are brushed down. She rushes forward upon seeing me and stops abruptly in front of me and Lolly, bouncing on her heels and holding her own hand behind her back.

'You came!' She grins.

'Figured I might as well.' I shrug, going over to my jacket so I can grab something to fasten my hair off my face, a smile toying with the corners of my mouth as I turn my back on her.

She follows me. 'You ride a motorbike?' she asks, tapping the top of my helmet with a finger.

'It's a soldier thing, back home.' I shrug again.

She hums. 'Very cool,' she says with a smile as she lets her hand slide off of it.

Maybe it's because of how we met, but every time Val smiles at me I feel my heart skip just a little in my chest.

This of course makes sparring her a massive problem later in the day. It's Lolly's suggestion because they want to see some of the combat applications of the forms I was doing earlier.

Everyone else I'm able to give tips or get in nice jumping kicks. Sparring Radwa is really fun because it's not often I get to fight girls that are taller than me. She's also quite fast, but she throws her arms out to counterbalance whenever she kicks or totally forgets about a guard when attacking. Lolly needs to learn to protect their ribs. They hold their hands in a somewhat useless position that makes them slow to block in either directions. Every single hit I got in on them was their ribs or their head – which feels like a cheap shot when sparring someone so short but Radwa did it to me! It also doesn't help that they can't stop laughing at themself reflexively whenever someone goes to hit them.

Val on the other hand is different. She's slightly slower than her sister but seems to have more power behind her techniques, which she pulls back just before she actually hits me. This is a good thing because her soft little smile and the way she sticks her tongue out as she thinks are so frustratingly distracting that she actually manages to create a few openings. She could properly hit me if she wanted to. I don't really care. I'm used to taking a wallop. But the control from someone fairly new to fighting is seriously impressive. Honestly it makes me even more aware of my own. Out of all of them I'm most stressed about hurting her – even though, if we are mates, it would be impossible to *seriously* hurt her – mainly because I want to be her friend, but I also think Mitch would fucking kill me if I did. He looms in the corner watching me carefully as we fall into a rhythm with each other.

Val manages to land a hit on me as I'm watching him behind her. 'You getting tired?' she laughs, doing that adorable nose scrunch she does when she smiles.

I grin, settling back into the fight, and manage to land four more hits before Mitch calls time.

'You too tired to spar me?' he asks, raising an eyebrow and joining me on the mats they've laid out on the muddy garden floor to avoid stepping on needles and pine cones.

'You, watch yourself.' Val glances up at him authoritatively.

I give myself a shake off before baiting him over. He shrugs at Val, grinning, as he taps his hand against mine.

To start with, Mitch is quite good at sparring. He uses his hands a little more than his feet and starts on the defensive to see what I fight like. Though he *is* surprisingly fixed in his stance for his size – usually, smaller people benefit from using their size for speed and agility. Making people move around you isn't a bad thing. Magnus is an expert at it and usually has you dancing in circles while he prowls like a panther before he strikes, but it doesn't seem to suit Mitch. He's hesitant with it and seems reluctant to actually hit me? Like he's being too careful with me.

'Lolly!' I shout, nodding them over. Out of everyone, I think Lolly – ironically – seems the most cautious to fight. It works like that sometimes. At the party, they were high and defending Radwa, but when forced into a fight, stone cold sober with no apparent reason, their body seems to freeze up. 'Get behind Mitch.' Then I turn to Mitch. 'Stop me from hitting them.'

This is actually how we got my cousin Lycaon to be more aggressive. I figure Lolly must be one of Mitch's mates. From gathering info on the pack prior to meeting with them, I know that Lolly has been living with him on and off for a while. I figure maybe it has something to do with how their parents took them coming out. They also have matching semicolon tattoos, so it's a lucky guess.

Admittedly, choosing Val would be a more sure fire route – we have very extensive notes on their attack and know she saved him when it should've been impossible – but she just fought, and I struggled to make myself do anything that could harm her.

Thankfully, adding Lolly to the equation is exactly what's needed to draw Mitch out a bit. He moves into me more instead of just baiting me over. It's actually going really well and I'm impressed with him before everything goes to shit.

I aim a kick at his centre, slightly lower than normal but I intend to pull it anyway. That is, until he moves into it, trying to keep Lolly behind him. It lands hard in his lower stomach and he doubles over, eyes bulging, before staggering to the ground.

Fuck. Shit. Fuck.

'I'm sorry – I didn't mean – you moved into –' I cut myself off, realising how much of a dick I sound.

Lolly crouches next to him, putting an arm around his shoulders and holding their hand out for him to spit his mouth guard into, then signalling to Radwa to go and get something from the house. Val comes over and kneels beside them both with his water.

It was an accident but it was just a kick. Surely he can take a kick? He clearly trains *something*. If he can't take a tiny kick we have *big* problems. He's supposed to be the alpha.

Shit, how are they gonna let me help train them now? My heart starts to hammer in my chest and I realise my hands have gotten sweaty again. They're gonna freak out – I look like an asshole I—

I'm gonna go. They need space, okay, I should leave. I'm – yup.

I grab my leathers, my boots and my helmet from the side

and start to walk off down the path after apologising one final time.

None of them are ever going to be okay with that. I always fuck friendships like this up. How do I always do that?

About halfway down the path, I hear footsteps following me, and smell a rather distinct mixture of sandalwood, weed and hair dye.

I bring my hand up to wipe tears that I can't seem to stop from falling before I turn around.

'Can you slow the fuck down? I can't keep up!' Mitch shouts, hobbling down the path behind me.

I didn't realise I hurt him that badly. Surely that's not all me.

Fuck. Shit.

God, why is it so hard to figure out where the line is with the new wolves? Back home, I was good at all this, but here, where I don't know anyone, where I can barely hear anyone because they're not in my pack, I'm shit at this. Tears bubble in my eyes again, a lump growing in my throat.

'Hey!' Mitch's voice has a calm kind of authority that doesn't feel the need to announce itself. He sort of reminds me of Magnus like that. 'Can you name anything around here that's red?'

'What?' I splutter, pulling out of my monologue almost immediately stunned by the question. 'Your hair,' I say stupidly. 'You have red hair.'

'Good.' He nods, then he moves onto orange, then yellow and so on, leaning back on a blackened tree trunk that's been struck down by lightning as we go through each one.

'Something that me and Val do,' he explains after I'm done. 'I moved into that by the way. It was my bad. I'm usually faster on my feet... but recovering from a flare-up, so I'm a bit sluggish.'

I grimace, crossing my arms and itching my shoulder awkwardly. 'Probably my fault for calling Lolly in. I wanted to see if protecting them would make you less hesitant to go on the offensive.'

He scrunches his nose up looking at me through the sun. 'Just less scared to get hurt.'

I feel the guilt twist in my stomach again. 'I am sorry, by the way. I know I've given you nothing but stress the past couple days but I just want to – I only intended to help.' I wince as I say the last word. It sounds so fucking stupid.

'It's fine. I can normally take a hit. It's just that a hit to the stomach is the last thing I need after an endo flare.' He smiles awkwardly, leaning back against the trunk and lowering himself to the floor so that he can tuck his legs up.

'Endometriosis?' I ask, feeling even worse than before despite his attempt to comfort me.

'Yeah, it's a condition where—'

'I know. Phelan used to do presentations on different illnesses as a kid.' I chuckle. 'That one sounds particularly shit,' I add, joining him on the ground just across the path. The pinecones that litter the floor are enlarged and opened so wide I can push my fingers between each section.

'You know, your brother is—' he starts.

I tense automatically, letting the pinecone I was fiddling with drop to the ground. Any time I have made human friends they've hated Phelan as if it was something intrinsic. Tyler couldn't stand him.

'I know he's weird, but he's still my brother,' I cut him off, picking up the pinecone again.

'What? No,' he laughs. 'I mean, maybe a little different, but in a good way. We like different. I was just like him when I was his age. Well no – not just like him, because what I was gonna say is he's so fucking smart.'

I feel my beam growing on my face despite myself. 'He's pretty great, isn't he?'

We fall quiet for a second, the only noises surrounding us

are the chatter of the birds, the roar of the river and each other's steady breathing.

'You gonna come back to the clubhouse then?' he asks eventually, pushing himself up.

'You want me at the clubhouse?' I ask, sounding sheepish even in my own head.

'No shit, Sherlock.' He offers me a hand to pull me up. 'Someone has to teach me to fight better. And besides' – he shrugs – 'you're one of us now.'

And it's then I realise what I failed to pick up on when I was panicking earlier. Four voices now louder and easier to reach in my head than before. Some voices even louder than any I've known previously. Another pack. *My* other pack.

Chapter Eight

Mitch

Maybe it makes me a bad Christian, but I've always taken the Bible to be mostly metaphorical. Some of the people sitting around me in the Bible study group that Saturday afternoon seem to wholeheartedly believe that every single word of it is true, but staring at the peeling wallpaper above the altar I don't really think that's what matters most right now.

At the end of the day, it doesn't really matter if we believe that giants like Goliath really existed. What matters is all twelve of us sitting around this table, heads bowed over leather bound books, fingers following the text across the page in order to keep up with the complicated speech and tiny writing, are feeling the same things reading about a hero going up against a seemingly impossible feat.

I mean, I believe in Heaven, Hell, God, Jesus and all of that. But the Bible for me is just a collection of stories which challenges your perspective on morality.

Esther is talking about the overall message of the text next to me while Reverend MacIntosh nods thoughtfully. He has the kind of face you'd expect a priest to have: an open kind of warm face that lacks any judgement for each person's interpretation of the text. Though even his eyebrows furrow slightly when Nathan says something about how uncovered dinosaur bones are actually just the bones of a Goliath put together incorrectly.

I think the story is about leadership. King Saul was too afraid to stand for his people against Goliath. And David was courageous, yes, but I think saying he wasn't afraid is too simple. Even Jesus was afraid going to the cross. I think what it's saying is that what makes a good leader is someone willing to risk it all for their people, their family, their livelihood – to put themself on the front line instead of someone else. Not that David ended up being the least problematic figure in the Bible – but in this story at least he's intended as the hero.

Thankfully the Reverend doesn't make me speak today. He must take the bags under my eyes as a sign that I don't want to talk. I'm getting there after the flare but between that, fighting Wren, and the whole 'acting alpha' thing I'm too overwhelmed to actually contribute much today.

I hang back for a moment helping pack away the stationary and the Bibles while everyone else leaves. We're carrying some Bibles back to the little bookcase by the door and chatting about the next food drive, which I usually bring spare fish from work to, when I notice a new missing poster on the board.

I hadn't really paid much attention to what was going on when I was out of action, which sounds shit but when I tell you all I can do is crawl to the toilet to throw my guts up for like three days and then sleep for about five to make up for it I mean it. And I think everyone else was just so distracted with Wren's news that they didn't realise or think to say.

The girl in the missing poster is about seventeen. I think she was actually in Radwa's year – just moved schools last year actually. She has long brown hair and, though her makeup is quite severe and slightly too dark for her face, her eyes are kind.

Emma MacIntosh.

I turn to the reverend behind me, who is holding a stack of Bibles waiting to hand over. Taking them from him I try to tactfully bring up the poster.

'So um…' I start, giving a nod towards it.

'My niece.' His face grows severe, jaw setting in place, eyebrows bunching together. 'That picture was taken just before a party about a week ago, and then one day later she was gone.'

'I'm sorry.' I murmur, slotting the last book into the thin crevice left on the shelf.

He shakes his head. 'Don't be. We'll find her. "Faith is the assurance of things hoped for, the conviction of things not seen."'

Then he hands me a flyer for a search party they're having for her tomorrow evening. These things never do any good, if anything they just cause more issues for us when they coincide with moons, and I swear half the people that actually go missing are usually part of them. The rogue surely gets their scent in the wood and follows it until it can corner them alone.

Still I take it from him and say that I'll pray for her safe return. Maybe it makes me a bad Christian, but I'm feeling a remarkable lack of hope and faith in the face of these posters recently.

When I get to the car I turn on my phone to let the rest of the pack know what I've found out, and it's then I see a message.

```
LOLLY
I need you to take me to my mams
```

Fuck. Fuck. Fuck! I hit the palm of my hand against the steering wheel, then rake my hands through my hair before tugging the handbrake up.

Lolly

We're just about to leave the clubhouse when my phone goes off.

> LOTTA
> Can you come home tonight? Mam's drinking again. I'm scared.

Lotta is my eleven-year-old sister. It wasn't my choice to leave her with Mam.

The night I did I had been sitting at the table next to her as she quietly coloured in, looking as though she was in some kind of trance. I had that look about me a lot when I was growing up too. But at least she wasn't afraid anymore – until the shouting started.

Mam had flipped out because I told her a story with two princesses who fell in love, and I mean she had properly flipped out. In a way she hadn't since she saw me kissing my ex girlfriend and took my door away. Lotta's head barely came up to my shoulder, as she tucked herself behind me to shield herself from the noise, hands on my hips, eyes wide.

Of course, she was never the one Mam took it out on. I knew she'd be physically safe when I left her, at least more so than I was that night showing up at Mitch's house with a broken nose and black eye, but that doesn't stop the lump forming in my throat as I picture her little face.

I still wish I could've taken her. But Mitch says it's like when they say on TV shows that in a plane crash you have to put on your own mask before helping anyone else. Sometimes you have to be selfish to survive.

I don't like being selfish.

I nearly didn't apply to uni. What happens if I do get in? If I called the social for her, who's to say anything would come from it? Mam might just stop letting me see her all together again. Or she might get put with some like … with someone who *hurts* kids. I could be putting her at more risk.

'You okay?' Radwa asks me, tilting her head to the side.

'Yeah, fine I just – it's nothing.' I shrug it off, feeling my heart rattle against my rib cage. I slip my phone in my pocket after sending Mitch a quick text.

It doesn't take long for him to come and pick me up. Barely twenty minutes pass between me texting him and me sitting in the passenger's seat of his car with my backpack hugged against my chest.

'Will I wait outside?' The sound of his fingers drumming on the wheel are the only indication of his feelings on the situation. Driving me here makes him anxious. He doesn't like the thought of me at home alone.

'I'm gonna stay there tonight.' I throw him a smirk. 'Give you two some space.'

He shoves my knee then he drives around the corner into Mam's part of town. It's not the most idyllic place to have grown up. I once found a bloodstained knife under the slide in the park here.

When I walk into the house I can tell how bad it's been. It smells like wine, vomit and dust.

Some old and broken blinds fall and spew out from their resting place - propped against the corner of the hallway – when I walk in. A cloud of dust rises from them. There is a new red wine stain on the carpet. It looks like it's not been hoovered in a while.

I peer into the living room. It's half-wallpapered, and some new shelves are hanging above the couch flimsily. Self-help books on mindfulness line them. I walk in further, nearly tripping over a pair of rollerskates.

Mam sits on the floor of the kitchen, with an overfilled

glass of red wine. Every time she lifts it it leaves another ring stain on the tile. She's humming softly and has a large canvas propped against the washing machine and the overflowing basket next to it.

'Dolly.' She looks up with an eerie calmness. 'Do you like my painting?'

It's a bunny. I think. It's a bit shit. I stifle my laugh. 'Yeah Mam it's really good.'

I go to sit down next to her, moving her glass of wine out of the way. I take up a paintbrush and start to paint with her.

'That's a lot of washing though. Need me to wash Lotta some clean clothes?' I ask calmly. Trying not to seem accusatory. Mam can be quick to anger when she's like this.

'I know how to parent, Dolly.' I hate it when she calls me that. 'I raised *you* didn't I? Fuck all help from your Dad.' I wince. My father is a good man. 'Besides, my books say it can be good for anxiety to go out with stained clothes. It stops you from caring about what other people think.'

'It's also good for bullying when you're eleven, Mam,' I retort.

'Dolly!' She slams her paintbrush down. 'I said I know what I'm doing! Just let me be happy for a second, let me have my me time. You don't see me complaining when you're out all night, not coming home for weeks hanging out with those—'

I want to rage at her. Tell her not to say that word. That she's not allowed to talk about Mitch and Radwa like that. Hell, tell her she's not allowed to talk about *me* like that.

'Probably with who knows who doing who knows what—'

She gets so bitchy when she's defensive. I'm about fucking done, but I see Lotta on the stairs. I wink at her.

'You know my thoughts. Sex to a girl is a very precious thing and when you're out all night—'

Sex *with* a girl is a very precious thing. I remember my

first time with my ex, Kat. It was far from perfect, but it was special for us back then. We only broke up because she also had a lot of baggage and we were destroying ourselves emotionally to support each other. Besides, her parents were super homophobic and we couldn't exactly chill out at mine.

'But no, I let you, because you're happy.' Mam pauses, pursing her lips thoughtfully in a way that tells me the incoming bitchiness is because she is hurting herself. 'You're *not* her mother you know.'

Mam's good at telling me that when it suits her. She's bad at acting like that when it doesn't.

Sometimes I think I would prefer to have a mam who cared. She wasn't always like this. It wasn't until her friend did something a friend should never do. I was very young. Seven years old. Lotta had just been born. Mam's friend was babysitting me.

When Dad found out what she did to me he killed her. That's why he's in jail. He beat someone to death with his bare hands for doing the one thing we all know justifies it.

I go upstairs and lay in Lotta's bed with her until Mum cools off. She smiles when she sees me and jumps into my arms.

I catch her and give her a big embrace. She refuses to let go even when I sit down so I tickle her.

She catches my arm. 'You got a new tattoo!' She traces the healed lines with her finger to see if they feel any different. My first one is scarred so she always does this now, looking for a different texture in the skin. 'She's pretty. What's her name?'

'Medusa.' I smile, wrapping her in my arms and kissing her hair. It's matted badly. 'She was a powerful creature in Greek mythology who could turn people to stone with one look.'

'I got a book on Greek mythology from the library last

week! Can you read it to me for a bedtime story?' She looks up at me with her big brown eyes.

I hesitate looking at the size of it, the tiny words. The last time she asked me to read to her we were doing picture books. 'How about I make one up instead?'

'What would it be about?'

'Werewolves.'

She smiles and nods. I get her to agree to let me brush and pleat her hair while I tell it.

'So what most people don't know is that werewolves are usually friendly, and our story is about four – no, five – of these friendly wolves…'

I know it will be the same tonight. She'll beg me not to leave, and I know that after a week here I probably will. It's too hard to stay here after everything that's happened. But for now, for tonight. I just want to hold her in my arms and tell her it'll be okay.

It won't ever be okay with Mam in the house though. I go downstairs to see what she's doing when I finish putting Lotta to bed.

'Why are you going through my things?' I ask, reaching the second step from the bottom.

'I knew it.' She's in the toilet with her back to me. 'You let them get to you.'

'What do you mean?'

'That's why you hate to see me happy.' She shakes her head. 'Because they're pumping you full of these zombie pills.'

I race down the stairs, only to see her taking my meds out of the sheet and flushing them. I catch her as she gets rid of the last one.

'I can help you feel happy again, okay?'

Her sincerity makes me feel sick. A hand closes tight around my throat. It takes at least a week to get my meds into the chemist here. A full week of spiralling out of control, a full week of my skin prickling all over and every small thing feeling like a dagger in the heart.

My jaw tenses, locking tight as my canine teeth push through my gums. I close my eyes, knowing that they must be glowing by now as the tears threaten to bubble over. Even though I want to rip her fucking throat out I make no attempt to fight Mam as she hugs me, nor do I hug her back. I just stand awkwardly in her arms, hands balled in fists by my sides, looking at Lotta's muddy school backpack sitting in the corner.

Once she lets me go I make my way back up to my bedroom. Sitting on my bed breathing shallowly, I unfurl my fist, wincing as my claws pull out of my fleshy bit of my palm.

I *hate* my mam. I know it's bad to say, but it's not because she's sick. I'm the exact same brand of fucked up. I don't hate her because of what her friend did to me. That wasn't her fault. I hate her because I was the one who was hurt, but she got to be the one that was hurting. I hate her because I needed a mum. I hate her because she refuses to try and get better. Even if she couldn't get better, or it was too hard to do *while* raising us, our grandparents would gladly take us. But she's too selfish for that. I think, in her own way, she thinks she owes it to us to try. But the thing is she's not trying. Not really.

I turn over in my bed later, wrapping the cover tighter around me. I feel like a child. A small frightened child. I feel like that every time I enter this house. Waiting for the next time I try to leave, knowing I'll inevitably get pulled back.

I notice a letter sitting on my bedside table. It wasn't there before. I push my finger into the top corner and rip along the seam. The word **Congratulations!** blinks at me like a flashing light. The logo for Heriot-Watt stands proudly in the corner.

Oh. I didn't expect to actually get in. An unconditional

offer – so it doesn't even matter what results I get from this year.

I'm in. This is my escape ticket – like we planned. I'm *in.*

There's another note there, a folded white piece of paper. I open it up, it's one of Lotta's drawings, along with a letter written in blue crayon.

I miss you ♡

Well fuck. How can I even dare to think of leaving her?
My phone flashes from where it sits on charge.

```
MO LEANNAN X
Wanna talk about what's wrong?
```

I smile as I see her little icon light up my screen.

```
                              HABIBI <3
           Nah I just want a distraction
           right now. What are you up to?
```

She shows me, letting me in to hear what she's thinking about. Her room is mostly white, with an orange accent wall and little orange accessories dotted about. She's sitting on her bed with her switch. The lights in her room are all warm and soft. A fireplace screensaver crackles on the monitor of her gaming computer which sits across from us nestles between two large bookshelves. She brought these from her parents' house.

Radwa has her issues with her parents too but the great thing about her dad is he loves her enough to let her have this space to grow and find herself.

I know admitting to my feelings for Radwa has to mean keeping a distance physically. It would be hard if we were in a relationship because touching people is how I show them that I love them.

But it's not all about wanting to kiss her. It's about right now wanting to feel so small I disappear, curled up in a ball, my head on her shoulder, her arms around me. She's a whole seven inches taller than me so that wouldn't be hard.

I want to lay in her room when I need comfort. I want to smell the coconut oil that sits on her bedside table, the citrus fruit candle she always burns, and all the old books that line her shelves. I want to hear her sappy old music. I want to feel the heavy weight of the blanket she sleeps under when she feels overwhelmed, and the soft ears of the teddy I bought her. Radwa has the warmest hands, and I want to feel them giving my arm a gentle reassuring squeeze.

I know telling her means giving up any chance of that kind of comfort again for a while at least, but I also know I owe it to her. I respect her too much not to let her know.

But not tonight. Not when I'm out of meds and back at my mam's. Tonight I just need a friend.

I wanted to talk to you about something—

I got into uni.

We think at the exact same time.

What did you wanna talk about? I ask.

You got into uni? She tries to seem excited, but Radwa is terrible at faking any emotion. She just is how she is. I like that about her. I like that I never have to second guess what she means because she gives herself away constantly. And right now, I can tell something is wrong.

Is that okay? I check, confused.

When Radwa and I were younger we planned to run away together to Edinburgh. We'd get as many pets as we could, and take turns cooking, and eventually we'd save up enough to buy our own place together. That was the plan. Alcohol would not be allowed in the flat, but weed would. She'd have her laptop set up in the living room so she could game while I watched TV. We'd make blanket forts together and stay up all night and if we ever had a disagreement we would sit in the blanket fort and talk about it without being mean or giving each other the silent treatment.

Okay? Lolly, that's amazing! When do you start? I see her room start to distort and slip away from focus. She's blocking me, or trying to.

Not this September, but next. I deferred. That was always part of the plan we were meant to go together. Why is she mad at me? *Radwa, what did you want to talk about?*

She shakes her head violently. *It doesn't matter right now. Hey, listen I'm so excited for you but I really need to go help Val's mum with something. I'll chat later, okay?*

That's a lie. I know that's a lie. Why is she lying to me?

Okay? I hesitate. *I love you*, I whisper to myself as the room fades around me and I find myself back at Mam's house.

Wren

The youth group is loud when I get there on Saturday. The sound of many voices filled with joy and hyperactivity radiates across the room, each louder the last, as though they are high on the drug of being recognised for who they are for the first time.

Dad thinks *these* humans will be enough to convince me they're not all bad.

If anything, being thrown back into a room with people I don't know – people who I can't read – just makes me feel out of control again.

Sometimes I like feeling out of control. Like earlier, sitting next to Val by the campfire with Lolly and Radwa. Sparks of the fire twisting and curling in the air illuminating our faces; the heat kissing our noses and cheeks. I sat watching the little gold ashes that broke free from the flames reflecting in Val's wide eyes and knew she felt the same adrenaline as I did.

It's thrilling to be that close to a fire. I've always thought so. It's like you're on the edge of something dangerous. Like in a moment everything could be snatched from your control. I feel the same way when I walk by a flooded river. Sometimes I want that feeling in my life. Since the war ended I often feel weighed down, and I patiently wait for something to snap me up and let me float out of control. Is that strange to admit? Surely I should savour peace.

This lack of control here and now is nerve wracking. I can feel my heart hammering in my chest as I play with the zip pocket of my cargo trouser. I'm sitting with my back pressed against a barely working radiator in the town hall, debating whether or not I should just leave, when the door opens, nearly hitting me in the face.

'Sorry!' A hand, stained with oil pastels just below the pinky catches the door as I step back and lift my arm to stop it. 'Eason, be careful, you plonker!' the boy attached to said hand exclaims, shoving his friend with his elbow. His voice is unusual for a human. There's a more deliberate inflection in his tone that highlights his words are more fond than mean towards his friend.

Eason – who I think was in my year in school – holds his hands up, apologising, but walking awkwardly through so the people behind him can get through the door.

'Are you okay?' the first boy asks carefully, still holding the door for the people coming through. There's an urgency in his dark brown eyes when he looks up at me. His heart is beating fast. Maybe he's feeling a little out of control too.

He lifts his other hand, running it through his hair and I realise I've still not said a word. My cheeks flush warm. I nod quickly.

'Oscar, come on!' A short girl with silvery blonde hair motions over from the beanbag. She's from my school too. The unsettling feeling lingers.

I think the thing about losing control is the context entirely depends on who you're with. Who wants to take the wheel? Is it a friend letting you get way drunker than them because you need it after a breakup? Is it the boy who finds you way drunker than you should be? Is it the boy who put something in your drink and forcibly took control of the situation?

My mind always wanders back to Tyler when I have to interact with humans. For a long time after what he did, I felt out of control: in my life, in my body. I think I'm just starting to get that back again.

He was my first boyfriend, you know, the first person I had sex with too. Consensually at first. He left after that first time, though. He left me in my bed alone. It was on and off after that but I guess you should be able to get drunk around someone you're dating regardless. You should be able to fall asleep next to them and have nothing happen.

The door swings open again and I take that as my cue to find a new hiding spot, pushing myself up onto the wide bay windowsill and leaning against the cold glass of the window. Even just being pushed out of my comfort zone like this can make me want to dip out of social situations nowadays. My brain can be inconvenient like that.

I wedge myself into the corner, sort of wishing I had someone here with me. Phelan did offer to come, and I feel bad for rejecting his offer. He really needs to make some friends here, but hanging out often feels more like babysitting an angsty fifteen-year-old who's mad because he had to leave his boyfriend back home. I know that sounds mean. He struggles to make friends because he's really quiet, and well… him. And who he is is great! But when I'm this nervous I don't want to have to do all the talking for him.

I tried asking the pack, but all of them had their reasons for not wanting to come. Val had plans with Mitch since he's not working tomorrow and had been at church all afternoon. Radwa said she would've loved to but often feels shut out in places like this because she's religious as well which seems to put people's guards up. Lolly was down but then they got a text from someone that changed their mood entirely.

One second we were sitting around the fire pit and I was trying to show them how to play a guitar that I had found and tuned in one of the bedrooms of the clubhouse. The next they looked distraught and we went home pretty immediately after that. No one really told me what was going on. Just that they had a family thing, but it seemed pretty massive from how much Radwa clung to their side.

I wonder if it would be different if I met them sooner. If any of them would've come or even let me know what was happening.

I cast a furtive glance at the groups of people gathering around me. The boy from earlier – Oscar, I think the girl said – is sitting with his friends on some beanbags talking animatedly with his hands about *Doctor Who*. I wonder if he's seen the classics; those were one of the few VHS tapes we had back home during the war.

He smiles warmly at me, catching my look, and gives me a wave.

Eventually the group leader calls the groups together and gets us to go around the circle offering our names and pronouns.

I can't help but feel like this might just be for my benefit since everyone was already chatting anyway – as if I didn't already feel like an outsider

Oscar sits across the circle from me. He glances up and down, looking at me. I expect him to look away when I catch him but he nods in my direction and smiles at me then turns to talk to his friend.

He's cute. His dyed blond hair curls tightly. His complexion is slightly lighter than my own but not by much. Four badges sit on his shirt. One is a pronoun badge, and the other three are Pride flags: pan, polyam, and trans.

It's his turn to catch me staring. He blinks and pushes his golden-framed glasses up his nose.

It's his turn to introduce himself next. He looks directly at me when he says it. 'Oscar, he/him.'

Once we finish the formal introductions, Oscar comes over to informally meet me. He crosses through the busy room of people and takes a seat on the windowsill by my side. My pulse quickens but, for some reason, even though everything in me wants me to run, I... don't.

'Hey Wren,' he says conversationally. 'First time here?' His eyes flicker up as he asks the question and then he looks down at the windowsill between us again.

Tyler never made eye contact when he spoke. So when people avoid it, it instantly raises my defences. I scan him with my eyes. What does he want? What isn't he saying?

I nod. 'I thought it was obvious. Wasn't my appearance responsible for that ordeal?'

'Nah, we always do that. Some people change their pronouns so gotta stay up to date.' He waves it off. 'So how'd you find out about us?'

I shake my head with a small chuckle. 'You know the door didn't hit me right? You don't need to come talk to me because you feel bad.'

He lets out a little exhale with a dumb little smile that makes the long dead butterflies in my stomach stir.

'Straight to the point.' He nods. 'I have a feeling we're gonna get on well.'

I cross my arms, more amused than not. 'Oh you do, do you?'

He grins when he nods, sticking his tongue behind his teeth in an effort to suppress the smile. 'By the way, I'm not talking to you because I feel bad about Eason nearly hitting you. If anything I feel bad you're sitting on your own but I'm also partially chatting to you because I think you're pretty and I like your badges,' he says, looking up for a second before letting his eyes fall as I meet his gaze, 'if you want full disclosure.'

Despite still wanting to catch another glimpse of that brown colour so dark it's nearly black I feel myself relax a little. People aren't usually that forthcoming with their intentions like that. Humans, at least, hardly *ever* let you know what they're thinking.

I feel a soft pink heat prickling up my cheeks. My hand comes to fidget with my badges on my tote bag. There are two button badges there: a trans flag, and a bi one. Along with three enamel pins, a TARDIS, one reading 'Black Girl Magic' and the polyamorous heart – it's easier than explaining that most werewolf packs don't operate under the assumption of monogamy.

'Thanks.' I smile, as he flips the TARDIS the right way around. 'My parents and their partners got me loads of them. I figured they were conversation starters.'

'Same.' He laughs, gesturing towards his own on his shirt. 'About them being conversation starters – my parents aren't that cool.'

'Mine and their partner Magnus are actually the ones who *made* me come here,' I confess, delighting a little in the wide grin the sentence plasters across his face. His eyes flicker up for a second longer than usual as if to confirm he heard me right. I nod and continue. 'Dad found it. He wants me to make some queer friends before starting college.'

He's still looking at me eyes wide when he asks which college I'm going to. When I first moved here I wouldn't have understood his amazement, but after seeing what Phelan has gone through this last year I get it.

'The one in town,' I smile, turning hot until his more steady look, 'doing music.'

'Hey, I'm starting an art diploma there this year!' He beams. Then he adds a little lamely, 'I draw—'

'I know,' I cut in too fast, looking at his smudged hands again. Then I point. 'Oil pastels, right?'

'Yeah.' He flushes, rubbing at the mark with his other hand. 'Do you – uh – do you do anything – art-wise I mean, you obviously do things – you play instruments right?' He looks down once more trying to recover himself.

'Yeah,' I fidget with one of my braids feeling strands of hair catch on my blistered finger tips. 'Drums and ukulele. I know a bit of guitar too. Never had the patience to draw though.'

'But the patience to play three instruments isn't a problem?' he asks without looking up, a smile playing with his lips.

'Okay, maybe I just don't like it when I'm not immediately good at things.' I wrinkle my nose. 'If you're due to start college did you just finish high-school then?' He nods, so I add over eagerly. 'Which one? I've not seen you around.'

Trust me, he has the kind of face you would remember.

'Well I was away for a bit because I was ill.' He scratches the back of his neck. 'But I…' He chuckles. 'I went to an all-girls private school.'

Oh, that must've been Hell. It explains a lot. He must be from up the back roads behind town. In other words, he comes from money.

'I know what you're thinking.' He winces. 'But that's my dad. And he doesn't know about all this yet.' He gestures to himself. 'Yeah he works away, and he's probably not gonna like coming back to this, so I'm not counting my uni fund just yet.'

'Maybe he'll surprise you.' I smile, and he wrinkles his nose, unconvinced. It suddenly becomes very apparent why he was so awestruck by my parents.

He looks up. 'Do you have any plans after this?'

I bite my lip. 'Probably meet my friends. They hang out in the woods a lot in summer down by the distillery.'

'Cool.' He nods. He asks about my friends, what we get up to together.

I tell him we've been doing martial arts recently – leaving out that it was part of my training as a child to fight in an unseen supernatural war.

We were both raised sporty. He used to do competitive gymnastics as a kid but isn't really into anything like that now.

The night wraps up and we're still sitting, blabbering – though by now we've moved onto *Doctor Who*. His knowledge of the topic rivals Phelan's regarding Spiderman.

His friend Eason comes over so that they can leave together and makes a point of apologising for the door that didn't even hit me once more.

'Can we walk you some of the way?' Oscar asks me as he hops off the windowsill. 'People keep going missing lately. Safety in numbers, right?'

They're heading in my direction anyway so I allow them to even though I'd probably do a better job of protecting them. Oscar makes sure I stand on the inside of the path away from the road. We part ways at a crossroads.

'See you next week then!' He waves to me as he crosses the road.

'Who said I'm coming back?' I shout back. He holds his arms up and shrugs.

I know it's too early. I know I'm not ready. But something about his grin gives me butterflies.

Radwa

My breathing is heavy and racing as I push Lolly out. I curl up into a ball on my bed tucking my knees to my chest and covering my ears to try and quiet it. This was always the plan, I know it was, I just— My chest aches as I take a heaving breath.

Water. Water will help me breathe normally so I can hear myself think. I reach out a trembling hand to grab my flask from the side, only to knock it over on its side.

Argh! I let out a yell of exasperation and throw myself down on the floor with it, sobbing, before taking a slow and deliberate sip.

I didn't mean to push Lolly out. It's just, I didn't want them to think bad of me when I saw that I wasn't happy or excited for them but instead mad and upset.

Whatever I do I can't let them know that. They would hold themself back for me. I am *really* not the kind of person who would want them to. Or I don't want to be.

My reaction has nothing to do with my feelings for them.

Or maybe it does, I don't know.

I just – we've been going back and forth for three years and now I know they like me too, now we have a chance and it's slipping through my grasp like water.

That makes me angry.

And the worst part is I'm mostly angry at myself because I don't think I'm going to get into uni. I worked as hard as I could but I'm just not good at maths and how exactly am I supposed to be able to devote myself to studies entirely if I'm spending a good portion of each month coping with transforming into a wolf? What reasonable adjustments could the education system ever make for that?

If I knew I was going with them, it would be less of an issue. But the not-knowing makes everything worse. Even if I was confident I'd get accepted, I'd still need to wait another year to find out for sure. I know that's the case for literally everyone, but I've never coped well with uncertainty.

Even if we got together now, could we do long distance? If I don't get into uni, could we make it work?

Not that I think they'd cheat on me or I on them, but how would we see each other? Isn't uni supposed to be about partying all of first year, and sex and drugs and alcohol anyway? What if they want that experience? Would they resent me because they couldn't have it?

And does any of this even matter right now if we can't even talk about our feelings while we're in the same town?

Radwa?

I mean how would we talk about our feelings across one hundred and twenty-eight miles – yes, I googled it – if we couldn't do it in the same room? There isn't really a cheat code for this – you can't exactly up, up, down, down, left, right, left, right, B, A, start a relationship!

Radwa?

Have they thought about all of this? What if they have and that's why they haven't said anything?

Radwa? Wren's voice echoes loudly in my head, snapping me out of my thoughts.

Wren, I am spiralling. What is it? My mental voice has a bite to it that I don't quite intend.

You are thinking very loudly about Lolly right now, they point out. *And I know it's probably not my place to say, but I don't think you want them to hear all this, considering you haven't spoken to them about it yet.*

I can see Wren clearly saying this, putting their phone down, eyes gentler than they usually are. Their thoughts lack their usual snark, and just a few seconds in their head are enough for me to feel the excitement rushing in them like a newly lit firework.

I lean back in my bed, taking up my Switch again and running about my island on *Animal Crossing*.

I know, I say as I bump into Mabel and attempt to trade bugs. *I just...* I pause for a second. Should I be talking to them about this? Their friendship is new, yes, but they're literally in my head so there's no sense lying to them. *Why can't they talk to me? I've already tried once, and it's like the second I find out they like me, they have to move in a year which is next to no time at all and what if they like the idea of being in a relationship but don't like what that would mean with me?*

Wren sighs in my head loudly. *Maybe because you're the one who knows they like you? I can hear that you do but Lolly – they have no idea.*

I scoff. *Surely they must. Besides, I...* I stumble for the words so instead just show them the amalgamation of doubt my mind has been conjuring up about long distance, about uni, everything. *I don't want to implode their life like that.*

That, Wren thinks with a smile, *is their decision.*

I groan, putting my Switch down and covering my face with my blanket.

Wren laughs. I can hear some of what's going on around them. They're walking home, and the wind is blowing in their face. The heels of their shoes are clicking on the pavement. They're feeling buzzy.

Is your group over? I ask, changing the topic. Just talking to Wren is making me feel calmer, less alone.

Honestly, I wish I'd had queer youth groups when I was younger. Not so much now that I've found my people – frankly there is only so much socialising I can take in a week. But when I was being bullied it would've been nice. The thing is, I've found I exist at too much of an intersection for people to understand. One of the first things me and Mitch bonded over was the fact that we've both been shut out of queer spaces for being religious.

I felt even less able to engage with the 'community' when I started wearing hijab too. That held me back from doing it at first, because it's not like I could *hide* the fact I was religious anymore. In the end, I decided my faith was more important to me. I just wish there was more space for people like us.

I think Wren can hear the resignation in my thoughts because they move on quickly.

Are you guys still at the clubhouse? Their thoughts sound light and happy. The night air feels cool on their face.

Nah. I shake my head. *Did you have fun?*

They smile to themselves, and then they start to tell me about their night. The excitement carrying in the air around them smells like pine, nail polish and bubblegum.

Val

It's always quiet when Lolly goes to their mam's house. Not only is Mitch's house less lively than usual – his mum and dad have also gone on a date so it's quite literally just the two of us and the rats – but it's also quieter in our heads. I'd assume they were just blocking us out but it kind of seems like more than that is going on. No tiny little Lollyisms slip through the cracks, no random impulses, no stupid jokes or larger than life ideas.

It's like they're just… not there. Until they actively think about reaching out it's like they're just … numb … dead but still walking around. And for all the messy emotions and intrusive thoughts I think the worst part of being able to get inside of Lolly's head is when they're not there at all. I *hate* not being able to hear them. I *hate* not knowing if they're okay.

After shooting Radwa a text to see if she's heard anything, I toss my phone back down on the table. It's my only means of checking in for now. Mitch is pretty adamant we can't force our ways into Lolly's consciousness to lure them out when they're like this. It's too personal. Even he *won't* go there.

He comes over to stand next to me, pressing two kisses to the side of my head.

'I can tell how hard you're trying,' he whispers into my hair. 'I'm so proud of you.' He gives me another two kisses, placing a chopping board down on the breakfast bar next to my arm where the rest of the stuff he's prepared for dinner sits.

We're making pizza for dinner tonight. Honestly, this

might be the only way forward when we do live together. I swear this, cheesy pasta and chicken nuggets are the only meals the man has in rotation. It's sort of sweet how much of an effort he still makes when I come over though. He even went out of his way to get olives for my pizza, despite hating them.

Sitting down across from me, he pops the lid off the jar then slides it across the table with a grimace. 'You can cut those if you want any, I'm not touching those things.'

'Dare you.' I grin, piercing one with a toothpick and holding it out to him.

He leans forward to inspect it then recoils in disgust.

'You know,' I say, crossing one leg and turning to face my ingredients as I pop it into my mouth, 'I've heard T can change your taste. Like, not just making you hungrier but giving you weird cravings and stuff. Maybe you'll like them one day.'

He screws his face up once more, crinkles forming between the freckles along the sharp bump in his nose. 'Well it's doing *some* things but I *don't* think that's gonna be one of them.'

I raise my eyebrows, taking my pizza base out of the packet. 'Some things?' I ask.

When Mitch blushes he does it in this cute way that sort of covers his whole face and the tips of his ears. He clears his throat. 'Just you know hungry, kind of tired, grouchy and itchy. I also feel a bit – like – crampy and stiff, and my throat is sore. And other stuff.' He scratches the back of his neck. The red shade grows deeper as he shoots out of his seat to go and grab some passata from the cupboard for the base.

His t-shirt rides up on his hips as he stands on his tiptoes reaching for the top shelf. It exposes a thin smattering of curly ginger hair marking a pathway through his collection of hot water bottle scars.

I swear it looks thicker than usual. It did look that way the other day when we were training with Wren. He kept flashing it when he pulled his tank top up to wipe the sweat from his face. I scan over his broad shoulders with my eyes, they look square and well defined but I'm not sure it's any more so than usual. Things surely don't change that quickly.

'Other stuff?' I ask as he slides back into his seat across from me.

He nods without looking up from his plain-ass pizza. A few moments pass in silence as he spoons some sauce out for both of us and starts sprinkling cheese on his own.

My brows furrow. We used to watch documentaries about trans celebrities and their experiences on HRT before he started so he knows he can talk to me about *whatever* it's doing to him and I won't bat an eye.

'And,' I say, cutting the silence, as I peel a slice of salami out of the packet, 'anything interesting?'

'You know, just the stuff we would have expected.' He scratches his face, lifting his base onto an oven tray, then taking mine from me so that he can put them in to cook together.

'Meaning?' I ask as he straightens up, turning back around to look at me.

'A couple things.' He shrugs, picking up the rubbish from the table and tossing it in the bin. Then he pauses in front of me, standing between my legs. 'One, which I really hope no one has noticed, being that my thoughts are kinda all over the place.' He chuckles. 'Especially with you in that dress.' His fingers come down to fidget with the hem of my sundress where it sits on my knee, rolling the string of my fishnets between his fingers.

'Oh is that right?' I laugh, tongue coming to fidget with the medusa bar of my cyber bites. He nods, coming closer and placing his hands on my hips. 'How long till the pizza's ready?'

''Bout half an hour.' He cocks an eyebrow up, and I

pretend to think about it for half a second before we race up the stairs together determined to make the most of our alone time.

The inappropriateness of our timing doesn't really strike me until we're laying together in bed about twenty-five minutes later, both in some state of undress, only top half on his part. It's only ever the top half, and even that took some coming around to. He lays with his head on my thigh for a little while before crawling up and offering me one of two joints he keeps behind his bed frame to slow my racing heart. I usually don't smoke – I don't like the way it tastes – but after sex, and days like today I'm sort of okay with that.

He lights it and I take a draw, sprawling back out on the bed. 'What was the other thing by the way?' I ask, flicking the ash off the end into an ashtray on his bedside table.

'Ah – it's – related, but it's not really something anyone else would notice.' He shrugs, gesturing vaguely to the crotch area of his buttoned up jeans as if that answers the question.

Ah. That stings a little. I know there's nothing I can do to change how he feels about me being anywhere near … that … part of him. Two years into dating and he's not let me touch him there at all, not using my hands, not using toys — nothing. He's not even into the idea of doing something to himself while we're making out or whatever. We've spoken and it's definitely a dysphoria thing. I know he likes me, and is into me like that. I just wish *something* would change his mind, cause fuck if I don't want to make him feel half as good as he makes me feel. But I know it's not something I can push, this isn't quite as simple as olives.

'I'm sorry,' he whispers, hand tracing shapes on my leg. 'I wish I could – I just get too—' he stammers.

'You have nothing to apologise for,' I promise him, reaching for a kiss, 'except maybe these pillows,' I add as I lean back.

He rolls his eyes, gesturing for the ashtray so he can tap

off his ash. I reach across to grab it from his bedside table. When I do, a crumpled flyer falls out from underneath it with a picture of a girl who was in Radwa's year at school. I say *was* because underneath her picture there are thick black letters declaring her missing.

'God, that's such a shame. She was actually really genuine,' I whisper, lifting it from the floor and pulling the covers back over myself.

I wish it was more of a surprise. A girl our age going missing is a tragedy. But in this town, as the years have gone by since Mel's death and more bodies have shown up, nothing can pack the same punch as the first one. It's become normal.

'Shit, yeah.' Mitch sits up, taking the ashtray from me. 'I meant to tell you about that earlier but I got distracted with Lolly's message.'

I suddenly feel quite guilty for goofing off together tonight. Not that I regret any moment of my time with him, just that I feel bad for getting so easily distracted when our friend is going through some shit. When people are going missing and turning up... mauled.

I grab my phone from the side to check to see if Radwa has messaged me back. She hasn't yet but the timer for the pizza is about to go off. Mitch jumps up to go and get them, pressing two kisses to the side of my head.

I shoot Radwa another message before raking through the drawer Mitch has cleared for me in his dresser to see if I can find some pyjamas. My pyjama shorts are there but I can't find a shirt.

That's strange. I thought I left my one with a blown up picture of Nancy from *The Craft* here. It must be at the club- house, I guess.

I toss my hair up with one of the bobbles I left on Mitch's bedpost before stealing one of his oversized dysphoria hoodies and heading downstairs.

Chapter Nine

Wren

The gate clicks a little too loudly as I come into our garden. I was hoping to avoid being interrogated by Dad about how the group went so I cringe, trying to tiptoe my way up the path and in the door.

Honestly, I don't think I could handle the smug grin that would cross his face the moment he realised I made a human friend. Nope. Not telling him.

Thankfully he's upstairs reading to Conan when I come in. Whenever we move, we line the bedroom walls with silver panelling that sound proofs them. So, with the door shut, outsiders can't hear anything happening inside and vice versa. This means Dad won't have heard me come in.

I sneak upstairs feeling the corners of my mouth turn up of their own accord as I imagine Oscar's wide grin as he shouted to me about coming next week from across the street.

A door opens as I'm halfway upstairs. Phelan emerges on the landing. Despite my best efforts to fight it, my cheesy beam must stay on my face against my will because he pushes one side of his headphones off of his ear.

Enjoy your night? He laughs, taking my glee in.

Met a guy. I repress my grin as best I can. *Maybe humans aren't so bad.*

The change in Phelan's features are miniscule: his lips press together, his eyes harden, and he pauses momentarily as if talking to someone in his head. He lifts his phone from his pocket hanging up the video call he'd been on with Harley before pushing his earphones off entirely.

Go on then, he thinks, attempting to offer me a smile.

So I do. I tell him about the door *not* hitting me and the stupid little smudge mark on Oscar's left hand when he caught it. I tell him about the badges and his *Doctor Who* obsession. And I tell him how he refused to let me walk roadside on the way home.

All the while Phelan just sort of stares blankly at me, his eyes watching my every movement.

And, I finish excitedly, *he just says what he's thinking. He doesn't make you guess or try and read him for it.*

Phelan gives a small nod, lips pursing together tightly, not meeting my eye.

I stop suddenly, piecing together his hesitation. *What?*

Nothing. He swallows, making to continue downstairs. *He sounds… almost too good to be true.*

Pup… I start feeling the tingles that were running up and down my arms fizzle away. *I know I don't have the best track record with guys but—*

It's not that. He shakes his head. *It's just, humans* never *let you know what they're thinking. He has to be hiding something, they all do.*

And just like that, the butterflies die. Crumpling as though their wings were made of paper. I win my battle with my smile.

Wren— Phelan starts.

I shake my head. *Forget it. It was stupid, I'm gonna go shower,* I tell him, then climb the stairs before he can stop me.

I spend ten or so minutes standing under the boiling water of the shower, willing it to bore into my skin and wash away that naive part of me that wants to trust humans in the way my Dad does.

After I'm done I wrap a towel around myself and pick up my phone to check the time. The screen has fogged up because of the length and heat of my shower. I wipe it down.

The first notification on my phone screen reads:

```
OSCAR MACMILLIAN HAS SENT YOU A
FRIEND REQUEST.
```

What is he trying here? I'm hesitant. If he *said* he wanted to talk to me because he found me pretty then what was he *thinking?* After everything with Tyler and everything that followed, I don't really do this anymore. I'm tired of being lusted after but not really wanted.

I fall in love so quickly as well. I know it's not healthy but I'll easily make someone else the centre of my universe and give up everything for them. Maybe I like just being my own sun. Maybe I'm scared that his stupid dimpled smile is exactly what will send me into orbit again.

He does go to my college.

I do need more friends.

I press accept and start drying myself. I'm reaching for my shea butter body lotion when my phone dings loudly.

```
OSCAR
Hey! Just wanted to make sure
you got home safe tonight.
Message me when you're good. :)
```

I reply straight away. It might not just be the dimples that get me.

```
                              WREN
         I'm home safe. Thanks for
         checking in
```

OSCAR
We gotta look out for each
other. Can't be too safe rn ;)

I hesitate to decide whether I need to reply to his message. I don't want to seem overeager. He sends another message before I can second-guess myself.

OSCAR
Wyd?

The question stares at me. I decide to test the waters.

WREN
Just out of the shower now. Was
thinking about maybe practising
ukelele. What about you?

OSCAR IS TYPING…

I can predict his response. '**Pics?** **x**'. That's where this always leads.

OSCAR
Ukelele! I remember you saying
you played some instruments. I
couldn't remember which ones. I
was saying to mum I wish I
played something. I'm painting,
but I'm frustrated with it so
I'm forcing myself to look away.

Or maybe not.

WREN
What are you painting?

OSCAR IS TYPING…

Maybe this is where he pulls the cheesy line.

> OSCAR
> My dog. I'm good with people but
> not animals, he's also a black
> lab so it's hard to make his
> face look like anything other
> than a shapeless blob with big
> eyes.

Maybe not. He attaches the image. It's not terrible, but you can tell it's not exactly his forte. I text him back as I carry my clothes to my room, chucking them in the washing basket in the corner before climbing onto my bed and nestling myself between the many pillows that sit there.

> WREN
> What's his name?

> OSCAR
> Sammy. Do you have any pets?

> WREN
> I have a husky called Luna and a
> sun conure called Soleil.

I attach pictures. Providing more victims for his paintbrush to butcher.

> OSCAR
> Luna is so cute! However …
> something you may not expect
> from me … I'm positively
> terrified of birds.

My hand slaps over my mouth to stifle a laugh.

> WREN
> No! I've had Soleil since she
> was a baby. She's trained to
> give kisses. She is not scary.

> OSCAR
> She is descended from dinosaurs!

I mean, technically he's not wrong. I shake my head laughing at him. I lay in bed chatting with him until about one in the morning, when I realise it's definitely time to sleep. I wrap my braids up in a silk bonnet to stop them from getting frizzy while I sleep.

I send him a selfie. Maybe it's a test. Maybe I just want him to expect something other than *those* kinds of pictures from me.

> WREN
> Right, I am officially ready to
> sleep but talk tomorrow?

OSCAR IS TYPING…

He sends a selfie back lying on dark grey silk pillows. He's cuddled into his dog who loves the attention.

> OSCAR
> Night Wren! Sweet dreams! :)

∽

Our text exchange continues for days uninterrupted.

> OSCAR
> Morning! I saw this video of a
> sun conure who hates men. Are
> you sure this isn't Soleil's
> secret account?

Halfway through the week, he's sending me pictures of his actual artwork. It's great. He's working on a folio called 'Boys Will Be Boys' about trans identity.

Then before I know it the following Saturday has rolled around.

OSCAR
Hey! You gonna be at group
tonight? Would be nice to
see you.

                                       WREN
      I have plans with my friends
      today but should be done by
      tonight. Would be nice to see
      you too :)

OSCAR
Val and the gang?

                                       WREN
                        As always!

OSCAR
Keep me updated on our favourite
ship.

                                       WREN
      Eh, not much to update. Lolly's
      at their mum's rn to look after
      their sister Lotta so they're in
      a foul mood. But they got into
      uni and Radwa's now super
      nervous she won't :/

I hesitate, looking at the message. Maybe I shouldn't have told him that.

Val filled me in the other night on what was going on with Lolly. We were sat next to the fire chatting while the others went to go and pick up food after an intense training session. She had flushed warm after saying it, despite the night air being so cold that she had tucked herself under my discarded biker jacket. She then admitted she didn't really know why she'd told me that, and that I am too easy for her to talk to.

If the others hadn't got back I'm sure I would've scared her away forever by beginning a ramble about how our friendship was basically written in the stars.

A new message from Oscar flashes on the screen.

>   OSCAR
>   Oh no! Congrats to Lolly tho! If
>   you're at your hangout in the
>   woods today, be careful. Did you
>   see the news?

>   WREN
>   No?

He attaches an article. Another body has shown up with pieces missing. The article just says it's been dismembered.

At first my stomach sinks, thinking Emma must've been found. She was so nice when I met her at the party, and my dad's had no luck tracking her down since she was reported missing. But this victim is male, a young guy.

That's weird. The rogue must've turned more than one person this moon if it's responsible for Emma's disappearance, too.

We'll have to be careful on the next moon. Be careful we're not attacked by the rogue. Or by targets of the mass hysteria this article will cause.

When I turn up at the clubhouse everyone is lounging around outside, exhausted by the heat.

Mitch has stripped down to his binder and a pair of shorts. He's sprawled out on a huge tree stump next to Val. I don't think I quite realised how scarred he was until now. Angry red burn marks cover his lower stomach, thick wolf scratches from one side of his torso to the other, and thin methodical lines on his hips. I try not to stare. I don't want to make him uncomfortable.

Radwa is lying across a log, spraying herself with water and catching Pokémon on her phone. Val has tossed her usual knitting aside in favour of a sketch pad. The wool sits across the empty fire pit from her. Her hair is slung over one shoulder and falls loosely in her face while she works. I notice, somewhat hilariously, that she sticks her tongue out as she shades with the pencil, just like she does when she's sparring, eyebrows bunched together in focus.

'Hey,' I call out to them as I approach, helmet under my arm.

Val tosses her sketchbook down and beams warmly. 'Hey!' She waves.

I feel heat rise in my cheeks but decide to blame the weather. 'Where's Lolly?' I ask, yanking my leathers off as if they've caught on fire — which to be fair they might as well have considering how fucking warm they are.

'Hyper-fixating on martial arts,' Mitch replies. 'They said they're "overwhelmed to the point of being angry at everything" and will come over if they want to socialise. I *was* gonna train with them but I've sweat through two shirts already. Can you calm the fuck down!?' he shouts down towards his own body.

Val shoves him, laughing, then wipes her hand. 'You're so gross right now. Such a fucking man.'

He grins widely, and his whining ceases for a moment.

I join Radwa on her side of the pit. 'You okay?'

Her eyes don't leave her phone. 'I will be once I catch something other than a Pidgey.'

I don't push. Radwa has been quiet lately. I'd be confused if she hadn't accidentally let me into her entire thought process during her meltdown. Lolly found out they got into uni and Radwa isn't sure she'll be joining them. The thing is, while Radwa is very capable, she's also been through a lot in the past three years. She's burning out, and you can't exactly add 'werewolf attack' to your personal statement, can you?

Instead, I open my phone.

SNAPCHAT FROM OSCAR.

I open it. He's captioned the picture, 'Rate my fit?'

He's wearing a white t-shirt with an open leaf-print shirt and some light green shorts.

'Is that Oscar?' Radwa nods to the picture, sitting up.

'Yeah, that's him.' I turn the phone to her, hoping she didn't see me talking about the situation between her and Lolly. It's not like I was bitching but we've just gotten closer and I don't want her to feel like I'm betraying her trust. 'He's pretty cute right?'

Her brow furrows as she bites her nails. She scrunches her nose. 'Not into men.'

Val laughs, then gestures for me to show her, nodding approvingly.

'Listen, I'm not into men either, but that is a pretty man,' Mitch agrees, sitting forward to look at the phone properly.

I snap him back one of me using the filter that tells you what temperature it is and some fire emojis. I want him to know he's hot… but I also want an out in case he doesn't want me to flirt with him.

Lolly comes up behind me and places their hands on my shoulders as I take it, diving into the photo themselves.

'You work through that energy?' I ask as they sit down between Radwa and me. Radwa scooches down the log a little away from us.

'I dunno, it's so weird, it's just that! Too much energy. I have so much fucking energy and nowhere to put it and it's making everything overwhelming and then making me angry. I can't even fucking sleep Wren.'

'I get like that all the time, don't worry.' I check my phone to see if Oscar has replied to the chat yet.

    READ: 5 MINS AGO.

Oh well. *That* was fun while it lasted. I sigh.

'I'm fucking starving by the way,' Lolly groans.

Mitch bolts up. 'You're hungry? Can we go get food now? I'm *so* hungry.'

'Fuck yeah.'

'I love you so much.' Mitch smiles tilting his head up towards the sun.

'Can I come with you to get the food?' I ask, getting up, leaving my phone by the log in the hopes Oscar will message me by the time I get back.

I could just message him again. Maybe he just opened it and got distracted and forgot to reply.

Or maybe he thinks you were saying too little, a voice in my head whispers. Or maybe you were saying too much.

Mitch

Lolly and I sit in the front two seats of my car and Wren hops in the back. I crank the stereo up as we drive from the entrance to the woods where I parked to the main road, and then down to the high street.

Wren keeps glancing at Lolly. 'What's going on with you and Radwa?' they finally ask.

Bad timing, bad question. The air around us grows thick with tension.

I wait for Lolly to explode, but they don't. Maybe they've just tired themself out for now. Sometimes they manage to burn themself out just enough that their emotions seem to succumb to their exhaustion. Or at least their reaction does.

They roll their eyes, annoyed. 'Urgh, that.'

We drive again in silence. I feel like I should've chosen a better song. I can feel their skin crawling just being trapped in a car and having been asked that question. They're on edge, energy building in them, bubbling to the surface and threatening to spill out.

'She's pissed off I got into uni I think, and honestly, I think I'm a bit pissed off that she's pissed off, so let her be like that, because I really don't have the energy.'

But that's a lie. Lolly has nothing but energy right now and they can feel it building so much they want to scream.

Wren looks over to me, and I shrug in response. Lolly is agitated about everything right now.

'I don't think she is pissed off,' Wren tries. 'I was talking to her just after she found out that you did.'

'Well, you'll know she's not happy about it, is she?'

'I think it's more complicated than that.' Wren smiles gently.

Lolly scowls.

When they found out, their reaction was that they couldn't leave their little sister, but I think now that they know that freedom is an option and it's close, the idea of not chasing it makes them feel very stuck. The thing is, Radwa would never ask them to stay. Radwa is actually leaving for Edinburgh herself next year if she meets the entry requirements for her course. It's very clear to everyone except Lolly that Radwa is just nervous she won't get in, and nervous about losing them.

We're silent for the entire drive to Morrisons, and most of the trip around the shop is spent talking about snack preferences.

When we eventually get in the car, after having time to process things Lolly finally speaks. 'I'm not actually pissed off at her. Just frustrated that she's icing me out,' they admit.

'I don't think she's trying to,' Wren offers. 'She just doesn't know how to express what she's feeling or why yet without sounding like an asshole.'

'She's just acting different around me.' They shrug. 'Like I've done something wrong. She doesn't sit next to me anymore, or hold my hand or…' They shake their head like a dog. 'It's dumb.'

It's not dumb. Lolly is a very touchy person. In both senses, physical touch is their love language. They are constantly hugging us, laying on us, kissing our cheeks or foreheads, and they are also very sensitive even though they pretend they aren't. I believe that they would be the first to notice if Radwa was acting differently in that regard but also the first to take it personally.

'I thought your skating date went well,' I say, checking my mirrors and flicking my indicator to turn into the clearing by the woods.

'So it was a date?' Wren chimes in.

I give Lolly a meaningful look. 'Babe! Talk. To. Her.'

At this rate, Wren and the new guy they're talking to are going to be together before Lolly has even attempted to talk to Radwa.

'Fine!' they concede. 'But not right now, my brain feels like it's vibrating off my skull.'

Wren laughs and walks ahead.

I grab Lolly and pull them back. I know they don't like other people overhearing their family stuff. 'Please come back to mine.' I want to protect them. I feel like it's my job.

'I can't.' They pull their arm back. 'I've got Lotta to think about.'

'Okay.' I don't push it because I don't want to push them away. 'Can I hug you?'

They sigh. 'Not right now Mitch.'

Something is definitely wrong.

'There you guys are.' Val smiles, coming to greet us when we eventually make it to the clubhouse. She slots herself under my arm and puts both hands around my waist.

She has been very lovey with me lately. This has been funny because, between my heightened emotions with hormones and keeping my proposal plans a secret from her, I feel like I've been the same. It's like I'm sixteen with a huge crush on her all over again. I pull her in close and kiss her forehead twice. She only does kisses in twos, unless she's too distracted to care.

Lolly glances at us and rolls their eyes. 'The heteros are at it again.'

Radwa laughs, and they smile at her for a moment.

'I'm bi!' Val pouts. 'It's not my fault I fell for a straight man.'

Lolly shakes their head and tuts disapprovingly.

'Did you miss me that much?' I laugh.

'Actually, I was hoping you knew where my t-shirt was. You know, the *The Craft* one?' I do know that one. 'I know you don't usually borrow it because of the cut but Radwa definitely hasn't—'

Radwa shakes her head, confirming that she doesn't even *like* the film. I've not seen it, but tell Val I'll help her look.

'You know, it's weird. My hijab went missing the other day, too,' Radwa adds.

'I'm sure it's nothing to worry about,' I promise, giving Val another two kisses before going upstairs to the room we've claimed as our own in the clubhouse.

There are three. Ours is the closest to the stairs, with a window that looks out to where the front garden would be. Our room is really a cluttered mess of things: random clothes we brought here before transforming on moons, shelves of our books, a practise dummy with a shirt over its head (not the right one unfortunately), an acoustic guitar which has been newly restringed, and a double air mattress with some bedsheets in the middle of it. Sometimes we camp out here after particularly rough moons so we all needed a bed even if we didn't have a bed frame for it. We thrifted most of it.

I check on her side first and then mine in case it got thrown over there. Nothing.

I sit on my side of the air mattress. It's then I notice something else is missing.

My journal. It's a small leather book that usually sits on the box I used as a bedside cabinet. Everything else is there. Loose change, a black ring, nail polish, and a cup holding two Pride flags I got at a parade one year: demisexual and transgender. A book by a trans YouTuber I used to watch religiously about his journey to starting testosterone.

Two things might be a coincidence, but three…

'Guys?' Lolly's panicked voice comes from across the hallway. 'I don't suppose anyone stole a shot of my hairbrush?'

Make that four.

My journal. Where I wrote about my first kiss with Val. Where I wrote everything about falling in love with Val. All my old pictures of Mel. Where I documented everything about the attack.

If someone finds that, it could be bad for us.

I rush downstairs. 'My journal's missing.' I throw myself down onto the couch. I'm pissed off. At myself, I think. For putting us all at risk.

'You keep your journal here?' Radwa looks up as if to ask why.

I'm even more annoyed. 'I don't want my mum to read it.' She would. She'd mean well and just be frustrated I was shutting her out. But she would.

'What is in this diary?' Val looks at me, her silver eyes wide. 'Stuff about us?'

'Us, trans stuff, pack stuff, Mel stuff.'

'*What* about us?' Her eyes widen.

'*Everything* about us – did you miss the fact I wrote about us being fucking werewolves?'

Val lets out a breath. We're fucked. And it's all my fault.

Radwa

Just when I think Val might die of embarrassment Lolly comes downstairs. Their heartbeat is a little elevated. They smell like dry red wine and dusty waiting rooms. Panic. They smell like panic. 'It's not up there.'

I can tell they are trying to keep calm but they are in the same boat as me. Stealing a hairbrush specifically from Lolly is a very personal message.

Everyone finds comfort in believing in something, and

Lolly believes in three things. These three things have kept them safe since they were eight years old, in the garden believing they could talk to fairies. Lolly believes in nature, themselves, and nearly a decade later they still believe in, and work closely with, the creatures we call fairies.

They are Pagan, and if I understand anything about their faith, it's that having someone's hair, middle names or blood is practically a bold, capitalised, underlined threat.

I look at Mitch, sitting with his face in his hands. I look at Lolly who is clearly struggling to regulate their anxiety. Val looks defeated – there's a sadness, a grief in her thoughts. I remember locking myself in my room upstairs when I couldn't find my hijab.

I have a thought. 'Val, where did you get the t-shirt?'

She smiles softly. 'Mel got it for me.'

It's a pattern.

It's all things tied to faith. Val isn't particularly religious. The closest she comes to worship is how attached she gets to things her friends give her because she believes that wearing them will keep them safe. Mitch only believes in God or Heaven because he wants to believe in somewhere Mel isn't hurting. His journal had pictures of Mel, evidence of a time when she didn't hurt. Lolly's hairbrush. My hijab. Whoever took them selected items specifically to hurt us, to render us hopeless. But also items we used or wore a lot. Items that would smell of us.

'This was a message,' I say out loud. My voice comes out shaky. I'm shivering – no, it's too warm for that – I'm shaking. My body has realised I'm afraid before it's even fully registered in my mind. 'We're being hunted. Whoever took this stuff knows us, or one of us. They're intimidating us.'

'It's the rogue,' Wren whispers, eyes narrowing.

They press their lips together in an attempt to control their expression, but I catch the look that washes over it: intrigue.

Lolly

We decide pretty immediately that we have to get out of the clubhouse.

We regroup at Wren's and sit in the kitchen with their oldest brother, Phelan, and their dad.

'Where are we gonna go for the next moon? It's in two weeks,' Val starts.

'How are we gonna protect ourselves against that fucker?' Mitch keeps it going.

My brain feels buzzy like it's going to burst out of my skull. I feel sick like my skin is covered in oil.

I can't breathe, I'm so overwhelmed. God it's not taken this long to bring myself down in a while. Frustration bubbles in me looking for a way out.

'Guys?' Radwa starts.

'They know about the clubhouse so we can't go back there.' Val shakes her head, taking the coffee Wren's dad hands her.

'Well where are we going to go? I think the locals will notice a wolf pack roaming up the highstreet.' Mitch takes his tea.

The inside of my cheek tastes like blood, the skin there is raw from me biting it.

'Guys?' Radwa's voice comes from across that table again.

'The woods are big. We go somewhere different, somewhere they can't find us.' Val holds out her palms next to me. Her shoulders rub against mine.

'Guys!' Radwa is shouting now.

I feel the tears on my cheeks without realising that I've started crying again.

It's too much. It's all too much.

My leg jiggles restlessly. So much energy.

I'm sitting in a corner, trapped again. I want to run. I want to leave.

I feel twitchy. Restless. Like I'm on drugs or something.

'They have our scents.' Mitch tuts, shaking his head.

'Can you both shut up!' Radwa yells.

Everyone looks at her in stunned silence. She gestures to me with her head.

I hate the attention that comes with people noticing that you're crying. I feel myself put the smile on, it feels like my eyes are sucking the tears back up. I straighten up. I'm a little annoyed I've been called out.

'I'm fine.' I shake my head.

I am not fine. Wren's youngest brother, Conan, toddles over to me with some water, and I just about fall apart at the act of kindness. But I manage to hold myself together.

'I think, for this moon, we should take a trip and be with my pack,' Wren offers. 'We can get weapons there, do some training, make a week of it.'

'People might get hurt, and we won't be here to help.' I feel the words come out of my mouth without meaning for it to happen.

'We've noticed that the killings usually happen the week after the moon. So the rogue can heal themself. Besides, you're no use in this state, and without proper training,' Wren's dad says gently.

But I wasn't thinking about the alpha or the killings.

Phelan's ears prick up. 'We're going home?'

'My friends and I *might* be going for a *visit*.' Wren looks at him sternly although there's a hint of amusement in their eyes.

'Can I come? Please. Please please please please please. I'll do your chores for a week.' He gets up immediately, knocking his cat-ear headphones off and putting his Switch on the table with a loud clatter that rings in my ears even after it's over.

'Pup,' Wren sighs.

'I'll be with Harley the whole time! You won't even know I'm there,' he practically begs.

Wren starts trying to figure out how we're gonna drive down and eventually agrees to let their little brother come. They're gonna take their dad's seven-seater car so they have room to take weapons for training.

A wide grin splits Phelan's face. He picks up his phone and starts typing furiously as he makes his way out of the room.

I get a kick out of that. I feel happy for the kid. It's the first uncomplicated feeling I've had in days. Most of the time I've just felt pissed off. Only I'm not pissed off, I'm overwhelmed because I have too much energy and I don't know what to do with it, and I feel trapped. I need a project, a hobby, a pet. I should get a pet. I've always wanted a lizard.

Usually when I get like this, all energised, I use it all on partying, and girls. Lots of girls. But now I don't feel as though I want to. There's only one girl I really care about anyway.

I just wish she'd actually talk to me. I'm not the only one who knows how to speak, you know?

'Let me up I need a fag.' I pat Mitch on the shoulder three times. It's our code.

It started when Mitch started getting more ill. I remember the dull clink of his rings hitting the side of the toilet three times, tears streaming from his eyes as he could barely breathe for being sick. Make. It. Stop. Three taps. I guess it's kind of obvious to anyone who has ever done martial arts before. He only did it then because he was so used to that being all he had to do to stop something from hurting. I'm tapping out. This situation is too overwhelming.

The garden is quieter. I can hear the wind, a drain running, and Phelan up in his room. His window is open, and he is talking to his boyfriend. I try not to listen in. All I hear is him telling him that Wren is the best sister ever.

Didn't know that's what they preferred to be called. I don't know what I prefer. I think that I'm more of a big sister to Lotta than anything else. That label comes with expectations of emotional labour and second parenting and that's what I *do* so I suppose that's what I *am*. I think I prefer just Lolly.

The door opens and then closes again.

'I've not been meaning to shut you out,' Radwa says as she sits next to me.

'It's fine.' I shrug.

'It's not,' she insists. There is an unusual amount of space between us on the step, we're not touching at all. It's noticeable. Trust me; it is. 'I've been storming, but I'm not upset you got into uni. I'm just nervous I won't.'

'You will,' I assure her, even though we both know I can't promise that.

A silence falls between us but it is not an awkward one. What I like about me and Radwa is we never have to be entirely focused on each other. We just exist in our own minds but we want to do it together.

'For the record I am just trying to figure out what's allowed because I h—' she starts.

'My head is full of bees,' I say at the same time. My thing is more shocking.

'Bees?'

'Bees,' I confirm.

'What are they doing in there?' She looks amused, eyes wide with mock concern.

I shrug. 'I don't know. Buzzing I guess.'

She laughs. Then I laugh. I think her laugh must be the most beautiful sound in the whole world, especially when it's been so long since I've made her laugh. A week is very long for us. When she laughs she sort of squeaks, like she's trying to catch her breath. It's ridiculous and contagious.

I give her a kind of half smile once we stop. I hope she gets into uni too, because it would really suck not having this.

'Are you thinking about Lotta?' she asks.

And I feel bad because for a second I wasn't. For a second I was just Lolly, hanging out with my friends, and making a pretty girl laugh. Just Lolly. I resent myself for it.

Now that the plans have been set into motion I check my phone.

NO NEW MESSAGES.

Strange that Lotta hasn't messaged all day.

'She hasn't messaged,' I say to Radwa.

'You should call her.'

Mum doesn't know she has a phone. I know she's not silly enough to leave the ringer on but still. I hesitate.

'I think I'm just gonna go home and check in. Figure out how to tell her I need to leave for a bit.'

Radwa nods. 'Lolly…' She pauses for a moment. '…Are you okay? Will you be okay?'

She always sees right through the bullshit. The stupid act. And I don't know why I refuse to let her. I guess I just want to be Lolly. The funny Lolly that makes pretty girls laugh and not the problems-at-home, alcoholic-mum, traumatic-childhood, mentally ill Lolly.

'I'm fine.' I give her a huge smile. 'She's probably just annoyed I didn't bake with her like I promised this morning.'

Val

Mitch drives Lolly back to their mam's first. The door is already open when we get there.

The plan is to take me and Radwa home, but, just as we're about to pull out of the car park, I notice Lolly pick something up off their step. They wipe their hands, look at the item, then I watch as it clatters to the floor and Lolly bolts into the house.

I glance at Mitch, but he has already put the handbrake back.

He throws himself out the door and follows after them. It seems instinctive, like he knows something we don't.

Radwa wrenches her door open and I follow suit.

When we get to the step I see what had Lolly so panicked. A hairbrush.

I pick it up, and it is coated in a thin liquid. The smell burns my nostrils. Gasoline.

It's strong enough to block any other scent. Whoever left it knows. And they do not want to be followed.

I hear Lolly upstairs, slamming themself against something hard.

It breaks.

When they scream, time freezes.

Only it's not a scream exactly. You scream when you're terrified because you don't know what is going to happen. The noise Lolly makes speaks of terror, heartbreak and knowing. They wail.

Radwa looks at me eyes wide. We race up the stairs.

We find Mitch and Lolly in the room directly right of the staircase. The window is wide open. The entire room smells of gasoline.

I put my hand down on the bed sheets. They're wet. Everything is wet.

On the wall, around an A4 sheet of paper with

written in crayon bubble letters, there are easily twenty drawings. In the bottom right-hand corner of each of these in purple crayon, there is a name. Lolly's sister signs her name in full on her artwork as all kids her age do.

Charlotte Saoirse Kearney

I look as Lolly collapses into Mitch, knees buckling under the weight of their sobs. His face is stony and pressed tight to their head. He mutters something to them that I don't hear and then kisses their head, holding them tighter.

It's then I realise why Mitch reacted so instinctively. I realise what he knows that we don't.

Chapter Ten

Radwa

I don't know how Mitch gets Lolly to pick themself up off that bedroom floor. I really *really* do not.

He takes them down to the car while I grab some things for them from their room. They aren't coming back here tonight. They have no reason to.

I can't see their meds anywhere so I assume they must be in their backpack already. Most of their stuff will be at Mitch's. They might have spares there.

I think of one more place to check. I open the bottom drawer of a unit next to their bed that doubles as a bedside table. Its bottom caves in as I do. Everything in this house is falling apart, I realise.

There is only one thing in this drawer. An orange tie-dye hoodie.

It's been sitting there gathering dust for a while. I pull it out.

This is –
This was –
Mine.

That first night I met them they didn't have a jacket and it started to rain.

Why have they kept this for so long? And why folded neatly in a drawer of its own, when nothing else is? It sits there staring at me like a modern art display commemorating that night.

On top, there is a folded yellow Post-it note.

It has a number written in blue pen. My number. Above it, there is a name. Well, a surname. The first name (my deadname) has been scratched out in black ink.

I pause for a moment staring. How long have they liked me for? Maybe this isn't because of *that*. No, this is surely more a memorial piece of when the pack became... well, a pack.

I shut the drawer, unable to shake the feeling I wasn't supposed to see that. Like I wasn't supposed to hear them thinking about me being their girlfriend that day we went skating. But I have now, and I have no idea what to do with that information.

'Radwa?' Val calls from downstairs.

'Coming!'

We head to Mitch's straight after Lolly's. The three of us sit together in the living room while Val lets Wren know what's happening. They, Phelan and their dad have been given Lolly's keys to try and find something with a scent strong enough to follow to find Lotta.

Lolly hasn't left Mitch's side since we found their sister's room like that. They currently lie on the couch, with their head resting on his chest. The vacant look in their eyes makes them seem absolutely miniscule. Usually what they lack in size they make up for in enormous energy. But now it's as if someone has taken the spark that once lived inside and, in one mighty exhale, blown it out entirely.

Mitch lifts his hands to their head, twiddling the ends of the longest parts between his fingers.

They breathe out slowly, leaning into him. That's something I've never understood about them, the way they like being touched. When they're panicking, they need to be held.

'What I don't understand is how the alpha knew about her.' It's the first thing they say after discovering their house like that, their voice hoarse and hopeless

Mitch's hand stops moving in their hair. I hear his heartbeat rise.

So do they.

Their entire demeanour changes. They let in a sharp breath and hold it. 'Did you write about her?'

They don't turn to look at him. Their entire body has stiffened. Mitch's face has gone paler than it's ever gone before.

'In your journal? Did you write about my sister?'

Mitch is quiet.

'Mitch?'

I'm watching him. Val is watching him. Lolly has not turned to look at him.

'I can't remember,' he finally says.

It's the truth, and I think that's what makes it so hard. Mitch is desperate for it not to be, to at least know.

'Look, I worry about you when you're at your mum's, so, truthfully, I might've mentioned her existence in passing. But I honest-to-God cannot remember.'

An unreadable emotion washes over Lolly's face. They sit up off of Mitch.

'Lol…' he starts. 'I'm sorry I—'

'Are you fucking kidding me?'

'Babe I—'

'No Mitch, don't babe me. How fucking stupid do you have to be—'

'Don't call him stupid,' Val interjects. 'How was he supposed to know?'

'He knew we had to look out for her,' they start, then glare at him through the corner of their eye, not turning their head to see him properly.

Just because your sister—

'Fuck sake Lolly!' Val shouts. 'Do you always have to take it too far?'

Her voice makes me flinch. She rarely loses her temper.

Lolly shuts us out, shutting their train of thought down before anything else comes out. But we all heard where it was going, and it was going way too far. They're not in a place to admit that right now, but their cheeks flush with embarrassment.

They hold up their hands, dark claws creeping out from their nail beds. 'I think I want to be on my own right now.' Then they make their way up the stairs.

I can feel the anger vibrating off of Mitch. He doesn't turn to look at them as they climb the stairs.

Lolly gets like this. When they get hurt, or let down by someone. The strength they push against them with, push them away with, is the same strength they love them with. They're learning where to draw the line but sometimes we hear them before they shut us out.

'Fuck.' Mitch looks hopelessly at his hands. He moves the pillow Lolly was lying on off his chest and puts his head in his hands. If Mitch was able to cry I think he would be. But he can't seem to do it right now.

Then he sits bolt upright, picks his phone up from the table and dials a number.

'What are you doing?' Val asks him.

In response, he asks, 'Where was Lolly's mum?'

Mitch

'Hi, Saoirse.' I'm calling Lolly's granny. I don't know why, but it's bothering me that their mum wasn't there.

She asks how I am. I can hear a child on the other end of the phone so I ask her where she is.

'Just at mine and Gerry's, love. Deborah just dropped Lotta off, wouldn't tell me where she was going, does Lolly know?'

Relief washes over me like a flood, cleansing my body of all anxiety and fear. I collapse onto the couch.

'No,' I croak out, 'Lolly doesn't know.'

The door was stuck when we first went up like it was jammed. The window was open.

We weren't alone in the house. That's the only explanation. The rogue ran into Lotta's room when they heard us coming, doused it in gasoline to mask their scent, then, once Val and Radwa had entered the house, jumped out the window and made a run for it. It's the only explanation. I tie up the conversation quickly, and then I run upstairs.

'Lolly.' I hammer on their door. No answer. 'Lolly, I'm sorry, just open the door. I know where Lotta is.'

The door wrenches open almost immediately. Lolly stands in the door frame, eyes bubbling like molten silver and blood shot red. 'Jesus fucking Christ, Mitchell!' they shout. 'Lead with that!'

I place a hand on their shoulder. They glance at it threateningly. I remove it. 'She's at your granny's. It was all a coincidence. A scary coincidence.'

They look like they're about to float away. I know this doesn't mean I'm off the hook completely for potentially endangering their sister. We don't really know what came first. Did the rogue go to Lolly's because he found out about Lotta from my diary? Did they find out when they were at Lolly's house?

I hand them the phone.

'Lotta?' they ask, holding it tight to their ear. I can see the relief wash over them. Their shoulders fall, tension disappearing even in how they hold themself. 'You didn't message me, I – Lotta… Sweetheart… Charge it then.'

They're laughing again.

'Yeah, I'm fine, I'm at Mitch's. Yes she's here. No. Lotta no!' They almost giggle, then their smile presses into a thin line once more. 'No, I don't know where she went. I know pet, I'm sorry, we'll bake next time okay? Okay.'

When they hang up, Lolly settles uncomfortably into silence.

'I dunno if there's gonna be a next time Mitch,' they say eventually. 'She's not safe there. She's not safe with me. Regardless of how the rogue knows, they know now.'

I nod. 'So, what next?'

They straighten themself up with a grim resolve.

'I think,' they start, voice shaking as their chest rises up and down rapidly. A hand comes up to play with the lapel of their shirt. The irritated red bruises on its knuckles are already fading before my eyes. 'I think we need to report her – Mam, I mean – I don't want to lose Lotta but – if we don't say something, aren't we just as selfish as Mam is? And we can't let her go back to the house not if the rogue knows where—' Their breathing gets faster, harder, their panic bubbling over like a boiling pot.

The therapy group they used to go to used that image a lot. When they got like this they recommended that people in their support network ask them to quantify the feeling on a scale. I feel like if I asked them that now, I'd get told to shove the stupid fucking continuum up my ass.

This is not a distorted thought pattern. This is a justified reaction to a shitty situation and I *hate* that I can't help make it better. If anything, I've made it worse.

That feeling gnaws at my insides that night as we wait with them for the call back from the social to take their statement. They dismissed the idea of calling the cops.

They've always hated cops, ever since they took their dad

away for protecting them, for doing what any good dad would.

'Can I do anything?' I hear Radwa ask as they sit on the step together, waiting.

'I just need a friend right now.' They shrug half-heartedly.

Radwa nods. 'Understood.'

Wren

Lolly's house is unlocked. Even still it feels kind of rude to be traipsing through it when they were so against letting anyone know what was going on. Luckily we don't need to look for long.

Dad finds a washing bag feebly tied to the machine and a half finished canvas by an intricate network of spiderwebs. He stays downstairs sorting through that to find a scent for Lolly's sister while I scan the upstairs. The rogue doesn't seem to have left anything noteworthy. There's a faint smell of fermenting fruit but nothing that we can catch onto.

Anything? I shout down to Phelan, looking out to the garden.

The sour smell of dust mixing with gasoline makes his asthma flare up inside.

Nothing. He holds his hands up in defeat.

Great. I groan and sit down on the bed, hearing the duct tape around the slats slowly pull apart under my weight. My phone buzzes underneath me.

It's Mitch. They've found Lolly's sister.

I don't know why he doesn't just hop into my head to tell me. New wolves are weird about privacy like that.

When we get home, I write up a report for the pack back home on what's been happening. Show them the rogue's getting desperate and that we're getting closer.

I lean with my head in my hands, holding my braids out of my face, and trying to decide what exactly to put in the write up of how I managed to befriend the pack – I don't think Uncle Cygnus needs to know I let my guard down enough to be spiked. Honestly, I'm surprised my cousin Lycaon – Cygnus's son, next in line for alpha – didn't grass me in when I told him about Val saving me.

I'm about to send it off when a message from Oscar lights my phone up next to me.

```
OSCAR
Missed you at group tonight.
Was looking forward to seeing
you :(
```

Shit. Amidst all the pack shit I forgot.

```
                                    WREN
          Sorry I totally forgot. I really
          wanted to see you too :(
```

```
OSCAR
Wanna call me instead?
```

I pause for a moment.

TV might tell you that people like me – people perfectly crafted into soldiers since they were preteens – don't get to have emotions. The truth is, we do. We yearn. We love. We laugh. Emotions are what separates us from machines.

And listen, you can try to detach them. Come back to me with the disorder you develop from the trauma. We feel just as much as you do if not more. We love harder because we lose more. We laugh harder because we live less.

Don't get me wrong, I'm not saying I love Oscar or anything. It's way too early for any of that. But I really like the way he's made me feel this week. Appreciated. Wanted. Seen.

```
                              WREN
              Yeah okay if you want :)
```

Oscar's room is dark when I answer the call. The only light comes from a couple of candles and some fairy lights that canopy over his bed. Oscar likes the dark. Most people fear it. Or maybe they fear what it contains. Maybe, like me, they fear that lack of control. This could mean one of two things.

Oscar MacMillian craves knowledge so bad that he values it over his own safety. He knows what the dark contains and yet he lures it out. Flirting, in his casually suave way, with what lies there, in the hopes he can learn something new.

Or, Oscar MacMillian is incredibly naive. The dark should always scare you.

I can't see his face properly. I tell him this and he turns the lamp on his bedside table. It emits a warm light that takes the shape of a sunset on his wall.

'Hey.' His breathing is shaky. He doesn't seem quite as put together as usual.

'Hey.' I smile. I hope he's okay. He seems… nervous? … Upset, maybe?

'Thought you were avoiding me tonight.' He smirks, but his eyes don't quite meet the camera. I can hear him shaking his leg up and down. His bed creaks underneath him.

He is nervous.

'I wasn't.' I shake my head and catch his eyes. 'I promise I wasn't. I was really excited to see you. I just had a friend-related emergency.'

His eyes flick up quickly. 'Did Radwa finally tell Lolly—'

'Tragically, that was not the emergency.' I laugh. They have fans all over town at this point. 'Everyone's okay though.'

'That's good. Shame about Lolly and Radwa though. They're goals.'

'Not talking about your obvious feelings is goals?' I raise an eyebrow.

'Okay, if they were together they'd be goals. Right now they're a mess.'

I laugh at him once more. 'Lolly has a lot on their plate right now though. They've been bottling it up for a while, and now…' I exhale and make a small poofing gesture with my hand.

'Are they okay?'

'They will be.'

We fall back into silence. I can still hear his anxious stimming.

'Speaking of bottling things up. What's bothering you? I can tell something's wrong. I'm sorry I couldn't make it to group. I didn't think you cared that much whether I came or not.'

He flushes. 'It's not that. It doesn't matter. I mean, I do care whether you come or not. I text you all day and every night until three and you think I'm not gonna jump at the chance to see you in person? But you had a friend thing, I get it.'

It's my turn to get flustered. He wants to see me. He wants to be seen with me.

Why is his breathing so fast?

'I – it's no big deal. If not, it's totally fine. But I did wonder if maybe you wanted to hang out later this week instead. Just the two of us? We could go get ice-cream.' His stimming slows once he says it. His breath is a whisper. Oh. That's why he's nervous.

'Oscar' – I can't help but smile – 'are you trying to ask me out on a date?'

'Would it be okay if I was?' he asks. He sits up straighter in his bed, hand reaching to scratch the back of his neck. He can't seem to meet my eyes.

'Oscar?'

He looks up. His eyes have a gentle beauty. They're dark

brown, the colour of hot chocolate. They pull you in, warm you up, and allow you to lose yourself in them.

'I was going to ask you tonight anyway,' he says by way of response.

'Just ice-cream?' I ask, raising an eyebrow.

His lips part for a moment before he splutters, 'Just ice-cream. I – I'm – eh – yeah just ice-cream.'

'Friday?' I ask.

'Friday sounds good.' He nods.

Radwa

Things are tense between Lolly and Mitch after the call finishes. Lolly hasn't lost their sister quite in the way they thought they had, but they still might lose her in a sense, and it still might be Mitch's fault. For now, Lotta is staying with their grandparents until the social services can contact their mam.

It's strange, Lolly never really gets mad at Mitch. And while they're not exactly fighting anymore and they're in the same room, we can still hear each other's thoughts. And we can hear them blocking each other out.

They never block each other out. They're the kind of people who FaceTime each other on the toilet. It's awkward. Lolly bites their cheek, Mitch picks his nails, and I want to scream.

Just when I think I can't take the silence anymore Lolly looks at me. *Wanna get out of here?*

Yeah okay. I nod. I can't stand sitting in silence.

Despite being past ten o'clock, it's still bright when we leave Mitch's house. Val elects to stay because while we both know Mitch messed up, we both know he didn't mean it at all, he couldn't have foreseen this. Besides, he has a guilt complex and Val doesn't want to leave him alone.

'Where are we going?' I ask Lolly as we leave the house together.

They shrug. 'Just needed out of there.'

I nod in agreement.

'Can we go to yours?' they ask. 'Just the two of us?'

'Of course.' They've been through so much today that I think I would give them anything.

It's the first time it'll be just us since that day skating. I've been avoiding it until I figure out how to talk to them, but I think about what they said, about just needing a friend, and decide it's fine because I definitely won't be talking to them about all of that tonight.

By the time we reach my house, the sky has started to get dark. The air has a chill to it as well. Goosebumps have raised on Lolly's bare arms under their t-shirt.

'Are you cold?' I ask as we walk upstairs to hang out in my room. Val's parents are watching a movie downstairs and I don't want to interrupt.

'A bit, but I'll warm up.' This is a lie. Lolly is always cold and their body never regulates back to a normal temperature without adding layers or cuddling someone.

'Here.' I pass them one of my hoodies from the radiator. Their own hoodie sits next to it, I think about giving it back but I don't want to. I wonder if they notice.

They smile softly, but it doesn't quite reach their eyes. They take their glasses off and roll the sleeves up their arms.

'Do you wanna talk?' I ask, sitting in my gaming chair as they sit on the bottom of my bed.

'I'm fine,' Lolly says from inside the jumper as they pull it over their head. Once it's on they put their glasses back on and attempt to flash me a smile.

'No you're not.' I can tell.

'No, I'm not.' They laugh derisively and then they start to cry.

Then they talk about something they never talk about: they talk about their childhood.

My claws, which I have learned to keep retracted, pierce their way out of my hands as theirs do when they're ready to fight. As though the wolves that exist in us recognise each other as friends to protect.

My skin prickles, burning hot with anger and disgust. But being angry doesn't change what happened to them.

'You know I love my Dad, but sometimes I think I'd rather he had just been there for the fall out.' They lift Bonnie off my bed and cuddle her close to their chest. 'To protect us from other shit. From mum and her shit. Then I wouldn't have had to protect Lotta,' they mumble, pressing their face into Bonnie's fluffy head, rolling her long ears between their thumb and forefinger. Their eyes are fixed in a dead stare at the bed in front of them. 'That's been my one job since he left you know? Protect Lotta and keep mum happy. When he left, when…' They fumble with the words.

I know what they're trying to say but I don't want to interrupt them; I want to let them say it however they want to. So, feeling as though I'm about to vomit, I press my tongue to the roof of my mouth to stop myself from speaking. It rests uneasy between the canines that have been pushed into its place by protective love, fiery temper and a tensed jaw.

'After everything that happened with Mam's friend – after they found out what she'd done and Dad lost it – that's when Mam changed, right? And nothing made her happy, and she couldn't look at me because me being sad – seeing me sad made it worse.' Lolly starts to ramble, heart beating fast. They sit Bonnie down in their lap so they can move their hands freely when they talk. 'So I found this dial – in my brain somewhere, right –and I cranked that shit all the way up, as happy as it could go. I made myself happy to keep her happy. Keep Lotta safe and keep Mam happy.'

It infuriates me that someone could look at a traumatised

child and force them to grow up, force them to pretend to be okay for someone else's benefit, to be an *adult.* I swallow the blood and bile that has pooled in my mouth as a result of my teeth coming through.

'But the dial fell off,' Lolly continues with a sniff, bringing their hands up to their eyes, 'or I – fuck—' They scoff at themself, trying to wipe the tears that have started to pour. 'I lost it or something and I have no fucking clue who has it now but it's not me, and they don't know how to set it in the middle, they just keep twisting between extremes.'

Seeing Lolly cry breaks my heart, they cry so quietly, but I will never tell them this because I need them to learn that they're allowed to.

'I'm not mad at Mitch. Not really. I mean I am a little, but it's not like he knew what would happen. I just needed someone to blame because I failed.' They shrug, lips trembling. Then they clap their hands down on their knees. 'Mam won't be happy about this, and Lotta isn't safe. And Mitch, he was just there, and it was easy. I just need some space to cool down and not be around him for a second. Because' – they let out a heavy sigh – 'if I am, I'll say something I can't take back. I already nearly did. And I don't really want to push him away because I love him. I'm just scared. And I can't talk about this shit without sounding like a complete fucking mess.' They shake their head. 'I'm sorry.'

They look up at me, biting their lip. They smell like the rain, like guilt.

'Lolly,' I start, taking a deep breath and willing my claws and my teeth to retract, 'I – you – please never apologise for talking to me about this. I know how hard it is for you to –' I stumble over the words. 'No one should have ever made you deal with that alone. And I am so incredibly proud of you for being able to talk about it. And honoured to be one of the people that gets to hear it.'

They nod, lips wobbling as they glance to the ceiling.

'You can stay here,' I assure them. 'I don't have the answers, but I'll give you space, or stay with you till you sleep. Whatever you need.'

They nod, bringing their hands up to wipe their eyes. The cuffs of my jumper come over their fingers. It's far too long for them. 'Can we do our own things together?'

God, I love them. Sometimes they just want to hang out in silence and simply share the space we're in. They'll play on their phone, I'll draw, they'll watch Netflix and I'll play games. It's my favourite time to spend with them sometimes.

'Okay, but I was gonna play Resident Evil when I got home sooo…' I trail off.

They tell me not to let them stop me, and load up Netflix on their phone.

They're about two episodes in when they look up at my screen. 'Holy shit that woman could step on me.'

I snort. 'Step on you?'

'She's hot!' They hold their hands up.

I laugh, putting the controller down and bringing my hands up to my face. 'Lolly she's like nine foot. I'm not even sure she's human.'

'Otherworldly magical women? Hot. Tall women? Hot,' they say decidedly.

I smirk, picking up the controller and looking towards the screen again, not daring to look at them for what I'm about to say. 'Thanks Lol didn't know you felt that way.'

They turn red and splutter, 'Oh fuck off.' They're smiling for the first time tonight, but it dies quickly.

We usually share this flirty banter, but they don't seem in the mood for it right now. So I leave it.

They eventually fall asleep where they're lying on my bed. I stand up, ready to walk through to Val's and sleep there.

I look over. They look really small. It's weird. Lolly is very small but they never seem it. They've got a big personality. But right now they look tiny, curled around my teddy, my jumper drowning them. Their knees are tucked underneath it and pulled tightly to their chest, and mismatched socks poke out the bottom. They always fidget until they fall asleep, rub their feet together, and roll the blanket between their fingers, but when they do fall asleep they sleep like the dead.

Their phone has fallen out of their hand, and their glasses sit next to their head. I pick up both and put them to the side. I grab my throw off the back of my gaming chair and put it over them. I whisper a goodnight as I leave the room.

Chapter Eleven

Lolly

I wake up gently, not really remembering where I am.

The room comes into focus. Radwa's room. I'm sleeping in her room, cuddling her teddy, wearing her hoodie. It should feel comforting. It doesn't. Memories of what led me here come fleeting back. I pull the soft but heavy orange blanket off of me.

Ew. I'm still wearing my jeans. Sleeping in jeans is gross. I'm gonna have weird indents from that. Mitch usually wakes me up to make me strip when I pass out like that.

Fuck, Mitch.

I sit up and reach for my glasses.

There is a knock at the door.

'Are you decent?' Radwa asks.

Urgh. I totally dumped on her last night and got all ugly and emotional. I'm not feeling much better today, but Lotta is okay and people are around so I guess I have to find that dial somehow.

'Morally, depends who you ask,' I scoff, 'but I'm dressed if that's what you mean.'

She laughs. 'Can I come in?'

'Sure.' I cram my glasses onto my face.

She carries a breakfast tray into the room. 'I made waffles and chai. Only, I can't cook and I didn't want to wake you up, so by that I mean I made chai and took the waffles out of their packaging.'

I don't deserve Radwa. I push myself up the bed so I'm leaning against the pillows.

She hands me a cup and sits down opposite me. 'My mum used to make me this whenever I was upset. Usually if we had had a fight.'

I smile tightly. It sounds bad but sometimes I'm grateful to have someone who gets how shitty parents can be. I lift the cup to my lips. It fills me with warmth. Not just literally. The taste is like liquid sunshine. This must be what the Greek myths mean when they talk about ambrosia.

'I'm sorry I fell asleep here. You could've kicked me out,' I say, just as Radwa has taken a rather large bite of a waffle. She chews frantically and I can't help but laugh.

'It's fine,' she eventually says. 'I just slept in Val's room.'

I appreciate her so much. Now I'm a bit more put together than last night, and I've eaten, I can sense she's holding something tight to her chest. She needs to talk about something.

'Something's bothering you,' I note.

She shakes her head quickly. 'Just worried about you.'

'But you want to talk about something.' I can tell.

She scrunches her nose and waves her arms. 'It doesn't matter.' Then she adds, 'I mean, it does, but I don't think I want to talk about it right now.'

I examine her face for a second, eyes following down to her lips. The urge to kiss her is overwhelming.

I imagine kissing her so strongly that I nearly convince myself I actually have.

Would it be so bad if I did? It's a bad time, I guess, but I can't really find a reason to care.

Before, I wanted to talk to her first, but now I don't care. I just want to do this. It would make me happy and I want to be happy.

I don't care, I want to be happy. My energy bubbles and I feel that impulsivity rising.

My heart rate pounds in my ears, building, and climbing and—

I shift in the bed and the teddy I bought her falls to the floor.

My eyes follow it. I breathe out slowly. I hadn't realised I was holding my breath till now. And there it is, a reminder of the last three years, of our friendship, of how much I value and *respect* her as a person.

I take a deep breath in. 'Radwa, I need to tell you something.'

She looks down at me. 'Yeah Lol?'

It suddenly hits me why all of that was so easy to forget for a moment: why I got angry with Mitch, why I was angry with Radwa herself yesterday, why I was willing to overlook years of careful respect for one second of bliss.

I want to chase happiness. But mine often comes from my friends, not in spite of them. Not caring about them? Not caring about her? That's not happiness. Not true happiness, just a high wave.

'Mam took my meds,' I finally admit.

She is not a fleeting high to chase when I feel like this. If I deserve her at all, it is not like this.

She looks a little sad.

Then she smiles.

'Okay.' She nods. 'That's okay, we can get you sorted out today.'

Mitch

I don't sleep after Lolly leaves. My heart feels heavy. I let them down. I fucked up. They're never going to trust me again. My best friend in the world will never trust me again. They literally ran away from me.

Val barely manages to coax me to bed. She tries to gently comfort me while she fights back sleep, but sleep eventually wins at about two in the morning.

I look at the clock now to check what time it is. It is finally, finally 9.30 am.

A normal time to be awake again.

I saw all hours of the clock waiting for a message or a random thought to come through from Lolly.

But nope. Nothing.

The worst part is I can't even fucking cry about it.

What kind of monster can't cry after everything we've been through in the last twenty-four hours? I need to cry. I want to cry. But I can't.

Val turns over in bed next to me. She's been tossing intermittently all night. The hair at the back of her neck and around her ears curls with sweat. She twitches and I run my thumb over her shoulder lightly.

Her heart is hammering in her chest.

I didn't realise she still had nightmares.

'Sweetheart,' I whisper, giving her shoulder a little shake.

She lets out a soft little moan but doesn't wake.

Sweetheart. I try harder.

She twitches hard into the mattress.

'Morning,' I whisper. My voice is hoarse. My throat hurts.

Her heartbeat is even quicker than before as she turns to cuddle into me, resting her head on my chest, her arm wrapping around my ribs.

'Morning,' she eventually grumbles, her eyes still closed.

We lay like that for a second. In times like this, it's usually easy to forget anything outside of us exists.

It's her that says it first. 'Have you heard from Lolly?'

She checked in with Radwa last night before dragging me to bed. They got to hers safely. Lolly was watching Netflix at the time and Radwa was gaming.

I shake my head. I wish I never even started that stupid fucking journal.

It had been my therapist's idea after Mel had died. I only started writing in it to make sense of it all. Then it had been about making sense of other things: relationships, friendships, trans shit, wolf shit.

I had written in there after my first transformation. I wanted to die. I wondered if that feeling would ever go away. I had written in there when Mum had found out what I was doing to cope with it all. And when I relapsed. And when Radwa had told me that when she was really bad, her dad would take her for a drive in the car, and that when she was struggling she just went for a walk to try and replicate that feeling. I had told her that I would sing along to punk music because I felt like screaming, and it was the most socially acceptable alternative. And I wrote about how that night she messaged me that she wasn't feeling great, and I hadn't been either so I drove to hers and told her to get her shoes. Then I drove us as far away from anything as I possibly could, and we got out of the car, walked into the woods, and screamed together.

Then it had been celebrating things. My first kiss with Val, promptly followed by the first time we made out. I felt like my head was going to explode. The questions about sex. If it was weird that I'd only ever felt that way about her and my ex. If it was weird that I didn't find celebrities, or anyone else attractive like that. If it was kinda fucked up the only two people I'd ever felt that way about were my friends first. Was I just that kind of guy? The kind that equates friendship with sex. If not wanting stuff in return was a trans thing or a Mitch thing. If I ever would. I also wrote about when I realised I was demisexual. Then about our first time together. She had been so nervous, and I had made her laugh. I had made a joke, she had shoved me away, then she pulled me close. I don't even remember what the joke was. I had written about it so that I remembered, but now someone else has it.

And Lolly, I had written about Lolly. About that first night, they showed up at mine, about how worried I was about them because of their mam. And I might have written about their sister. It makes sense with the other things I was writing. I must've.

Val has broken free of our cuddle and reached for her phone. 'Radwa is asking if we can come get them.' She sits up. 'Lolly told her they've been off their meds for about a week. They want to go get an emergency prescription.'

How the fuck didn't I notice? I must be a truly terrible friend.

Val looks down at me, a slight annoyance in her eyes. 'Okay Mister Pity-Party, your friend needs you. Are you gonna get up and help? Or are you gonna stay and mope? Cause you can't do both.'

I concede.

When we pick Lolly and Radwa up we discover that Lolly's mam has fucked off for a holiday.

'Yup,' Lolly laughs. 'Just decided to fuck off to Berlin. Fuck knows why.'

She does this sometimes but it is rarely this bad. She won't be home for another two weeks. Lotta is to stay with her grandparents as the social can't find a reason to separate them. Then it will go to court. For now, we have about a month of just waiting.

Val decides to stay with Radwa while I take Lolly to the pharmacy. We drive down the high street in silence. Complete silence. It's weird.

'Nice jumper,' I say, trying to break it.

'It's Radwa's.' They shrug.

I would normally tease them about this but instead, I just shrug back.

'I'm not mad at you,' they say as we park at the pharmacy.

'What?'

'I'm not mad at you. You didn't know what was going to happen. I just needed someone to blame. It doesn't really matter how the rogue knows now anyway does it? I was just scared.'

'You can be a little mad at me.'

'Maybe a little.'

I nod. I'm okay with that.

'You can be a little mad at me, too.' They whisper, 'I wouldn't blame you if it was more than a little. I'm trying to be better, but I know I pushed too hard yesterday. I'm sorry.'

I nod and give their hand a squeeze. I don't say it's okay, because it wasn't and they know that, and I'm allowed to be a little mad.

'Did you and Radwa sleep okay?' I desperately want to ask about the jumper.

'I dunno about her, I fell asleep while she was playing a game.' They shrug. 'There was a really hot, really tall woman in it.'

'Resident Evil?'

'You get it!' They laugh, and I thank God that they do. I thank God I can still make them laugh. 'You know me too well.'

I smile at them, because I do, and I've missed them. 'So, your mam's impromptu holiday gives us a chance to go see Wren's pack next moon then,' I note, taking the hand break off to start the car.

'Yeah, just gotta get through one more week alive.'

I drive past the turn-off to Val's, following the road straight down to Morrisons.

'Where are we going?' Lolly asks.

'Remember how you said you wanted to make it through the week alive? Well, Val's assignments are due tomorrow and she's out of coffee.'

They laugh, and I feel myself relaxing in my seat. We're gonna be okay.

Val

The fifteen and a half seconds it takes for the page confirming the submission of my final assignment are the most agonising of my life. Well, maybe not; waiting to find out what happened to Mitch after the paramedics took him the night we were attacked was pretty painful. Still, there's no reason for it to take this long to load a simple confirmation message.

I click out of the page, back onto my assignments tab.

Whenever I press submit on one I always have to go back and check the deadline just to make sure I haven't missed it. What if it was supposed to be 00:00 instead of 12:00? Why do they always make it noon or midnight? – It doesn't seem the most clear. What if there was another part I had to submit?

It doesn't matter how many times I check my own planner, or ask classmates, email the lecturer, or consult the course notes. I still end up convincing myself that I've somehow got it wrong and will have to tell Mitch, Radwa and everyone who actually believed I could get out of here that I've let them down. It doesn't help that I'm the first in my family to do the further education thing, and instead of doing something practical I took a chance on a dream.

After confirming I've sent everything off correctly – for the third time – I start getting ready to take my portfolio into uni.

I pull on a sheer maxi skirt and crop top combo that always makes me feel hot as fuck. Maybe it sounds shallow, but I like how I look. My body is strong, in a way that most people will never have to be. The legs that the long slit in the side of the skirt allow to poke out? Those are the legs that carry me off the floor of the clubhouse every single month. The stretch marks that poke out of the bottom of the top? Each one, each inch of them is proof that I *lived*. I survived all of that and got to be an adult. The hands that I adorn with golden rings and bracelets? Those are the hands that saved my boyfriend's life, and let me do all my favourite things – sewing, knitting, drawing. So yeah, I *like* how I look.

The only thing that makes me slightly insecure are the scars on my chest. They're proof that I survived which is a beautiful thing in itself. But they're also a reminder of the night my best friend died. Even then, I don't know if insecure is the word – it's not like they disgust me. It's just... a part of me I struggle to recognise some days. It's a heavy kind of feeling, not unlike what I've sensed from Mitch and Radwa before. I like my chest, it's just the scars themselves. It's a... disconnection.

Luckily this top covers them, so all I need to think about now is my hair. It will not stay straight in this humidity, there's no point even trying.

Radwa knocks on the door as I'm trying to figure out what to do with it to let me know she's going for a shower. She's in there for a few minutes, quietly singing under her breath in a way that she forgets I can hear, when the door goes downstairs.

I unravel the dutch braid I just did, which was honestly going too squint anyway, and go to get it.

Wren stands at the door, arms crossed awkwardly across their body. They must also be warm today because they're not wearing head to toe leather for once but instead a soft cotton tank top that hangs loose on their frame, the sides low enough to expose the dark outline of a flower on their ribs.

Hey— they start.

Radwa's in the shower— I think at the same time.

They look embarrassed, eyebrows pulling together.

Not that – no, come in. You can wait with me in my room. I instantly feel bad for accidentally writing them off entirely.

I lead them upstairs and then sit back down at my desk, propping my mirror up and sectioning the other side of my hair off. *I'm just getting ready to go to uni – you can sit down wherever it's fine—* I add as an afterthought seeing them awkwardly hover, swaying side to side. To be fair my other chair has a pile of clothes so high it nearly touches the bottom of the net of teddies that hangs above it.

Sorry I— They flush, sitting down on the bed and staring at their knees.

I look back at them in the mirror. *Make yourself at home, honestly there's plenty of space and you're allowed to take it up.* I laugh, then I turn back to the mirror and tug my hair back out, exasperated. The downside to having a Dad who is a hairdresser is that I've never quite got the hang of braiding my own hair like this.

Here. They smile, stand up and walk towards me. They gesture for me to watch my hands out the way and I concede, letting them take over. Annoyingly, it takes them all of five minutes to do the little half braid, half bunch look I've been attempting for about half an hour.

Damn. They grin, stepping back as I stand up to check the full look out in the mirror. *You look* gorgeous*! Mitch better watch his back.*

I see my reflection beam back at them wider than I had intended to smile. I shake my head, going to grab some clips from my desk to finish off the look. *Thanks, I know.*

They smile at that, and then they nod like I have said something incredibly profound when in actuality I just agreed with them. I think sometimes people expect me to disagree, because I'm fat, and I have thick, visible scars.

They shake their head. 'It's not that. I've just never thought of responding that way.'

I look at them. They are taller than me by about three

inches, but in a way that makes them look elegant, not just lanky. They have high cheekbones and gorgeous hair. They sort of look like a supermodel.

'Well, you should, because you are beautiful,' I say meaningfully.

They *are* of course. It's the first thing you notice when you look at them. And it's not just that they are hot. I think they know that they are attractive in that sense, but it's important to me that they know they're beautiful too.

'Stop it!' They shoo me away.

'You're supposed to say "I know".' I look at them, arms crossed and lips pursed.

'Shut up!' They reach out, trying to cover my mouth.

I dodge, turning my face so they only just catch me in their arms in a strange sort of side hug. I look up at them, heart hammering as if we're actually fighting, not just mucking around.

'You're beautiful, Wren,' I insist, catching their hands as they try to cover my mouth again.

'I…' they start. I glare at them. 'I know. Thank you.'

I nod. My work here is done.

They do look gorgeous today. There is a hardness to their look. An edge, but also a softness. Their eyes are round and gentle. From this close I can see their purple highlighter. It's their favourite colour, and they have a little dot on the centre of their nose. I think that's so telling of who they are. They're all motorbikes and leather, they're literally trained to kill but they're also kind, and soft, and I don't know that they could ever actually do it.

You okay? they ask, letting go of me finally.

God, I must've been spacing out on them like a knob. I glance over to them, just catching my bracelet box behind them and thanking God for small mercies that get me out of situations like this.

Bracelets, I say.

Their eyebrows knit together, confused.

I finished yours, I say, giving myself a shake and crossing the room quickly. Why am I acting so awkward? I'm never this awkward.

The box topples as I yank it out of the cupboard. Fuck. What's wrong with me today? This does not bode well for an exam day.

I grit my teeth, turning around in an anti-clockwise circle as I lower myself to the floor to reverse the bad luck. If Wren notices, they don't say anything, but they do follow me to the floor to help me pick it all up.

Are those pronoun earrings? they ask, scooping some bags up to put in the little red basket of prototypes.

Yeah, new design. Do you like them? I ask, sorting through the organza bags I keep my orders in to find them.

Yeah. Could I buy some when they drop? they ask.

I nod, telling them they can just have some whenever I next get the stuff in for them.

Can I get 'she/her' too? they ask, pausing for a moment, their hands closing around the products they've scooped up. *I've been experimenting privately – if that makes sense – and I kinda…* She trails off, heart hammering, but that's okay.

I think I understand exactly what she means.

She smiles hearing me think that. *You can let the others know, it's okay if they hear you thinking… Actually sometimes that's less awkward that having to say that—*

I've got you. I wink, plucking a bag from the floor. This is definitely hers. Trans, nonbinary, bi and—

Did you try to come up with a polyam design? she asks, examining the bag as I hand it to her.

I fiddle with the inside of my lip piercing. *Saw it on your bag. Shapes are kinda hard, so it's not perfect, sorry.*

I love it, tie it on me. She holds her wrist out, and I get a whiff of her perfume. It's strong, but not in an overwhelming way, in a bold way. It smells kind of earthy, like sage.

I tie it, securing the knot tightly.

Radwa's knock at the door is enough to make both of us jump. I don't know why it feels like I've been caught doing something wrong.

'Sorry.' She grimaces as she apologises to Wren. 'I thought I had more time.' She joins us on the floor, sitting cross legged and pulling out her phone, checking to see if Lolly has messaged her while she was showering. 'Val, you do realise you have like half an hour to get to uni right?'

Shit.

My time management is usually much better.

I make the deadline by the skin of my teeth then walk out through the art bay. My time here is already over. It's hard to believe.

I go to pick up some supplies I left here when I notice something sticking out the fabric bin. A black t-shirt.

I lift it out. It is wet. It smells like gasoline. I turn it to see Fairuza Balk staring at me. Nancy was always my favourite from *The Craft*. One of those characters you just love to hate. Mel disagreed. She hated her all around.

I pick the shirt up and put it in my bag. I'm not even mad that the shirt smells like gasoline. Or that the alpha knows where I go to school.

I'm just happy to have a tiny piece of Mel back, and for a moment the air smells like freshly peeled oranges.

Chapter Twelve

Wren

Oscar meets me at the ice cream shop the following Friday. He looks like he's been there a while. A sketchbook sits on the little circular table in front of him. He's trying to draw the bearded collie that's lying in the doorway of the taxi office next door. Trying to.

He really *is* much better with people.

'Hey.'

He looks up as I speak. Then he pushes his chair out and stands to greet me. 'Wren.' My name sounds smooth like honey in his mouth.

He's wearing a brown shirt that matches his Converse. He sits down, crosses his ankles and rubs the back of his leg with his foot.

'You look beautiful today.' He smiles softly.

This man is going to kill me. Where does he find the nerve to make me blush like that?

I start to say something like, 'Oh shut up,' or, 'It's nothing.' But his confidence makes me want to be more confident.

I think about what Val would say if Mitch said something like that to her.

'Thanks.' I smile, then add, 'I know.' It feels a little forced on my end but he grins.

We order and sit talking about group stuff until it comes out. He tells me it was actually his friend from group Eason who convinced him to ask me out.

There's something about him talking about me to his friends that makes me a little giddy.

The food doesn't take long to arrive. He gets an Irn Bru ice-cream float, with bubblegum sauce which he swears by. I get a cookie dough tub with raspberry.

'What have you been drawing?' I ask him, right as he's taken a sip of his float.

The bubblegum sauce sticks to his lips. He awkwardly tries to dab at it with a napkin, then catches my eye and starts laughing. I feel like we could make each other laugh a lot.

'It's supposed to be a dog. I thought they were getting better,' he moans.

I suppose they are. It looks better than the one he showed me that first night. He flicks back in his sketchbook to compare the two.

'See, Sammy looks a bit like a seal in this one.' He chuckles to himself. Then he shows me a picture of him on his phone. He lets me scroll through his Sammy album. 'Do you want to meet him?'

'Does that line work on all the girls?' I smirk, raising my eyebrows and handing him back his phone.

'I wouldn't know. You're the only person I'm talking to. You're also the first person I've been on an actual date with.' He pings a strand of his hair.

How does someone, as beautiful as he is, make it eighteen years without being asked on a date?

'I don't believe you.' I narrow my eyes, take a scoop of my

ice cream. The universe made boys like him for kissing in the rain. 'Have you ever been in a relationship?'

He itches the back of his neck. 'Kind of? I mean, high school romances, right? I used to hang out with this other trans guy in my old school a lot. We'd sometimes make out, but it was just that. Nothing more serious.' He pushes up his glasses. 'We were circumstantial. Besides, *he* never met my dog.'

I laugh again. He's good at making me laugh and making me feel less awkward.

I eventually agree to meet Sammy, taking my ice-cream tub with me as we walk out. He leaves his cup over half-full, insisting it's too sticky to hold. He holds my hand as we walk to his car.

His parents' house is huge. There's an electric fence to get in. I can't help but feel underdressed in my faded black jeans and cropped t-shirt. I feel like a ball gown would look less out of place.

He lives in an honest to God *manor*. It's the only way to describe it. The clean cut grass, the perfectly trimmed hedges. It's the kind of place you'd either expect to attend a ball or die in a murder mystery. I'm used to homes that can house eight or nine people but this one can do more comfortably, and it isn't gridlocked with a neighbour on either side. Hell, it doesn't have *anything* on either side for *miles.*

'What do your parents do!?' I laugh, running my hand up the stony bannister of the staircase leading to his front door.

'Mostly just born into the right families.' He laughs, juggling with his keys. 'Dad's a criminal defence lawyer though. Mum is a private psychiatrist, but she also volunteers at women's shelters to help people who have been through domestic abuse and sexual assault.'

I wonder how that dynamic came to be. Those are two very different career choices.

The inside of Oscar's house is very bright. It's busy, and a bit cluttered, but when you're rich I guess that's called being maximalist. It's the kind of mess that shows you the people that live there care more about living life than looking perfect.

'Sorry about the mess,' Oscar laughs, trying to defend himself from Sammy's excited kisses.

It's odd, because he and his mum seem so relaxed about it that I wonder where I learned he had to apologise for living. Then I see a picture of a stern-looking man hanging in the hall. He looks nothing like Oscar, this pale white man with thin cropped red hair. Their only similarity is their freckles. His are a muted orange whereas Oscar's are a darker brown.

'That's my dad.' Oscar shifts uncomfortably. 'He's not home right now. Mum's through here though.' He tilts his head.

His mum lounges across a chaise, reading in the living room. 'Darling,' she calls out distractedly, not putting the book down, as Oscar starts to show me up the split staircase, 'I hope you're not planning on sneaking your friend up to your room without saying hello.'

She puts her book down and rounds the corner. His mum is a short, round woman. She wears an orange patterned scarf around her head and hair. The brightness of the orange makes her dark skin glow.

Oscar brings a hand to his head, pinching the bridge of his nose. I hope it's not my fault. Is he embarrassed to be seen with *me*? Or is he embarrassed of his mum?

'Mum, this is Wren. Wren, this is my mum. We're gonna go watch TV in my room.'

'You are just in such a hurry to deny me the pleasure of this young lady's company.' His mum tuts, then turns and smiles warmly at me. 'Make yourself at home, sweetheart. I love your braids. I used to wear them like that. This one can braid like no one's business.' She grins like Oscar does.

I smile back. 'I'm getting them redone soon for Pride. My

cousin's gonna help, but next time it's your turn.' I nudge him.

He looks up at his mum with a smile. 'See what you've done, are you happy?'

'Oh on you go.' She shoos us away, shaking her head fondly at her son.

'Sorry about her,' Oscar says, his fluster fading as we climb the stairs. 'Do you want to go up to my room and watch Netflix?' I must pull a face because he stutters over his words for a minute before adding. 'Just Netflix, I promise.'

I agree and we make our way into his room, it's so oddly empty. Like a blank canvas – as if no one actually lives here. And yet it's clearly the same one from our calls. He throws himself back on the bed, clicking on his fairy lights and pulling his Macbook into his lap. Then he looks up expectantly for me to come and join him.

It feels like a weight has been placed on my chest for just a moment.

I lower myself cautiously onto the edge of the bed.

We sit watching a queer comedy together. One scene genuinely makes me laugh so hard I get the hiccups, which makes Oscar tear up with laughter while he blindly searches for a pack of water bottles he keeps by his bed.

My eyes are streaming by the time I get rid of them because Oscar keeps making me laugh again. Firstly it was by quoting the scene and now it's just every time he looks at me. Sammy's frantic whining at the fact I was crying does not help the situation at all.

'I don't think I've laughed this hard in forever,' I sigh.

I'm not quite sure when I got this far over to his side of the bed but I realise I'm basically leaning on him. His face is far closer to mine than I expected when I look up at him.

'I – um…' I start to say something but I get distracted by the simple fact that I can feel his breath on my lips.

He has such beautifully full lips. They look like they would fit with mine perfectly.

He tilts his head up. I lean forward.

Oscar's kiss feels like coming across a deer in a silent forest. His breath is baited. He is hesitant, gentle, and careful. He waits to take his next cue from me.

I kiss him back, pulling him closer to me. He sighs gently when I do. His muscles relax against mine as his anxiety fades. One of his hands comes up to lightly cup my face.

My nose bumps his glasses. He pulls away, only very briefly to take them off, before kissing me more deliberately. Kissing him now feels like playing a duet as we fall in and out of time with each other, perfectly harmonising.

My hand hovers before landing on his jaw.

I pull him closer.

I can taste the bubblegum sauce on his lips.

'Oscar?' his mum shouts as she walks upstairs.

I pull back away from him, letting him reply.

'Yeah Mum?'

'Door open!' she calls back.

He flushes. It looks like he's never been more embarrassed by his mum in his life, searching frantically for where he tossed his glasses. He walks over to the door and opens it.

'It stays open. Especially when you have such pretty girls over.' She looks over at me then back to him. 'Have you asked your girlfriend if she'd like to join us for dinner?'

'Mum!' He widens his eyes at her, visibly flushing. I'm now starting to believe it is just that his mum has a habit of accidentally embarrassing him.

'I actually have plans, but thanks for the offer Mrs. MacMillian.'

'Oh, please love, I prefer Ada.' She says it so genuinely but it seems touched with sadness.

Oscar looks after her when she leaves.

'Are you okay?' I ask.

He swallows and nods. Giving himself a little shake. 'Again, I'm sorry about her. Do you have time to finish another episode before you go?'

I nod. I feel a little heavy.

I try not to take it personally but something has clearly upset him. I remember him saying something about his dad being away a lot at group, and how his parents fought because of it.

He gives me a lift home that night, and he walks me to the door, hand in hand, to say goodbye.

'Thank you for today.' He smiles, his thumb circling my hand. 'It was nice to spend some time with you. I'm sorry if I seemed off at the end there.'

'It's okay, it happens. You too.' I smile. I look at him, he looks at me. For a moment we're just looking at each other. I'm ready to awkwardly laugh and head inside when he looks down at my lips, back to my eyes and then starts to say something.

'Can I—'

I kiss him. He kisses me back.

I pull away before he is ready for me to. 'You were saying?'

'That –' he stammers, flushing, 'that was – yup.'

'Night.' It is my turn to grin at him.

'Night.' He just about gets the word out.

I collapse against the door when I get in. I sink down it. Then I bring my hands up to cover the absolutely gigantic beam I'm wearing. I squeal and kick my feet in front of me. I cannot hide this feeling.

Phelan walks in, looks down at me on the floor and removes his headphones.

'The human?' he asks, cocking an eyebrow.

I take a moment to look at myself from the outside in and realise exactly how fucked I am. I'm falling again.

'He's different,' I insist, and I'm not sure if the promise is more to him or myself.

Mitch

I called it. Kind of. Wren and Oscar are a thing before Lolly and Radwa even talk. At least, I think they're a thing, because they text all the time and hang out all the time.

It's been going on for about a week by the time we leave for the moon. Wren smiles so cheesily when they talk about him. I have not met Oscar yet but I'm willing to bet he does the same. Wren says they've not defined anything yet but they're *talking* which has always confused me. Why do people say they're *talking* when they mean late-night texting, making out, or pre-dating but not talking about it at all? Isn't the issue that they're *not* talking?

What I do know is that whether you take *talking* literally or figuratively, Lolly and Radwa are not doing either. Lolly's head has been all over the place lately. I think Radwa would love Lolly regardless of where their head was. I mean, she does, we all do. But it would make for a rocky foundation for their relationship.

Still, it's insufferable to watch them sat with one seat between them, sharing earphones, wearing each other's hoodies and not fucking talking about it.

We're travelling down south together. Wren's pack has a base in the middle of a mountain range where no one will bother them. The forest expands forever. I have heard rumours of wolves down here. I never knew they meant werewolves.

Wren drives us down. Their brother sits up front with them for most of the journey. He is bouncing off the walls for at least two hours, then we get an hour of calm when we stop for food.

But as soon as the service drops and the dark green hills, littered with fir trees, start rolling past, he's bouncing off the walls again. He also has the aux cord and his taste in music is sending me back years. I'm not ashamed to admit I can sing along to all of the songs he plays, although I admittedly shouldn't right now as my voice squeaks every time I speak louder than a whisper and has a range of about three notes before it spirals out of control.

Radwa has taken to bullying me for this. She and Lolly sit in the middle of the car in front of me and Val.

Lolly turns to face me, four hours into the journey. 'Twenty-one questions. I'm thinking of a character.'

'Lady Dimitrescu.'

'How did you know?'

'Lolly I can literally read your mind.'

'Oh yeah.'

Radwa laughs at them, finally turning away from the window she has been staring out of for the past hour, trying to catch glimpses of the deer herds as they prance past. I was looking with her for a while, but then the road led up a hill, and the side next to our window was a sheer drop into a valley below which sent a shiver down my spine.

'Have you noticed,' Wren asks, checking their mirror and blending into the fast lane, 'that you can hear some people more easily than others?'

Val examines her nails. 'Not really. I mean I've never accidentally heard your brothers, or your dad but—'

I agree, reaching forward to grab sweets. 'Are we supposed to?'

Wren presses their lips together looking thoughtful. 'Well, in larger packs, like mine, you can hear some people more loudly than others. Usually your *mates*. That's what we call wolves whose souls are tied together. You can usually only tell for sure when you end up drawn to them in a moment of need. You'd be compelled to save their life. But you can often hear them a lot more loudly than any others.'

I don't think there's much of a difference between how

everyone sounds in my head. But maybe that tracks: I know I've supported Lolly in times they desperately needed it with their BPD; Radwa and I have our woods tradition. I wonder if things like that count.

Obviously, there can be no denying the fact that Val saved me from the rogue. And she acted so instinctively, despite knowing next to nothing about first aid. She managed to figure out exactly how to stop the blood before there was too much, before it choked me out. Our connection definitely deepened that day, in a way I always assumed was shared trauma but maybe was something more, too.

'Like a soulmate?' Radwa asks.

Wren nods. 'They can be multiple, though. They *usually* are. And they can be platonic, queer platonic, romantic, familial or anything else really.'

Val's expression softens. 'Do you have a mate back home?'

Wren's jaw tenses. 'No.' She shakes her head. 'Never have, but we're pretty sure Harley is Phelan's.' She takes her hand off the wheel to ruffle his hair.

He huffs, batting her away.

I've always felt like Val and I were soulmates. Being Christian I kind of believe in the whole 'greater plan' thing, but the confirmation doesn't go amiss. I turn to offer her a smile following this revelation but she's looking down somewhat confused, eyebrows knotted together.

'Babe.' I nudge her with my knee. 'Pretty cool right, about us being "mates".'

She looks up, nodding, a smile on her face as she links her fingers through mine. I resolve to ask her what was on her mind once we have a moment alone.

We arrive at Wren's uncle's house shortly after. It's three stories high, and the walls are made of exposed wooden logs. There are long windows that reach floor to ceiling, and balconies coming out the second and third floors. This seems to be the same for every house on the street. The gardens and parking spaces seem to be communal too. There's no inflated sense of importance about it, nothing to indicate that this is the *alpha's* house. It looks like it could be any other village in the highlands – except for the little announcement podium and the separate medical and training huts we pass on the way in.

Frankly, I'm surprised no humans have accidentally wandered in.

It's because when we turn we leave a scent, Wren explains. *Humans usually find it very off putting unless they're our mates or whatever. It makes them anxious. You'll notice the same with the clubhouse,* she adds, turning the car off and popping her door open.

Phelan all but jumps out of the car and makes to start running down the street.

Wren grabs hold of him by the back of his shirt collar. 'Settle down, Pup. Grab your bag and take it in, then you can go.'

He huffs and shrugs their hand off of him.

I'm not sure he likes the nickname considering Wren is barely three years his senior. I also think they know this and purposely do it to annoy him. It makes me miss Mel.

I take a minute to have a smoke while we all stretch our legs. Just a fag. Wren warned me against bringing weed in the car. Which is fair considering they're driving and have their little brother with them.

Wren pauses leaning against their car and checking their phone. Then they smile.

'Oh, Oscar!' Phelan drapes himself dramatically against the side of the car. 'It's been hours since we last spoke! I believe I may perish!' Wren pushes him away trying to cover his mouth to shush him. He dodges. 'A week without you is simply too much to bear!'

'Why are you making me a posh white lady?' Wren stops fighting to laugh. 'Go see your boyfriend.'

Phelan grins and runs off. We all know Wren *is* actually checking in with Oscar from the way they smile at their phone. They tuck one of their braids behind their ear. It's sweet. Their happiness is contagious. I hope he deserves it, I hope he's worth it.

They then pocket their phone and grab their bag from the back. 'Mitch!' they shout for help.

I stub out the fag and come round to see what they want. They hand me my bag and then a long thin leather case. The martial artist in me lights up. Toys.

'I needed someone else who's trusted to carry weapons.' They laugh. 'Got too many.'

I strap the case across my body. It must contain a staff of some kind because it's about six feet tall. I have to lift the bottom of it under my arm to stop it dragging on the floor. There are scuff marks on the bottom of the case anyway, so I imagine Wren has the same issue. They can only be a couple inches taller than me.

Wren's cousin, Lycaon, meets us in the garden. The alpha's son, the first in line to inherit the title. I recognise him from their memories – I thought at first he was her brother because they look so similar.

He's throwing two tennis balls for a huge dog. It's thin, black and tan with soft floppy ears. I think it's a Doberman. Each time the dog returns one of the balls he bends over to wrestle for it, silvery twists falling in his face as he does. Then he straightens up, holds a lean, muscular arm out behind him and tosses the ball forward across rows of communal garden space. When Wren walks into the garden he looks up with a wicked grin and drops the balls, opening his arms up to give her a hug.

'Oh hey, you made it!' another man says, coming out of the door swirling a glass tumbler of coffee in one hand – ice cubes rattling as he does. He brings a hand up to shield his bronze eyes from the sun. Neither of them have bothered to hide the way their eyes glow. 'Does Harley know yet?'

We hear excited squealing somewhere in the distance.

'I'll take that as a yes,' the man says, lowering himself to the steps.

Wren, who had put their bags down to greet the dog, now straightens up and smiles. They gesture to their cousin. 'This is Lycaon, his mate Ash, and their dog Wulver.'

Lolly's eyes light up and they go to greet the dog. Radwa smiles at them affectionately as they do. I get the impression Wren does not just mean that Ash and Lycaon are friends, they mean that they are mates in the wolf way. I wonder if that is a platonic or romantic relationship. I wonder how they came to know they were mates. Considering what Wren's said about the war, I figure it's probably pretty traumatic, so I don't ask.

Lycaon crouches to help Wren carry the bags over to the door of the next house over.

'Wren's told me a lot about you guys,' he says to me and Val, jostling a bag onto his broad shoulder. 'I'm really glad that you were there for them. They've been through a lot with the humans, you know?' he says, looking down at Val who flushes a little under his gaze.

I can hardly blame her. The emotional intelligence only makes him more attractive. Even my cheeks flush warm when he tells me that he's happy to chat if I'm ever stressing about the whole 'acting-alpha' thing.

Radwa

We end up back at Wren's uncle's house around lunch time after dropping our bags off at her parents. The front communal garden is crowded with groups of teenagers and older children all sitting together around picnic blankets. Some of the older kids play games together, where the teenagers sit in small groups lounging lazily on each other, basking in the sun.

Phelan is there too, tangled up with a boy his age whose shoulder length black hair is the only thing remotely dark about his otherwise sunny exterior. His smile even coaxes Phelan's own out of hiding.

Most of the groups are quiet. Some talk out loud, but most you can walk past and hear nothing but an eerie silence where conversation should be.

Wren said that the people who lost their families to the war tend to come over to the alphas house around lunch time and they all make something together. I didn't quite expect this many people, though. The sound of so many heartbeats, so many people breathing but not speaking – or at least not in a way I can hear – is slightly nerve wracking. It kind of feels like being bullied again, even though I know they probably couldn't care less about my being here.

It's worse inside. People are actually speaking there because they know that we can't hear them. The others try to offer a helping hand with making lunch. While being able to hear them is comforting, the amount of noise is just too much. My ears ring. My pack huddle around the kitchen island helping cut veggies and butter bread while Wren and their family dance around grabbing stuff from the many kitchen cabinets dotted around, washing the dishes as they go.

'If it's too loud, you can go upstairs,' Lycaon offers on his way past, stooping so I can hear him better. 'There's a spare room on the left. Uncle Art and Uncle Mags lined the rooms with silver a while back so they're soundproof if you need a second.'

Cringing, I thank him, while silently wondering how awkward I must've looked for someone outside of our pack to pick up on it.

I don't think I quite realised how big the house was until I properly went into it. It looks sort of cabin-like on the outside because of the woodwork exterior. Warm. But inside the paint is a fresh white colour. In an odd way, despite Wren's house being void of almost all of its usual inhabitants, the small glimpse I got when we dropped bags in the door seemed homelier than this building could ever.

That's particularly true of the room I find on the left of the staircase that Lycaon said would be free.

It is quieter, that's for sure. No one has been in here for at least a few months. All the furniture is boxed up aside from a teddy which is sitting propped up on one of the boxes.

The thick layer of dust on top of everything chokes me as I walk in. It doesn't have the same scent as the dust that litters Lolly's house; there's no bitterness and lost love, but there is anger and mourning in there.

My heart, which had only just slowed, drops when I see the wallpaper. It's peeling away from the wall and is faded and sunbleached from the light coming in from the window but there is an unmistakable pattern around the border halfway up the design. Little cartoon moons, planets and spaceships. There are glow in the dark stars on the ceiling when I look up. This is a kids room. A kids room that smells like mourning in the base of a pack that's been at war.

I swallow back a heavy lump in my throat, hand coming to my chest as if simply placing it on top of my heart will aid the dull ache that resides there.

I'm about to leave to go downstairs when my phone starts ringing. Rather than go back into the abandoned nursery room I decide to take it in the hall, leaning back against a wall next to an open office door.

It's Mateo. That's weird. He never usually calls any of us. His usual mode of communication is texting a bunch of emojis for us to decode. My heart seems to pick up on the little danger alert before my brain does, drumming my ears like that foreboding music that starts playing before a boss battle in a game. Everything with Lolly's sister last week has made me concerned where the rogue might go – what it might do – next.

'Hello?' I answer urgently, bringing the phone to my one ear, covering the other with my hand.

'Hello Radwa,' Mateo's jolly voice blasts through the speaker. 'There is a letter here for you. It's from the NHS so Karen said we should phone just in case you wanted it opened. We can send you a picture if you want, or we can just leave it till you're home – it's up to you.'

A nervous laugh escapes my lips. *Alhamdulillah*. They are okay. I let out a sigh of relief, leaning my head back against the wall behind me, suddenly very glad I wasn't just sent a hospital emoji with no other context.

It's about another gender clinic appointment in a couple of weeks. I've had about five appointments by now. Last time they said this one would be to discuss fertility stuff and then hopefully I can get on hormones. I'm glad we checked when we did so we can arrange travel and a hotel. Since I'm still under eighteen I'm with a clinic down south.

I thank Mateo for letting me know before hanging up and then take a second to catch my breath again needing a moment to be alone with the news but also recover from the scare the phone call gave me. Mitch and Val's grounding exercises are good for things like this so I decide to give one a try.

I look around the barren cream-coloured hallway with its dark wooden doors trying to name five things I can see. Losing faith in finding anything of note in the hallway I let my eyes wander to the exposed portion of the office behind me.

The first thing I notice are the tall bookshelves lined with titles I've never seen before. Books on wolf customs, and laws between packs, peace treaties and wars. I wonder how that works. Do different packs have different constitutions, so to speak? Ways to stop the alphas from abusing their powers?

Maybe it's a little rude, but since there's no one else

around I can't help but take a closer peak. When I enter the room, I notice a board, standing right infront of the desk. It's a corkboard with clippings, pictures and maps. There's even a picture of Wren on it. Admittedly it's an older picture. I'm not sure how I know, she looks exactly the same, same eyes, same nose, same lips… I'm pretty sure she's even got the same colour synthetic hair in her braids as she currently has. But, there's less severity in her look, more hope. I can't explain it any other way. It's the kind of change you only see by looking in her eyes.

The picture has a violet string attaching both it, a stapled document, and an old newspaper clipping to where our town sits on the map.

There are other faces in different areas of it. A woman, with whom Wren shares her high cheekbones, sits lower down alongside a round ginger woman with curly hair.

Right on the top of the board there is a flower engraved. Wolfsbane.

These must be the aconite soldiers.

'You know,' a voice sounds from behind me, making me jump about a foot in the air. 'They've waited their whole life to be on that board. I rather thought they'd want to move around it a little more.'

I turn around to see a man leaning against the doorway, arms crossed. He's tall and broad enough that when he stands and walks into the light he has to stoop slightly and turn his shoulders.

His golden eyes land on me as he does so. Wren's Uncle Cygnus – their alpha – has caught me exploring his office.

'I'm so sorry – I saw the books and I…' I start, unsure how I'm going to explain myself. Maybe if I explain that I needed somewhere to take the call he'll be glad I came here instead of the kid's room I found across the hall.

He waves his hand dismissively. 'You're one of theirs, aren't you? Radwa Hashmi.'

'Yes sir.' I nod, looking down at my own feet on the dry hardwood floor.

Cygnus runs his hand over his head compulsively, then he tuts, looking away from the board.

'You like books, Radwa?' he asks, walking around the room, fingers along the shelves gently caressing their spines until he finds one he's looking for.

I nod once more. 'I'm hoping to study politics, and I just wanted to see what kind of stuff transferred over,' I whisper, crossing my arms and rolling my scarf between my thumb and forefinger.

He backs around so he's behind the desk and tosses the book he's chosen towards me.

'Well, the first step to understanding pack power dynamics is to understand those of your own pack. Yours is rather tumultuous.' He smiles glumly. 'Maybe something in there will help you assist my niece in their effort to settle that.'

I glance at the book title. *Choosing Violence: Understanding Rogue Wolves and the Packs They Create*. I pick it up cautiously to flick through the contents.

'You can borrow it.' He nods, gesturing for me to pick it up. 'If you need some more space before you go downstairs, feel free to use the spare room,' he says dismissively, sitting down on the chair behind the desk. 'Though I must apologise for the mess. It's been like that for as long as I remember. Unfortunately, I've had more pressing matters to attend to. As I do now…' He gestures to the door.

I feel my cheeks turn warm, and rush forward to pick up the book before making for the door.

Val

We finish up lunch pretty quickly after Radwa comes downstairs. Everyone rallies around the kitchen, under Lycaon's instruction, to erase any trace of the fiasco that just occurred from the pristine white countertops. Fortunately, there isn't too much mess. Not even Mitch and Radwa can mess up sandwiches. Mitch and I gather up the food waste in a compost bag while Lolly takes up post doing the dishes with Radwa, Ash and Ash's sister Amber.

A warm hand gently placed on the small of my back pauses my mission of trying to gather up the onion skin from the kitchen island.

Can I squeeze into that cupboard? Wren asks softly, pulling her hand back. She's wearing all four of the bracelets I made her.

I press my lips together in an effort not to smile as widely as I want to. 'Yeah sorry let me just—' I try to move around her, as she moves to the same side. 'Sorry I—'

We both try to move out of the way at the same time. She laughs, and I know she's not just laughing at me by the way her face flushes.

Placing her hands on my shoulders, she directs me to the side and steps around me with a giggle before squatting down by the cupboard to get some antibacterial spray.

Mitch comes to stand next to me, giving the back of my arm a little squeeze. *Are you okay?*

I nod again, hearing my heart hammer in my ears.

Ever since Wren first mentioned the whole concept of 'mates', I've not been able to think straight around her. Every one of her thoughts seems to echo, clear and loud in my mind. Obviously I *knew* that everyone sounded different, but I assumed Radwa and Mitch just sounded louder because I'm closer with them than I am with Lolly.

But then I heard her, and it was confusing, sure, but I never imagined that … I *hate* the idea of fate. I've never believed in it. I'm the kind of person who second guesses every one of my actions. My daydreams are filled with how things might have ended differently if I'd done something different. Hell, I spend half my life doing little rituals to change the course of it. To be told it all follows some predestined plot makes everything feel futile.

Then there's the question of how far it goes. If I was always destined to save Mitch that night does that mean that Mel was always destined to die? Because *that* is bullshit.

But, hearing Wren's thoughts in my mind, feeling what I did that night when she was in danger, I can't help but feel that *if* fate exists and there are people on this Earth woven tightly and securely into the fabric of your life, she is one of mine. And I don't know *how* or *why* yet but I know I am happy to have her.

She straightens up, taking out a half full spray bottle. I know it sounds odd, but I half expected the cupboards to be empty here. Everything else seems to be wiped of any evidence of inhabitants with a chemically clean precision.

When the door opens, she drops the bottle to the floor with a clatter.

I instantly whirl around to see what's causing her distress. But instead of a threat I'm met with the friendly face of a man I recognise from her thoughts. Magnus.

He catches her in his muscular arms as she launches herself on him. He can only be an inch or so taller than her, but he lifts her on her tiptoes as he embraces her, holding her tight to his chest.

Of all of Wren's parents, I think she thinks about Magnus the most, so seeing him act like this with her is enough to turn the corners of my mouth up. It's nice to see another one of my friend's parents show love for them so clearly and overtly without making them fight to earn it.

When he finally releases his daughter Magnus turns to us. 'The new pack, I assume?' he asks, with a chuckle straightening his glasses and flicking his long greying locs back over his shoulder. 'Art has told me all about you.' He gives Mitch a nod as he sits down in one of the barstools by the island.

'Wren said you like martial arts. I just finished one of the kids' sessions. You'll have to join us for the adults' class later tonight.'

I had wondered where he was when we got here. Him being the only one of Wren's parents actually on base I'd expected him to at least be here when we got here.

All Mitch can do in response to his offer is nod, eyes wide as he takes in the man in front of him, mouth hanging slightly open as if he is meeting a celebrity. His blush reaches the tips of his ears. The man was gone from the moment he heard 'martial arts'.

The funny thing is, Magnus doesn't look like a particularly violent man. Even the bite mark scar on the crook of his neck just visible under his tank top looks tender and loving in comparison to the harsh and jagged scratches across Mitch's face.

Wren must sense my thoughts because she leans in to talk to me while Mitch and Magnus start going through the backstory of their individual martial arts at high speed. As much as I love Mitch I start zoning out when he starts talking about how his is like the second cousin twice removed of Kung Fu and brothers with Taekwondo and Karate.

The scar is from when he was turned, she admits. *It was my dad that gave him it, to save his life. He had no choice in the matter. It was instinctive because they're mates. There's usually a massive difference between that and the scars people have from rogues.*

I mean, for starters, Dad only just bit enough to turn Magnus. It's not like he consumed any of the blood, or he'd have turned rogue.

I nod, hesitantly, again not loving the idea that we are something predetermined, that we have no say in how our fate plays out.

And you're right, he's not very violent. He's actually pretty pacifist, she tells me, watching on with a smile as Magnus bounces up and down in his seat while they talk about the four fundamental weapons of Tang Soo Do. *But he was a gay teenager in the nineties, and bullying mixed with watching* The Karate Kid *too many times creates...* She gestures up and down in front of her.

I glance over towards Radwa and Lolly who stand doing the dishes together. After the bullying started for her, Radwa was so timid, but the man in front of us is so laid back and yet brazenly and unapologetically queer. He mentions to Mitch how his wife got really into helping him develop the different martial arts he knew to factor in werewolf strengths and weaknesses, and then in the same sentence says that their husband was exhausted with all of the new ways they both found to injure themselves. I wonder how much he knows about his own son's bullying, and how hard it must be hitting him to see him go through the same thing.

It becomes evident at training that night that Phelan's bullying is hitting Wren pretty hard, too. I watch as she paces around him, striking a punch which he blocks lazily, staying standing still in something which looks only remotely like a fighting stance and moving his hand ever so slightly up to push her fist out of the way.

'Move,' she warns him, bouncing up and down on the balls of her feet as she steps elegantly and purposefully behind herself to circle him.

I'm inclined to think the only reason Phelan even agreed to train with us was so he could watch Harley, who is currently sparring with Mitch in a scrappy combat oriented way that doesn't care for legal target areas or point scoring. His black curls bounce up and down as he dives out the way of one of Mitch's hits aiming a swift, low kick at the side of his knee. Mitch lifts his leg out of the way just in time, giving the boy a cheeky grin.

Phelan staggers back, nearly falling on Radwa and I, and brings my focus back to the fight in front of me.

'Ow,' he growls through gritted teeth, shaking himself off and approaching his sister again.

'I told you to start moving and countering better. Other people *aren't* going to go easy on you. I'd be a dick if I let you train under that assumption. Move,' she says forcefully, baiting him back over to her.

I catch Magnus glancing over only very momentarily, but otherwise letting her continue with the lesson, grimacing. It's as if it's something that needs to happen, something that needs to be learned. I wonder if Phelan being bullied can be considered a fixed event in his life. If it is that's pretty fucking shitty.

I'm jolted back to my fight when Radwa throws a very light punch at me, pulling back before actually making any contact.

We train until about nine at night, after which point everyone is pretty much ready to go to bed. Since Wren's house only has one spare room Lolly and Mitch are given it to share while Radwa and I share Wren's with them.

I'm making my way upstairs to say goodnight to Mitch when he meets me halfway coming down to brush his teeth.

'Hey.' He smiles upon seeing me, pausing on the step above.

'Hey,' I return, leaning my head against his chest expectantly waiting for him to wrap his arms around me.

You okay? he asks, leaning his chin on top of my head as he does, kissing the side of my head twice.

I nod, sitting down on the step. *Just been thinking.*

He joins me on my step, giving me a steady look and scratching his neck contemplatively. *About the mates thing, right?* he asks.

He knows me so well. I wonder what betrayed my feelings on that. I thought I was doing an okay job at blocking everyone out.

Yeah, I sigh, leaning my head on his shoulder. *I mean, the night I saved you...* I feel his muscles tense underneath me but he nods for me to continue. *If that was always predestined to happen then,* I continue, *that means that Mel was always destined to—*

No, he cuts me off. *Not like that at least. I think God has a plan but humans have free will. He doesn't control all variables. You were destined to save me but not necessarily in that way. And what killed Mel was partly an animal, sure, but mainly it was a human exerting that same free will.*

He thinks it firmly, as if it's something he's considered at length, so I don't question it. It's nice that he has something to believe in, something to ease the pain, and if that's how he explains the coexistence of a loving God and grief beyond comprehension then I'm glad he has that, too.

You know, I think, quietly steering the topic ever so slightly off course, *I think Wren is one of my mates,* I confess.

Yeah? he asks, turning his head to the side to take me in properly. He doesn't look enraged or upset at all at the confession. Actually, the idea seems to have painted a gentle smile across his expression. *Explains why you were so defensive of them from the get go.*

It... does actually. I hadn't considered that. *Their voice is really loud in my mind, like yours and Radwa's.* Not quite like Radwa's; it doesn't have the same feeling. Radwa feels like family. Wren doesn't quite.

Mitch nods thoughtfully. *Makes sense.* He tails off for a second, fidgeting with the elastic cuffs of the joggers that he wears to bed. *She seems to really get on with Magnus.*

She loves him, I nod with a soft smile.

He glances at me for a second with narrowed eyes and an amused kind of look on his face.

What? I ask him.

He shakes his head with a laugh, looking away. *It's nothing.*

What? I prompt, nudging him with my knee.

Is it bad I kind of wish her mum and dad were here? Even just to know how that dynamic works? he asks, turning around to look at me leaning with his back against the wall. *I mean, I know it's pretty common here, but I've never really seen a relationship like that in real life before, you know? I mean I've heard about them – polyamory is very common in ace spec spaces online but—* he starts.

Do people seriously add someone new to their relationship just because their partner doesn't want to…? I trail off. I hope he can hear from my tone of thought how disgusted I am by that idea. He needs to know that I wouldn't… we're not… Even if I would like other things from our sex life, him not being able to give those to me wouldn't make me want to *replace* him.

Usually it's not like that. It's more that both deal with a different range of relationships outside typical conventions of romantic and sexual attraction, he explains. *And Wren's parents' situation seems to be quite healthy and… loving and supportive, instead of just sexual, you know?*

One conversation with Magnus enough to make you curious if there's space for one more? I joke, scooting my bum to the side to make space for us to cuddle. *I get that he's attractive and into martial arts but damn.*

He scoffs, giving me a light shove with his elbow. *No! Not like that!*

Why does it matter? I ask, leaning my head in his lap. *It's not like we're like that.*

It doesn't *matter.* His silver and gold eyes bulge at the suggestion. He brings his hand to my hair automatically as if fidgeting with it is enough to calm him down. *But like – I dunno, it's just, what if you turned out to have another mate you felt that way about? Like if you ended up fancying Wren or something? I just wanna know how that would work, what that would look like.*

I straighten up, taking one of his warm but boney hands in mine, the other comes to his face. I need to make sure he's looking at me when I say it. *I wouldn't – Even if I did have feelings for someone, we'd work it out, but you know, I'd never...* I pause.

Mitch's ex cheated on him before they broke up. It really destroyed him for a while. The guy she cheated with was cis, I think that's what fucked him up the most. Especially because it was his first sexual relationship, and only other one before us.

I think that's why he was so mad that the same thing happened to Mel. It's also why I've felt so odd about the slight awkward familiarity, maybe even flirtiness, that Wren and I seem to have.

He takes my hand in his, giving it a squeeze. *That's not what that would be though. It's the fact it was behind my back that I took issue with. If she had asked I probably would've been fine with it. Even if you did have another romantic mate I'd be okay with that.* His eyes flicker up to mine again meaningfully. *Don't get me wrong I want everything we've discussed before—*

Images cross his mind of a black wedding dress spinning in unison with a kilt while ceilidh music plays, martial arts suits small enough to fit a toddler, a couple of cats and a family car with doors that all match each other. The simple things we've both been dreaming of.

It's just... he continues. *Well, if there* was *someone else that came into it, I've never known anyone who had both and...* He shrugs with a small smile. *I guess I thought it would've been pretty cool to see what that looks like.*

I get you. I nod in agreement, taking his hand in mine and giving it a squeeze.

It feels like we've unlocked a new level of understanding between us and the exhale I release as I lean on his shoulder makes me realise I've felt like I was holding my breath ever since Wren first brought up the concept of mates.

Wren

Despite the fact that my lungs are burning, I have to say I've missed waking up early to train with Magnus. He's been my favourite person to train with since I was about six years old, and no amount of time away from base is gonna change that.

The sound of his laughter plays in my ears as I slump myself down on our front door step the moment we get home, exhausted from our training session. My top sticks to me where my armour straps were tied around my body.

At least this session went better than our recent video calls. I feel like training with the pack has brought back some enjoyment for me that I've been missing for a while, especially after everything with Tyler.

Just a few days here has been enough to make me feel like normal: training with Magnus every morning and a full combat class every evening.

Yesterday afternoon we even went to the target range and Val took a keen liking for a set of throwing knives I showed her how to use – which are only actually effective for wolves like us that have enhanced strength, or dexterity – and Radwa found harmony with a compound bow. Honestly, there's only really one thing missing to make it feel like home.

I'm sorry your mum couldn't be here, Magnus says, pushing himself onto one of the communal garden benches. The moss ridden wood creaks under his weight. *She'd have loved that bo staff sequence. Especially the overhead hit and the circle back. Wait 'til she sees the video I took.*

I grin, uncapping my water.

Mum was supposed to finish a mission just after we arrived and we thought we might get a day together, but Cygnus predictably sent her straight on another before she even got home. She's been gone a while this time.

Her not being here the past two years hurt at first. When she was first sent away I was completely livid. She was always supposed to be there for my first mission but she'd managed to piss Uncle Cygnus off enough that she couldn't be and I was furious at her. Then that anger turned to hurt when she wasn't there for when Tyler – did what he did.

I needed my mum. More than anyone else I needed my mum. And the shitty thing is, I couldn't even tell her. We're forbidden from telling people any bad news when they're on missions like she is, at least until they're home.

She's an aconite, like I am, but she's tracking a pack who all went rogue together and have a strange sort of belief that they're better wolves because of it. They have this whole underground system for turning people. It's crazy.

Anyway we've not really seen her and her mate Ailsa, who she bonded with on the mission, for longer than a day or two at a time since we first left. By now, I think I'm used to it, but Phelan is still pretty cut up about it. You'd think with him being a healer he was my dad's shadow growing up, but he is *such* a mama's boy. He's gonna be so upset.

Yeah. Magnus nods with a sigh, then he claps his hands onto his knees pushing himself back onto the overgrown grassy floor of the long shared garden. *I should go let him know. Don't say anything 'til I find him, yeah?*

I nod, lounging back on my hands in the doorway as I watch him leave, pausing only momentarily to check a scuff on his motorbike in the carpark in front of the garden.

It's only about seven in the morning when I check my phone so I don't expect to see any messages from Oscar. He was trying to call me last night but my service here is unsurprisingly shit, we don't really have any reason to call people here because of the telepathy. I did manage to connect to the med centre's Wi-Fi to message him for a while. His sister Heidi was in town so he was sending me videos of them together. Evidently, Oscar showed her my Insta because I got several videos of her screaming down the phone about me being out of his league while he giggled his ass off in the background.

Watching them back makes me laugh too. Oscar looks like he was sculpted out of clay, perfectly crafted by an incredibly skilled artist.

Then, I suppose you're supposed to think that your partner is a little bit hotter than you. Is that what we are? We've kissed a couple of times now. The Saturday after we went on that date he, and his friends, didn't leave my side at group, and he gave me a lift home and kissed me goodnight again. We've made out since then too. Once that first time at his and then once at mine just before we left. Maybe that's all it's about. That's all it was about with anyone else.

But he's not tried to take it further or anything, and we go on dates and hang out together around other people. And the whole time we were hanging out he looked at me with this lovesick expression and everyone knew something was going on. But it's not like he was showing off that he got with me because he hasn't, he just isn't hiding that he likes me. So maybe we are dating. I don't know. We've only known each other for a few weeks. How would I even ask him that anyway?

In my experience, Val thinks, descending the stairs and coming to sit next to me, *boys are dumb and have to be told what to do.* She rests her chin on my shoulder, looking out at the garden with me. *Just say something like, 'Hey I'm pretty hot so if you wanna keep doing what we're doing you're gonna have to lock this down.'*

Imagining myself forcing those words out my mouth actually makes me laugh out loud. I struggled with 'I know' let alone *that*.

Instead of fighting Val on the whole me-being-hot thing – a battle I've already lost – I just lift my wrist to showcase the bracelet she made for me. 'Don't think the idea of me having someone else is much of a deterrent.'

She flushes, lifting her chin off of me, immediately embarrassed. Her blush is deep, burning hot on her cheeks when I turn to look.

'It's okay,' I assure her. 'You hardly meant anything by it.'

Obviously she didn't mean anything by it. She wouldn't have gone out of her way to make such an intricate bracelet if she had a problem with polyamory in general; she's just not used to the idea of it, which is a different thing entirely.

'I'm sorry.' She laughs at herself in a small exhale, letting her forehead thud on my shoulder. 'I'm trying to learn more! Me and Mitch were talking about it last night. Well that and the whole mates thing,' she confesses.

I feel my heart flutter in my chest. Does she know?

Why were you...? I start to ask, looking at the ground in front of me rather deliberately, wrapping the grass around my fingers. This feels so awkward. Surely the whole point of *having* soulmates is that this isn't awkward.

Val adjusts her top, a small smile creeping up her face. 'Felt important I guess. Mitch seemed oddly intrigued by your parent's relationship by the way,' she says with a laugh. Then she scoots forward so she's sitting with her feet just out in the sun, back leaning against the doorframe.

Val looks different in the morning: the lack of eyeliner on her face makes her eyes look softer and wider. More of the rough and jagged scar on her chest is showing than I've ever seen in her low cut Hello Kitty pyjamas. And I don't think I've *ever* seen her in colour before but the matching bright pink pyjama shorts hug tight around her thighs.

'Does everyone here ride a motorbike?' she laughs, pointing forward at the carpark and snatching my attention away from my examination of her.

There are four infront of us currently: Magnus's, Lycaon's, Ash's and another – which looks slightly less badass and more like a scooter – I think belongs to Harley. He's a few months older than Phelan so he'll be learning soon, but since he's only sixteen there are some restrictions on what type he can ride exactly.

'Kinda like the martial arts thing.' I tilt my head to one side, with a fond smile. 'Pretty much everyone wants to be like Magnus.'

To be honest even I fall into that category. The kids hero-worship him because he can do so many flips and tricks, *and* he's just really good with them. He kind of has a thing about respect – regardless of age he makes sure all of his students feel respected and it earns him complete and utter adoration in return. It goes really far when you have people who lost their parents like Harley, or people who have parents like Lycaon's.

'I've always wanted to ride one,' she admits, brushing some of the baby hairs the wind has blown into her face back behind her ear. 'It's hot.'

I raise my eyebrows. 'Well,' I nudge her with my elbow, 'maybe I'll take you out for a ride one day. We'd need to get you some leathers though.'

She scoffs. 'Have you seen my wardrobe? I have plenty of leather.'

'Motorbike leather has to cover a little more than that tragically.' I raise my eyebrows.

She scoffs, tapping her top labret with her tongue. 'Tragically yeah?'

I feel my cheeks turn red, pressing my lips tight together to stop the corners turning up.

'Tragically,' I say again, covering my mouth with my hand and pretending to be distracted by some people walking by.

A moment of pregnant near silence passes between us.

Eventually the house starts to wake up behind us and people cross the garden to the dining hall to make preparations for how much tonight will take out of us. I've missed full moons at home. Everything is so much easier when you have a community behind you.

Mitch

Turning at Wren's place is actually almost tolerable. For starters, there's the fact that the doors of her house are wide enough that we can fit through them in wolf form, and their handles are pretty much a one pounce job to open. Which means we can turn inside without getting that locked in sense of cabin fever.

As much as I love the clubhouse, there's something about actually being able to prepare in a warm house with private rooms that makes it much more bearable than having to strip at an old drug du in the woods hoping that no one sees my ass.

Manoeuvring around the unknown forest and mountain area is a little more difficult. Before, if we were running somewhere unfamiliar, so long as we could smell other wolves up ahead we were pretty much fine. But here there are a thousand scents of wolves everywhere, and wolves look pretty similar.

Still, there's no mistaking the pair slightly in front of me on the track.

A jet black one with lighter brown patches where her back legs become shaggy who keeps curling protectively around a fluffy white one with grey markings on its back and face, slightly smaller than last month.

I've always thought Lolly's form changed a little every moon. They usually seem smaller – almost like a puppy – after they've been back home, and if they're ready to fight they seem a lot larger than life.

It didn't really make sense until the other day, in the car here, when we were chatting about souls. Wren says that your wolf form is very much a reflection of your soul, of who you are inside, your deepest understanding of yourself.

Which is kinda funny, because while every other part of

transforming into a wolf feels like a violation, the idea I have a dick in this form is fucking sick.

Anyway, I'm starting to wonder if that's why Lolly changes. People with BPD don't really have as firm a sense of self. It flickers like a flame. It's not the same as having alters – a system would, however, be an interesting study in lycanthropy – but it does explain why Lolly can go from seeing themself as strong, independent and capable, to child-like and vulnerable, especially when their trauma is fresh in their mind.

Val stalks up behind me as we head back to Wren's, tucking her snout under mine affectionately. The moon is starting to fade in the sky as the sun starts to paint colour through the clouds. I have a thing for artsy people, creative types, but I think the image of the sun cutting through the moonlight will always be my favourite picture.

Thankfully this month testosterone and my meds seem to have worked in unison to ensure that I don't have to deal with a full blown flare up with my endometriosis.

Wren has been extremely concerned and sort of on me like a hawk all day because she has a horrible panicky feeling and everyone *else* is fine as far as we can tell. But I seem to be good. No sickness, no blood. Just quite sore, both from the moon and just from a constant baseline pain endo gives me.

I try to just get through it for a bit, hoping to give my body a break from all the medication I constantly have to throw at it. And I manage for the first couple of hours, while sitting trying to comfort Val, who's feeling very guilty about being able to enjoy this moon and is half convinced we must've done *something* bad.

But eventually the pain gets more than a little annoying so Wren takes my place comforting her, and I manage to walk myself to the medical centre on camp while the others start making breakfast. It's a small building, older and overcrowded. The corridor is thin when I go in; the room to the left juts out too far. I'm almost convinced I've gone the wrong way until I hear voices.

'Say something. Or let me in just—' a small voice whispers, belonging to a younger boy. I barely have time to register that it's Phelan before his boyfriend replies.

'Phe.' He exhales shakily. 'I … Not right now.'

Phelan swallows. I can hear tears in his voice. My fist clenches at my side, I take a breath in releasing it. As much as I appreciate Wren's family and feel for Phelan, I cannot deck a sixteen-year-old just because the guy is crying.

'Please don't leave me,' Phelan sobs once more.

My heart drops for him. Jesus Christ, maybe I don't need any painkillers. I don't wanna walk in on this. Trying to be as quiet as I can, I turn for the door again.

'I saved you didn't I?' Harley scoffs. 'I'm not going anywhere. Besides I'm not the one who—' He trails off abruptly like how Lolly does when they've realised they're going too far. He doesn't sound bitter but he sounds fuck-angry.

If he saved him, doesn't that make them mates? I can't imagine any situation where someone would be mad at their mate for being in danger … I mean maybe when Val has to patch me up after I've tried something stupid with Lolly on a bet … actually yeah no now I can imagine that.

'You're not gonna tell anyone are you?'

I wonder what could be so embarrassing that he doesn't want anyone to know, even if that means not telling people that they're mates.

'Phelan, I—' he starts.

Then a door bangs open in the hallway along the way. Yelling and the smell of blood tears through the air, as the two boys jump to their feet.

Immediately I feel sick, my heartbeat raising. Someone is hurt. Is it one of us? I dive around the corner to see what's going on without really thinking about being caught lurking.

Phelan jumps back in the chair he's sitting in. 'Mitch,' he gasps in a whisper, looking up at me through wet eyelashes.

A bell rings out over a tannoy system, the voice coming out of it is distorted and made metallic by its speakers. 'Can all healers report to ward five, healers to ward five please.'

'Fuck,' Phelan groans, wiping his eyes on the long sleeves of the yellow jumper he's now wearing and pressing his pinkies to his eyes. Then he gets up, making his way across to the ward.

His boyfriend reaches out a hand, tapping his wrist to hold him back gently. He wipes the tears that remain from Phelan's cheeks, pressing a kiss to the side of his head, and then ties his long black hair back so it no longer casts shadows on his face.

Then he leaves without any audible words being exchanged but I get the feeling he's let Phelan know what he needs to before he disappears around the corner behind a row of steel lockers.

Once he's gone the other boy looks at me concerned, eyebrows pinching together in the middle of his forehead causing wrinkles beyond his years.

'None of yours,' he says plainly, folding his arms and leaning back in the chair. 'Checked with Wren for you. They're all good. Harley's just checking if they need me.'

I nod in thanks, my pulse still galloping in my ear. It's pretty hard to name different things you can see in a plain white corridor.

'So,' – I grimace, taking a seat next to him – 'you guys are mates,' I try to casually make conversation as I slide my hand through the neck of my hoodie to rest on my thundering heart.

He glares at me, silver eyes wide. 'Not so loud.'

I thought it was a *good* thing. 'You must've done something really stupid if you don't want anyone to know he saved you.' I meet his glare with a softer look, conspiratorial. 'You know, me and Lolly once tried to backflip out the second floor of the clubhouse – neither of us actually know how to backflip but we figured the height might help. It didn't. Val was so mad when she had to help clean me up.' I laugh, showing him a scar along the bottom of my tricep where she had to cut it open to get the glass out. In my defence I didn't think I'd land on the table. 'She forgave me eventually.' I nudge him with my knee in what I hope is a reassuring way.

His lips pull tight. 'Thanks Mitch. I hope he does too. It was *really* stupid.' He pauses, scanning over me with his eyes for a minute. 'You know, the mates thing is kinda a big deal here. And it can change things a lot. How people see you and what they expect from you – as a couple and on your own. I think I want me and Harley to be able to process it before everyone knows, so could you maybe not mention it to Wren until I do?'

'Course.' I smile, giving him a wink. 'I didn't actually come here to spy though. I need drugs. The pharmaceutical kind. Know where I can get any?'

He cracks a smile finally and gets up to find some.

I think I get what he means about the mate thing. Even with me and Val it feels different knowing that I'm guaranteed to have her *forever*. Not that there was ever much doubt in my mind. I've always known that no matter what happens she will be the love of my life, Hell I want to marry her. But I think part of me has always been a bit worried that one day she'll realise she could do so much better. I mean *look* at her. She's the most gorgeous person I've ever laid eyes on. But she's also so fucking *smart* and *creative*. She's going places for sure and every single day she takes me along for the ride I'm grateful.

The idea that, even without being married yet, we are

strapped in forever makes me feel so lucky but also so... relaxed. There are things in our relationship that fear was holding me back from fully committing to – even when the demisexuality did finally allow me to think of her like that. So I can get why a couple might want time to cool off and figure out what the whole mates thing meant for their relationship before wanting to share it with their family. It seems like a huge commitment for two teenage boys especially.

We sit in a quiet understanding silence for a moment after he returns with the water before Harley comes racing around the corner by the lockers again combat boots squeaking on the cracked linoleum as he does.

'You guys are gonna wanna see this,' he says, and the urgency in his voice makes me forget my pain entirely.

Lolly

We all gather in the hospital, staring at the body laying in the bed in front of us. Her brown hair is matted in a cloud behind her. The monitor to the right of her beeps to a steady beat that disappears into the background noise of the room. I barely recognised her without the fake eyelashes and heavy contour covering her freckles.

There are wires going in and out of her skin. The scars that run down her face and the centre of her stomach are still healing, thick scabs lining them. It looks like she scratched one and pulled the stitches out. It must've irritated her while she was turning.

From what the healers can tell this girl – Emma, the drunk girl from the party where I got into a fight – was turned last month and most of her injuries are from her freaking out during her first moon. She's one of the people that went missing in our town. Mitch figures that she must've escaped the rogue and been hiding out for a bit, moving south. He knows her uncle, says her parents are religious and quite strict, so maybe she knew she was turning and was worried what they'd think.

'We've tried to make her comfortable,' a slender girl with ginger hair called Willow tells us. She looks a lot like Ash. 'But it's only a matter of time…'

Then they clear the room for a little while to give us space to talk.

Only no one says anything for a good few minutes. Mitch, who is sitting with his head in his hands pinching the bumpy bridge of his nose between his fingers, is the first one to say anything at all.

'Someone should let Reverend Peter know.' He rubs his eyes quickly as if trying to wash the sleepiness from them. 'He was so worried about her.'

Val props herself on the arm of his seat carefully, placing a hand on his shoulder. 'How would we explain—'

Mitch sniffs, eyes flickering up to the blinking hospital light. 'I don't know but he deserves to know if she's gonna…' He trails off, as if the word is too heavy for his mouth to form.

A tense silence takes hold of the room. I hate this waiting shit.

Just… waiting. Waiting for someone to die, powerless to stop it. Someone should be here, someone who actually knows her.

Sure, we're connected to her in some stupid wolfy way but we didn't *know* her. The most I had to do with the girl was when I had a thing with her best friend Aimee.

Radwa shifts where she's perched beside the bed, a leather bound book in one hand which she scans carefully as though it will help her decipher the map of half healed, new and re-opened scratches along the girl's body.

'I don't get it.' Wren shakes her head.

'Me neither,' Radwa agrees, pointing to a line in the book deliberately. 'Normally rogues want to cause as little damage as possible when turning people right? So that they don't use too many healing cells before they get to them. The serious damage comes later, when they're trying to kill them, if I'm right?'

My stomach turns a little at that as I catch my best friend shifting uncomfortably, his face pales under his myriad of scars.

'So unless she had some kind of beef with the rogue... then her injuries shouldn't be this bad?' I ask, eyes lingering on Mitch and Val for a second longer before snapping back to the girl on the bed.

'Yeah, but the thing is she was so sweet.' Wren wrinkles her nose, confused. I remember Wren and her had briefly bonded at the party. 'She was popular, yeah, but the kind of popular that *everyone* liked. So it makes no sense that someone would want to kill her.'

Mitch noticeably stiffens on the armchair, the cheap cream leather squeaking under him. 'But it makes sense for someone to have killed Mel right?'

Wren's eyes widen. She sits down on the blue blanket at the end of the bed. 'God no. But it makes sense for a rogue to have discovered a new power and used it to kill the first person they saw without rhyme or reason.' Her lip wobbles, nostrils flaring in disgust. 'That's just the kind of people who become rogue.'

Val eyes Mitch carefully. He has his head in his hands. After another tense moment of silence, he slaps his legs and stands up, pacing back and forward.

Whenever things with Mel come up he gets antsy like this.

To be honest, I get it. From the moment I walked into the room, to now watching Radwa brush Emma's matted hair from her face, all I've been able to picture is Lotta laying in her place.

'Did she have a phone?' I ask, looking up. 'With her things? Did she have a phone? Maybe we can figure out who might have motive from there?'

Wren crosses the room to a table behind the door where there's a phone on charge. 'Password protected.'

Mitch looks at me with a knowing smile.

Hacking used to be a hyperfixation for me. It's actually *why* I applied for maths and computer science.

'Give me an hour,' I say to Wren, taking a look at the phone.

While everyone waits for me to get into the phone – which seems like a far more socially acceptable thing to wait for – the others scan through her public social media to see if there are any hints of conflict there.

Nothing is very obvious. It's a private profile, so most of them can only see her profile picture updates, her birthday, her relationship status, and when she started dating her boyfriend. I make a note of both dates to try on her phone but they don't work as her passcode.

'How do I know Aimee Barnes?' Mitch asks, looking down at his phone. 'Apparently we're friends online.'

Val glances over his shoulder. 'Oh, her and Lolly used to—'

'Okay!' I interrupt.

Radwa lets out a small cough, cheeks flushing warm.

Nice, Val, just casually bring up my hypersexual past in front of the girl I like, thanks a bunch for that by the way. Gods, as if things between us haven't been awkward enough recently.

'Why do you wanna know who Aimee is?' I ask, rubbing my eyes and looking back at the phone.

Mitch shows me his screen. It looks like Aimee has been posting on Emma's wall nearly every day since she went missing.

From what I can tell, they both went back to Aimee's after the party we were all at. Seems like Emma walked home alone the next day because Aimee had the hangover from Hell after being spiked. Nothing happened to her – thanks to

Emma – but she seems really torn up that she wasn't with her. That seems to be the last time anyone saw her until now.

'Wait,' Val pauses looking at Emma's profile again. 'Her bio.'

She turns the phone to Mitch who takes it from her.

'"Seek peace and pursue it",' he murmurs. 'Hey, Lolly, try thirty-four, fourteen for the passcode, will you?'

I type it in. There is a click – it fucking worked. The lucky bastard.

We all huddle together scanning through her text messages and Instagram for some sort of indication of who exactly she was arguing with.

They all end the night she went missing. Maybe she never got the chance to charge it. Maybe she was so scared of what she'd become that she had started to run away.

There's nothing in either app that actually answers any of our more pressing questions, and her Facebook and Snapchat have been signed out and password protected.

That will take a bit longer to figure out it seems.

By the time an hour is up I'm basically begging her to wake up and give me the damn password. By the time two have passed, she's gone.

Chapter Thirteen

Wren

A blanket silence seems to fall over the pack after Emma's passing. Even Phelan is extremely quiet on our drive home, folding his arms and tucking his legs into his chest, leaning away when I offer the aux cord. But he says he just has a stomach ache.

Mitch eyes him carefully from where he sprawls in the seat behind him, legs wide and arms crossed. Until this moment he had been laying with his head back and eyes closed. I feel, for the first time since he welcomed me to the pack, a little uneasy around him today.

We fought last night. Well, argued.

It was when we were walking home from training together. Caleb told me that the medical centre weren't quite ready to release Emma's body yet. They needed to perform an autopsy to study the injuries from the attack and see if they could find any reason for the change in the rogue hunting behaviour – which is perfectly procedural. I mean, it's just part of the process – someone dies, you analyse why, and then less people die, ideally.

But Mitch didn't really see it like that. I mean I don't know what he was expecting. It's not like we could drive her home and show up on the church doorstep.

But then, maybe seeing her body like that did something to him – Phelan says it's probably that. According to him, Mitch's stubbornness on this is likely related to his PTSD stemming from Mel's death.

He also says my 'absence of emotional reaction' could be to do with mine over growing up in wartime. I don't like when he does that. I *told* him to stick to psychoanalysing our friends.

Regardless, the car ride home is quiet.

And when we do get back, it takes a few trips to the club-house – where we mainly focus on training, installing CCTV, and setting up a target for Radwa and Val to practise shooting and throwing – before the tension caused by our opposing reactions to death dissipates from Mitch and I's relationship.

The awkward energy means that by the time I'm ready to introduce Oscar to my friends we have already known each other for over a month, and we have been making out occasionally for more than half of it.

We decide when texting one Friday night. We're talking about Lolly and Radwa and he says he wants to meet my friends.

WREN
I dunno Lolly has been dealing
with a lot rn. They've not
really been focusing on that
whole situation rn.

It's true. Their mum is still AWOL but they are worrying about their sister, and spending a lot more time visiting back and forth between Mitch's and their granny's.

> OSCAR
> Aw, that's fair. They sound
> awesome though. I really want to
> meet them.

I think for a second.

> WREN
> Come into town early tomorrow
> before group and you can! I
> can't come bc Mitch is having a
> party for his birthday.

> OSCAR
> Aaaaah okay! I'm gonna misssss
> youuuuuuu

> WREN
> You're literally still going to
> see me

> OSCAR
> Still :(((((((

He's ridiculous. He's just gonna miss sneaking off to make out with me when the group starts debating about controversial trans YouTubers.

We talk until I fall asleep, and then I meet him off his bus at about two-ish the following day.

He looks cute as ever. He's wearing a band t-shirt under one of his many patterned shirts. I ask him about their music.

'Oh, it's punk – folk punk, to be precise.' He pushes his glasses up his nose. 'I was hoping Mitch would appreciate it since you said he likes that kind of thing.' He scratches the back of his head. 'I'm really trying here.'

'Dork.' I laugh at him.

He nods in agreement and then laces his fingers through mine as we walk down the high street. We pop into a newsagent on the high street so he can buy an energy drink.

He also buys me one and asks if any of my friends would want anything.

'You are really trying aren't you?' I ask him. He flushes awkwardly and starts to stammer out an apology. I cut him off. 'You don't need to buy them anything for them to like you.'

'I'm not paying, Dad is.' He pings a strand of hair from his forehead. 'He gives me an allowance because he never sees me.'

The more Oscar speaks about him the more I get the impression that while he loves his dad, he doesn't like him. I know he does love him – he has a picture of them together on his bedside table – but I think he also resents him a little too.

I tell him what everyone drinks. Lolly likes Pacific Punch Monster. Val likes the Ultra Rose. Mitch and Radwa don't drink caffeine but will probably take something else. He grabs snacks, too.

The pack decided it was better to meet at the pier by the clubhouse today. They said it was because it's hot and they were having a water fight on the beach. I think it's also because they want to get a feel for Oscar before bringing him back to their den. It makes sense. Us wolves can be pretty territorial.

Oscar's heart hammers as we walk up to the ruins on the end of the pier that Radwa is sitting with her back pressed against. Is he really that nervous? Does he really like me that much? It's kind of sweet that he cares. I guess that means he cares about me and wants me in his life.

I call out to Radwa, giving her a wave as we approach. There's a funny contrast in how she is sitting – legs curled to her chest, Switch resting on her knees – and the old crumbling watch tower she's pressed against.

She looks up on hearing her name. 'Wren, I'm dying! It's too hot!' she groans, slouching down the wall as I come up to her.

'I brought drinks!' Oscar offers. 'Cold, just out the fridge.'

Radwa sits up and smiles, as he hands her a can of juice. 'Oscar! It is so nice to meet you.' She presses the cool can to her forehead. 'I'm Radwa by the way.'

'Oh my God Radwa you were right, this heat is ungodly!' Mitch jogs over, scrambling up the wall from down on the stoney beach. His bare legs and stomach are covered in sand and grit. He pulls a bobble out of his hair and gives his head a shake, allowing drops of water to fly from it. Then he collapses down onto the path. The stone must be cool against his skin because he smiles in triumph. 'Hey, Wren.'

It's nice to have confirmation we're still friends after our fight. 'Hey, Mitch. This is Oscar. We brought juice.'

'And we also brought snacks,' Oscars adds, blushing a little as Mitch sits up, shielding his eyes from the sun with one hand to look at him.

Water droplets still cling to Mitch's skin. A chain necklace holding a silver cross and a golden 'V' sits flush against his sodden binder.

'Val! Oscar's here and he brought snacks. He's coming for your man!' Lolly shouts.

They clumsily clamber up the wall with a green and orange plastic water gun in one hand. Once up, they playfully squirt it at us, prompting Oscar to take several paces backwards, even though it doesn't actually come anywhere near us.

Radwa's keen gaze fixes on Oscar, suddenly alert, as if mentally assessing him. Though she could just be avoiding looking directly at Lolly. Lolly is also wearing swimwear and soaking wet.

Val is the only one sensible enough to have used the steps to get up. 'Oscar's gonna wish he stayed home,' she laughs, crouching to grab a towel from her bag.

Her hair is tied back in two pleats, and it curls where it got wet. She's wearing a black and white polka-dotted swimming costume, with a cut-out just under her chest. The fabric is secured in a knot above this. Her soft, scarred skin pokes through a little. She looks gorgeous.

I turn to see if Mitch has noticed me looking. Of course, he hasn't. Over the past month or so I've realised that whenever Val arrives anywhere, Mitch's eyes never leave her. She throws him and Lolly towels.

It doesn't take long for the pack to decide that Oscar is welcome back at the clubhouse. I don't expect him to take them up on their offer; most humans would run twenty miles in the opposite direction the second they smelled a wolf den. But he surprises me, joining us in the house despite his nervous leg shaking and his racing heart.

I hoped it wouldn't make him anxious – which I know is stupid. The only way that would happen is if he was my mate. I can't expect every human I'm even a little attracted to to be my destiny. Even still, I'm happy that he makes an effort despite his evident anxiety.

He fits in well with the group. He bonds with Radwa over art, disarms her and Lolly with dog pictures, and his t-shirt works perfectly with Mitch and Val. Mitch loved him from the second he mentioned snacks though.

It gets to about four when Val starts to complain that it's cold and we need to start getting ready for Mitch's party.

'Oscar, do you wanna come party with us? My parents are out of town so we're throwing a massive one,' Mitch says with a grin as he helps Val with her boots.

'Won't your parents be mad when they catch you?' he asks, looking up from his phone which he's using to show Radwa and Lolly a video of Sammy. 'One time Heidi had an end of year party at ours but she forgot about the camera on the gate and Dad went absolutely mental.'

'The camera on the—' Lolly starts, shooting Mitch an incredulous look, but he doesn't seem to be paying attention to them.

'They know about the party. I honestly think they lined their trip up with it so they wouldn't have to listen to Frank's drunken rendition of The Cranberries. They said it was because they didn't want to cramp my style but I know the truth.' He laughs, running his hand through his hair as he turns to Oscar again. 'I mean it, you should come. Frank's singing isn't that bad.'

I don't need to be able to read his mind to know exactly how excited Oscar feels about this because I can already read the grin plastered on his face.

Mitch

I don't know why I decided to invite Oscar, but I did. I like his general vibe. I dunno. He seems to fit in with the group in a way not a lot of people manage to.

We head back from the clubhouse. Lolly tells me that they, Radwa, Oscar and Wren will pop to the shop to get drinks while we go sort the house out and get changed. In a way it feels weird to be doing this now, considering that someone just died. Our town has gotten all too used to that recently. Maybe we just need something to blow off steam. I know I do, and it *is* my birthday.

The pack have been joking that we should all wear red to my party since it's basically the only colour I wear other than black. Val doesn't seem to own anything red because when we go back home to get changed she pulls a silky black dress out of her bag. God, I love that dress on her. It's got two slits on either side and hugs her body beautifully.

'You're staring,' she laughs, as she comes into my room after getting changed and doing her makeup in the bathroom.

I am halfway through getting dressed at this point, in my binder and boxers. I want to point out that I am on T and she is wearing that so no fucking shit I'm staring but instead I say, 'You're not wearing red.'

She smirks deviously and raises her eyebrows. 'Am I not?'

'Unless I've gone colourblind.' I am in wolf form but usually not when human. I reach past her to grab my new shirt out of my wardrobe.

'Mitch.' She pulls the edge of her skirt up to reveal a thin line of red fabric.

Oh. OH!

She puts it down. 'Your face!' She smirks, coming to kiss me.

Her kisses are soft and hard at the same time. The kisses are instructions. Keep. Kissing. Me.

And all I can think is 'as you wish' as we fall back onto my bed together with her landing in my lap. Well, not all I can think, because testosterone has turned my brain to mush. Right now I can think of a hell of a lot of other things I'd like to be doing with her. Things I'd like her to be doing.

She pulls back and I chase her lips forward.

'Your thoughts are' – she pants and pushes herself up, then pulls her hair over one shoulder – 'very loud.'

'Shit, sorry.' I feel my cheeks flush. I mean she knows I think of her like that but we've never done it like that before. Not how I was imagining at least…

'We probably have some time before the guys get home if you want me to—' she starts.

I can actually feel my heart beating in my chest. Every other time she's offered it's been a 'no'. Admittedly, testosterone has made it a much less sure 'no'. That, mixed with the whole 'forever' part of the mates deal, has me second guessing myself.

'I mean,' I hear my voice shake a little as she sits back on her knees, 'you don't have to do *that* if you don't want to but—'

She touches her tongue to her piercing, trying to suppress a smile. 'Oh I *want* to.' She grins despite herself.

'Really?' I sound a little too excited. I reel it in a bit. 'I mean only if *you* wanted to.'

She laughs, coming close to kiss me again. 'I've wanted to for two goddamn years.'

Val

My head gently rests on Mitch's leg as I trace over all the new hair that has grown there.

'That was—' he starts. His heart races and his voice sounds ragged.

'Yeah.' I laugh and press a small kiss to the inside of his thigh. 'Happy birthday I guess?'

He chuckles at this, absentmindedly stroking my hair. I'm probably going to have to fix that now, and my makeup.

This feels like our first time, only I am not so nervous this time around. I was a little, but it makes it easier when you can communicate telepathically and so you know exactly what to do.

But in a way it is a first time. The first time he's let me do anything to him. Maybe we should talk about it but it also feels serene like we don't need to. I can tell he's happy about it and feels comfortable. I wonder what made him okay with it this time.

'T.' He laughs. 'And I'm fine. Actually, I'm *way* more than fine. Stop worrying.'

I smile and nod.

He gives me a wink.

'I think your voice has gotten deeper,' I comment. Is that a weird thing to notice right now? 'I mean, I was watching videos of us the other day and it sounds so different. And I can't help but notice when you won't fucking shut up.'

'Val!' He covers his face with the pillow and lets out a muffled scream. Then uncovers it. 'For real though?'

I nod enthusiastically and push myself up a little, reaching for my phone which he insisted on placing out the way 'just in case'. I lay on his stomach, his legs wrapped around me, to show him the videos. He grins, listening, as he hears the change with each one.

'We should get dressed before the guys get here,' he says, still playing with my hair.

'Yeah,' I agree, but we just sort of lay there for a second longer.

'Come kiss me.' He nods his head gesturing for me to come up to him.

I sit in his lap again to do so.

'This is a dangerous game. It's how we ended up here in the first place.' He laughs.

It's true. I kiss him anyway.

He kisses me back and then groans. 'Please brush your teeth before our friends get here.' He brings his hands to his face, turning redder by the minute, and I laugh.

As if they were summoned by name we hear the door open downstairs.

'I AM LOUDLY ANNOUNCING OUR ARRIVAL!' Lolly yells as they walk in. 'PLEASE STOP SHAGGING AND PUT SOME CLOTHES ON!'

Mitch turns as red as his binder, which happens to be the only thing he's wearing at all right now.

'Be down in a second!' I shout down on his behalf.

'Oh my God, they were actually shagging, weren't they!'

Mitch hides his face on my shoulder. Eventually, we get up and dressed. I go to brush my teeth and sort my makeup while he makes his room acceptable for having people stay over.

Lolly

We got a variety of spirits and mixers at the shop. The real reason I wanted Mitch to bugger off was so we could get him a birthday cake, which Radwa took charge of while Wren, Oscar and I paid for the alcohol since she is only seventeen.

I'm putting candles in it when Mitch eventually comes downstairs. Wren chases him out of the room. Once we all sing happy birthday to him and cut the cake for everyone that wants some (including Wren's little brothers who we have to pass it over the fence to) I go upstairs to get changed.

We all agreed to wear red today so I find a band t-shirt with a red logo on it and a red-and-black flannel. I decide to put on a little makeup, just basics and some eyeliner, but I fuck up the eyeliner. I poke myself in the eye and it streams down my face so I have to go get a tissue from the bathroom.

The door is shut when I get there. I knock.

Radwa opens it. 'Sorry, I was just finishing my makeup,' she says, grabbing her things and stuffing them in a bag. Then she looks at me, and I want to die.

She is standing there in this gorgeous red and gold dress. Her highlighter matches the shade of gold perfectly and she has some on her cheeks, the tip of her nose and one spot right on her cupid's bow. Nothing is out of place. She looks unreal. And here I am with eyeliner halfway down my face and one eye red and puffy.

'Are you okay?' she asks.

'I—' I grab the tissue and hold it to my face. 'You look really pretty,' I say.

'Thanks!' She smiles softly.

'Eh – you're welcome.'

It looks like she starts to say something, but I'm already walking away as she does. Or running, make that running. I run away before the ground swallows me up.

∼

I've never known how he does it, but Mitch always seems to end up with half the town at his birthday parties. It's been that way since we first met.

Jesus gives me a wave from the smoking corner in the garden where a group of stoners are clinging to his every word. Guess there's no skiving work with a hangover tomorrow.

Making a mental note to thank Mitch for the heads up later, I reach into the kitchen cupboard to grab a tin of juice, squeezing past Mitch's elderly coworker Frank who – true to form – is looking for Mitch's phone to blast 'Zombie' over the Bluetooth speakers. I actually quite like The Cranberries but if I have to hear that same song butchered one more time by an elderly man slashing Tennent's about the place I might rip my eardrums out.

Fortunately I manage to locate the phone and slide it into Mitch's pocket with a wink before anyone else catches me.

On my way back out the room I narrowly avoid a red wine collision, glaring daggers at the drunk girls who nearly spilt on me, and manage to weasel my way out of a conversation with Val's middle aged neighbour Vickie about how she 'might be a lesbian, you know' because she 'can't stand men' and kissed a girl once in her teens.

Most of the kitchen guests are wildly drunk, including Mitch himself who is dancing with Val, and by that I mean they are swaying to the music while holding/falling over each other. They seem to find this very amusing.

Wren and Oscar haven't been drinking. Well, I know Oscar hasn't. If Wren has, they're not drunk anyway. Last time I saw them they were making out in a corner somewhere.

I cannot find Radwa anywhere. Trying not to let it panic me, I start to ask the usual questions.

Where would I be if I was Radwa?

I move towards the back of Mitch's living room where he

keeps his rats. Usually this is where the less drunk, slightly more stoned, neurodivergent people can be found.

Radwa is sitting on the floor next to the cage.

She reaches through the bars to give the smaller one, Edmund, a scratch on the nose. She has a book propped up on her knees, cover concealed by a makeshift linen jacket. It must be the one Cygnus gave to her. She's been reading it obsessively since we got back.

'Thought I'd find you here,' I say as I sit down next to her.

She doesn't look up. Her eyes scan the page in front of her, then she places her finger down to hold her place. 'They're scared of water. Hydrophobic. Like rabid dogs.'

My head pounds from the music in the next room. I feel my eyebrows knit together to combat it. 'The rats?'

'Rogues,' she mouths deliberately. 'Do you have your water gun? We could rule out half the town if we—'

'Oh yeah,' I scoff, placing my hands on the book and setting the Post-it note she was using as a bookmark where her finger was previously. 'We could really narrow it down to serial killers and people who don't like wet clothes.' Half of this room would be fucked for sure.

She scrunches up her nose, annoyed but also trying to figure out another way around it.

I can practically hear her brain ticketing away like clockwork. 'You know,' – I smile at her affectionately – 'you'd probably get a better indication of who it was by talking to people than you will sitting with the rats.'

The fact she is here is so typical. If Radwa is missing at a party you look for a dog, or a cat, or a rat, or a chicken or a lizard – you get the point. The saved videos on her phone are basically all animals. Her love is so all encompassing she changed her entire diet because the idea of eating meat made her feel so bad.

Her face relaxes slightly. She purses her lips. 'Well I had to make sure they weren't scared! And that no one fell into them.'

'You doing okay?' I ask, wondering if maybe she is projecting onto the rats.

She says she's fine, she just likes being on the floor, which is funny because we both like sitting places that aren't made for sitting. I'm a counter person.

We sit for a while just watching people. Parties are more fun when you're sober. People are so stupid when they're drunk. We watch as people scream at their friends about how much they love certain songs or each other, they swap secrets they never would sober. I think the main reason I find drunk people funny is they do what I do sober. They're too loud, they overshare, and they get over-emotional. They're too much. It's funny to see it on someone else.

'Don't you think?' Radwa shouts over the music. 'That drunk people are really cute! I love how passionate they get about everything!'

I blush, even though she does not know what she just implied. Then she comes close to my face so I can feel her breath on my cheek.

'I have to go to the toilet,' she shouts in my ear. 'Look after my drink!'

Her breath smells sweet and warm and it makes my heart flutter. I can see the sparkling gold eyeshadow she's wearing from this close, and I don't think I've quite mentioned how fucking gorgeous she looks tonight.

She looks at me, rolls her eyes then tries to say something over the music.

'What!?' I shout back.

'I can't hear you!' she says.

'I can't hear you either!' I shout back.

'No, I said—' She sighs. *Nevermind*, she thinks, *I'm just going to the toilet. Watch my drink, will you?*

Okay! I give her a thumbs up.

I sit on the floor for a minute alone until I notice Oscar come in. He looks overwhelmed, his eyes are wide and he's fidgeting with the end of his shirt. I get up to check on him.

For a second I try to communicate with him telepathically and then I realise it's not going to work so I drag him into the hallway.

'Are you okay?' I ask.

'I can't find Wren.' He looks around at the drunk people anxiously. His nose is scrunched.

I feel for him. It smells like my mum in here. 'Last time I saw them, their face seemed rather attached to yours,' I joke, to try and calm him down.

It doesn't seem to work. His gaze flits around and he scratches the back of his neck.

'I'll help you find them,' I promise, feeling my own heart race a little.

Maybe it's just everything we've seen recently but I don't like the idea of one of us being out on their own.

'They went to theirs to grab their meds before Conan settled down for the night.' He adjusts his glasses. 'They've not been back.'

I gesture for him to follow me into the kitchen so we can go around to theirs.

As we round the corner into the hallway, I notice a crowd has inexplicably formed around the kitchen door. I push my way through, trying not to gag on the sour smell of drunken sick clinging to a girl's hair as I squeeze behind her.

I turn back to Oscar. 'Maybe Frank's finally decided to perform "Linger" instead,' I joke, trying to pull a smile from him.

He simply swallows, looking as nervous as I'm starting to feel. The smell of vomit, Oscar's furrowed brow, and the nauseous churn in my stomach combine into the kind of instinct I know not to ignore. Wolves are instinctive creatures, after all.

How bad could it be? Wren's trained to kill right? Literally. But then they have been hurt before – and if they weren't expecting it—

'Oh my Gods, can you *move?*' I lose my temper, pushing my way through a group of popular boys and dragging Oscar with me 'til we reach the end of the crowd, standing shoulder to shoulder with Jesus.

We walk into quite the scene. Val's glare is sharp and sober, and she has her hand against Mitch's chest, holding him back. I notice an unwelcome face among Mitch's uninvited party guests wearing its signature smarmy smile.

'Relax!' Tyler holds his hands up to Mitch. 'Was just doing a drop-off.' Tyler is a dealer. Not our dealer, but a dealer nonetheless.

'Out!' Mitch barks, pointing towards the door.

Then he squirms and looks deliberately down at the floor to hide the metallic blaze in his eyes. The hand he is pointing with shakes from his wrist all the way down to the blackened claw forming at the tip of his finger. Blood beads on his lip where his teeth must have pierced it.

Images of a girl whose picture hangs unchanging in our hallway flash across his mind. He blames Tyler for Mel's death. She never would've been out that night if he had kept just kept it in his fucking pants.

Tyler looks down at Mitch, directly into his eyes – which he has thankfully forced back to their normal muted colours.

Then he sort of laughs. Tongue in his cheek. 'I'm leaving.'

He smirks, downing the remainder of his redbull and vodka. Some misses his mouth and a light red spit trail dribbles down his chin. He wipes it on the back of his sleeve then staggers to the door.

He walks out the door right as Wren stumbles in. Next to me, I feel Oscar exhale a breath he's been holding. I'm relieved to see them, but my heart still pounds in my chest as I wait for them to get past Tyler.

They bump directly into him and they actually apologise and move out the way back flat against the door before they notice who it is. Then they shrink. They visibly shrink.

'Tyler,' they say. Their voice sounds so small but the music has stopped.

'Hey Wren.' He licks his lips and smirks, brushing against them as he walks past. 'Surprised to find you downstairs and fully dressed at a party,' he mutters, loud enough for everyone to hear.

Everything happens very fast.

Wren shrinks further down the door. Radwa, who just came down stairs, rushes past us to go to her.

'The fuck did you just say to them?' Mitch lunges forward.

But Val catches him. 'Leave it,' I hear her whisper. 'There are too many people around right now,' she says even more quietly.

She wipes the blood from his mouth, thumb brushing against his exposed teeth. His hand balls in a fist by his side but he relaxes under his girlfriend's instruction, closing his eyes and taking a deep but shaky breath.

Oscar, on the other hand, starts shouting. 'Who on earth do you think you are, exactly?' He makes to go after Tyler.

Val puts her other arm back to stop him coming forward. I can't help but notice her own claws have started to protrude from her nail beds. She's half ready to fight herself. I grab Oscar.

'No, because who does he think he is? Talking to them like that?'

'Oscar!' I say, then I point to Wren.

She sits hyperventilating on the floor. Mitch and Val have joined her and Radwa. I get the feeling that – even if it wasn't for the wolf thing – a fight breaking out above her would be entirely too overwhelming for Wren right now.

'Let it go. For them.' I pull Oscar back by his shirt. 'Come on, we'll go and get some air.'

He steps towards Wren and tries to ask if she's okay but she can't breathe to speak.

Mitch stands up. 'They'll be fine, but we need to give them some space right now. Come on.' He puts his arm around Oscar's other side and pulls him towards the kitchen door.

I think seeing Mitch calm down makes Oscar less angry, but he keeps looking back to Wren. Their face is tear stained and their eyes ablaze. Radwa looks worried.

As we walk through the house Mitch shouts, 'Right lads, I don't care where we're going but we can't stay here because I have to tidy up before my mum gets home, please take all your leftover alcohol and fuck off thanks very much for coming!'

And, 'No, no you're fine, I've enlisted the help of these lot to help tidy, I've got it.'

'Please leave out the front door, we have a spill in the back we're gonna need to sort out,' he lies, leading the crowd away from Wren while trying to avoid the onslaught of drunken birthday hugs.

When everyone's out and we're sitting on the doorstep he turns to Oscar. 'Sorry, I know I'm coming off rude, but I *hate* random ass hugs, and I just wanted to get everyone away from Wren.'

I don't point out that this is only half true. Mitch hates hugs from people he doesn't love. If he does love someone, I swear he's more touchy than me. I think it's just because he sucks at being fake.

Oscar waves him away distractedly and he paces in front of the doorstep shaking his hands up and down.

'You okay?' I ask.

His heart is pounding and I kind of just want to let him go after Tyler because I think with this righteous anger he would win. I can hear Val, Wren and Radwa moving in the house. At least they have got them up off the floor.

He shakes off. 'I'm fine. I'm just worried about Wren. Who on earth was that?'

'His name's Tyler,' Mitch says. He looks at me.

I shake my head. Wren gets to tell this story however she wants. We are not taking that from her. 'Wren will probably explain when you guys get a second alone.'

Oscar nods. We sit in silence for a moment. Mitch starts rolling a joint.

'Sorry, that wasn't the best direction to take you in when you were overwhelmed.' I nudge Oscar's leg with my foot.

He stands just across the path from me. 'That obvious, huh?' Oscar chuckles. 'Yeah, loud noises can be a bit much for me sometimes. I'm autistic, so parties can be a bit of a sensory overload.' He casts an uneasy look Mitch's way as if trying to figure out if that was rude. 'I was having fun though before I lost Wren though!' he adds, glancing up at him again, a slight flush warming his cheeks.

Mitch waves him off. He is harder to offend than that.

'Radwa gets like that,' I tell him. 'like how you were. She's trying to figure out if she's autistic.'

Oscar nods. 'I could see that.' He looks up at the stars, getting lost in them for a second. 'Are you two together yet?' he asks rather abruptly.

Mitch barks out a laugh and lights his joint before handing me the lighter so I can do mine.

'Not you, too,' I sigh and put my head in my hands. I take a draw before answering. 'I wish. But I think that's pretty obvious.'

Oscar nods. 'It kinda is.'

'To everyone but her apparently,' I mutter.

'Didn't you just say she's autistic?' Oscar raises an eyebrow. 'Don't muck around waiting for her to pick up a tiny sign, just tell her.'

Mitch shakes his head, swallowing hard. 'No, Radwa knows.'

'I don't think she knows.' I turn to him. We've been over this a hundred times.

'Babe, I'm telling you. She knows.' He gives Oscar a look, and Oscar shoots the same one back meaningfully.

I roll my eyes. I don't think I'm that obvious. 'Anyway, enough about me and Radwa.' I glance anxiously upstairs, hoping she can't hear us talking.

I can hear her trying to convince Wren that, even if Oscar has taken anything from what Tyler said, he doesn't seem like the type to judge.

'What about you and Wren? What's happening there? Have you guys made it official yet?' I take another draw.

Oscar wrinkles his nose at the smell so I waft it away from him. 'I dunno. I've been wanting to ask them about that but I don't know if I should or not. What do they say about me?'

I look at Mitch. This boy is more helpless than me. At least I wouldn't straight up make out with Radwa at a crowded party then doubt whether she wants to go out with me.

'They said you're *talking*.' Mitch rolls his eyes.

'What the heck does *talking* mean?'

Mitch's eyes widen, and he pats Oscar's shoulder. 'Dude, I've been saying the exact same thing. Like are Lolly and Radwa *talking*? Because I assure you, they're not actually talking.' This makes Oscar laugh.

'It means you both know you like each other, and it's maybe implied that there's like, romantic or sexual intentions there,' I explain, done with their shit.

'So… are you and Radwa talking?'

I splutter. I mean my intentions are definitely romantic but – 'One relationship drama at a time please.' I hold my hand up, then gesture for Oscar to keep speaking.

'I mean like, I really really like them, and I don't want to scare them away. I don't know if they do the whole in-a-relationship thing. Do they?'

Mitch rubs his eyes. 'I swear to fuck if people don't start

actually talking to each other in this friendship group.' He pinches the bridge of his nose. 'Yes Oscar, they want you to ask them out. They want to be shown off. They want more than casual dating and making out.'

'Oh.' Oscar glances at me.

I nod. He resolves to ask them but not tonight because they're a bit all over the place.

Then he looks at me again. 'Is that dope?'

Mitch loses his shit laughing. 'I take it you don't smoke?'

Oscar shakes his head.

'Do you want some?' I hand him the joint. It might calm him down, it might make him worse, but I know he's in safe hands regardless and assure him of this fact.

He eyes the fence, as if to see if it's tall enough to cover him, probably worried someone will see. Then, he takes it. He's never smoked before so I show him, reassuring him that I'll look after him.

'Like this?' He tries to talk while also holding his breath then coughs smoke everywhere.

He's a mess but it's hilarious so I take pity and explain again. Mitch shakes his head at us and finishes his own joint before heading inside to start tidying up.

Radwa

By the time we get downstairs everyone else has left. Mitch has cleaned most of the living room since me, Val and Wren are sleeping in there tonight. Upon seeing us arrive he goes upstairs to get into his pyjamas. I am glad he didn't get into a fight and expose his lycanthropic strength or healing tonight but I also feel kinda sad that Val stopped him beating Tyler up. Is that bad?

I find Lolly and Oscar in the kitchen. Lolly is climbing on the kitchen worktop.

'What snacks do you like?' they ask, looking down at him. 'I have a basket up here.'

Oscar drums his fingers on the worktop and tells them he doesn't really snack. They look appalled.

I freeze in the doorway. It *is* weird. Who doesn't snack even occasionally? Maybe I have been reading too much of that book Wren's uncle gave me because my immediate instinct is to toss him some silver just to see how he reacts. Rogues don't eat human food either, but I don't suppose you can accuse someone of mass murder just because they're not hungry.

Lolly wobbles on the worktop, trying to reach their basket, and clutches their chest dramatically. Oscar seems to find this hilarious because he starts giggling uncontrollably, and his laugh infects Lolly as well.

I roll my eyes. 'Get down.' I grab the basket for them.

They are both still giggling when Wren comes in. She looks at Oscar, then bends down to look at his eyes. 'Are you high? Lolly, did you get him high?'

Lolly looks guilty. 'He was overloaded! I calmed him down! Besides, he likes it!'

'It's true, I do!' He kisses Wren's cheek then leans his head against her chest. 'Your hair is wet.'

Wren nods. Their braids are wet because they had a shower. They got into their pyjamas after being sick. They tell Oscar this. They leave out that they were sick because they had a full blown panic attack, and that they had another one while showering. I had to sit by the door and talk to them while they showered.

'Are you okay?' Oscar asks, his voice muffled by Wren's chest. 'Like, from earlier?'

'Can we talk about it tomorrow?'

He nods and kisses her cheek again. Then he goes upstairs to find Mitch in order to get something to wear to sleep.

Mitch

After everyone is sorted downstairs, I go up to my room to get changed. When I get there I notice something on my bed. A small, leather bound book.

My journal!

I open it, and a picture of Mel and I, from my sixteenth, falls onto my bed. There is a note on the back that wasn't there before.

Happy birthday Mitch

The rogue, the alpha, they were here tonight. Hot shame floods me, just like when we thought Lotta had been taken. How could I be so stupid? I cannot tell anyone about this.

The worst part is I recognise the writing. I just can't think from where.

There are notes on three more photos. They're just generic shit.

Love this one

One of me and Val from our last dance.

Excited for the gig

One of me, Mel and Val outside The Ironworks.

Pretty

One of me and Mel's eyes. We both had heterochromia so they looked really cool in the sun.

The weird thing is the notes just look like captions. Like I could've written them myself, but I don't remember them being there before. And they aren't on any other pictures. Besides, it doesn't look like my writing. The ink is smudged across it as if written by someone left handed.

I hear a knock on my door. I jump.

'Who is it?' My voice sounds fucking weird. Scared.

'Oscar, sorry,' he calls from the other side.

Well that's a fucking relief. I stuff the pictures in my journal and slam it shut, banishing it from both my sight and mind 'til I have time to sit down and figure out whose writing it is.

'Don't apologise, come in!' I've decided tonight that I definitely like Oscar. I like how he makes Wren smile. I like how ready he was to fight Tyler earlier.

'Hey, man.' He comes in awkwardly. 'I was wondering if I could steal a jumper or something to sleep in. I'd steal one of Wren's, but their Dad and brothers will be sleeping by now, and I don't wanna disturb them. I'll give it back. I just didn't know I'd be staying over and I can't not bind in this.' He gestures down to his white t-shirt.

'Shit,' I sigh. 'If you didn't know about the party you must've been binding way too long.'

He half smiles.

'Twat.' I roll my eyes. 'You should've asked for something earlier, but I get it. Here.' I grab my Vans jumper off the pile of ironing I still have to put away.

'Well, I'm the dolt with sore ribs now, aren't I?' He shrugs.

Been there. The desperation to pass can be fucking awful sometimes. It doesn't help that there's this whole notion in the community that if you're not practically breaking your ribs you're not trans enough, or not binding well enough. It's total fucking bullshit. Not that you can tell dysphoria that.

'Do you want a blanket or something? Or if you're really sore, I have paracetamol downstairs? No ibuprofen though, sorry.' My medication for endo contains ibuprofen. It's a fucking pain in the ass.

'I'll suffer, but some blankets would be super.' He smiles.

I grab him one, then he goes to change in the bathroom. I look at the notes again.

'Mitchell!' Val shouts from downstairs. 'Are you dressed yet?'

I cast a final glance back at the journal. 'Just coming! Sorry! I got distracted.'

Val

We regroup in the living room and play party games.

'Oscar! Truth or dare!'

We have been picking on Oscar all night. It's hilarious. He's the only one we can expose because we all already know each other's secrets.

'Truth.' He is laughing. Him, Lolly and Mitch have just had a smoke again and it turns out high-Oscar is blunt and giggly.

'Describe your ideal type.'

He rattles off a list of characteristics that could easily describe Wren. Tall, bright hair, piercings, tattoos, generally alternative.

'We have the same type!' I shriek in a giggle, holding his hands in mine.

The alcohol is definitely getting to me again. I feel so warm, despite being in a shorts-and-vest pyjama set with my hair tied up. Radwa passes me a bottle of water.

'We do! Mitch is well fit!' Oscar all but screams.

I laugh harder at this, especially because it makes Mitch turn ridiculously red. 'I know right!? I've thought so since – like – I met him.'

He does look exceptionally hot tonight, but maybe that's just because earlier is on my mind. His hair is tied back. His shirt sleeves actually fit his arms quite well instead of falling down to his elbows like usual. He's always had nice arms – they're strong, covered in tattoos. But they do look a little more refined than usual. Every time I look at them for too long I want to be wrapped up in them. Can't blame Oscar for looking.

Besides, we've already established he has good taste. I look over to where Wren sits, joggers riding up her long legs, sitting low on her waist. Her belly button is pierced. I didn't know that before now.

'Wren is also insanely hot,' I add. It is true, she undeniably is. When she and Mitch sparred I nearly died.

He nods rapidly, pulling my hands closer as we laugh together.

'I will never understand types,' Mitch chimes in. 'Like, Val is my type because she's Val.'

That'll be the demisexuality.

'Thanks babe,' I laugh.

'If T makes me gay I'll be sure to give you a call,' he adds, and winks at Oscar.

Wren tells him they'll give him his number.

If Oscar flushes any hotter I feel like steam might come out his ears like in a cartoon.

'Are you four done flirting?' Lolly laughs derisively. Then they say, 'I don't think I have a type.'

Mitch starts listing off characteristics which describe Radwa perfectly: smart, emotionally intelligent, independent, nerdy. Lolly tells him to fuck off. Oscar then dares Lolly to stop picking dare all the time because 'people only do that when they have something to hide'.

I agree enthusiastically. I like Oscar more and more by the minute. I wonder if he's only like this when he's high, or if it's just because he's calm enough not to care.

Lolly asks Wren how many piercings they have.

'Six,' they reply, at the same time Oscar confidently says, 'Four.'

I tap the top of my lip with my tongue by means of stopping myself from laughing. Lolly doesn't try to stop themself.

'Where?' Oscar turns his head quickly.

'Seconded.' I turn to look at them.

They raise their eyebrows in response. I wonder if it's the ones I want.

Wren just got a little bit hotter.

'I'll show you if you want,' they offer me, casually.

Mitch laughs hard as my face grows hot. Radwa throws a pillow at us.

Wren then asks Mitch's favourite tattoos: his semi colon by his ear, which matches one on Lolly's wrist, a mountain range on the back of his left elbow, and his bumblebee on his forearm which matches one on my wrist. We got them for Mel.

I start falling asleep on Mitch's shoulder before we go to bed. It's about three in the morning.

He shrugs to shake me awake. 'Babe, I'm gonna go up to bed. Are you gonna get yourself sorted and tucked in?' I groan in response. 'Want me to wipe your makeup off for you?' I nod and close my eyes to let him wipe my face.

I hear him reach for my makeup remover and cotton pads. I take off my false eyelashes and hand them to him. He gets the case out my bag and clips it shut so they don't get ruined.

'Right,' he says, then he's finished. He takes my hand and leads me to my bed for the night – a mattress on the floor – and kisses my head. 'Night, sweetheart. I love you.'

I smile, my eyes still closed. 'Love you too.'

'You guys are gonna make me cry,' Wren comments.

Lolly gags from the corner. I hear a dull thud. Then, 'Ow!' Mitch must hit them over the head.

'Night!' Oscar says, then I think he kisses Wren.

'*Oidhche mhath* guys! Val, Wren, *tha goal agam ort*, Radwa, *mo leannan, tha mo ghion ort.*' Lolly always speaks *Gàidhlig* when they've been drinking or smoking at a party.

I hear them leave the room. I don't fully register that they've pointedly said a different thing to Radwa until Wren points it out. I open my eyes to see them wrapping their braids into a bonnet. Radwa is closing the door so she can take her hijab off now it's just us.

'They like you,' I say.

'I know they do,' she replies, folding the scarf over her hand, not looking up.

Finally, I think. And then I fall asleep.

I wake up to the smell of burning.

Who let Mitch in the kitchen?

He is attempting to make pancakes. Lolly comes in and takes over before he sets something on fire. We sit at the table with a whole host of different toppings, lemon juice, icing sugar, maple syrup—

I point at Mitch with my fork. 'Making pancakes and taking my makeup off last night. You trying to wife me up over here?'

Mitch chokes. Lolly and Radwa both look at me. Then for some reason, they all start laughing.

Chapter Fourteen

Wren

Oscar and I head over to mine not long after the pancakes. Mitch had to go and put his T on and the party dispersed. I know we have to talk, I do, but I just want to spend time with him right now. I'm still feeling emotionally raw from last night and I need a second before I just dive into it.

We sit on my bed for a while, petting Luna and listening to music off his phone. Oscar keeps side-eying Soleil's cage in the corner, but she appears to win him over when I show him how I've trained her to touch her beak to my nose and make a kissy noise.

A little while into chilling out together, once Soleil is back in her cage, we start talking about the party.

'What did you think of my friends?' I ask, scratching Luna behind the ears.

He grins. 'They're lovely.' Then he thinks for a second. 'I mean, you didn't tell me Mitch and Val were so hot which was rude but—'

I laugh. 'Val I get. Sometimes she flirts with me and I think I'm going to pass away. But Mitch?'

He groans. 'I know, I'm terrible.' He buries his face in Luna's side.

I'm going to enjoy taking the piss out of him for this.

A shout comes from downstairs summoning Luna. It's Conan, so she leaves in the hopes of hoovering up some dropped food.

I shuffle to close the space between me and Oscar and lay on his chest.

'Um... careful. I'm not binding right this second. I hurt my ribs pretty badly yesterday.'

I sit up quickly. 'Sorry, I didn't mean to make you uncomfortable.'

'Oh, no.' He shakes his head. 'You didn't. Just be careful you're not laying on Mitch's jumper because it pulls it tighter.' He pulls the material away from his chest, then lays his head on mine as I cuddle in.

'You alright?' I ask, as he lifts his arm to let me lay on his chest again.

'A bit dysphoric. I hate not binding.' He winces.

'You look very flat if that helps,' I whisper, cuddling in.

He smiles so I guess it did. 'Actually. It feels flat when I'm lying down in the middle, I lay my hand there when I'm having a bad time, sometimes. It's really stupid.' He laughs and scrunches his nose. 'Here, I'll show you.'

He lifts my hand from where it lays on his stomach to the middle of his chest under his jumper. It does feel very flat. His heart hammers under my fingertips. I tap gently in time with it.

'Sorry,' he laughs. 'I've never shown anyone that before.'

'Thank you for trusting me,' I say, reaching to kiss him.

You know, it's funny. I think I'm Oscar's first for a lot of things. There've been times when we've been making out where I know that was definitely a first for him. Not that he's bad, just he's very easy to make nervous. I guess it's the trust he's putting in me that makes me start talking.

'So about last night…' I start hesitantly. I look at him to see if he realises what I'm talking about. 'That guy.'

'Yeah!' He looks annoyed, but I don't think it's with me. 'Who was that? And where the…' Oscar's brow furrows and he takes a deep breath. 'Excuse my language, but from whence the actual FRICK does he find the audacity to talk to you like – well, like that?'

I press my lips together to stop an inappropriate giggle from bursting free. 'You know how much time I spend with Mitch and Lolly, and you want to excuse "frick"?'

I'm pretty sure Lolly would argue that the c-word isn't technically a curse in Scotland yet Oscar is concerned about 'frick'.

He folds his arms indignantly and mutters something about only using 'swears' when talking about people he REALLY doesn't like. His 'grumpiness' is so hilarious that for a minute I forget what we're talking about.

I grin. 'Whence,' I giggle, putting on a posh voice. 'From whence does he get the audacity?'

He folds his arms and huffs. 'There's nothing wrong with speaking properly. Anyway I meant to ask where he gets the—'

'The nerve. I get it.' I sigh and look over at Soleil, half-praying for an interruption.

But she's still nestled under her wing, unbothered by Oscar's 'outburst'. I guess living with a pack of werewolves and one excitable dog will make you unflappable. Pun not intended.

'Tyler,' I say into the silence. Something about the way I say it makes the grumpiness slide right out of Oscar in a matter of seconds. 'He's my ex-boyfriend. He, uh, kinda sucks.' I swallow.

That seems like a lame way of phrasing it but I'm not sure where else to start. Saying *that* word out loud always feels so dramatic. I never feel like I'm allowed to say it. Like I haven't earned the right. As though my story isn't traumatic enough.

'You seemed scared of him,' he notes. His hand comes up to my shoulder and gently traces shapes on it.

It calms me to focus on the feeling. I want to close my eyes so I can't see his face change when I say it. 'I am.' That is all I manage.

He waits patiently for me to continue. His breathing is now calm and steady. The shapes on my arms have stopped, and the moment feels frozen while he waits for me to tell him something I am nearly entirely sure he's halfway to figuring out himself. But I know I should tell him.

I swallow. 'I'd tell you what happened, but the thing is I can't remember. I was asleep, or maybe half asleep, and high. He'd put something in my drink. I just remember waking up to it happening, and then that it had happened. I don't think I was awake enough or sober enough to remember the bits in between. That's the truth, and I'm not sure how I'm supposed to heal from something when I can't even remember half of it. There's just this scary black point in my memory and I don't know what happened there. I'm scared to know what happened there. All I know is it happened, and it hurt me.'

He is very quiet for a moment. He looks livid. He takes a deep breath and swallows. I can feel the seconds ticking by until he says something. 'Are you okay?'

'I'm getting there.'

'Did you report him?'

And of course, he asks that, because everyone asks that. It's like if you don't report it no one will believe it was as bad as you say it was.

'We were in a relationship,' I say.

And we continued to be in a relationship for about a month after that. See what I mean? Not traumatic enough.

'I didn't really realise what had happened until it was too late.'

He was showing our friends videos of the party, and people were laughing at how drunk I'd been. I regretted it, sure. But that's all I saw it as. Sex that I regretted, or didn't remember too well.

I mean, he was so chill about showing everyone how drunk I was. How could it have been anything other than that? He wouldn't show that off. I mean, sure, he wasn't mentioning the sex part but I figured if it was something worse he would've wanted all evidence of us being together that night to disappear. I did.

And eventually people were more interested in the rumours he spread. No one sent me the videos. I had no evidence and thanks to him I had a reputation. Who would believe a girl like that?

I only realised what had happened when I was watching Netflix with Phelan one night after Tyler and I had broken up. Something similar had happened on screen. I felt like I couldn't breathe. I felt like I was choking. Phelan had got Dad.

Dad was the first person I told. He had wanted me to report it too, even though he knew it was a case we'd never win. Magnus had wanted to kill him.

'Besides,' I continue, 'I live here, and look like me. And he lives up your end, so...' I blink rapidly and bite my lip, feeling tears welling in my eyes.

Oscar pulls me closer and kisses my forehead, stony understanding crossing his face.

This makes me actually start ugly crying. The fact that he doesn't care and still wants to hold me close to him. He is gentle in a way I'm not used to. Sitting up, he grabs some tissues from my side table. He hands me them and rubs my shoulder gently.

'I'm sorry. This is so dumb, it was literally like a year ago,' I sniffle, pulling the saturated tissues from my eyes.

He wipes the rest of my tears with the sleeve of his

jumper. 'Not dumb,' he assures me. 'Mum works with lots of women who've been...' He pauses, swallowing hard as he takes me in carefully for a second, his brown eyes flicking up and lingering on my face. 'She works with a lot of women who've been raped. It's traumatic. You're allowed to take time to heal.'

There it is. That scary word. Rape.

It feels like too heavy a word to use. A word reserved for true crime documentaries about kidnappers and serial killers, not boys you were naive enough to fall in love with.

I know that's what he did. If something like that happened to any of my friends, I'd fucking kill the guy who did it. I'd go mad. I would have no problem with them calling it that. It just feels like a big word for me to process. Calling it that makes it somehow more real and tangible. It turns it into something I have to address and confront.

Oscar reaches for my hand to give it a gentle squeeze, breaking me out of my trance. 'Can I do anything to make you feel safe? Anything I should know?'

I scrunch my nose. 'I know I'm safe, it's just hard to talk about.' I lay my head on his shoulder.

'Okay, but in terms of things that might trigger that trauma. Is there something I should know or avoid? Not that we're having' – he pauses, looking at me hesitantly before his eyes flick down – 'intercourse, or anything. But when we're kissing, and whatever this is we're doing...' A deep flush creeps between the freckles that coat his cheeks like sprinkles on a cappuccino. '...Maybe that's a bad time to bring it up? I – I just want to make sure you're okay and know how to avoid accidentally upsetting you.'

I try my hardest to stifle the laugh that comes out at his poshness but it erupts out of me so forcefully it knocks new tears from my eyes. I can't help it. Thing is, it's a valid question, we have been making out a lot lately, and I appreciate his concern, but God why did he phrase it like that.

'Sorry,' I giggle again, reaching to squeeze his hand. 'It was just the phrasing. I promise,' I try to tell him between laughs.

He hits me with a pillow.

Eventually I recover myself. 'In terms of sex' – cue Oscar turning even more red – 'I don't do that shit when I'm drunk. Making out is fine until we hit like three drinks, then I'm out, but you know that from last night. I think that's all I can remember that might cause issues. But stuff might come up and unlock a memory so I really just need you to communicate with me and learn to read me.'

He nods. He is still scratching his neck, embarrassed.

'For the record, I don't think I'm ready to have sex again yet,' I continue. 'I probably will be one day. I just can't even nap next to men outside of my family right now. I just stay up and panic.'

I've slept next to men in my pack since then. Well, Ash and Harley. And I would probably sleep next to Mitch if I had to for wolf shit because I can hear his thoughts. But other than that, men I'm not related to are a no-go, and I've never slept next to anyone outside of a group setting since then.

His expression softens. I can see him pitying me and I hate it.

'Well, I'm sorry to hear he messed up naps for you.' He holds my hands in his, then pauses for a moment. 'You know, I want you to know, with whatever we've got going on, with the making out and that – I don't – I don't expect more. Like I don't expect you to want to take a nap together. If you never want to, that's okay. I mean I've never napped with someone else anyway so—'

I feel like he might be talking about more than just napping here but I appreciate it all the same. I reach forward to kiss him, and to my surprise, he doesn't kiss me like I'm made of glass. He takes my lead, like he always does, but when I kiss him hard he kisses me back with the same strength. He meets me where I want him.

Something has changed with us today. I feel closer to him. I feel like I'm starting to trust him.

'You know…' I pull away from him. 'I don't know what you've heard, but I have a reputation, and when we go to college, people might talk about you if you keep me around. If we keep kissing.' I feel my face grow hotter.

Tyler spread a lot of shit about me when we broke up. Some of it was true. I suppose I am 'easy', I am naive. Most of it was just to ruin me, I think, so that no one would believe me if I did come forward.

He looks at me, straight at me. 'I don't care about the person I've heard about. I care about the person I know.'

'What if they're the same person?'

'Then they're the same person. I still care about them, and I still want to be seen with them, and kiss them… kiss them a lot.'

That makes me smile. I play with the end of my braid. 'I'd like that.'

'You know,' he continues, 'people who are so dedicated to kissing each other like that usually have these terms that they call each other. Maybe you've heard some. Partner, that's one of them—'

I laugh and push his shoulder gently. He grins. That fucking grin.

'Girlfriend,' I say. 'I prefer girlfriend.'

'Hmm.' He nods. 'That is interesting. How about if I called you my girlfriend, how would you like that?'

I put my head in my hands and look at him. 'Yes Oscar, I'd like that.'

He nods once more. 'I'd like to be called your boyfriend.'

I laugh at him. He is so goofy. 'Okay,' I agree, and then I kiss him again, relaxing into it this time as though he has undone a knot inside of me.

I can still hear my heartbeat in my ears but this time it is accompanied by the fluttering wings of butterflies.

We sit there cuddled together for a few minutes before Dad calls me downstairs to plan dinner. He asks Oscar to stay, in a way that doesn't seem like he's offering because he's here but because he genuinely wants him to. I wonder if he heard me telling him about Tyler.

Oscar politely declines, saying that he should go home to his mum given that it's just them in the house, and he doesn't want her to eat alone.

My dad smiles gently at that as if he's never been happier to have a dinner offer rejected.

What a gentleman, he thinks, raising his eyebrows at me.

We sit in the kitchen together while Oscar waits for his mum to come and pick him up. My brothers seem very interested in what is going on, despite my dad's attempts to shoo them away.

Conan pads through as he's peeling the tatties.

'Is you Wren's boyfriend?' he demands of Oscar before Dad has the chance to take him through.

'Pup, leave your sister and their friend alone,' Dad warns.

Oscar smiles warmly and nods.

'Is you a good boyfriend?'

This catches him off guard. He looks at me sadly. 'I'm going to try to be,' he promises, taking my hand. Then he turns to Conan. 'What do you think a good boyfriend would be like?'

Conan launches into a long-winded story about how he brought his 'girlfriend' cake in nursery one day and that made her happy, and concludes that maybe Oscar should bring me cake.

Oscar nods along and agrees to but only if Conan helps him make it, which seems to have him delighted.

Before long, Oscar's mum is here for him and I see him to the door.

Phelan speeds through from the living room. 'Not that I was listening, but can we talk about how sweet that man is, and how smooth, Jesus Christ? I like this one Wren.'

I laugh.

'He's gonna try, huh?' Dad asks me, pulling me in for a hug against his chest.

Yeah, I think. *He's gonna try.*

Mitch

I'm sitting on the step having a smoke when Oscar leaves Wren's.

'You got a lift?' I ask.

He nods and tells me his mum is in the car park round the corner. 'I'll wash your jumper then give it back.'

I wave him off. 'Whenever you can is fine.' I'd be one to talk about stealing clothes. I'm pretty sure my wardrobe is mainly made up of Val and Lolly's hoodies.

He smiles and turns to leave.

I wish we got to hang out more last night. I like his vibe, and I don't have many guy friends. I haven't really had any since I was a kid. Does that sound stupid? It's not stupid to want a friend that gets it, right?

'Oscar! Wait up.'

He turns around.

'Did you wanna maybe hang out sometime?'

He grins a wide grin that reaches his eyes. I don't think I've ever seen someone have such dark brown eyes. Maybe Val, before she turned. 'You free Saturday morning? I'll be in town before me and Wren's group anyway.'

'Yeah,' I splutter. I don't know why I feel so awkward. 'Yeah, I'm free Saturday.'

Chapter Fifteen

Mitch

When Saturday eventually rolls around, I feel kind of nervous. I don't know why. Oscar messages me loads, and he is ridiculously easy to talk to and be around.

I think I'm just excited. I really want to be his friend. Is that dumb to admit?

I guess it's because he seems to fit in so seamlessly with the pack. A large part of it is to do with how ready he was to kick Tyler's ass.

I sit on my floor raking through a drawer of band t-shirts trying to find one he might like. It'll give us something to talk about. I hate small talk.

The Front Bottoms one for sure, Wren pipes up in my head.

I flush with embarrassment. I don't know why it makes me blush. I guess I just don't want anyone to think that I care that much.

My phone lights up.

> OSCAR
> Leaving now! :)

I think about asking him what sort of car his mum has so I can look out for it but I don't want him to think I'm weird. His car has been in the garage or I would know what to look for from his Facebook.

She ends up dropping him in the front car park today. As it turns out she drives a black Range Rover. I think it's the most expensive car I've seen in my life. It looks out of place in the scheme car park next to my shitty wee red car which has one door a different shade from the rest.

Oscar doesn't seem to notice. 'Hey!' he calls, shutting the car door behind him and reaching through the back window to say goodbye to his dog.

I open the gate and go out to see him.

'This is Sammy,' he tells me, as I scratch the lab behind his ears. Wren has mentioned Sammy before.

When Oscar's mum drives off, we head into my house, then go straight upstairs to my room.

Oscar, as it turns out, isn't a fan of small talk either. He admires my book collection pretty much as soon as he walks in, and starts going on about all the books he's read from the shelf. It's not like he's bragging, or trying to dissect it in a way he assumes I haven't. There's not an ounce of pretension about it. He bounces on his heels and taps the spines of each book excitedly in turn as he talks about them. He gestures about in an over-the-top way, grinning the entire time, a sparkle in his eye. I think this is the most genuine I've ever seen him act. He comes to life talking about them – he's excited.

It turns out we're both fans of Wilde, although I'm more into reading his socialist writings, which as Oscar points out are admittedly flawed at points, whereas he's obsessed with *The Picture of Dorian Gray*.

He stands on his tiptoes to read the titles of the books on my top two shelves. He's short, shorter than me, shorter than most of the pack except Lolly. I take the book he's looking for off the shelf for him and hand him it.

'You crack the spines!' He turns it over in his hand, looking at it in disgust.

I take it from him and open it. 'I also wrote in it.' I point out the highlighted passages.

He mock-gags.

'It's well loved!' I clutch it to my chest pretending to be hurt.

He rolls his eyes and puts his hand out for the book.

'This ones my favourite. You'd probably like it,' I tell him. Everyone should read this book. 'It's about these two guys who fall in love in the eighties.'

'Sounds morbidly depressing,' he says bluntly.

I agree. It is. But it's also beautiful, and poetic, and the main character falls in love like I do. Maybe he's meant to be demi.

'One of the boys is definitely autistic coded,' I tell him. 'And it's got a happy ending.' I lay back on my bed and put my hands behind my head.

'It's *your* favourite?' He turns it over in his hands.

'It's one of them.'

He nods decisively. 'I'm borrowing this.'

I laugh. 'Sure, but you'll have to ignore my notes. They're not very academic.'

He's about to turn away from the bookcase when something on the bottom shelf catches his eye. He drops to the floor immediately, landing in a kind of 'W' shape on the floor and pulling a heavy book into his lap.

It's one on reading and writing in code – not computer coding, like what Lolly studies, but coded messages. Mel and I used to write each other letters and notes in class in code, and pass them to each other in the hall. One time she wrote me a sentence of gibberish that curved around a spiral and only made sense if you folded it into sixteenths.

Oscar looks up at me now grinning. 'I adore coded messages – their history in the queer community is –' He interrupts himself, looking up at me with wide sparkling eyes. 'Do you ever write in code?'

'I used to.' I look down at him, then at my hands, scraping the black nail varnish off in specks.

'That's so cool! Did you know that—' he starts, seeming to bounce where he's sitting before he catches my eyes and stops suddenly, seeing the awkwardness in them.

He puts the book down, sliding it back into the shelf, and scratching the back of his neck awkwardly.

'Did you maybe want to listen to some music?' he asks, nodding towards my record player.

I smirk, standing up to pick a record. After pressing play I lay back on my bed again. The sun is flooding in from the open window.

'Mind if I smoke?' I ask him. I feel like it would be rude to assume. He did come over to hang out with me.

He looks up. He has nestled himself comfortably on the floor. He is reading the book already. 'You sharing?' He grins.

Oscar has the kind of grin my mum would call cheeky. It gets him what he wants. My mum would call him a charmer.

I dread to think of what Oscar's mum would think of me and Lolly corrupting her son like this.

We sit on my windowsill looking out at the garden quietly.

'You read a lot of gay books for a straight man,' he says rather abruptly.

I shrug. 'I figured out I liked girls before I figured out my gender so I guess I did at that time and some of them just kind of stuck. And it's not like I couldn't imagine myself in that situation, it's just that I happen to be straight, unfortunately.'

He looks up at me out of the corner of his eyes, brows furrowed, then looks back outside. 'They helped you discover stuff then?' He smiles, taking a draw and then passing it to me. 'It was YouTube for me. That and my ex-boyfriend, Kaiden. He was really into a particular side of YouTube though.' He scoffs. 'If anything, it confused me more watching these guys that thought there was a set way for us to be men. It actually delayed my coming out because I *wasn't* like that. I mean I tried to fit their box but... it's not really made for people like me.'

See, this is why I've not spent a lot of time in the online community. There's a lot of infighting. I know exactly the kind of guys Oscar's talking about. They *hate* people like me: trans guys who like to dye their hair, and wear makeup and crop-tops.

Thing is, I know I could easily fit into that thin white binary box that Oscar's talking about, but it's just not for me. I came out to feel more like myself, not less. And when I grew up idolising the front men of punk bands, it seems stupid to expect me to fit the same model of masculinity the rugby lads subscribe to.

'I'm not like that anymore though, promise,' Oscar adds dumbly. 'Trying to be like that was really bad for me actually. I wish I'd had a space that wasn't so volatile, maybe the books would've been a better shout.'

I nod in agreement, taking the joint from him. Then I notice the smudges under his pinkie. 'Are you left-handed?' I ask, pointing towards it with the joint before I take a draw.

'Gosh, I didn't realise how bad that was.' He flushes, embarrassed, trying desperately to wipe it off on his trousers.

'It's chill.' I shrug. Mel was left-handed too. She didn't draw, but she wrote a lot, so she always had black ink there. 'Is it oil pastels?'

He looks up at me for a moment, a sparkle of excitement in his deep brown eyes as bright as a star in twilight. 'Do you like art?'

I chuckle, itching my neck. 'I like artists.' Val isn't the first artsy person I've dated. I think it's just an attractive trait to me.

Oscar grins as I tell him this. 'That makes sense. You seem like you'd be a pretty good muse.'

I choke on the joint as I breathe in. Shit, that was smooth, I'll give him that.

I pass him the joint as I take a spit of water but he shakes his head, saying his head has started to spin a little. Probably my bad, maybe it was a little strong for him since he doesn't normally smoke.

He climbs off the windowsill and lays on my bed on his front, propping himself up on his elbows to read the book I lent him. I sit on the windowsill until I finish.

'Do you smoke every day?' He asks, looking up from the book.

'Yeah.' I exhale out the window. 'It helps with my PTSD.' I don't know why I told him that, and I don't know why I keep talking. 'Or at least it makes my brain less loud.'

'Less loud?' Oscar laughs, pointing to the line he was on with his finger. 'I can hear your fridge right now.'

Okay, that's fair. 'I mean in terms of – I dunno, I get a lot of unwanted memories from back when me and Val were attacked, and there's less when I smoke.'

'What happened to you?' He looks up from the book again.

'Like I said, we were attacked.' I shrug, let him take from that what he will. I don't know why I'm telling him this much, or why I continue to. It feels like the words are spewing out of my mouth. 'I had a sister. Her name was Mel.'

At this point he puts the book down, sitting up. He smells of something I can't quite pinpoint, alcohol, tweed and night air. 'What was she like?'

God, that's a question. She was like a safety net for me. My closed captions for what was expected of me when we were out together. Then there was her laugh. It filled you with warmth like hot tea with honey. It was infectious. If she started, then I started, and that had a knock on effect on Val until we were howling and clutching our sides.

'She was my best friend.' I hop down from the windowsill and show him the picture I keep on my bedside cabinet. 'That's me, with the black hair... it was an *interesting* choice I know.' I laugh awkwardly. God that looked awful with how pale I am and the ginger eyebrows. 'That's Mel. She died that night. Hell, I nearly died that night.'

I lift my chin to show him the scar across my throat. He looks at it in shock. Then puts a hand on my shoulder to look closer. It's warm. I don't hate it.

He leans back. 'How did you survive that?' he asks, his voice barely a whisper, as his eyebrows pull together.

'Great question. I still don't know why.' I shrug. Val saved me. Val held on tight until the ambulance came. 'Sorry, I – I don't know why I'm telling you this.'

Oscar shrugs. 'I'm glad you feel like you can.'

We fall into silence.

It feels comfortable, despite the heavy topic. It doesn't feel like there's any expectation to know what to say or how to act.

We just sort of exist together. I don't remember falling into this comfortable a friendship with someone so quickly since Lolly and I first started hanging out.

At one point he closes the book and hits me over the head with it.

'Dude!' I groan. 'What was that for?'

'Telling me nothing sad happens. That was a lie.'

'In my defence, I didn't say that *nothing* sad happened. I just said it had a happy ending.'

He side-eyes me, trying to decide if he's still mad.

I decide to pick up my copy of *Dorian Gray* while he reads. I've never actually read this one. I just own it. But he seemed so excited about it, and grins seeing me pick it up, so I guess

I'm committed now. I pick up a green highlighter and allow myself to be submerged. It turns out to be a story about a beautiful, rich, blond boy and his sordid bisexual affairs. I don't think I like any of the characters except Basil. They scream rich-people's-problems.

'This is totally why you dye your hair blond, isn't it? Just taking that final step towards being him.'

Oscar snorts. 'You calling me a pretty boy?'

I take my turn to whack him over the head with the book. We sit reading for what seems like no time at all but is actually about two hours, when I suddenly get really hungry. It's like an itch I can't shake. This has been happening a lot lately.

'If I don't get a snack right this minute I'm gonna die,' I decide, closing the book as Basil and Henry discuss the opera.

He asks what I want and I tell him I don't know so he starts suggesting foods. His suggestion of an ice lolly gets a cold reception because, like I said, I'm hungry. The rice cakes he has in his backpack for a snack don't even dignify a response. What in the rich people shit is a rice cake supposed to solve? Cheese and crackers wouldn't be amiss, but I'm craving something sweet. By the time he suggests bell peppers and hummus I realise our snacking options are not compatible.

'Who the fuck smokes a joint and craves hummus man?' I laugh, putting the book down.

He laughs awkwardly and scratches the back of his neck.

It's the first time during this hangout that the air starts feeling weird. I think I've touched a nerve. I always say the wrong thing, I never mean anything by it.

I apologise and he waves me off. He seems to just understand in a way other people don't, except for the pack who have just sort of had time to get used to it.

'Should we go down the street for a snack run?'

He looks out the window to check the weather and then puts down the book and nods. I offer him another hoodie so he doesn't smell like weed. He takes the original one out of his bag and asks if he can just borrow that one again. I laugh and let him.

We go to the sweetshop. I have to hold myself back from ordering everything there. I settle for some blue raspberry bonbons. Oscar gets some bubblegum, which comes in bright retro packaging. Apparently, it's the best for blowing bubbles with.

He stops as we're about to leave, his eyes lingering on a poster on the notice board.

Emma's face stares back at me. The poster is new, the paper not yet sunbleached.

It fucking kills me that they don't know yet. Going to church and Bible study feels almost impossible now. How do you lie – even by omission – to a priest? How can I withhold information about someone's family from them?

But Wren says their family needs time to investigate, and to make sure nothing comes back to them. They made me promise not to tell, and I'm trying to be a man of my word.

My eyes are torn away from the object of their guilt as Oscar rips a ticket off another poster with a phone number written on it. Looks like the ice-cream parlour is hiring part-time after school hours.

'Looking for a job?' I ask him, contently shoving sweets into my mouth. Given the car his mum drives and the fact he's trying to get into university, I can't imagine why.

'Me and Wren had our first date here. I thought it might be cute.'

People don't get jobs because they think it would be cute. 'I didn't know you were looking for one.'

He sighs. His hands are balled into fists and he's rubbing his nails against each other. 'Dad's home in a few weeks, for good this time, and I'm gonna come out to him. Just trying to set up a safety net just in case.'

Ah, I stop. I feel a bit stupid. 'You worried he's gonna kick you out? For real?'

He taps his knuckles together. 'Aren't we all?'

That's fair, I suppose. My parents were always alright about it. *I* was never worried about them cutting me out of their lives at least. I didn't even need to worry about them 'mourning the loss of their daughter' because they had done that once before and knew nothing could ever compare.

'What about your mum?' I ask.

'Oh, she's great.' He smiles, popping some gum into his mouth.

'Wouldn't she support you?'

'Yeah, but Dad is…' He trails off. 'I think they're gonna get a divorce and any financial support mum could provide will probably be tied up with that.' He adjusts his glasses. 'If Dad is weird about me that might just be the thing that breaks them. And even if he isn't outwardly, and acts like he's fine, I have a feeling he won't be. I don't wanna live in a house with that energy.'

I nod, not knowing what to say. Radwa would be better at this. I offer him a sweet. He shakes his head and blows a bubble with his gum.

We walk in silence for a while. Then I have a thought. I take a pen out of my trouser pocket and grab his arm. I scribble on it.

'My number.' I smile as he looks up at me confused. 'In case you need me then and can't get online.'

He grins. 'Now Wren doesn't need to give you mine.'

I shove him, as we walk back to mine together.

Lolly

Anna is on the phone in the kitchen when I walk in from work. I hang up my jacket next to Mitch's in the cupboard and tuck the weed-turtle Jesus sent me with into his backpack. She leans on the counter, hand crossed over her body, clutching her cardigan close to her.

I can always tell when Anna has had some bad news just by how she holds herself. She moves more slowly and, like her son, she wears her emotions on her sleeve. Her face betrays anything she might try to keep from us. Fuck knows how she manages to hear so much gossip because the woman cannot keep a secret.

'Yeah, thanks Saoirse. That's Lolly in just now if you want to speak with them.'

My blood turns cold in my veins hearing my granny's name, shoulders tensing, as Anna hands me the phone.

Time seems to freeze over as my granny tells what's been happening. I press the phone against my cheekbone and have to steady my elbow against the counter to keep my hand still. They found out Mam has been on it again – I pretend to act shocked about that one. There was enough evidence in the house to create a case for neglect, so they're applying to the court for full custody through kinship care. They reckon they need to cut Mam off entirely but they're pretty okay with that. She'll get served with the papers tomorrow.

After we finish the call I sit down at the breakfast bar to sort the thoughts in my head. They swim through the heavy air around me in slow motion.

'You know, if you wanted to be adopted with her, you still can be. I was looking into it a couple of years ago,' Anna advises, shimmying into the seat across from me and scooting a mug of tea across the table.

I pause for a moment, watching as she picks up her gossip magazine from the chair tucked most tightly into the corner. A couple of years ago? That would be around the time I started staying over.

She smiles softly and squeezes my arm. I feel my eyes get wet. There's a lump in my throat.

'Are you okay, pet?' she asks, popping her magazine down in her lap

I nod, rubbing my eyes under my glasses. My elbow knocks the mug as I do, splashing a little tea on the counter. 'Fuck.' I wipe it up with my sleeve. 'Shit, sorry for swearing.'

Anna laughs. 'Fuck's sake Lolly,' she teases, tapping my knee with her magazine and deliberately emphasising the curse like a child being told they're allowed to swear. Then she gives me a soft look. 'Would you like me to take you over to your mams so that you can see how she's doing tomorrow?'

She knows that will be a distinct fuck no. I glare at her.

'I thought as much.' She pats my leg. 'I just wanted you to know. And I also want you to know, whatever happens, there is always a room here for you.'

I nod. 'I know.' I feel a little choked up so I add, 'Unless you decide to look into adopting someone again and end up giving it away.' I dramatically fake sob.

'Lolly' – she takes my hands in hers – 'it was never just about adopting *someone*.' Then she squeezes them and leaves me there, sitting on the counter.

I eventually make my way up to my room.

That was a lot. As much as I love Anna, that was a lot. I sit back on my bed. The room is spinning, and Mam won't be happy. Lotta might be safe, but she is going to be so confused.

Happy place.

I look for my happy place.

I message Radwa.

```
LOLLY
Hey. Are you free right now?
```

For me, happy is less a place and more a person.

She doesn't appear to be online because forty minutes pass and she still hasn't replied. I open my messages, refreshing the tab. I even message our group chat with a meme I found online, just to make sure my messages are going through.

Val heart-reacts to it. Wren replies.

I groan, turning my phone off and sliding it across the floor. I hear the gate open downstairs, and Wren's husky barking accompanied by voices.

Shortly afterwards, Mitch appears at the door, holding a book in one hand. He looks at me, then raises an eyebrow.

'Yes?' I ask, crawling back over to my phone.

'What?' He looks confused.

'What do you want?' I ask, looking up.

'Nothing, why?' He looks down at the book, inspecting something on it.

'You're standing in my room,' I remind him.

'I'm not in your room. I'm in the hall.' He's trying to be awkward now.

'You're actually not funny.' I reach for my backpack with my rolling stuff in it. I need a joint right now.

'I actually am, by the way.' He comes into my room and lies with his back against the computer desk.

For a while he just sort of sits there reading his book. Both he and his mum are like that. They don't say anything to cheer me up, just appear and decide we're hanging out.

It makes me feel better, even when I didn't know I felt down. Sometimes I just need our friendship. Even if we're not doing anything that exciting, we're next to each other, smoking, scrolling, and showing each other memes. Around him, I'm just Lolly, and that, somehow, for once, feels like enough.

He climbs onto my bed as I light my joint, taking his from behind his ear.

'Look at your fucking leg hair,' I laugh, reaching to feel it.

He pulls his gym shorts up to show how high it goes and how fluffy it is. 'Fucking T for you man.'

We chat shit about his changes for a while, shit he wouldn't tell anyone else. He asks me if I've ever thought about hormones and I tell him yeah, but I wouldn't because I'm no closer to a man than I am to a woman.

Then we talk about top surgery, and how I have also thought about that because I like binding, but I like tits.

'Hey, I like tits too, just not on me.'

I nod, pointing towards him with the joint. 'That is a point.' Then I laugh. 'I dunno man,' I shrug, flicking some ash into the ashtray. 'Gender shit, and Radwa shit, that's all taken a back seat with family shit right now.'

'Heard about your sister,' he says, stubbing the roach in the ashtray and then laying back on my bed with his hands behind his head. 'Are you okay?'

I check my phone again while he's talking.

NO NEW MESSAGES.

'I will be once Radwa replies to me.' I put my phone face down on the windowsill and sit back down on my bed, crossing my arms huffily.

He nudges my side with his foot and tells me to talk to him instead.

I shrug it off. Then I point to his book. 'What are you reading anyway?'

He turns it noncommittally to show me the cover as he picks up his own phone to reply to a message, apparently realising getting me to open up is a lost cause. *The Picture of Dorian Gray*.

'Isn't that like *the* gay book?' I ask.

He scrunches his nose, not looking up from his phone, smile growing more and more prominent on his face. 'It's bi, technically. And it's one of Oscar's favourite books. We're reading each others'.'

'That's somehow gayer.' Teasing him makes life a little easier.

I glance at him again. I can always tell when he's messaging Val because of this soft lovestruck look he wears on his face. He flushes pink, twirling his fringe around his fingers like a teenage girl and, though he tries to fight it, a massive toothy grin sneaks across his features.

I nudge him hard with my elbow. 'That's a Val smile. Can you stop being straight for five seconds?' I laugh. 'I thought we were having a moment here.'

'I don't have a Val smile,' he snickers. 'Does that look like Val to you?' he asks, turning his phone to reveal a picture of Oscar holding his hand up to show a shiny smudge mark just under his left pinky. It's captioned: **No bc this was last night! It happens every flipping time!**

'My bad.' I shrug. 'Can you stop being gay with Oscar for five seconds then?'

He pushes me away. 'Oh fuck off, I'm just excited to make friends with him. I really like him.'

'Uh-huh and does Wren know that you're going to be sharing a boyfriend with them?' I nudge him and he laughs.

I look down at my phone. Still no replies.

Radwa

The pile of papers lining my bedroom floor nearly trips me on the way out the door. They're all arranged in a mind map around my bed. Different things I've learnt about rogues from the book.

They're hydrophobic – that means they're scared of water. Genuinely terrified. So they often smell bad because of it. That's one of the only actual indicators I've managed to find so far.

Another is that they don't eat human food after a while. It starts to make them sick.

There are other things that have come up: the fact they usually turn people in the least traumatic way possible in order to savour their healing cells; their annoying charm and ability to manipulate people.

Apparently, they will often appear under the noses of the pack they turned, swindling their way closer to them in order to get past their defences so that they have an easier time getting in their head and controlling them.

I have a horrible theory that's how ours might be able to stay so close to us.

Unfortunately, I don't have time to organise my notes before I leave. I arranged to meet my parents for dinner today so that I could tell them about my GIC appointment. It's tomorrow. They don't even know I've started these appointments.

Val offered to drive me to the restaurant, but I walk so that I have time to be alone with my thoughts. I run over everything in my head as I do.

If they tell me that I'll regret it, I have the information on the rate of detransition. Gender-affirming care has less of a regret rate than knee surgery. Actually, it's ten times less. And they didn't seem to have an issue with Nani getting that, so…

I also have pamphlets on the health risks that most people tend to fabricate. Obviously, my bones will become more brittle, but I'm pretty sure menopause is doing that to Mum anyway. I'll be no more at risk than a cis woman is.

The thoughts race through my head, illustrated by imagined arguments, as I cross the junction to theirs.

I'm so focused on them that I barely notice Oscar until I basically walk into him.

'Sorry,' he murmurs, wearily looking up from his phone.

'Oscar?' I ask, giving him an awkward sort of wave.

'Oh, Radwa.' His eyes flicker up distractedly before glancing at the floor again. 'You alright?'

'Yeah.' I eye him up and down. He looks slightly dishevelled, hair streaky with dry shampoo. Is that because he hasn't showered? Is he having issues with water? 'What are you doing here?'

Did that sound rude? Part of me hopes it didn't. Obviously I want to make a good impression on Wren's boyfriend, but everyone seems suspicious right now. Maybe I do need to stop reading Cygnus's book.

'Oh.' He rubs his eyes tiredly. 'My mate Kat, her parents kicked her out so we were getting her moved into a flat with her girlfriend. But listen, I've gotta get going. Mum said Dad's talking about coming home. I've gotta go find out what's happening.'

I nod sympathetically as he races past me, quickly bringing his phone to his ear.

By the time I get to the restaurant, I have a text from my own parents to say they're running slightly late, so I go in to claim our table before our reservation is given away.

My hands feel hot as I sit down. I wipe them on my skirt and watch out the window for them. It's not long before I see them arrive.

Mum wears a purple kurta with golden beadwork, and a golden head scarf to match. I've always been jealous of her clothes. They look so beautiful, and she wears them with so much grace and elegance.

The headscarf, in particular, I swear I recognise. The pink flowers on the bottom hem are imprinted in my memory for some reason.

She looks down at the table when I come in.

'Radwa!' Dad smiles, reaching down to give me a hug.

I feel a weight slip off my shoulders.

We're halfway through dinner before Mum decides to ask.

'So' – she pauses to take a sip of water – '*beta*' – she always calls me this; she's not quite come around to using my actual name yet – 'what did you want to tell us?'

Dad nods, leaning back and putting his arm around her chair.

'Well,' I start, my heart jumping into my mouth. I tuck my hands underneath me to stop myself from fidgeting nervously with them. 'I've been seeing a psychologist at the hospital.'

Dad's brow furrows a little. He leans forward, concerned.

Mum crosses her arms and legs, then bounces her foot up and down. 'Go on.'

So I do. I go on until I think I'm going to run out of information, getting louder and louder to be heard over the droning sound of the patrons surrounding us. I tell them about how I should be ready to start hormones soon.

I go over everything. Everything the appointments have detailed, every change, every little risk factor that's been assessed, every different way it can be taken to minimise them. I want them to know I've covered it all. I have my stats ready, I have all the information memorised, and I even have pamphlets in my tote bag to show them.

My hand shakes a little as I bring them out, dropping a couple onto the floor. 'Sorry, I—' I begin, scrambling to pick them up off of the sticky pub floor.

Mum puts her hands up with a harsh finality as I drop to my knees. 'Enough.' She shakes her head. Her eyes look teary. 'I'm sorry Faraz.' She turns to my Dad. 'It's too much.' Then she gets up and takes her bag with her.

'*Baba.*' I look at Dad as she stands up.

He stays seated. He takes my hands in his. 'She just needs time, *beta.*'

'It's been years.' I feel my eyes burning. There is a lump in my throat. 'She can't even say my name.'

He tuts. 'Radwa, it's...' I wait for his next excuse. That's one thing I always admired about them. They're a team, but there's only so many excuses he can make. 'I will support you no matter what,' he promises, squeezing my hand. 'But I think if you want her on board, you need to give her time to adjust to this before doing anything drastic.'

My nails fight their way through my nail beds, making a

horrible squeaking sound as they pierce the corkboard of the pub's thin red placemat.

It's not drastic. It's been over three years that I've known this. I've waited this long already.

He puts the money down on the table and gets up to follow her. 'I love you *beta*.'

'Yeah.' I nod, biting my lip so hard my canines pierce it in my effort to hold back the venom threatening to spill from them. 'Yeah, love you too.'

I walk back to Val's. It's a mile and a half but I need the air. It takes the first half mile for my teeth to sink back to their normal resting place. The other mile is spent coaxing my nails and willing my eyes back to normal.

When I get home Val is waiting up in the living room.

'How'd it go?' She untucks herself, putting her coffee down, when I come in. 'I told you to text me for a lift.'

I don't respond. No words seem to fit what I want to say.

'Oh, sweetheart. You're shaking,' she says as I sit beside her on the couch. Her hand comes up to wipe tears from my stinging cheeks, tears that I hadn't realised were falling. 'What happened?'

I just shake my head in response, unable to force my mouth to form the words. When I fall to the side, leaning on her shoulder, she opens her arms wide to receive me.

We lay there for about an hour before my phone buzzes in my pocket. Pulling my consciousness forward to respond is almost as hard as unravelling myself from the tight orange cocoon Val has wrapped me in for comfort. But by the time I've fought my way out of the blanket I feel ready to look at least.

It's Dad. He reiterates that he will be there no matter what, and asks I text him when I decide what to do. As if it's a decision.

I don't see it as one. All I know is that before I came out I couldn't stay clean from self-harm for a month. I was suicidal. And now? Now that I'm out, I've been clean for three years.

Medical intervention and suicide prevention isn't a tough decision. In fact, it doesn't feel like a decision at all. It's a necessity. I'm doing what I have to do to survive.

While checking my notifications I see a message from Lolly that is five hours old.

I bite my lip and open it.

> RADWA
> Sorry!!! I ended up meeting Dad for dinner. Is everything okay?

I've kind of been ignoring them cause I needed the mental space. Val gives my shoulder a rub as I lean on her.

Mateo walks in and puts down a chai for me, and a fresh coffee for Val. They have quick conversation, but my mind is too tired to focus on any of the languages I speak *fluently*, let alone one I'm just learning like Spanish. He gives me a smile and sort of pats the couch next to me and gives me a wink.

> LOLLY
> Okay so basically…

The start of Lolly's message lights up my screen.

Their message keeps going on for paragraphs. I'm so tired right now, but I force myself to keep reading.

Which proves to be a good decision when I read somewhere in the middle of their paragraphs that they have finally managed to hack into Emma's Facebook. For a moment, excitement builds in me as I anticipate firing up my laptop to scroll through months of messages and clues, but it's quickly dashed as I read through the rest of their message and begin to register just how emotionally drained meeting with my parents has made me.

The gist of their messages is that they found out their grandparents are adopting Lotta and it all went downhill from there. They seem pretty worried that their mum is going to freak out about the whole situation.

I don't know what to say in response so I spew out some generic shit.

```
                                    RADWA
            Aw that's good for Lotta but I
            get why you'd be worried :(
```

They send another few paragraphs, but their bubble shows they're still typing so I put my phone down for a second.

My eyes are so heavy. I feel them close.

Then I jerk myself awake.

Val wraps her arm around me. 'You okay?'

I nod, then lean back on her shoulder. My eyes feel heavy again.

Val

Radwa falls asleep on my shoulder after half an hour or so of fighting it while trying to message Lolly. I take her phone off the couch so it doesn't fall. Then I get back to packing our overnight bag for Glasgow. Her phone keeps vibrating on the side table so I turn it onto silent mode. I'm sure Lolly will understand that she's tired after the day she's had.

I fold a pair of her trousers over my arm. This colour suits her skin tone so well. I smile to myself. It's such a pity the rogue took the scarf I made to match them. Maybe they'll return it. Those little pink flowers were a bastard to embroider so I almost hope they do.

When I get back down, she's woken up and is sitting over her phone.

'I have packed you *the* cutest outfit for our trip.'

She doesn't look up.

I sit down next to her, tucking my foot under me as I do.

'Lolly okay?' I ask.

She shakes her head and keeps scrolling.

'Lemme see?' I put my hand out, lifting my reading glasses from the chain I hang them on around my neck. It's decorated with little bat charms. Mitch got it for me because I kept losing them when I was sewing.

God. That's a lot of paragraphs.

At one point Radwa replied telling them she had been out with her dad, and that she had a **mad stressful day**. Lolly doesn't even ask, they just reply **Offt same** before continuing.

My lips pull into a tight grimace.

'Don't,' Radwa says before I say anything. 'They've had a rough day, they don't need any more stress.'

I bite my tongue. Neither does she. She has also had a stressful day and Lolly knows family shit can be a trigger for her. Lolly's not even talking about Lotta anymore – that I'd get – they're just bitching about their mam.

I hand Radwa back her phone and bite the inside of my cheek.

She gives me a sideways glance. 'Don't.'

'I'm not saying anything.'

She raises her eyebrows, then pouts. 'You're being judgy.'

I scoff. 'I am not. You *know* I love Lolly. They're one of my best friends too. That doesn't mean I can't critique them a little. In fact, that makes me a better friend if anything.'

Radwa opens her mouth to protest, but then Dad comes in the door announcing that Mum will be home from work in thirty minutes so we leave it there to get ready for our trip down to Glasgow.

Chapter Sixteen

Radwa

Most of our drive to Glasgow is spent with me buried in my phone, scrolling through Emma's every message, status and notification. I make myself more and more car sick until I have to relinquish my devices to Val for my own good.

The last thing I manage to see is a friend request Oscar sent Emma after she spent months offline for some reason. I sit uneasily, staring out at the passing landscape and taking careful breaths through the nausea, with the awful feeling that things are adding up to a suspicion I don't know what to do with. Could we really have a rogue amongst us that *no one* suspects?

We get into our hotel at about midnight. My appointment isn't until the following morning, so Val and I spend most of the night watching anime and eating sweets in our hotel room. We only get about two hours of sleep before we have to force ourselves up.

She still manages to make the effort to straighten her hair and pull on a somewhat presentable outfit before I've even managed to wearily search the suitcase for whatever she packed me.

She and Fairuza Balk both glance back at me in the mirror as she fixes her eyeliner.

'You found your *Craft* t-shirt?' I ask, examining her as I pull out the white turtleneck and the baby pink t-shirt she packed for me.

She replies, but I don't quite hear what she says because I'm too distracted by something else to process it.

The trousers she's packed for me are a dark orange colour with pink flowers embroidered along the hem.

Suddenly I realise where I recognise the scarf mum was wearing from. It was one of mine. The one the rogue took. Those flowers took Val days. My mouth falls open.

If the rogue took the scarf back to my old home, that means the rogue knows my parents' address. The rogue has been in my parents' house. The rogue knows where they live.

'Radwa?' Val asks, seeing me pausing, clothes in my hand, dumbfounded.

I don't say anything. I wordlessly back into the toilet and close the door behind me, hands shaking as I punch in the number I was taught to memorise in primary school.

It rings twice.

Then it rings again.

I start silently praying the next ring will bring an answer, or the next one, or the next one.

After what seems like an eternity a voice answers on the other end.

'Ammu?' I ask hesitantly as she answers the phone.

She pauses for a second. 'Beta, is that you?'

I let out a breath of relief that I can practically taste her chai on. 'Yes, it's me. Are you and Baba okay?' I continue.

'Yes, yes fine. Can we help you with something?' she asks.

The words sting a little, serving as a cold reminder of how distant my family has become.

'I was just wondering, um, when we were at dinner – you had a headscarf I liked – with the flowers – where did you get that?'

She lets out an exasperated breath of confusion. 'I don't know. I think it got mixed up with my stuff when I went to the ladies' swimming class with your Nani for her arthritis. I found it in the car with my other stuff just before we came to meet you and it went nicely with my outfit so I decided just to wear it out. Why? Is someone looking for one?'

'No – No—' I laugh, relieved that the rogue doesn't seem to know exactly which house my parents, brothers and grandparents live in.

Even though the idea that my scent has been removed from their house so completely after years of absence hits me hard, I'm glad that it's at least protected them.

'I just liked it, that's all,' I offer as a throwaway excuse, and try to wrap the call up quickly so I can get back out to Val – without telling my mum that I'm currently on my way to my hormone appointment.

By the time I get back out we have about ten minutes 'til we need to leave. To Val's credit, she's unperturbed by my sudden exit and return. She's used to me and my ways. She just raises her the dots that used to be her eyebrows at me in the mirror.

'Sorry!' I say to Val, putting my hands up in apology. I grab my clothes again and duck behind a half-closed door to get dressed as I'm talking to her. 'So when did you get the t-shirt back?'

'The rogue returned it to the art bay,' she confesses, pausing for a moment with a makeup brush held at eye level. 'In uni.'

'You didn't show it to Wren? Me? We might have been able to trace a scent—'

But Val shakes her head. 'It was like Lotta's room. Doused in gasoline. Maybe I should have said something but… Mel gave it to me and I just got kind of caught in my feelings seeing it again' She smiles so sadly that I drop it. She's right – Wren's family didn't find anything at Lolly's mum's house to help trace the rogue.

My eyebrows knit together. 'How many people do we know who study art in the uni?'

'Just me?' Val purses her lips in the mirror, drawing a guide line over her shaved eyebrows. 'Oh, and Oscar now.'

A horrible feeling settles in my stomach, wrapping around my every sense. 'Do you know if Mitch ever got his journal back?'

'Not that he told me.' Val shakes her head, moving onto the other eyebrow. 'Why?'

I sigh, resting my clothes over my arm. 'Don't laugh at me.'

She puts her pencil down on the veneer desk the hotel has set in front of a mirror in imitation of a dressing table, turning to look at me properly now.

'I saw Oscar yesterday,' I start.

Val's eyes narrow as she scans me up and down.

'He was hanging about my parent's bit,' I continue, watching her cautiously for a sign that she's judging me for jumping to such wild conclusions. For a moment I think I see her expression waver so I set off at high speed. 'And then my mum was wearing the scarf the rogue took the other day at dinner. And then there's your t-shirt and the fact he refused to snack even when he was high – even *I* know that's weird. And he's getting so close to Wren so quickly it just seems like —' I look up, seeing her face has started to fall, her mouth hanging open for a second.

'But –' she starts, eyebrows furrowing as she toys with the bottom of her lip piercing. 'Surely Wren would—'

I sigh, laying back on our bed and reaching for Bonnie – who stowed away in our bags for moral support. 'I think

Wren sees everything Oscar through rose-tinted glasses,' I confess, pressing her lavender scented fur against my face.

Her eyebrows crease in the middle for a minute. 'But—' she starts.

She's interrupted by a rap at the door. It's Mateo, advising that we have to leave in five minutes.

We bookmark our talk and decide to see what Mitch and Lolly think before taking it any further. This proves a good foresight as we barely make it to the GIC on time after Mateo takes an hour to park the car.

We run into the waiting room with less than a minute to spare, which does not help with the adrenaline that I'm already drowning in.

The loudly clattering air conditioning offers very little reprise from the swampy heat the unprompted exercise left me with. Sweat sticks my trousers to the back of my knees as I sit down with Val in the plastic seats, under excessively bright lights, after giving the receptionist my name. I pinch the hem, pulling them down a little. It only takes a second for them to climb halfway up my shins. I love Val but these are getting way too short for me. I yank the hem down more aggressively this time, and then I open my phone.

4 NEW MESSAGES.

One each from Mitch, Lolly and Wren, and Aadilla.

She sends a gif wishing me good luck. Mitch says the same with more words. Lolly tells me that they're thinking of me. Wren sends a longer message covering both of these things and telling me to call her later if I need to chat. I smile softly to myself, then show Val Mitch's message. She places her hand on her heart and then gives my leg a squeeze.

The doors open. An older woman walks in. She is beautiful and tall. Her hands are laden with rings and costume jewellery. She has long grey hair with a streak of pink in the front. Her tote bag has the trans flag on it, and a pronoun button. She must only be in her fifties or sixties, but I think she is the oldest one of us I have ever seen.

It's strange to think she's older than my mum. She's probably seen more change in her lifetime than I can ever hope to. I wonder what it was like for her coming out back then. Did her parents accept her? Did anyone? Or was she forced to hide herself for years? Maybe that's the only reason she survived when so few others did.

She sees me looking at her. She smiles, and I smile back.

'Excuse me sweetheart,' she says, shakily, as she sits down next to me. 'I think we might be family,' she says once sat down, giving me a knowing wink and tapping the trans Pride bracelet Val made me with a pale and boney finger.

My smile splits my face fondly at the word. 'Yeah, I think we might be.'

'I like your trousers,' she whispers.

'I like your bag,' I say, in a voice so hushed she must barely hear me.

She gives me a wink.

A doctor walks in. 'Radwa Hashmi.'

Val nudges my knee with hers.

Lolly

One downside of working in the only witchy shop in town is the sheer amount of ex-hookups I have to serve in a day. You know that thing where people ask what you would do if you walked into a room and everyone you've ever shagged was standing there? Yeah, well my answer is clock in for my shift, I guess.

Thankfully, by the time Aimee has finished buying her moldavite pendulum, Jesus has already started to lock up for the night. I barely held it together knowing exactly who she thinks it'll help her find.

The town still thinks Emma is alive, and being the only ones who know otherwise fucking sucks.

The windchimes rattle as Jesus hits his head off of them, taking in the stacks of bracelets that were propping the door open to let some air in.

'What's with those anyway?' I ask, wandering over to help him bring in the rest.

They seem tacky, the kind of stuff tourists like with gemstone beads and Celtic knots on thin bracelet elastics. One of the charms burns my stomach where my top has rolled up as I hold the pillar it's on against me. Fucking silver! I wince, popping it down just inside the door frame and fixing my shirt.

'Those are protection bracelets,' he scoffs. 'Some of the kids are getting a bit hysterical over the animal attacks. There's a conspiracy that it's a werewolf. I'm surprised you didn't hear. It was all over the gossip page on Facebook.'

I grimace. The pack grew very well acquainted with that gossip page the year Radwa came out. I got banned for sending people hate comments – but they were literally posting transphobic hate about a teenage girl and nobody took any issue with that.

'Apparently, people figured out they happen at the same time every month, so there's been a bit of a demand for silver. Load of crap if you ask me, but it brings money in. You want one?' he asks, fingering through them.

As much as he's laughing at the theory, I can't help but notice that he is wearing one bracelet on each of his wrists along with several of the gemstone ones: selenite, amethyst, hematite, aventurine and carnelian in turn.

My hair stands up on end – I feel not unlike the first stages of turning on a full moon. My skin feels as though it is made of a million tiny creatures crawling over one another. I swallow before I reply, choosing what to say carefully.

'Got plenty, thanks.' I smile, fingering a selenite bracelet on the other post. 'What about these?'

'Wellness.' He shrugs. 'It was a deal with the supplier. Anti-addiction, anxiety, stress, things like that. That one's for restoring relationships.'

'You reckon they actually work?' I ask.

This kind of thing tends to be where I draw the line with magic stuff. That probably sounds daft coming from a werewolf, mind you. Like sure, some herbs and crystals have calming effects and can reduce some general anxiety, but I don't think some tacky jewellery is going to change the fact I have a personality disorder. At least, not as much as going to therapy and putting the work in will.

Jesus shrugs as he walks past, patting down all of the pockets on his jean vest for his keys.

'I dunno man,' he starts. 'I think it's like anything in here. Depends on the intention of the person using it. You can't help people who don't want to get better.'

'And you intend to go sober?' I ask, tossing the bracelet in my pocket and sliding a fiver under the cash register for it. 'No more weed?'

Jesus scoffs at this, waving me away. He usually doesn't charge me for cheap things like this – just weed and books.

'Just the harder psychedelics.' He smirks, sliding the money back across the counter to me. 'Think you were onto something. I swear at Mitch's party I thought the man had claws. Was half ready to start siding with the kids screaming wolf and point the finger at your lot. But I figured it would cost me one of my biggest buyers and my only employee so...' Then he looks up and adds in a tone which is equal parts serious and joke. 'You'd tell me if you were, right Kearney?'

The thing most people might not realise about me is that I hate lying. Especially to Jesus, because he was the first adult to treat me like I was a person.

It sounds silly maybe. He's irresponsible, he's way too laid back and he's basically a big kid, but I remember meeting him for the first time as a kid coming in here with my ex, Kat. She'd just wanted something to piss off her catholic parents, but I'd left with something more important. The feeling of being respected as myself for the first time.

He didn't question when I said to call me Lolly, he didn't patronise or sexualise our relationship, he just let us be and chatted shit to us while we were paying. That was it. So simple.

But I'd thought he was really cool and so came back more and more. I think he noticed stuff was bad at home because he offered me a job. When things were really bad – before I met Mitch – Jesus would pencil me in for extra shifts so I could avoid going home. He'd help me get clothes washed for school so I wasn't singled out for the state Mam would send me in.

I have to swallow all of this before I reply. 'Jesus, if I wake up one day as a monstrous beast with an *unquenchable* thirst for human blood I *promise* you I will call in sick,' I say, hoping my joke is convincing enough to stop him asking any more questions. I turn the door sign over to **CLOSED** before pushing my way out. 'Besides, you'd be grand. Nobody kills the weed guy, that's just bad form.'

He shakes his head with a chuckle, turning the key in the lock and lighting a joint to walk down behind the highstreet with me. He lives in the street just above Mam and behind Mitch so we walk home together all the time.

We walk in silence for a moment as I contemplate what he was saying about the increased concern about the attacks. Maybe we'll have to lay a little lower this moon, go off our usual trail or even just hide out around the clubhouse for a bit.

As I'm worrying, my phone starts vibrating in my pocket, derailing my train of thought.

Withheld number.

Usually that means it's Dad. It's a bit early for our weekly call but I pick up, ready to go through the whole script about accepting the charges to my phone. Only it's not the same automated voice that picks up.

'Hello?' the warm voice of an older lady says down the phone. 'Hello, am I speaking to Miss Kearney?'

I put my finger in my ear to hear better. 'Lolly, it's just Lolly. Can I help you?' I ask, hearing my voice crackled back through the receiver – Highlands signal for you.

'Hi Lolly, my name is Mary. I'm one of the secretaries here at Raigmore Hospital's Emergency Department. We've had a patient come in, Mrs. Deborah Kearney. She's in a state of distress and you're listed as her next of kin. Is now a good time to talk?'

I feel my stomach actually flip over inside me.

Jesus must notice my face go white because he puts a hand on my shoulder to steady me. 'Kearney?' he asks, uncharacteristically concerned.

The voice on the end of the receiver – Mary – keeps asking if I'm still there, and I can't even find the words to explain that I'm not. Because I know my mind is about to go on strike without any warning or discussion. I can practically hear the blaring *'entering survival mode'* alarm.

I need you, I call out before my voice silences itself completely. It sounds shaky even in my own head but I don't care. *She's done it again and I need you.*

Okay, Mitch's voice returns almost immediately. *Stay with me. I'm on my way.*

I don't really compute anything between getting the call and getting carefully ushered into the front seat of Mitch's car. In fact, nothing really registers until I'm sitting in the passenger side, knees curled up to my chest, halfway along the A9.

It's probably shitty to admit but I don't really get sad

when Mam pulls this shit anymore. I did the first time, when at nine years old I first learned what a suicide attempt was, and saw what it looked like. Then, when she did it after racing me out of my own house for kissing a girl, I was angry at her for daring to play the victim. She probably thought it would make me apologise but the opposite was true. I actually told her that I hoped she tried a little harder next time – not my finest moment I admit. And now next time is here, and I can't bring myself to feel anything but numb.

'Lol?' Mitch asks. His tone makes it seem as though it's the second or third time he's tried.

'Yeah?' I give myself a shake.

'I was asking if you would message Radwa for me, to let her know I'm driving,' he says, nudging his phone my way without taking his eyes off of the road. 'She's blocking telepathy 'cause dysphoria.'

Reaching forward I grab his phone and punch in his password – he and Val's anniversary.

It opens on a message chain between him and Radwa that I hadn't expected to see. Nothing weird or anything, just Radwa venting about her appointment and before that about her parents, but it's all things she would usually tell me about.

'I thought the appointment went well?' My forehead creases as my eyebrows pull together, lips pulling so tight I can feel my dimple burying itself into my cheek.

Mitch takes a deep breath, chancing a quick glance at me. 'The fertility stuff can just be hard for a lot of people,' he says, looking back to the road and changing gears to pull out into the fast lane and overtake a tractor. 'Mine was hard going enough, and I've heard they're even shittier for trans women. So I checked in on her. I thought she would've messaged you about it.'

'Yeah, me too.' I shake my head, pulling my knees closer

to my chest and leaning my chin on them, tossing Mitch's phone back in the little pocket under the radio.

Even though I know I'm quite literally huffing like a toddler, I can't help myself. Why wouldn't she tell me? Why wouldn't she let me know what was going on with her dad? It's always been us, we've always been a team. Her not telling me any of this makes absolutely zero sense.

'Why wouldn't she—?' I look up at Mitch, my hurt bubbling into something more like rage as I untuck my knees.

Mitch itches his neck behind his ear, fingers grazing the inky black dot of the semicolon tattoo he got with me not long after I moved into his house more permanently. 'I mean, we *are* friends. It's probably just because I've been through the whole process,' he says, risking another look at me as if to see if I believe him.

The glance and the thin guilty grimace on his face is how I know that there's more to it than that.

'You know something.' My stomach drops.

I want to bolt, unclip my seatbelt, and open the door into oncoming traffic at the idea that two of my favourite people in the world are talking about me behind my back in a way that's anything less than favourable.

'It's not like that,' Mitch promises, drumming his fingers against the steering wheel.

'Sounds like that,' I snap back, before he can even get an explanation in.

'We've not even spoken about it. I'm just making an assumption because I know how it is from her side!' Mitch exclaims defensively, keeping his eyes on the road as we reach the bridge into town.

'Her side of what exactly?' I retort, hand braced against the door. There's no way in hell I'm really going to open it but my intrusive thoughts are apparently loud enough to make Mitch flinch.

'Jesus fucking Christ, Lolly! Can you please try to use

some of your STEPPS skills so I can keep my bloody doors?' he shouts back, darting forward to click the button on the dash to lock the doors from the inside out.

I huff, sitting back in my chair. I fold my arms across my body, feeling antsy, as though my skin is made of a million tiny beasties again. 'Her side of *what* exactly?'

Mitch looks at me with soft concern as we join the traffic jam leading up to the roundabout after the bridge. It's always awful here during rush hour, even sometimes outside of it. This junction and the bridge itself are constantly getting closed, so I know him running a hand through his hair and turning his shoulders towards me with a sigh is about a little more than the lane of cars in front of us.

Without saying anything, he pops open the glovebox in front of me, then rifles blindly through the collection of CDs, rolling papers and missing posters to find a pack of mystery flavour sweets which he hands to me.

Despite my best efforts I feel the corners of my mouth turn up. It's a grounding technique, one from the group I went to. On the inside of the glove box door there are five or six of the little cards I got for emotional regulation and supporting someone with BPD. I realise that, maybe unconsciously, in getting the sweets he's offered me another technique – look at the evidence. Mitch's love for me is clear. Even when I'm not in his presence I'm solidly part of his life, and an important part at that. Anything said behind my back would only be said with love or concern.

He grimaces as he places one of the sweets in his own mouth. 'Soap,' he chokes out, reaching for his Lucozade.

I grin wickedly, unwrapping my own and placing it on my tongue. Luckily mine is green apple which is my favourite.

'Please tell me what you mean?' I ask, sitting back in my seat tucking my knees up small.

'Lol,' he starts hesitantly, snapping the lid back on his bottle, 'I think you have enough to worry about right now.'

'I get that,' I nod as we progress out of the queue and turn down the exit for the hospital, 'but you know what I'm like. I'll only take it in the worst way possible and get butthurt about it until you tell me.'

He sighs, defeated, knowing that I'm right.

He pursues his lips, thinking how to start. 'You know how you go through phases of being really into things – things that you might *genuinely* love doing, things that make everything better? But, randomly, you'll stop getting that dopamine hit and get frustrated with it? Like when you spent a small fortune on guitar lessons because you were convinced it would add something to your personal statement and help you ask Radwa out in a cute way, but then you didn't do that and then gave up and forgot to even include it in your statement despite getting pretty fucking good at it?' he asks hesitantly. 'Then you moved onto learning hacking and code—'

'Which is helping with Emma *and* helped that one time our wolf forms were caught on camera,' I interject, chuckling at the memory, looking down and picking at my Converse as I wait for the next more painful part of his point.

He bites his lip, thinking. 'You sort of do that with people too. Usually me and Radwa.' He scratches the back of his neck, continuing, 'I mean, you've got better at the whole frustration thing don't get me wrong. I know you're trying and I love you for it, and I would still rather you spoke to one of us than dealt with it alone. It's just when it gets to the point where it feels like one of us is solely responsible for your mental health it can be difficult to open up in return.'

My heart sinks to my feet, the cars next to us move in slow motion, and it's as though a cloud has covered the sky on an otherwise clear and sunny day.

Suddenly I'm eight years old again, not allowed to have my own problems, not allowed to feel anything about what happened because Mam's feelings were taking up too much emotional space for mine to fit in the same household. I swore to myself I'd never be like her and yet—

'Oh.' My voice sounds small. I feel my lip wobble, so I catch it between my teeth, eyes flicking up to the ceiling trying to hold back a floodgate. 'I'm sorry that I've made it hard for you guys I – I'm sorry. I didn't know I was doing that. Shit, do you think she's mad at me?'

Mitch shakes his head as we pull into the car park of the hospital. 'I don't think she could be if she wanted to.' He puts a hand behind my seat so he can see properly to park. Then he gives me a smile. 'I'm not either, you know. I just think that might be why she's not spoken to you about *her* shit.'

I nod, resting my head in my hands and feeling my elbow push the selenite bracelet in my pocket into my thigh. Then I take a deep and shaky breath. There has got to be a way to fix this before they end up where I did.

Mitch

Lolly's mam is currently being kept in a private room in Accident and Emergency, a fact that has Lolly cracking up as we sit waiting in cold grey plastic chairs under yellowing lights. They sweep their mullet back with one hand, twiddling the dry ends which are now a washed out green colour. Then they lean their head back on top of mine where it sits on their shoulder.

'I dunno,' they whisper, trying not to laugh. 'It just seems kind of ironic for it to be called an accident. And the mental health system certainly doesn't treat it as an emergency.'

At first, I found Lolly's flippancy surrounding this to be really weird, almost off-putting, but over the years I've come to learn it's just how they cope.

As they bring their hand up to wipe the tears that their suppressed laughter has brought to their eyes, a nurse comes around the corner. He crouches by their side, mistaking them for tears of sadness, and asks if they're okay. All I can do is stare at the poster behind his head advising of the dangers of non-prescription antibiotics in a desperate attempt not to crack up.

Then the nurse takes Lolly around the corner to a little room so they can see their mam and drop off some pyjamas for her. Only one person is allowed in at a time and Debbie doesn't even know me so I'm happy to wait for them to come out.

I think I'd actually feel sorry for her, you know? If it wasn't for what she'd done to Lolly.

While I wait, I open my phone to see what's been going on with Radwa. She's asked if we'll come over when they get home. I'll have to mind and let Lolly know.

Oscar has also messaged me. My smile bites into my face as I notice it. My hands flex, fingers spreading out to let the happiness reach my finger tips.

I open the message. He's been drawing animals again. Bees on different flowers, specifically lilacs, green carnations and violets.

I grin and then message him back.

```
                              MITCH
                       Pride parade!
```

He sees my message before I can even close the chat.

```
OSCAR
Have you read Walt Whitman?
```

```
                              MITCH
                              Duh.
```

I rush to tell him my thoughts on the pictures so my message doesn't seem too boring to reply to. I look back at the drawings, before typing up a huge paragraph analysing the poems and hyping up his art. Then I have a thought.

MITCH
Let's see the damage then?

He sends me a selfie holding up his pinky. It's a mess as expected. His eyes are sparkling and I can hear the laugh behind them. I smile wide.

My inappropriate happiness earns me an appalled look from the older couple sitting together under the TV. Bashfully I pull my lips over my teeth trying to hide it, and brush the knot out of my hair which I didn't realise I had subconsciously tied twiddling it between my fingers.

When Lolly does eventually come back around they look a lot less amused. An ECG machine is beeping somewhere in the ward as they go over paperwork and leaflets with the nurse and I can feel their nerves being wound tighter and tighter with each repetitive noise.

The sky is kind of dusty by the time we get out. It's not cold enough for our breath to fog but the second we leave the doors I swear I can see Lolly exhale all of what they've just endured into the air.

'How *are* you doing by the way?' they eventually ask, having got all the way to the car park without a word being passed between us. 'With all the acting alpha shit and—'

I shrug. 'It's been… a lot, I guess. I don't know.'

It's hard to put it into words. The whole mate thing, the whole destined to save us thing, it's been a lot, but I guess I don't even feel like I'm allowed to feel anything about it. There's not really a choice, so my feelings don't really matter. Honestly, the idea I could let them all down or get them more hurt is kind of terrifying.

'Thanks for asking, though.' I nudge into them, pulling them in with an arm around their shoulders and kissing their head.

They push me away, pretending to be annoyed. I can tell they're not because their laugh is back.

'Did I show you the ring I bought for Val?' I ask them,

pulling up the link on my phone. 'Finally actually saved enough to order it.'

They look at me, eyes wide, stopping in their tracks while bouncing on their heels to give me a playful slap. 'No you fucking didn't show me!'

While I am I get a phone call from the woman herself.

Both of us stop, side-eyeing each other and cautiously wondering if either of us were thinking too loudly and have been caught, but as it turns out she just wanted to know if we'll meet her at hers because Radwa wants to chat about something.

By the time we get there it's late. Mateo and Karen are sat in the living room with a cuppa and a takeaway menu between them.

We find Radwa and Val up in Radwa's room. After double-checking we're good to come in, Lolly cracks open the door and I follow them.

It's been a while since I've been here. A lot has changed. It's far less sparse and much more personal now. Photographs of us all together line the small strip of wall between her wardrobe and the door. The big light and lamps have been abandoned in favour of fairy lights and a screensaver displaying a roaring fire on her gaming monitor.

What I didn't expect to see was her and Val sitting on the floor beside the bed in a pile of notes and photocopies so big it spews under her wardrobe.

'You're here.' Val looks up at me quickly, a purple Post-it note caught in her hair.

'The fuck is going on?' Lolly laughs, stepping over the pile to take a seat between them. They lift up a page from the pile. 'Are you reading about rogues?' they ask, eyes scanning over the page quickly. They hand it up to me.

During the period following the full moon, prior to feeding, the rogue is at its weakest. For this reason, it's not unheard of for the rogue to keep a 'supply' of freshly turned wolves on hand in a secondary location.

In all but one of the case studies, both the primary den and the secondary location of the rogue wolf were found underground. This is widely believed to be due to rogues in the late stages of sickness becoming highly photosensitive.

Once the rogue's den has been found and the rogue dispatched, history has proven that finding the new 'pack' is of vital importance for the hunter of rogues. These new wolves should be approached carefully—

I scan over it and then hand it back to Val who takes it from me carefully.

'So have you found a lead or?' I start, leaning back against the desk behind me.

Val rests her head against my knee. I reach down to pet her hair.

'Radwa thinks she's found something,' she says, screwing her nose up as if it's an idea she isn't very fond of.

I straighten up, feeling my muscles tense.

Radwa looks up. She sits with her legs crossed, holding them in the middle and rocking back and forth as she speaks, going over all the signs she's found out about: not eating, avoiding water, excessive nervousness and sensory sensitivity, normal healing, normal eyes.

'...So me and Val were talking and, we've both had our stuff returned, and I noticed a pattern, and I was wondering if you had got your journal back yet?' she asks plainly, not looking up but her heartbeat spiked as if she's nervous to tell me her hypothesis.

Even though I feel like I'm walking to a trap by answering, I know I have to tell them the truth.

'Yeah, the night of the party I found it in my room on my bed and it had—' I start, but Radwa cuts me off.

'I told you!' she points to Val, snapping up. 'See, Val got her top back at college. It was in the art bay. I noticed that my mum had my scarf when I met with her for dinner – just after I saw someone we know walking back from near their house. Someone who studies art *and* was at your party.'

When I put together the pieces, I feel the colour drain from my face all at once. My hand lands on the desk behind me to steady myself.

'It was a rager. There could be a lot of people at the party who also had access to the art bay,' I start, itching my face around my neck where new hairs have started to push their way through. Nothing makes you notice all the little things like being overwhelmed.

'Lots of people who have been getting closer and closer to us recently? Who don't eat? And are – by their own admission – sensitive to light and noise? And avoided water the time at the pier?' Radwa pushes.

The knuckles on my right hand go white where they're braced against the desk. 'That doesn't mean that... He's autistic and *no one* likes wet clothes,' I insist, feeling my face go warm.

Lolly must sense my frustration because they take a deliberately slow breath. 'What about me? Oscar had no way of knowing where Mam lived.'

Radwa turns to look at them, maybe a little hurt that they're not automatically on her side. She frowns looking at the floor, putting down a piece of paper. 'I think Wren might've told him something. I mean, I saw her talking about us in her messages one day when she was showing me a picture of him. And, I don't know what was said, but I figured since you know how to—'

Lolly holds their hands up sitting back. 'Woah. I was with

you until now but I'm not hacking into Wren's phone. That's a total violation of her trust.'

'Okay then what if we just asked her—'

Val lifts her head off of my leg to look at Radwa. 'Please do *not* mention this to them. Their self-esteem is already at rock bottom; they don't need their only friends suggesting that the only reason their boyfriend likes them is because he's secretly a serial killer.'

'He's *definitely* not a serial killer!' I exclaim decisively, sitting down on the floor to examine the papers. 'Now, we can sort through this to see if there's anything useful here, but it's not Oscar. End of discussion.'

'But—' Radwa starts.

'End of discussion,' I reiterate, picking up the papers.

Val gives me a careful look. 'Did you say there was something else up with the journal? Maybe we can use that to explore more options.'

My eyes flicker up from the paper momentarily. If it was just Val, if there weren't already accusations flying about, maybe I'd tell the truth.

But something about the image of oil pastels – of warm freckled skin – living in my mind makes me second-guess showing them the smudged writing on the back of the pictures I found that day, if only for Oscar's sake. It would only make them question him more.

'No,' I lie, shaking my head, not looking up from the page that I'm holding.

I *know* it isn't him. It can't be. End of discussion.

Lolly

By the time me and Mitch get back to ours it's getting late. Charlie has already gone to bed with a cup of tea and Anna is half asleep on the couch watching true crime documentaries when we come in. I'll never understand her and Val's obsession with them – to me they're either an exploitation of a vulnerable person pushed to the edge of morality or a romanticisation of a disgusting human being. She pauses it on our arrival, knowing that the interviews only irk me and that if Mitch sees blood, even on screen, it'll turn his stomach.

He actually used to panic every time he smelt or saw blood for the first few years into our friendship, which was not ideal given all his health shit. Even now, piercings, blood tests, and things like that are enough to make all colour drain from his face, the phrase 'sharp scratch' colliding with his stony exterior like a wrecking ball. It's even worse if he can taste it – or touch it. Honestly, I worry about how he's going to be with getting surgery sometimes.

He doesn't seem to be bothered as he perches himself on the edge of the couch cushion, trying to undo his boots with one hand. The other clutches his phone which his eyes are glued to. I don't think he even hears Anna offering him some leftover pasta for dinner. After undoing his laces, his hand comes up to fiddle with his hair for a second as he replies to either Val or Oscar.

The way Mitch looks when he messages Oscar makes me hope against hope that Radwa is wrong. It's almost too painful to watch him under the weight of that uncertainty. So, I decide to go and get some pasta from the fridge, riffling my way through it to find a lemon so I can use the zest and juice to garnish it.

That's when my phone starts ringing.

WITHHELD NUMBER.

My hands shake a little more than they did when faced with the same message earlier today.

I can't tell if I want it to be about Mam or not. They wouldn't call me unless something went south. Is it sort of twisted that I almost *want* something to come up that will sever that tie now that Lotta is safe?

Taking a deep breath, I force myself to press accept.

An automated voice on the other end asks me if I wanted to accept charges for the call to my device.

I press the option to confirm, walking into the hall for a better signal.

'Dad?' I ask, sitting down on the bottom step with a grin.

'Hiya Poppet, how's it going?' a thick and warm voice answers back.

In the beginning I used to close my eyes and imagine what Dad might be doing when we had our calls like this, or I'd imagine him next to me. But eventually it became too painful because I found that each visit saw him looking less and less like the man I imagined.

He was still basically a kid himself when he and Mam had me. My age, actually. Twenty-six when he was taken away. Now he's pushing forty, and every wrinkle in his smile that I forget to imagine is a painful reminder of just how long eleven years is.

'Sorry I'm late in calling. There was a fight in the canteen today so they locked us all down for a bit,' he adds offhandedly.

'Are you—'

'Och aye I'm grand. Keeping my nose clean from all that – gotta get out so I can kick your arse into gear about that girl you like—'

I chuckle, lifting the biro pen off of the end table next to me and drawing shapes on my hand. 'Her name is Radwa. I've told you this.'

'Am only teasing Pop.' He grins. Sometimes, despite my best efforts to not imagine him, his voice gives his actions away. 'How is she doing?'

My pen pauses on my skin as I reach my second knuckle when I imagine her face earlier while we all shut her theory down. The look of hurt in her eyes as she stopped rocking and looked at the floor. I'd reach out to her if I thought she'd actually talk to me about any of the emotional crap right now.

'Think that I've fucked it,' I admit.

There's a sigh on the other end of the phone. 'Not got your old man's charm?' Dad teases.

I breathe out in a short small laugh.

'C'mon,' he continues, 'I thought you said you were good? I know I can't do much from here, but I can still listen.'

'I know, I just—' I start, leaning down to draw on the rubber part of my shoes where my skateboard has scuffed them.

I bite the inside of my cheek as a moment of silence passes along the line. He calmly waits for me to continue.

Mitch is chatting to Anna about Val's ring in the living room, his voice gravelly and low as if he has a cold. If not for myself, for him and Radwa, I know I need to expand my inner circle to include more than just one person precariously propped on a pedestal at any given time.

I rest back against the step behind me, reaching into my pocket to toy with the bracelet from earlier. 'So, things with Mam haven't been great—' I start, and as I continue, I feel the spindly, suffocating arms that have cradled around me for eleven years slip slowly away.

Minus the werewolf shit, I tell Dad about everything that's been going on with Mam and Lotta since he left.

He's upset, understandably, but he assures me that it's more to do with what I've had to endure, and that he would much rather I tell him than bottle it up. I'm not sure I believe him. He wouldn't have any reason to be upset if I didn't. But his words, his emotions, they feel like permission: permission to be upset, to be angry, to mourn the mam I lost and to hate the mam I had. And when we hang up I feel emboldened with a new strength.

I pick up the phone one last time, standing up to pace in the hall as it connects. The receptionist lets me know the name of the hospital that I'm all too familiar with, running through her script as I balance the phone between my ear and shoulder, fishing the bracelet out of my pocket and rolling it down my arm.

'Hi, I'm wondering if you can help me. My name is Lolly Kearney. I'm calling in regards to my mam Deborah,' I say once she is finished.

'Oh yes, she's not allowed any phone calls right now. Can I pass on a message?' The receptionist sounds young and bright, though not in a way that is jarring or off-putting considering her profession.

'No, no that's fine,' I quickly assure her. 'I just wanted to know if you can delete my number from her record? I don't want to be contacted regarding her. I'll send the paperwork to the main hospital. I just wanted to let you guys know first.'

There is a pregnant pause on the line in which I can feel her judging me, wondering what kind of monster would cut off their mother while she's sectioned.

But I won't let her make me feel bad about it. Because when I look into the mirror right now, I don't see an eighteen year old with bloodshot eyes, who always smells like weed and can't finish a shift without running into a hookup. I see a seven-year old kid, who has just had their safe adults ripped away by drink and by flashing lights, and they are terrified, but ultimately I can see that they *finally* forgive me.

Chapter Seventeen

Wren

When Oscar and I get into the clubhouse a few days later, Mitch sits on the floor between Val's legs. She is practising braiding on his hair. He keeps looking up to catch a glance at her concentrated face. Then he gets told, while Val holds the hairbrush rather menacingly, to stay still. He looks at her with a strange kind of adoration and smiles like he just can't help himself. Val, who is of course kidding, catches this and smiles back. An understated sort of smile, shadowed by a blush.

How have they been together for three years and they're still like this?

'Oscar!' Mitch grins, looking up.

Val gives his hair a playful tug. He pulls a face. She laughs then ties the braid off and pulls him backwards, a hand on either side of his head and kisses his forehead.

'I don't get a hello?' I ask as Mitch stands up.

He smiles at me. 'Sorry.' Then he walks over to his backpack which sits next to Lolly, who is balanced on top of a crate of water with their legs crossed. 'I have a present for Oscar though.'

Oscar grins, looking at Mitch through the sunlight. Oh, this is going to make his entire day. I tap him with my elbow. He bites his lip and elbows me back.

Mitch hands Oscar a book with a fancy-looking man posed on the cover – *The Picture of Dorian Gray*. It looks well-read. Sticky notes are coming out of pages left right and centre. The spine is cracked, and the pages are yellow.

'What's this?' Oscar takes it from him.

'You wanted to know my thoughts.' Mitch shrugs. 'So I wrote them down as I was reading. It's no big deal but I thought you'd appreciate it since it's like a big interest of yours.'

Oscar's beam splits his face. His hands stretch out wide by his sides, and he bounces up and down on his toes as he starts to talk about it.

Mitch sits down next to him and puts his phone face down on the log across from him. 'Okay.' He nods, recognising Oscar's excitement. 'You have my full attention.'

I feel the corners of my mouth turn up. I fucking love that for Oscar.

I sit down on the ground next to Val's legs. I rest my head against her knee.

'I'm braiding your hair sometime soon,' I tell her. She has curly hair, not quite a tight coil like mine, or a loose wave like Mitch's, but curly, and she straightens it most of the time.

She nods. 'Okay.'

She smiles. Her smile is so pretty. She has one dimple on the left side of her face, and her teeth look perfectly white against her deep purple lipstick.

She leans forward to check her phone then nudges me to show me a picture Radwa sent her.

Radwa's buried in blankets playing Sims.

'How is she?' I ask, laughing at the face she's pulling. Radwa has now been on oestrogen for just over a week.

'Well, she cried for like half an hour this morning because

we ran out of waffles. And Dad offered to go to the shop, then she cried more because she was being "annoying."' Val holds up air quotes and leans forward to show Lolly the picture too.

Lolly jumps down from the water bottles, coming to sit with us since having been made invisible to Mitch by Oscar's arrival.

'She eventually just went back to bed for three hours and decided to try again later,' Val laughs.

I put my face in my hands. I remember it well.

'Oh! You'll probably know this,' Val says, casting a glance over to where her boyfriend is talking animatedly to mine before smiling softly and standing up to grab her throwing knives from the floor. She nods for us to follow so we can train together. 'Her hands keep cracking, like you know how she has to wash them all the time for prayers?'

I nod, following after her, pausing only momentarily to adjust the target. It's gained a fair few dents since the visit to my pack – both from her knives and Radwa's arrows. Both of them are progressively getting better at consistently hitting the target.

'Yeah, well her skin is really dry for some reason right now and it's annoying the fuck out of her,' Val continues.

That makes sense for the first week or so. 'You should've seen mine, it was awful! We'll have to get some face masks.'

Mitch looks up when we say this. Oscar has fallen quiet to look at all of his notes. The last thing I heard was him questioning why single letters had been highlighted at random through the book. Mitch had just raised an eyebrow and asked if he was sure they were random.

'I need one too for my fucking acne.' He lifts his neck, showing bumps all the way down it.

'Have you been shaving?' I ask, walking over to look at it. He tilts his chin up so I can see. There are nicks on his neck. 'Are you doing it right?'

Val laughs, and Mitch scoffs and paws my hands away.

Radwa

I'm sat scrolling through Emma's activity log on Facebook, having found nothing of note in her direct messages, when Lolly texts me.

> LOLLY
> Want us to pick you up on the way back from the shop? Xx

The guys have been hanging out at the clubhouse today because it's a full moon tonight. Oscar is with them.

After how my grand reveal went last night, I decided not to go.

Honestly, I'm still a little hurt that after all the research I pulled to show him, Mitch still decided to defend a guy he barely knows instead of hearing me out.

And I don't think I could watch Wren and Oscar interact in the same way anymore without wanting to blurt everything out to Wren. Val told me we shouldn't say anything yet, not until we have more evidence, because it would probably just upset her. But not telling her is stressing me out, almost as much as not knowing how they're going to get rid of Oscar before the moon is up.

> RADWA
> Sure thanks! x

I debate going for a shower before I see everyone but considering we'll be running about in the woods tonight I don't really see the point.

I see Lolly's jumper across the room. Last night I was kind of mad at them for shutting me down. But then they messaged me to check in on me and make sure I knew I could talk to them. I didn't reply properly, and feel bad shutting them out. It's just that so much has been going on, and everyone siding against me really drained me yesterday.

I smile softly walking over to it. I pull it on, hoping this will tell them what I'm not sure I have the words to yet. We'll be fine, even if it feels like we won't be, even though last night stung. We have to be. It's us.

I can't help but smile and feel my face flush as the soft fabric brushes against my skin.

All things considered, I'm still excited to see them.

Val

Wren absolutely insists that we need face masks for tomorrow after the moon.

Mitch also decides to pick up a razor. We spend about fifteen minutes looking at all the options in the toiletries aisle.

'Why are there so many!' Mitch hisses under his breath, his eyes wide with concern.

Lolly emerges from around the corner after going on an adventure around the shop. Their arms are full of pastries and they have Belgian chocolate waffles tucked under one of them.

'Just get the cheapest one,' they groan, reaching over my head to grab a coconut hand cream. Then they pick up a couple of face masks for themself. One is lavender-scented. They always smell like lavender.

I walk over to Mitch and stand on my tiptoes to kiss his cheek. 'I think you should get one of these two.' I point to two in the middle. Dad uses that brand.

He nods in agreement, then manages to make a decision in three seconds flat. Mitch is bad at decisions if he's got too many options.

We eventually make our way back to the clubhouse after dropping Oscar home. He has to go early because his dad is coming home this weekend.

I hear Wren asking him if he's okay, and reminding him that she's 'going camping' so he won't be able to get a hold of her tonight. He nods, and she comes out of the car with him to give him a cuddle and kisses his head.

I feel like I'm eavesdropping on a moment so look away.

I put my hand on Mitch's knee. 'You okay?'

He nods, then looks pointedly forward at them. 'Worried about Oscar. He's coming out to his dad this weekend. His dad is moving to working from home, so he wants him to know.'

That's oddly convenient, almost like an alibi. Then it's easy to judge from my position. And the hiss of breath Lolly takes in through their teeth serves as an abundantly clear reminder of the fact.

So I don't say anything, I just put my hand on Mitch's knee and give it a squeeze as he watches on.

Oscar gives us a wave as he walks up the road to his house. We wave back.

He feels further away with every step.

Chapter Eighteen

Lolly

'Oh my Gosh!' Radwa laughs when she gets in the car next to me. She gestures to the waffles in my lap. 'I was literally ready for a mental breakdown today because I didn't have those.'

I hand her them and the hand cream I bought her. 'They're for you.'

She smiles softly. 'Thank you,' she whispers.

I catch Val's eye in the mirror. She is smiling at me.

We barely make it back to the clubhouse on time before the moon comes up. Mitch rushes through the house taking his Docs off so he can go and get his binder off before his shoulders crack and twist into something distinctly more lupine.

By the time I see him next he is a massive rusty wolf, and the tips of my ears barely reach the top of his shoulder.

When we've all turned we run the route we usually do. Only this time we don't playfully chase each other, nipping at one another's tails. I feel much slower. It's like something is pulling me back.

Lolly.

I hear the voice in my head. Disembodied, not one I recognise. It sounds like sheets of metal sliding off one another. My head feels like it's going to explode.

It rifles through my mind, leaving no thought unturned.

Val

Radwa is the first to bolt after Lolly when they run. Her massive black paws scramble against the rocky floor as she runs through the heather and around tree stumps.

I race after them. Wren is just behind me.

Then I hear a voice.

Val.

It's discordant.

I recognise it. Where do I recognise it from?

I turn around to look at Wren behind me, but I find myself alone.

Isolated, with my back to the water, a sheer cliff face behind me.

Radwa

I can't find Lolly in the woods.

I can't see Val either.

The trees are too thick behind me.

Val? I ask into the void.

Radwa. A voice that isn't hers replies.

Wren

Stay here, I tell Mitch, watching as the others disappear from sight.

Something is going on here. Someone is calling us.

My instinct tells me to follow Val, and so I do, straight

down a thin deer path etched through the grass, all the way down to a clearing in the trees.

There is a straight drop in front of me, where the river meets the woods.

I peer over the edge. Waves rush by, the jagged rocks have been corroded by years of their harsh touch.

No sign of Val.

Mitch

I pace around the clearing alone for a moment.

I feel as though I'm being watched. As if someone is waiting just to see what I do.

Guys? Come back! Now! I look around desperately. *Please?* I think. I whip my head around looking for them between the trees.

Then I hear them getting closer, running towards me.

Did I just give them an order?

Val appears first. Her coat is so distinct that it's easy to spot her. Colourful like a calico cat, with threads of brown, grey, white and black fur stitched together like patchwork. She elegantly bounds over the tree roots which litter the floor to land by my side. The brown tips of her ears are turned down in distress. She tucks her snout just under my chin. Licking at, and rubbing her soft golden face markings against, my throat.

My eyes stay locked forward looking for the others. I let Wren know she is okay. They are next to come back to me, black markings on their face pulling together in an almost human expression of concern against their thick white fur. Lolly and Radwa are still invisible in the dark of night.

But I can hear them running because I know how to listen for them.

By the time we reunite, the moon is coming to the end of

her shift so we make our way back to the clubhouse to sleep for the night.

~

I'm the third to wake up downstairs. Lolly seems to be missing when I get up.

Radwa too, but she always wakes up some time before the rest of us and somehow manages to drag herself up the stairs to pray. I'm not sure where she finds the strength. When moons land on a Saturday, church the next day is getting missed. I'm sure God understands.

I walk out into the garden and find both of them sitting together outside. They've made a bonfire to combat the cold morning air. Lolly is toasting a waffle on a stick. Once again they are wearing a hoodie that is way too big for them, and Radwa is wearing one that creeps up her arms. They're sitting in silence with soft smiles and sleepy eyes.

I come and sit down next to them, reaching for a bit of bread to toast on the fire. I poke a sharpened stick through it and turn it on the flame. Val comes out shortly after me, wrapped in a blanket, coffee in hand, her hair slightly matted.

I look at them all. 'I was ready to fucking kill you guys last night.'

'Seconded.' Wren appears in the door frame wearing a tired smile and a silky shorts, vest and dressing gown combo.

Lolly laughs. 'I didn't even realise I wasn't with you guys.'

Radwa looks up from her waffle. There is worry in her expression, as if they have already told her what happened.

'There was this other voice.' They shrug.

Radwa nods. 'It called me, searched through my head for me, and it was like I blacked out. Then I heard Mitch.'

Val's eyebrows knit together, as she sips her coffee. 'I heard it too. I couldn't hear anyone else, just this weird voice, then Mitch.'

'So I take it neither of you recognised the voice then?' I ask, turning my head to the side knowingly and raising my eyebrows as I pull the bread out the fire before it actually gets much of a brown crumb.

Radwa crosses her arms, nose scrunching up in distaste. 'It was *actually* like someone was trying to *hide* their voice. Which would imply—'

'We know it's probably *someone* that we know,' Val cuts her off, cheeks flushing a little as she sits between the two of us holding her hands up. She gives Radwa a wide eyed look nodding slightly sideways towards Wren. 'Let's just take a second to think this through from all angles. Why couldn't Mitch hear it? And why could we only hear him?'

'It's because he's the acting alpha.' Wren shrugs, apparently not recognising the nod Val gave towards her.

There's that word again, that sinking weight on my chest. The heavy knowledge that all of this peace and serenity following moons rests on my shoulders.

Wren stands up, grabbing a pastry from the tree stump next to her to heat on the fire. Val's eyes seem to follow her before looking very deliberately away as she bends over blushing deeply. I cock an eyebrow at her and she turns more red.

'It sounds like the rogue tried to control you. It's good that Mitch stopped it but...' Wren continues, shaking her head, poking a stick through her croissant, then holding it over the fire, 'I'm gonna call for backup next moon, maybe get Magnus or Lycaon. I'd get Mum and Aisla but they're on a mission too right now.'

She reaches over for the cardboard plates and pulls her food off the stick, shaking her hand out as it burns her. Then she sits down next to Val. I don't know how she manages to look so put together after the moon. Her braids look slightly ruffled and frizzy but other than that her hair seems to have survived the night protected, and her post-moon 'comfies' have the elegance of a Hollywood movie.

Val looks up at her thinking the same thing. Her awe is evident in her expression.

Wren ruffles her hair. 'Told you to let me braid it.'

Val laughs awkwardly. Then she catches my eye, and smiles, leaning her head on my leg. I stroke her hair absent-mindedly, still more absorbed in what Wren said about me stopping the rogue with my order.

The rogue feels entirely too close to us right now. And I don't trust myself to be able to defend us again.

Chapter Nineteen

Wren

I tell Dad about what happened pretty much as soon as we get home.

He's on the phone to Mum and Ailsa when I come in and I catch the tail ends of the goodbyes and the love yous. I ask Mum about her mission. She tells me everything is fine and I tell her the same about mine. I couldn't really tell her that it wasn't. We're not allowed to share upsetting news with people when they're on assignment.

When I finally get to tell Dad about what happened he looks troubled.

'Well, Magnus is coming up for your brother's birthday,' he says thoughtfully. Phelan turns sixteen just before the next moon.

'So is Harley,' I offer.

Dad pulls a face. 'He's sixteen.'

I raise my eyebrows. It's the same age I was when I was first sent here.

Dad hears my thoughts. 'Yeah, and that is precisely why I don't believe in letting children fight our battles for us.'

I roll my eyes. I wonder if he'd say the same if what happened hadn't happened.

Eventually he decides to ask for Lycaon and Ash to come up as backup. I'm just surprised he doesn't think twenty-one and twenty-three is too young given that he has war wounds from when he was that age.

Dad folds his arms hearing this. 'Don't get smart. I know you're very capable, it's nothing to do with that. I just think it's a lot to ask someone so young to go through.' He pulls me into a cuddle and kisses my forehead.

I decide to leave Dad to the planning because frankly I am exhausted and need to fix my braids, so I make my way upstairs to relax for a little.

For some reason, I'm really struggling to unwind from this moon. My heart flutters in my chest and my body feels as though it is still running through the woods. The hairs on the back of my arms stand up. It's as though my wolf form is frustrated at having been confined. I'm laying on my bed attempting to decompress when my phone buzzes.

```
ONE NEW MESSAGE FROM GOFLB <3
```

Oscar's name in my phone is now a reference to a Queen song, 'Good Old-Fashioned Lover Boy'. This was in response to my telling him my dad said he seemed like a respectful young man when they met.

Oscar had found this particularly funny for some reason.

I open the message he sends me.

```
OSCAR
I just came out to my dad.
```

It feels like the world stops spinning around me for a moment. I sit up. I hold my breath as I type out my reply.

```
                            WREN
             How did that go?
```

OSCAR IS TYPING...

I count the seconds it takes him to reply, getting up to thirty before I get a response.

OSCAR
Bad

WREN
Are you okay?

I feel stupid. Of course he fucking isn't. My boyfriend probably feels like he's falling to pieces and all I've got is 'are you okay'.

I should go and get him. But would that make it worse? Does 'bad' mean he's sitting in his room waiting to talk once things calm down? Does it mean he's been kicked out? Is he alone? Is he safe?

I know what happens to people like us who don't get acceptance. I know where our minds go. I don't need telepathy to know how bad it could be for him right now, and I can't lose another person like that.

The wolf in my head has picked up a scent that it longs to follow, needs to follow.

'Wren?' My dad knocks on my door softly. 'You okay kiddo?'

I feel so panicked I can't speak.

'I'm coming in.' He opens the door after getting no response.

He looks worried. He crouches by my side and hands me a glass of water. He probably heard my heart hammering. He's always the first to the rescue when that happens. He was there for me a lot when crap went down with Tyler.

'Oscar came out to his dad. It went badly... And I have all this adrenaline. My body has to do something but I'm not sure what. I want to go to him but I don't know if that'll help or make things worse.'

My dad straightens up. He knows what's been going on there. I talk to him about it all the time. 'Get him over here. He can stay the night if need be.'

Dad never lets me have boys stay the night. I guess he knows how serious this could be. Magnus was born human and his coming out didn't go very well either. In fact, it's half the reason Dad had to turn him.

When I open my phone I see that Oscar still hasn't replied, it's been half an hour.

> WREN
> Sorry that was dumb. I know you're probably not. But dad says you can stay here tonight. I'll be over to pick you up as soon as I can if you want that. Just hang tight. Remember there's plenty of people who see you for you, your mum Heidi, me, your friends, my friends. We all care about you Oscar.

A bubble appears indicating he's typing then it disappears. I feel less panicked.

> OSCAR
> I will be.
> I'd like that, thank you. You have no idea how much I needed that.

Now I just need to get him here as soon as possible. As I'm racing downstairs to grab the car keys, my phone starts vibrating in my back pocket so violently that I'm half convinced it understands the urgency of the situation.

MITCH.

Something in me stops in the middle of the stairs.

'Hello?' I manage to choke out over the feeling of my heart pounding in my chest.

Suddenly everything feels far too loud, too... much. Conan throwing himself about playing at the bottom of the stairs with Luna on all fours. Phelan's voice in my head as he asks if I'm okay while squeezing past me on the staircase.

I need them all to shut up before my head bursts. Why can't they just be fucking quiet?

'Are you hurt?' Mitch's voice asks quickly, directly. The line is crackly and his breathing heavy so it's hard to make out exactly what he's saying after that.

'Hurt? No why would I...' I trail off, glancing at my open conversation with Oscar.

Mitch's rapid heavy breathing is almost unbearably loud.

'Mitch? What's the matter?' I ask, covering my other ear. 'I'm not hurt. I'm okay, I promise.'

'It doesn't make sense,' he murmurs, voice strained, wincing as though he's ran a marathon. 'I was out – couldn't breathe – out of nowhere – others – okay – no sense.' The next part comes through more rapidly, as though he had strung the words together on a piece of colourful thread. 'I-thought-maybe-it-was-a-mates-thing.' Then his voice slows, back to normal. 'But if we're all okay it won't be right?'

The question hangs in the air for a moment. I can feel Mitch waiting expectantly for an answer.

The picture on the wall above the stairs watches for my reaction. It's a picture of three teenagers, all dressed in their school uniforms. The girl in it has her silver eyes nearly closed in a laugh as she sprawls across her mates' laps. Another wolf is shoving her off, an affectionate grin toying with his lips. Between them there is a human boy who holds the girl in his arms, though his eyes remain locked on the other boy.

I wonder if they knew then their fates were tied, that he was destined to become one of them, and that one of them was destined to turn him in an effort to save him. That's usually how it works when wolves have human mates. He was theirs even then, before he was ever turned; their friend, their partner, their mate.

'Mitch.' My voice comes out in a hushed whisper. 'Where are you?'

'Up the backroads by all the fancy houses – Wren I—' he starts.

'Why?' I immediately cut him off with the question, because that's what I expected.

Because that's where Oscar stays.

There is a pause on the line, then a deep breath. 'I have no fucking clue.'

I have no fucking clue. It all rings in my ears. **You have no idea how much I needed that.** *No fucking clue.* 1 in 2. That damn statistic plays in my brain on repeat.

Is it possible that Oscar is Mitch's mate? And maybe also mine?

Mitch

I have no idea how I ended up driving to Oscar's. The only time I've been here was last night, dropping him off, and there are a million private roads and twists and turns which I needed him to direct me down. Honestly, it's a miracle we got back to the clubhouse before the moon.

All I know is that I was arguing with Radwa about him being the rogue one second, then I stepped out to get some air but ended up choking on my own breath, unable to make sense of anything. I checked in with the pack but every instinct in my body was burning, begging me to come here.

Just as Wren's call disconnects I pull up to an electronic fence in front of a three story house with a massive open gate and huge gardens. The sheer size of it makes me feel out of place.

There are voices in the driveway screaming at each other.

'_____!' A tall, ginger man shouts a name I don't recognise as he stalks down the front path, gravel crunching under his shiny suit shoes.

Oscar is in front of him. He shouts back. He's crying in frustration. He's not holding any bags on anything. He's not even wearing sunglasses or proper shoes, like he's just thrown himself out of the house.

It's not until the lights on a pristine white Audi blink in response to him raising his hand that I realise that that the shaking, red faced boy in front of me is planning on driving. And I don't know quite how but in that second I *know* that regardless of how fancy his car looks he'll be much safer behind my mismatched red doors.

My wheels skid on the stones as I park in front of the gate. Oscar's head snaps over upon seeing me. I reach over the handbrake to grab ahold of the handle and throw the door open.

'*Oscar*, get in.' My voice is steady, commanding.

He does.

I reverse quickly out of the lane just in time to see the man get a harsh scolding off of a woman who I assume is Oscar's mum. She throws her hands up and walks back into the house without the man. He's left standing there, hot in the face.

We drive in silence for a little while before I glance sideways at him.

'I guess you heard *it*,' he mutters under his breath.

I could just say I didn't or that I won't tell anyone. But he knows I did and knows that I wouldn't. I don't know what possesses me to do what I do next.

'_____,' I tell him, casually.

'What?'

'That's my deadname.' I shrug. 'For the record, only Val and Lolly know that.'

Radwa probably would, but she was three years below me in school and doesn't remember interacting with me before she knew me as Mitch.

He looks at me incredulously for a moment. 'Mitch! Ew! Why on earth would you tell me that?'

I shrug again, reaching to knock his mirror down as he screws up his face in the sunlight. 'Now we're even, I guess? I dunno, it just doesn't hold any power over me anymore.'

I turn the radio on, picking something on Spotify. It's a song by Wrabel I've not heard in a while. It was popular in trans spaces online when we were younger.

We sit in silence, Oscar starts to tear up. 'Man, I really needed this song.'

'I know.' I smile at him. 'What were you even thinking? Trying to go driving without proper shoes or sunglasses on the brightest day this year?' I gesture down to his sliders, trying to joke with him to coax out one of his signature grins.

Out of the corner of my eye, I notice his expression change, like a dark cloud passing over the sun. Then I see him start crying. It's silent at first, then it gets louder. His breathing gets faster, harder. He has his arms crossed over his chest, pushing down like he's trying to ground himself.

I put a hand on his leg and give him a squeeze while I look for a place to pull over. He puts his hand on top of mine and holds it for support.

By the time I've pulled over, he's crying, hard.

'I'm sorry—' He chokes through his sobs. 'I just don't know what I was thinking because I don't know what I'm supposed to do from here.' He's hyperventilating. 'I'm scared Mitch. What can I do from here?'

He repeats the question over and over again like he's losing it. It's terrifying. His eyes are darting around. His heart is racing.

I yank my door open and come around to his side. He throws himself out of the car and onto the floor with me. He leans against the hot metal of my car. He sits on his hands so they dig into the stony floor. I hand him some water.

I try to get him to focus, to name things around him like me and Val do, but it doesn't seem to help. There are not enough colours and he can't think about things to taste and smell and so on. I offer him my hand and he grabs for it.

I never want to be touched when I'm like this. But I look at how he's holding himself down, how tightly he grabs my hand, how he's pushing his back against the hot metal of the car.

At first it made me uncomfortable because it was like he was trying to hurt himself. But I realise he's not. He's just trying to find a sensation to focus on, like Radwa does with her weighted blanket or her earphones. I do it with music, too. He can't name things around him because there's too many to narrow them down.

I hesitate over what to do. I want to hug him.

'Oscar? Will a hug make it better or worse?' I ask.

He looks at me confused for a moment. Like I've stunned him out of what was happening. 'You don't hug people.'

I roll my eyes and pull him towards me.

'I'll hug you, Oscar,' I murmur into his hair as his head lays on my chest. Idiot.

His tears dampen my t-shirt. His hand holds it tight, scrunched up on my back in a vice-like grip. My arms wrap around him with equal strength, holding all of his pieces solidly together.

'I've got you,' I whisper, because I don't know what else to say. 'We're gonna get you through this, okay Oscar?'

I keep saying his name. Like it's a chant, a magic word that will make him okay, that will tell him he will be okay. I hope it tells him that I see him, that who he is is enough.

We sit there on the side of the road, him half pulled into my lap. My shirt is damp and crinkled. I won't let go until he does.

'I don't know how I'm going to survive this,' he murmurs, not looking up. 'You said we'd get me through but I don't see myself on the other side.'

His words hit me like a ton of bricks.

I look at where we've pulled over. We can walk to me and Radwa's spot in the woods from here.

I get up, grab his hand and pull him up. I lock the car.

'Come on. I need to show you something.'

He holds tightly on. He holds on.

Radwa

Sat slouched with my back against the couch playing *Animal Crossing*, I can't help but feel slightly useless. After he stormed out of the house for some air earlier, Mitch started to panic without really knowing why. Now it appears we have our answer because he just let Val know what's going on with Oscar.

Rogue or not, Oscar's personal situation has been enough to make my clothes feel heavy against my skin as though I've walked an hour and a half through a rainstorm.

The game's graphics usually make me feel so calm – not having any responsibilities other than catching butterflies probably helps – but it doesn't seem to work now.

It does, however, seem to ease any feelings of painful familiarity in Lolly. They make their character race up to mine and bonk my head with their bug catching net in an effort to capture my attention. I hit them back.

'Oh my God stop flirting!' Val laughs, picking up her phone to check what Wren and Mitch are saying.

'We're not flirting!' I blush.

'Apparently Mitch needs to up his game,' Lolly laughs.

Val doesn't react, so Lolly nudges her with their foot. She's frozen a little, eyes scanning over the texts.

'Everything okay?' I ask, putting my controller down.

She nods as she catches up. Then types a reply and locks her phone. 'Oscar's dad is a shithead. Mitch and him went on a walk to your woods,' she nods towards me, 'then to Wren's. His friends Eason and Kat met them there. Eason's left now. Kat's still there and has said Oscar can move into her spare room in the meantime but he's staying with Wren tonight.'

I nod and then pause. 'Is Wren okay with that?' They don't sleep next to guys.

Val shrugs, shivering a little then tapping her shoulders five times before checking her phone again. Then she turns off the Switch, much to Lolly's distaste. 'Oscar's just asked if we wanna have a group sleepover. Apparently he wants a distraction.'

It doesn't make a lot of sense but I guess you can't judge how people react to this sort of thing. I guess the pack is sort of like a family, and that's what he needs right now, isn't it? Family. At least this way I can both keep an eye on anything strange that he does and make sure Wren is okay but still be a good friend if I'm wrong in my suspicions.

Mitch picks us up a few minutes later. He looks stiff, serious. Val gives him a hug and asks if he's okay. He hugs her back, breathing out for what seems like the first time in hours, and confirms he is.

He doesn't look okay by any means; his eyes are dark and there is a wet patch on his t-shirt by his shoulder.

Looking back, I don't think Val was okay when it was me. Does this mean Mitch and Oscar are mates? If it does, that makes his haggard state even more understandable. I dread to think what I'd be like if something happened to Val or Lolly.

Not that I really *know* that Lolly is my mate, but it feels right.

Wren looks about the same as Mitch when we get to her house. She opens the door for us, then leads the way into the living room.

Oscar is laying with his head on the shoulder of a pretty girl with silvery blonde hair. She is short, pale, and thin, and her eyes are a light but stormy grey.

'Holy shit!' Lolly laughs, breaking the solemn silence. 'I didn't know you meant *that* Kat.'

'Lolly!' The girl looks up with a big smile.

'Mitch said Oscar was moving in with his friend Kat! Does that mean you finally—?' Lolly trails off.

'Yeah and I moved in with my girlfriend—' She nods.

'And Clyde!?' Lolly asks.

'Much happier, living with Nial. Is Lotta—' she starts.

'With family.' They smile.

'Did you get into—?' Kat doesn't even get the sentence out before Lolly nods vigorously. She takes their hands in hers and squeals then gives them a massive hug.

'Did you?' Lolly asks.

'Unconditional.' She flicks her hair off of her shoulders doing a little dance.

Lolly makes an excited squeaking noise I've never heard them make before. I look back and forth between them.

Oh. *That* Kat. Lolly's first—

'This is my...' They turn to look at me. Then falter.

'Radwa.' I smile awkwardly and wave. Then regret waving. Why am I so awkward?

She looks up at me, her eyes shake a little. 'It's nice to meet you.' She says it so genuinely. It annoys me. Of course she's *nice* as well.

Val

Promptly after we arrive, Wren decides it's time for a well needed cuppa. I follow them through to the kitchen to help with the cups.

'You okay?' I ask them, handing over the sugar from on top of the fridge.

'Yeah.' They smile tiredly, slouching to rest their head against my shoulder once I'm by their side. 'Just emotionally tired. Today has been a lot – more for him than me obviously but—'

'I get what you mean.' I nod understandingly, resting my head on top of hers in a show of solidarity.

She eventually sighs, lifting her head. 'I'm just glad he's okay, to be honest.'

'That's the main thing.' I smile, putting my hand on top of hers where it rests on the counter and giving it a squeeze.

The action makes her turn to look at me for a second. Her silver eyes look tired, maybe even a little bloodshot.

I remember how worried I was the night Radwa came out. I don't think I really appreciated the cloudy and uncertain weather forecast associated with coming out until Radwa did it.

Obviously, it was different for me. I'm bi, not trans, and my Dad was pretty great about it all. He actually said that liking all genders was only natural and wasted no time ordering a little bi flag to put next to the picture of me on his mirror at work. Even before Mitch passed most of the time he would defend our relationship to the death – he might call Mitch an idiot nearly every time he sees him but you best believe that is *his* idiot and he loves him like a son.

But now I can see that hurricane in all my friends and it is clear from red tracks down Wren's cheeks that today has been a day of turbulent and torrential showers.

I swallow, giving her hand another squeeze, and run my thumb over her rough, scarred knuckles before reaching for the coffee while she starts on the teas. 'Pretty lucky Mitch was about, huh?'

Her eyebrows pull together tight in concern, looking deep in thought as she pours boiling water into each mug. 'I wouldn't just put it down to that.'

'What do you mean?' I ask, pushing myself up onto the counter while she tries to coax some colour into Oscar's tea.

She presses her lips together, letting the bag settle, deciding it needs time to steep. Then she crosses her arms, leaning her hip against the counter. *It's trickier to tell with humans. But more often than you would expect, saving someone comes down to more than just physical danger.* She bites her lip, looking down at the floor. *If you saw what he looked like earlier you'd know what I mean.*

The corners of my vision start to twist and distort into the shape of her memory like fabric caught in a flame. They don't lift as easily as ribbon. Instead, they curl tight and heavy like leather. Their every fibre resists revealing the scene hidden underneath as if Wren is doing her damndest to keep Oscar's meltdown underwraps for his own sake.

I think about the creases and tear stains on Mitch's shirt earlier, the determination with which he rushed back into the house on feeling his breath pulled from his lungs, his unquestioning defence of him in the face of Radwa's suspicion.

You think that they're... I start. *I didn't even know a human could be...*

Wren rubs her face tiredly. *Well, it's not entirely unheard of. But, more often than not, they don't stay human very long.*

There is a flicker of fear on Wren's face, and I start to understand why she looks more terrified at this fact than relieved. There is *literally* a cannibalistic werewolf on the loose and she has been burdened with the knowledge that someone she loves dearly is doomed to be turned into one of us. It's nearly impossible to imagine a version of this where he doesn't get hurt *if* he survives at all.

I mean, look at my parents and Magnus – they were destined for each other long before he was ever turned. And I mean... She looks at the floor, twirling the end of her braid around her finger. *You were born human. And look at us.*

She pauses, looking up at me carefully, eyes studying my face before she continues.

I don't think you realised how important what you did that night we met was to me. If that had happened again I – I was barely recovering from the last time. I honestly think you might've saved me too.

She looks up at me with a small smile which makes her lips wobble so she pulls them tightly together.

Wren— I start.

She shakes her head, waving me away. Then she brings her hands up to her face, pressing her pinkies to her eyes.

I open my arms and gesture for her to come over towards me where I'm still perched on the countertop. She slots herself between my legs and rests her head on my shoulder. I kiss the side of her head gently and hold her tight to me.

The thing is, I did realise this before. I knew from the moment I heard her voice in my mind that she was a part of me – even before that, something primal in me knew she was mine to protect.

She pulls away first, pressing her pinkies to her eyes once more as she turns away.

We stand there quietly. The teaspoon against the cup is the only noise in the room.

Then I say, *It's kind of funny, isn't it?*

Us and the boys? she asks.

I confirm.

She shrugs. *It's way more common than you think. That's why polyamory is so normal with wolves. We tend to share mates, like my mum and dad, and their mates.*

My stomach flutters. *Don't get Oscar and Mitch too excited.*

She laughs, then looks at me for a minute. *You know, Oscar would be so down if Mitch wasn't so straight. He's poly anyway, and I think he genuinely has a crush on Mitch.*

I snort. *Honestly, when I see the two of them together, I'm not convinced Mitch* is *straight.*

She giggles, picking up some of the mugs to take them through for everyone.

Before she can lift them I stop her for a second. *Do you think there's a version of this where he comes out human? Where no one else gets hurt?* I ask her.

She stops for a moment, thinking. *I think we have people we are drawn to save, and unwilling to hurt – even though we sometimes do – but how exactly we keep and save them isn't written in stone.* She looks like she'd rather have another answer when she pauses. Then she gives me a knowing smirk. *But I do know that none of our stories are meant to be solo projects.*

Lolly

Kat disappears shortly after we arrive, just as we're starting to order food.

Oscar looks up after her uncomfortably. Mitch slides in next to him, wrapping an arm around his shoulders. He pretends to do the whole guy-at-a-movie-theatre thing, yawning dramatically. This gets a laugh out of Oscar, which makes us all smile.

'What do you want to eat?' he asks.

Oscar glances down at the menu, then back at Mitch. 'I'm not hungry.'

'Just pick something from the menu and you can eat it when you are. You need some kind of dinner,' he says flippantly.

'I don't – I can't focus on reading the menu right now because I have a headache.' Oscar waves him off.

'I'll read it to you then,' Mitch suggests.

Oscar shakes his head. Wren offers to order something for him and he lets them. They decide on something and then chuck the menu at me and Radwa.

The rush of air as the menu flies inelegantly past her face seems to jolt Radwa out of a trance.

I laugh as I scramble over the back of the chair to retrieve it. 'You with us?'

When I look up at her, Radwa has a guarded expression, one that I recognise. She's trying not to blurt something out. I can always tell by the way she tucks her hands under her knees, trying to physically restrain any reaction.

She widens her eyes slightly at me and presses her lips together, raising her eyebrows pointedly.

I flick my eyes between the menu and Oscar, who thankfully isn't looking our way, and I catch her meaning and send her a warning glare.

She waves her arms helplessly. She *knows* now would be the worst time in the world to say or think anything, anything at all, about her Oscar suspicions. But something Radwa and I have in common is a need to work carefully on our self-control. She's trying.

Is it suspicious that Oscar isn't hungry right now? Not really. He's going through hell. And we both know that; the scent of rain is as prominent in her mind as cheap red wine in mine.

But certain minds instinctively search for patterns more than others. Radwa has one of those minds. And once she gets a bee in her bonnet about something, she has to follow up.

I smile reassuringly at her. 'C'mon. Food will help.'

My eyes scan it even though I know what I want. Each dish is printed in bold with a description in italics, and nutritional information in a smaller font underneath. Honestly I think I'd rather if menus were a hundred pages thick with pictures of each dish instead of all this unnecessary information. It's no wonder Oscar finds it too overwhelming to look at right now.

Mitch and I debate what sides to get and share with each other. We have the same kind of taste in food. Usually something battered or fried. Tragically he's got no spice tolerance.

Val takes the menu and gets up to order for us. She's the one who makes the phone calls for us usually. Her or Mitch.

'So how did you meet Kat?' I ask Oscar, as Val walks out.

He drums his fingers against his arm. 'Used to compete together.'

Mitch looks down at him with a smile. 'No shit, what sport did you do?'

Oscar looks away, sitting up and then snuggling into Wren, slotting himself under their arm to lay on their chest. I know the answer before he says it: 'Gymnastics.'

I swear that's where Kat meets ninety percent of the people she knows. She used to spend more time with this one beam in her gym than she did with me when we were dating.

'Can you do the splits?' Mitch asks, turning his head to look at Oscar.

'Yes.'

'Can you do a handstand?'

'Yes.'

'Can you do a backflip?!'

Oscar, reaches a hand up to cover Mitch's mouth. Then he pulls him down on top of him to cuddle.

Mitch isn't about to complain, because Oscar starts playing with his hair.

Val comes in and perches on the arm of the couch next to Wren, who leans their head back on her lap and smiles up at her. Val smiles back, then reaches down to give Oscar's hair a ruffle. He leans into her touch.

There's an energy there. A dynamic I'm not sure I understand. I assume it's because they're just realising they're all mates, but then Val, Mitch, Radwa and I are all mates and even we're not that extra. I guess that's partly because we have more limitations on touch.

'If you're not hungry, I have a solution.' I smirk towards Oscar, standing up to go out for a smoke.

'Hmm.' Oscar smiles, his eyes closed. Val is still fidgeting with his hair. 'Probably not a good idea right now, mentally I mean.'

Mitch nods in agreement, and stays by Oscar's side.

Wren

'Well, this is the gayest shit I've ever seen,' Phelan comments as he walks into the living room. 'Which is a statement considering I've just finished calling Harley.' He throws himself down on the chair across from me, hanging his legs over the arm.

'Not true,' Val replies, lifting my head to shift her weight to the side. 'Mitch is sadly a heterosexual.'

Mitch raises his hands in defence as if apologising for the disappointment. 'How is Harley?' he then asks.

Phelan gets a sad kind of smile on his face. He misses him a lot. I can feel it, like there is a cord tied around his heart pulling him towards the shoreline, halfway across the country. He looks like he's worried about something.

'You okay pup?' I ask him.

He nods, sitting on the arm of an armchair.

I'll talk to him when less people are here, maybe when I'm looking after him and Conan next weekend.

Our food comes fairly quickly. We ordered for Dad and the boys as well, so we sit together in the living room, eating with our food on our laps.

Mates? Dad asks as he brings the food in, nodding towards the four of us lounging on each other on the couch.

I think so, I tell him. *Oscar doesn't know yet.*

Looks like he might need to one day, he thinks back, nodding to the pack around him.

He's right, but I have no idea how I would tell him that. Firstly I'd have to explain the whole werewolf thing, and then once we got through that we'd have to start on the fact that being mates with us means he's pretty much definitely fucked.

Dad brings through a blow up mattress and we fall asleep in the living room together.

Well, the pack does. Oscar is spooning me and snoring slightly. It's sweet, and the closest I've been to sleeping next to someone in a while. Mitch is cuddling both Oscar and Val in his sleep, Val's hair is all over both of them.

Lolly sleeps on one of the arm chairs. I didn't know it was possible for someone to tuck themselves into that small a ball.

Phelan sleeps on the other and is falling out of it. He must be getting to my height now, and he's lanky with it too. He's gonna be taller than me. I can't decide whether I like that or not. Little siblings should stay little. It's kind of cute that he wants to spend time with me and my friends like this. Maybe he was trying to make it so I was comfortable enough to fall asleep. Whatever it was, he is snoring now, quite loudly.

Radwa, who is the only one still awake, laughs at this, nearly waking Lolly up.

'Jesus Christ you scared me,' I hiss. 'I didn't know you were awake.'

'Yeah, my prayer is in, like, two hours. That's no time to sleep at all.' She waves her hands vaguely. She is still in her clothes, no wonder she hasn't been able to sleep.

'Shit, sorry, I didn't think. I was too caught up with Oscar. You could've taken my room.'

She shrugs. 'I was having a nice time. Aside from the whole circumstance, obviously.'

'And meeting Kat?' I bite my lip. 'I didn't know she was Lolly's ex, sorry.'

She looks at them, curled up in that ridiculously small position, and smiles affectionately. 'Nah, it's fine. I know they have exes. I can't really be mad at that.' Then she looks down at me again. 'You know, I'm awake. You don't need to worry about getting a couple hours of rest.'

I nod. My eyes feel heavy. I still don't feel like I could sleep.

But then, the cover is so warm, the mattress is so soft and Oscar holds me in such a close and gentle way.

Maybe I could.

Maybe I am.

Maybe—

I wake up with a jolt.

Woah. Phelan blinks wearily looking at me from his chair. *You okay?*

I fell asleep.

Yeah, genius. Radwa just woke me up because she had to go pray. You're fine, just go to sleep.

I shake my head, wondering how on Earth Radwa managed to wake my lump of a brother without touching him or waking anyone else.

I'm good, I'm up now.

Phelans nods and pulls his phone to his face, blinking in the harsh light.

Is Harley awake already?

It must be six, that's usually when Radwa prays in the morning.

He's on patrol today, he replies, anxiously checking his phone again.

I ask him who he's with. I'm told he's with Lycaon and a lot of very experienced soldiers. He will be completely fine. He's literally just checking the camp perimeter of any signs of a break in. Cygnus doesn't give Lycaon dangerous assignments.

How long till he's over?

Twenty four days.

And counting, I remind myself. I feel bad for dragging us here, for taking so long to figure out what's going on.

Is something going on with you guys? I ask him seriously, remembering how off he seemed last night.

He purses his lips. *I think we might be mates.*

Phelan and Harley have been dating since they were thirteen or fourteen. And before that they've been friends since before I can even remember. That happens in the pack, you grow up with the other wolves your age.

No shit. How'd you find that one out, did something happen when we were away?

He pulls his jumper sleeves over his knuckles. *He saved me. I don't wanna talk about it. Dad doesn't even know.*

I nod. I want to push, but I know it won't help the issue. If anything, in the past, pushing has only made him close off more. When we went to school together I knew he was being bullied but every time I tried to talk about it at all he would just slam his door, yelling at me to get out of his room. It took playing his Switch with him for four hours without trying to say anything on the matter before he even said a word about it.

But I dunno. He seems kind of off since then, and I don't want it to change anything with us, or – I mean I do but – it was a lot. He exhales. *And I just don't want him to resent me for it.*

I look after him thoughtfully. Talking to him now, I feel a little bad about how much I've been trying to separate myself from him recently. Like not inviting him to the group and that, it would probably have been good to take him.

Bad people don't tend to like Phelan because he can see through them. He's not easy to manipulate. Tyler couldn't stand him. Oscar loves him.

Besides, if Harley had to save him that must mean we came pretty close to losing him. And as much as I pretend he's one of the most *annoying* people to walk the planet, if we lost him I think that a pretty big part of me would go missing too. Since moving here, I think he's actually been one of my only friends until now.

I don't say any of this because that would just make us

both awkward. Instead, I try pointing out the obvious. *Does anyone here look mad at Oscar?*

His lips pull into a tight smile. *That actually helps, thank you.*

The door creaks open and he jumps round, even though he hasn't been saying anything out loud. It's Luna, just back from her walk with Dad. He taps the couch to bring her up, burying his face in her fuzzy fur.

Oscar pulls me closer as he starts to stir. I feel my smile turn into a giggle as he does.

'Hmmm, I heard a dog come in,' he mumbles into my shoulder. 'I would like to say hello to the good girl.' He lifts his hand up to call her over for a pet, which in turn wakes up Val and Mitch.

We're going to move Oscar's stuff into Kat's flat today. It's going to be emotional. I already know it. Oscar's not been up for two seconds and he's crying because Luna and Sammy have never been on a walk together, and now he has to leave Sammy at his parents'. Mitch and I try to tell him it's not going to be forever, that he can still visit his mum, she's still on his side.

It takes a lot to get him ready to go, but we get there, one step at a time. We drag him along. He will be alright. He has us.

Chapter Twenty

Val

'What's the password?' Mitch asks Oscar, as we approach a large electric fence together.

Lolly and Radwa went back to Mitch's house while we went to pick up Oscar's stuff from his parents'. We didn't want to crowd him too much, but we also wanted to support him.

'Password?' Oscar laughs, swinging his backpack over his shoulder.

'For the gate?' He taps on the box next to it.

'Hello?' A voice calls back. He jumps back in alarm.

'Heidi?' Oscar asks.

The gate buzzes. Mitch looks up in awe as the gates open for us onto a long driveway.

Heidi, as it turns out, is Oscar's sister, who is older than him by four years. She lives in Fife and studies Psychology, but came home upon hearing how Oscar's coming out went.

'Dad's out right now, but he'll be home soon.' She wraps her arms around him, pulling him close, as soon as we get to the top of the driveway.

Oscar's mum appears in the doorway. She comes forward to embrace both her children. 'Don't go,' she whispers to him, without knowing we can hear.

But his Dad's mind is made up and in turn, so is his. Leaving does not seem like a choice.

'You can come see me,' he replies.

I awkwardly play with the hem of my skirt and feel the fraying ends of my bracelet brush against my leg.

I remember when this was Radwa. When she showed up at my door in the pissing rain. She all but collapsed into my arms sobbing.

She was only fifteen at the time. Oscar is eighteen. I doubt that makes it any easier.

Oscar leads us to his room. It's chemically clean and minimalist. The only trace of his presence is in the art supplies that are neatly tucked away under his bed. I only notice they're there when he pulls them out and starts packing.

I grab a bag and help him stuff some clothes in. His wardrobe is much larger than what we see him wear and expands into another small room.

'I actually wear shit on this side,' he directs me, pointing to the left.

The clothes on the right are a chaotic mix of sizes, styles and colours. There's an insane amount of Lycra and velour, several heavy kilts and blazers, and a few cosplay pieces here and there. As well as that, several pieces have been thrown in the corner, including an expensive-looking woollen jumper and a t-shirt which is inside out with several tags showing.

I pick up a pile of jumpers in varying shades of green and put it in the bag. 'Do you make your cosplays?' I ask, folding a patterned sweater vest over my arm.

'Sometimes.' He shrugs, pulling open a drawer and taking out piles of socks. 'I cut my hair for the first time when I was thirteen because I wanted to dress up as Scott McCall. Dad was *pissed*.'

I can't help but laugh at the irony of the situation. The only *human* in a group of werewolves cosplaying as a werewolf.

Wren decides to go through to Oscar's bathroom to start packing his shower supplies.

'Wait! I think I left my dick in the shower,' he laughs, jumping over his bed to run in ahead of her.

'I'm sorry what!?' I laugh.

'My packer. I did leave him in here!' he shouts triumphantly.

'Why is he a *him*?!' Wren yells.

'Oh my God, what's his name!? Can I see him!?' says the straight man.

'Mitch, stop going after my boyfriend's dick,' Wren cackles.

'His name's Chad, and yes you can come in,' Oscar shouts through to Mitch, who scrambles over the bed as elegantly as an over-excited German Shepherd might.

Wren rolls her eyes, exasperated, and shrugs comedically over at me.

Oscar comes out of the bathroom pink in the face with something oddly phallic stuffed in his t-shirt. Mitch is laughing still.

It's funny. I think it's the most energised I've seen any of us in the past twenty-four hours.

'Can't believe you let him see your dick before me,' Wren quips.

Oscar's face turns scarlet. Mitch laughs even harder.

'Val definitely gets to see my piercings first now.' I feel my face get hot as Wren comes to stand next to me with her arms crossed sarcastically.

'I'm gonna start taking some bags down to the car, considering it's a half marathon to get there,' Mitch says, winking at me, then pulling at his crust pants so he can squat enough to pick up the box of art supplies, tossing some sketchbooks on top.

Oscar hovers for a second, holding his hands out and reminding him to be careful as he straightens up and swaggers to the door.

The boxes are stacked too high for me to see, from my position on the floor, what makes them both take a couple of steps back at the doorway. But it becomes clear when Mitch shifts the boxes onto his hip.

A tall ginger man stands there, wearing a polo shirt, with a jumper tied over his shoulders. It feels as though the second he arrives all the air in the room leaves. 'Who are you?'

Mitch looks up, rolls his eyes and then tilts his head to the side. 'I'm Mitch.'

'Your name is Mitch?' The man looks down.

Mitch is not short – he's actually average height for a man as he constantly reminds us – but Oscar's dad is very tall. His Docs don't even bring him up to eye level.

He straightens up. 'Yeah, is that a problem?'

I watch as Oscar's dad's eyes scan over the room. They glance at me and Wren – I stand up – and then they land on Oscar.

I don't want to know Oscar's deadname, so he better not pull any shit.

Oscar walks up and puts a hand on Mitch's arm. I see his dad's expression tense uncomfortably at the act of affection.

Let it piss him off. I want Mitch to lean into him just to get under his dad's skin.

He moves to the side, letting Oscar pass, while glaring at his dad.

'We were just leaving,' Oscar says.

'You're really gonna do this to your mother?' his dad retorts.

'Mum is welcome to visit me. You are just experiencing the consequences of your actions for once in your life.'

His dad scoffs, his tongue in his cheek. 'How long do you really expect us to indulge in this little tantrum, honestly? Are you not embarrassed? I bet your friends wouldn't talk to their fathers like this. Would you girls?' He looks at me and Wren, completely ignoring Mitch.

He seems to have decided, probably based on his appearance, that he is a lost cause.

I hear the moment Wren starts holding her breath as if the tiniest exhale of air from her mouth is going to out her.

I probably wouldn't talk to my Dad like that, no. But that's because my dad isn't a massive knob.

Part of me wants to say this to him, to curse him out for daring to act as though he has any sort of moral high ground right now. But I don't think he'd take too kindly to being berated in his own home, and I want Oscar to actually have a chance to grab all the shit that matters to him instead of being raced out of the house.

So I bite my tongue, feeling the sharp edges of my canines threatening to pierce their way through as I do.

Oscar's dad seems to mistake our stunned silence for an answer, because he smirks, shakes his head and says, 'Didn't think so,' before turning his back on his son and walking down the hallway.

He walks with a limp in almost the same wobbly imitation of nonchalance that Mitch has after a moon. Even though I don't like to think of myself as spiteful, I find myself privately hoping that it fucking hurts.

Oscar collapses back onto his bed, less upset than yesterday, more just tired of it all.

Mitch

We drop Oscar off at Kat's that evening once she is home from work. I feel really uneasy leaving his side. I can't quite describe why.

I give him a big cuddle as we leave, and Wren gets a big cuddle too. It's been a very long weekend.

I think about what Phelan said when he came in to see us all lying on each other on the couch. Gay. I wonder what he meant by that. I was just comforting Oscar.

'So, Oscar's your mate,' Val says as we walk into hers together. She leads the way straight up to her bedroom because she knows we are destined for a nap right now.

'Apparently so.' I smile. I feel like I should ask if it's weird even though I know it's not. Lolly is my mate and that's not weird.

'Platonically?' she asks, taking her jeans off to get into bed.

Damn, she's gorgeous. Her thighs are soft and dimpled slightly. It creates perfect dips for my fingers to sit in when I hold her.

'Sorry what?' I ask, giving myself a shake.

'Platonically? You guys were very cuddly yesterday,' she notes, pulling her jumper off.

I can't help but look for a minute. Well I could help it, but I know I don't have to, I'm allowed to.

She nudges me, rolling her eyes. 'Mitchell Reid!'

'Sorry.' I hold my hands up. 'Yeah, platonically. I like women. *Clearly*. And I'm cuddly with everyone I love.' I punctuate my point by wrapping my arms around her waist and pulling her down into my lap.

She gives me a wicked grin. She is another one of those people whose smile wins hearts and gets her everything she wants.

She rests her arms on my shoulders. Her hair is swept to the side. She is so beautiful. I tilt my chin up.

She reaches down to give me a slow, chaste kiss. Her hand cups my jaw gently. She gives one more gentle peck then pulls back.

'I'm so tired,' she groans, leaning her forehead against my shoulder.

I laugh. My hand comes up to her head to hold her. I press two kisses to her temple.

The sun is warm on my back, and I lean back into it. I tuck one of her pillows under my arm. God, every time I lay on her pillows I realise she's right about how crap mine are. She turns to lie with her head on my chest and her legs between mine.

'What about you and Wren?' I ask her, fingers stroking her upper arm.

'What?' I see as she tenses, her face getting hot. It's sort of adorable to see her almost bashful again.

'Well,' I smirk, 'you and Wren were cuddly too. Have you spoken to them about the whole mates thing yet?'

Her blush deepens as she toys with the bottom labret of her cyber bites between her teeth, nose scrunched up. 'Yes,' she eventually says. 'They brought it up yesterday.'

'And do you think that you guys are strictly platonic, or…?' I trail off.

Honestly, I'm not sure where Val sits on the whole concept of polyamory yet. Last time we talked about it she seemed hesitant, but more so about upsetting me than anything else. Thing is, I think I've always sat kind of halfway between poly and monogamous – like, I fell for Val when I was still with my ex.

So I could definitely be poly, especially with someone I trust like Val, but I'm so rarely attracted to people that the opportunity has never necessarily presented itself.

'It kind of seems like you might've been checking them out lately, which is okay, but like, do you find them hot?'

She looks up at me, eyes seeming to study me for a moment as if to check that I'm actually okay with her answer. Then she raises an eyebrow. 'Do you *not*?'

I shrug. I don't really think of them like that. I mean sure they are objectively gorgeous but we don't have that kind of dynamic.

Val looks borderline offended that I'm *not* attracted to Wren.

I wonder if she has any feelings for them, more than just finding them attractive. I don't think I'd have a problem if she did. Maybe some boundaries, but no problems necessarily.

I mean, look at their parents. They seem pretty happy.

As long as we're with each other through it all at the end of the day, in sickness and in health and all that, I don't really care who else is involved.

She tells me it's not really like that. At least, not right now. She thinks, for now, she just really wants to be closer to them, but she does find them extremely hot.

I laugh at this.

'Although,' she starts, 'I don't know if they were hitting on me earlier or if I'm reading too much into it.'

'With the piercing thing?' I wrap her hair around my fingers as I talk.

Her eyes bulge. 'I didn't even think of that. Nah, I meant yesterday. We were taking the piss about you and Oscar and they made a comment about us being like their parents because we're all mates.' She pauses. 'Like, poly.'

'Well, if they weren't joking I'm not mad,' I promise her first of all. I want to clear that up right off the bat. 'If you do develop feelings for them, that's okay, and we can talk about that.'

She nods, feeling reassured.

'Besides' – I decide to make a joke – 'kinda sounds like I get Oscar too.' I put on a silly kind of voice when I say it so she knows I'm joking. I tuck my hair behind my ear and purse my lips.

She sighs dramatically. 'And here I said it wouldn't work because you're straight.'

'Ah, see that was before I saw his house and his dick.' I shrug. 'He's turned me, what can I say?'

She starts giggling and paws me away. I tickle her sides.

She catches my hands and holds them right until she's sure the threat has been neutralised. Then she relaxes.

She's a lot less tense than earlier and lays more comfortably on my chest. Her hand comes to rest on my ribs, rubbing up and down in circles.

Lolly

Radwa and I go back to Mitch's while the rest of them go to pick up Oscar's stuff. I figured he might want some space. I know I only like a select few people around me when I go to my mam's. Hell, until recently Val and Radwa didn't even know where it was.

Radwa did offer to help Oscar out but he politely declined. His Dad could be a bit of an arsehole and he didn't want to subject her to any of the shit he might come out with, considering that she's already been through it all once, but he was very grateful for her offer of a friendly ear if he needed to talk about it.

We're sitting in my room listening to music together when I decide to say something. 'Are you okay?'

Radwa looks up at me. She's sitting in my beanbag, underneath my psychedelic smiley face tapestry. I have lots of different ones hanging from my ceiling. There's that one, and the nonbinary and lesbian flags on this wall, then a frog above my headboard. I'm sitting on my windowsill.

She picks the skin around her nails, playing a game on her phone. 'Why wouldn't I be?'

I push myself down onto the bed so I'm closer to her. 'I dunno, I guess I was worried Oscar's family shit might be a trigger for you.'

She shrugs.

'Do you still think that he's…' I trail off. 'Do you think all of that was just for show or—?'

She scrunches her nose up, not looking up from her

phone. 'I still feel off about him – he checks too many boxes for me not to. Like the fact we've still never seen him eat is *weird*. But maybe if *he's* not *the* rogue, he's *a* rogue, and being controlled by the alpha? I dunno.' She tails off, then she lets out a soft sigh and shakes her head. 'But there's no way yesterday was fake. We *both* know you can't fake that level of pain.'

The spite in her tone feels fresh. Normally I would just let her leave it here, but since talking to Mitch I've become overtly fucking aware that that isn't going to cut it anymore. If I want Radwa to talk to me I need to make it clear that I care about her shit too, that she can rant to me too.

'How did your dad take you starting hormones?' I try.

She looks up, thinks for a second. In the time it takes her to answer I can almost see the invisible thread our friendship hangs precariously from. What if it's already gone too far? What if she's already ready to give up on us forever? Or worse, she thinks I'm only asking so I can turn it around to be about me like a self absorbed asshole.

Then she leans forward, putting her phone down and her arms on the bottom of the bed to lean on it.

'He didn't say not to,' she starts. 'But he keeps telling me a million and one different risk factors as if I've not been on the waiting list for three years, and through psychology, and went through the whole figuring myself out process. I know it's just because he cares, but it's just *annoying* because it feels like another way I need to justify myself you know? Like to prove I know myself better than anyone else.'

I nod, sympathetically, trying to hide the sigh of utter relief that passes by my lips.

She actually talks to me, rants even, and she goes on for longer than she did in her messages to Mitch. It's like when we used to stay out all night together, back when we were both living with our parents, ranting to one another and planning our great escape.

I feel my mouth pull into a smile against the palm of my hand which fortunately covers it. She's *talking* to me again. Wait – fuck, what is she talking about?

' …And he keeps telling me that it'll permanently change some things, and I'm over here like … okay … good?'

I tune in just in time to chuckle at her expression.

'But it's annoying because while I really am looking forward to all the little things, right now I just feel tired, and my skin is awful, and my chest hurts, *and* I'm literally so emotional, all the time. And I feel like I have no right to be. Like I have to be happy all the time or I prove the point that those articles are making about hormones making us all depressed, or unstable, when I'm literally just *hormonal*.' She's sort of panting when she gets to the end. 'Sorry I know I'm ranting, once again,' she gestures up and down, 'hormonal.'

I chuckle to myself, and then I catch her eye. 'It's okay, you don't have to be the fix-it person all the time.'

Her brow furrows. She crosses her arms. 'What do you mean by that?'

Radwa

What do they mean by that?

They shrug. 'Mitch told me I dump shit on you guys all the time and it feels like you have to be the fix-it person quite often. You know, without your own problems, and I don't want you to feel like that. You can vent to me whenever you want to too.'

I groan, uncrossing my arms. 'Mitch should not have said that.' I don't want them to shut off from me and try to deal with everything on their own.

'He didn't use those exact words, and I'm not shutting off, I promise. Just not focusing on one person. I know I do that with you and Mitch way too much. I did it with Kat as well, when we were dating.'

I feel my face tense at her name. I know I'm not being reasonable here. I know I'm just very hormonal, and Kat is really lovely. It's just that she represents all the things Lolly can have, has had, should have when they go to uni. She is all the things I won't compromise to give them. Kat represents exactly why I won't ask them out.

'Oh my God,' Lolly laughs. 'You don't like Kat do you? Is it because we dated?'

I flush and shake my head. 'Why would that make me hate her? I'm fine, I'm just being hormonal.'

Lolly tuts, holding up their hands. 'I didn't say hate. I just meant because you're my best friend and she's an ex. I was going to say she's not one that we dislike but okay.'

I feel my cheeks get hotter.

'And fuck out of here with that "hormonal" bullshit. I've told you. I'm here to listen to you, and your feelings are your feelings regardless of why you're feeling them.' They fidget with the duvet cover where it sits between us. 'You can choose how you act on them, but I want you to know you are *allowed* to feel your feelings, and I want you to talk to me about them.'

I tap the bottom of the bed frame with my nail. 'Well, I want you to talk to me about your feelings regardless of what Mitch says. I just want you to know I have problems too, and don't always have all the answers.'

'Okay.' They nod, a smile on their face.

Then they breathe out and lay flat on their chest. They turn their face away from me so that it is masked by the covers.

'Well, if, hypothetically, you were feeling upset, or didn't like Kat, for some other reason, I do have something to tell you, that I've been keeping from you for a really long time, years actually – uhm—' Their heart races.

I cut them off. 'I know where you're going with this, and I agree we should talk, but—' I see their face fall and I feel like the worst person on the planet. 'I did mean it when I said I feel entirely unstable right now. With my Dad, and the hormones, I – I don't know how to feel about anything, and I'm really scared to have this conversation with you like this.'

Their mouth pulls into a tight smile, and they nod understandingly.

'I just think if we're going to start this we need to come at it from a better place. This – the conversation I mean.' I blush. 'Can you give me like a month, and then check in?'

They nod and give me a smile. 'I'll give you all the time you need.'

Wren

I stay with Oscar for a while, helping him unpack his boxes. He, Kat, her girlfriend and I order takeout, and then we disappear into his room for a bit.

We lay, shoulder to shoulder, across the width of his bed, his head half hanging off the edge of the mattress, in silence for some time. The room looks a little bare, with half unpacked boxes piled in the corner. But the easel and canvases that sit in the corner instead of hidden in the wardrobe and Mitch's copy of *Dorian Gray* on the bedside table make it look more like Oscar's room than the one at his parents' house ever did.

There is a skylight over his bed which we have strung fairy lights around.

'The moon looks really pretty tonight,' he whispers.

Waning. A tiny crescent, just after a new moon. I tell him this, and he looks surprised that I know how to tell.

'Have you seen my tattoo of the moon phases?' I ask, knowing that he probably hasn't because we haven't got quite so far as taking each other's clothes off yet and most of my tops don't show it very well.

He shakes his head. 'Do you wanna show me it?'

I flush. 'I'd have to take my shirt off.'

His gaze roams away for a moment, then he looks at me. 'Well, you can still show me it if you want.'

I think for a moment, then sit up and lift my top up at the back, over my head.

He sits up. 'Can I?'

I nod.

He runs his finger down my spine, pausing where each of the moon phases sits. My face grows warmer. It sends a shiver across my skin. Then he kisses my shoulder. It's a gentle kind of kiss that doesn't have any underlying implications.

'I thought it would feel bumpy for some reason,' he laughs half-heartedly.

I pull my shirt back down and turn around.

He wraps his arms around my waist, then rests his head on my shoulder.

'You okay?' I ask, pressing a gentle kiss onto his temple.

'Thank you for letting me stay last night. I know it was a big deal, and you probably didn't sleep—'

I smile. 'I did,' I whisper.

'Oh,' he replies, with a soft kind of excitement, happiness, and comfort.

'I was actually thinking,' I say, drawing shapes on his knee with my finger, 'maybe we could do it again, just the two of us.' I feel his eyes on me and continue, 'My dad is pretty strict after everything, but he's out of town next weekend. I'm babysitting my brothers. It would very much just be a sleepover, but it's a step I feel ready for.'

'I'd really like that,' he whispers, pulling me in for a kiss with a hand under my chin.

I climb into his lap and feel the butterflies rise in my stomach. 'Okay.' I nod and a smile creeps onto my face.

I know I've only known him for a couple of months at this point, but I'm really starting to trust him. Is that dumb?

I get attached to people far too quickly sometimes. I'm trying to not be too much or scare him away, he just makes me feel... I dunno... safe. Especially since he came out to his Dad. I feel such a strong connection to him. I'll never forget the feeling of dread that came over me last night, the panic, the need to do something. Anything.

I dunno. It's hard to explain to someone – someone who hasn't grown up knowing everything I know – why that changes everything. It might be early for other people, but for me? I think I might love him. Really love him.

Our phones then start going off like crazy in the corner of the room. He looks at me, concerned, and motions for me to climb out of his lap then walks over to get them.

'Thirty-two new messages to my group chat with Lolly and Mitch,' he says, passing me mine.

'Fifty-four to the one with Val and Radwa.'

He opens his phone, and I see him reading for a moment. Then he looks up at me, with so much joy in his expression, eyes genuinely sparking over someone else's happiness. 'I think *it's* gonna be happening soon!'

He pushes his glasses up and begins replying to Lolly's ramblings.

Seeing him this excited for my friends definitely confirms it. I feel my heart flutter so hard it might burst out my ribcage.

I do love him.

Chapter Twenty-One

Wren

My butterflies have not disappeared come the following Saturday.

Dad leaves early in the morning, after triple-checking that everything is okay with us. I assure him we will be fine, and that I will give him, Mum, or one of their mates a shout if I need anything. There is a week until the next full moon.

I walk into the living room, doing my makeup in the big mirror. It has better light.

Conan sits in the kitchen eating his cornflakes.

'Is Oscar coming over?' Phelan asks, looking up from his Switch.

'Yeah, probably,' I say, not looking away from the mirror as I blend my eyeshadow.

'Are you gonna be upstairs all day?' he moans.

'No. Oscar isn't like that.' I think Phelan remembers more about me and Tyler than I'd like.

'I think I like him,' he says, looking deliberately back at his Switch. 'I've not decided yet. But I think I do.'

I smile, putting down my phone. It's pretty obvious they

both get on quite well. Oscar likes playing games with the boys when he's over sometimes, and Phelan always asks for a run down on how he is and how it's going after I get back from his.

'Why?'

'He doesn't get annoyed at me and Conan.' He shrugs. 'And he doesn't treat you like a booty call.'

'Phelan!' I throw a pillow at him.

'Am I wrong?' he laughs, blocking it and sending it to the floor.

His phone suddenly lets out a loud vibration. He looks at it, biting the inside of his cheek.

'How's Harley?'

He picks at the chipped black nail varnish on his nails. 'He's fine,' he eventually says.

'Did you talk to him yet?' I ask, giving him a smile.

'None of your business,' he retorts.

That makes me laugh. He can ask me questions, but apparently I can't check in on him.

Oscar appears a couple hours later with ingredients for baking.

Conan clings to him the second he's through the door. Phelan's like a spectre haunting the kitchen, unwilling to leave but not interacting with anyone.

While the cakes are in the oven we go through to the living room to watch a movie. I pile blankets on top of Conan then take one over to lay with Oscar.

I rest my head in his lap.

'Don't fall asleep!' He warns me the movie is too good to sleep through.

I promise him I won't. But part of me wants to see if I could. Falling asleep when he's also asleep and someone is actively watching us is one thing. Falling asleep on him would be much scarier. I shut my eyes.

I wake up to the sound of Conan's frantic giggles.

'Oh no! You got me!' Oscar groans dramatically from the garden.

I find him collapsed in a heap on the path outside. Phelan is laughing. His smile is so wide it splits his face. Luna frantically checks if Oscar is okay.

He scratches behind her ears and then beams up at me. 'Cakes are cooling. Conan wanted to have a NERF fight.'

'I fell asleep on you,' I say, somewhat shocked.

'You did.' He sits up, smiling.

'He tucked you in and paused the movie,' Phelan offers, before running away from Conan with a high-pitched squeal.

'That's so embarrassing, I'm sorry.'

Oscar holds up his hands. 'It's nothing.' But he is grinning.

'Yeah, don't worry Wren, you weren't snoring like you usually do.'

I flush and put my hand out for Oscar's NERF gun.

After I pelt Phelan with bullets we go inside to ice the cakes.

'Is Oscar staying for a sleepover?' Conan asks, getting more icing on his arms than on the cakes.

I glance at him out of the corner of my eye. My heart flutters. 'Yeah, he is.'

We play Mario Kart with the boys all night until Conan gets a bit too tired and starts to tear up. He demands Oscar read him a story before bed. Oscar agrees to be dragged off for story time, claiming that he can do all the best character voices.

'I might go to bed too,' Phelan offers when they leave. 'I don't want to be in the way.'

'You're not!' I promise him despite wanting a little alone time with Oscar before the morning.

'Okay.' He smiles. 'But I *am* tired, so unless you *want* me to stay up.'

'No, that's fine.'

He says goodnight and heads up shortly after Oscar comes back down.

'Should we go up to bed?' I ask.

He taps his finger on the arm of the couch, deliberately avoiding eye-contact in a way I'm beginning to find endearing. 'Do you want me to go upstairs with you?'

'Upstairs is fine with me.' I smile at him.

My heart is beating hard. I've not slept next to a boy since – It means a lot that I can trust him like that. He's amazing, and I kind of want to kiss his stupid face.

For a while I just lay on his chest listening to his heart beating, feeling it rise and fall. I nestle myself into the crook of his neck and place a slow and gentle kiss behind his ear.

His breath hitches. 'Sorry,' he whispers. 'Just a big fan of neck kisses.'

'Oh yeah?' I smirk.

'Yeah,' he whispers.

Then I kiss him harder. My – thankfully still human – teeth scrape against his skin.

'Wren,' he gasps. I can see his pupils are dilated even though his eyes stray between me and the ceiling. He grabs me but tilts his head back, making it easy for me to gain access.

When I pull away there is a red mark on his neck.

'Get up here.' He gestures with his head, asking for me to kiss him.

He kisses me in a way that's new. It's more needy in the way he holds me. At first, his hand is urgent around my face, then we pull apart again for a moment. He looks up at me, panting gently. His lips are swollen from how much we've kissed, and his hair is tousled.

I reach a hand up to twist a strand around my fingers. He

grins at me, bumping his nose affectionately against mine before letting his own hand fall down to my hips to pull me closer, and then we're kissing again.

I realise more and more as we kiss that I'm not afraid of where this could go. The next time we pull apart for air I take the opportunity to climb into his lap.

We're not apart for a very long time at all, seconds really, just enough time for me to see how blown out his pupils are as I sit back down on my knees. It's that, and the soft little gasp that the action pulls from him that makes me realise I actively *want* this to go further even though I know it shouldn't right now.

I don't know when my top comes off, but when it does he kisses the side of my jaw, down my neck, my collarbones. Places he's never kissed before.

When we pull apart he is breathing hard, and I am as well. He grins. I smile. Then I lean my head on his shoulder and laugh, and he does too, a low and shaky laugh.

'You are,' he whispers into my hair, 'so extraordinarily beautiful. Has anyone ever told you that?'

No, I want to say, no they haven't. But I believe him.

His fingers trace down the side of my ribs gently, over the tattoos that sit there.

'I wondered if you'd notice them or my piercings first.' I sit up to look at him.

He looks down. It's too easy to make him flustered. He can't even see my piercings properly, it's not like I'm completely naked or anything. They're just noticeable through fabric sometimes.

I got them done to celebrate having been on estrogen for a year. It was also after I broke up with Tyler. I was in a bad bitch phase.

'I – I'm – not that I was – but I did – I didn't not notice,' he stammers in response.

'Babe—' I laugh. It's too funny not to laugh.

He huffs. 'Am I allowed to notice? Was I even supposed to be looking?' he rambles.

'Oscar? I wanted you to notice.'

I kiss him again. This appears to make things better, because he uncrosses his arms to pull me close again, his hands on either side of my hips.

Then we're kissing with a kind of intensity we've never had before.

Part of me wants to laugh. Like I can't take it seriously because that means acknowledging it, and that makes me nervous.

I nearly do when I notice one hand that was on my back is now resting on my ribs, as though he's subtly trying to work up to something. It's strange, though. I can't tell if it scares or excites me more. Things definitely feel like they're going further.

I can feel goosebumps forming where his skin touches mine. We kiss in a way that doesn't just involve our lips, but our entire bodies, all instruments working together in unison to create a song. I feel myself flush feeling his body move against mine. My stomach feels tight, and my leg twitches a little.

He bites my bottom lip. I feel a shiver run down my spine. I gasp softly and feel him smile against my lips. Bastard.

I know he knows what he's doing to me. It would be impossible for him not to know, especially when our bodies are pressed together this tightly. I didn't think I wanted more than this until we got here. Now we're here, I'd be open to talking about it.

Just as I'm starting to think that I definitely wouldn't be mad if this went further, he pulls back. His cheeks are flushed, and his lips are swollen. He rustles his hair, which is now very much messed up from my hands running through it.

'I –' He looks down, biting his lip. He straightens his glasses, which have been knocked squint.

'Need to slow down?' I whisper.

He looks up at me, grateful, and wrinkles his nose. 'Yeah, I'm sorry.'

I shake my head. 'Don't be. That's not why I invited you over.'

I hop out of his lap, and tuck myself into the covers next to him, resting my head on his chest.

'It's not that I don't want to,' he whispers into my hair, hiding his face behind thick braids. 'I just—'

'It's fine if you don't. You don't have to explain yourself.'

'No, I do,' he admits, lacing my fingers through his. 'I just feel like we should maybe, talk about things first, if you also want to.'

I nod, pulling one of my decorative pillows over to cuddle. 'I want to. I wasn't sure until now, but I think I want to. But we should definitely talk. I mean, it's your first time.'

He starts on sort of a spiel about how virginity is a social construct and he really doesn't care about making his first time special because no matter what it's bound to be awkward anyway.

But I want to make it special, and he says he'll let me try.

We talk about protection. Getting tested, other shit. It's an awkward conversation to have as a trans couple but I'm glad we're having it. He's on the pill already for trans shit but says something about needing to make sure he's taking it right for it to act as a contraceptive as well.

He also says he doesn't know how he feels about anything that would require that yet. Sometimes he thinks he wants to. Other times he thinks it would make him dysphoric. Other times he gets annoyed at himself for wanting to try it anyway.

We talk about what else would make him dysphoric, what would make me dysphoric, and what might trigger my trauma.

'You know,' he whispers as we lay together in silence, after saying everything we could possibly think to cover. 'The girls aren't home next weekend. If you wanted to plan it together and make it special. I'm working on Friday 'til seven but I could give you my keys and you could let yourself in if you wanted.'

I can hear my heart beating loudly in my chest. 'I'd like that,' I agree.

We don't go back to making out. It feels like it might get a bit too heated, and I do want to wait.

Besides, I'd really rather our first time didn't happen when I was supposed to be babysitting and stressing about being the responsible adult in the house.

Instead, we stay up all night, until we are beyond tired, laughing at absolutely ridiculous shit because we are so sleep-deprived. Oscar falls asleep eventually.

I stay up longer, sitting on the side of my bed that's pressed against the wall, window cracked open just a smidge. I can't sleep. But not because I'm scared of sleeping next to him.

It is because I'm going over every detail in my head. Every possible way to make next Friday perfect.

Eventually, I must've fallen asleep because, a few hours later, I wake up to voices in the garden.

Fuck. It's already eleven? How did I sleep in this late?

'Wren?' Dad calls, as he opens the kitchen door.

I look at Oscar, who is still asleep, in my bed, where I'm not allowed boys. Double fuck.

Coming!

I pat Oscar awake, he clumsily reaches for his glasses.

'My Dad is home!' I mouth, trying not to make any noise.

'Fiddlesticks!' he says too loudly. Dad definitely heard that.

'It's fine, it's fine, we can just say you came over this morning. Phelan will cover for me.'

He nods, then pushes himself up the bed.

It's then I see his neck. Oh, triple FUCK.

'Wren, could you come down here please?' I hear Magnus.

'Who?' Oscar mouths.

'Magnus. Dad's partner.'

Oscar's eyes widen. I've told him about Magnus, and martial arts training. He looks scared for his life.

'Now!' Dad sounds angry. 'You can bring Oscar down too.'

Oscar looks like he might actually start praying.

Mitch

I'm sitting on my windowsill with a cup of tea and a Virgina Woolf book when Oscar comes out of Wren's looking flushed.

'Hey!' I shout down.

He looks up, then behind him, before letting himself into my garden. I tell him to come upstairs.

I'm still sitting on the windowsill when he comes up. My bed's not been made. My laptop and headphones still sit on the edge from last night. I let myself fall back onto it when I hear him come in.

'What's up?' I look up at him, upside-down on my bed.

The first thing I notice is the mark on his neck.

And as I notice that, I hear Art and Wren shouting at each other from next door.

'No, Wren, I leave the house for *one* night and you try to turn your boyfriend.'

'I didn't try to turn him!'

'No? Then why does he look like he's been *mauled?*'

Phelan appears to find this hilarious. Magnus calmly

suggests that Art is perhaps more scared, or even protective than angry, which gets him snapped at too. Of course he is. I think anyone would be.

I start to laugh a little myself before I remember that Oscar can't actually hear this.

'Sleepover went well then?' I ask, turning over.

Oscar flushes before rushing over to my mirror. 'How bad is it?'

I lean back on my bed putting my arms behind my head watching for his reaction.

He groans. 'I have a shift at the ice cream shop tomorrow.'

'Thick woolly scarf is gonna be your only option,' I say, unhelpfully.

I feel like I should be giving Oscar some kind of speech about not hurting Wren, but he's my mate, so that would be impossible. Someone who would hurt Wren wouldn't be someone I'd want in my life forever.

I'm also just fucking proud of Wren for coming this far. I'm happy for her in a weird way.

'Take it her dad isn't happy.' Dad? Dads? Is Magnus Wren's stepdad, I guess?

He groans dramatically and puts his head in his hands, sitting on the edge of my bed. 'I wanted her parents to like me so bad.'

'So you decided to take the first opportunity you got when they were out of town to shag their daughter?'

'Can you not be so crass!' He hits me with a pillow. 'That's my girlfriend! We didn't, you know, have – sex.' He whispers the last word as if scared he might be overheard even though he doesn't know he could be. 'It was just about her being comfortable sleeping together – not like, sleeping together, but like—' He flushes.

I laugh at him, and he covers his face again.

His knees are pulled to his chest. He lets himself fall to the side so he's laying on my legs. 'I mean, it was close. We were making out, and – okay so… Can I ask your advice on something?'

I eye the wall, knowing fully well Wren's family could hear. 'Absolutely. Let's go for a run in the car.'

I decide to drive us to the nearest drive-through. I don't think Oscar cares where we're going because he's too busy panicking about seeing Wren's family on the way out.

I check my phone before heading off.

```
WREN & THE PACK

WREN
Like who the fuck gets grounded
at eighteen
```

The little writing next to the bubble tells me there are seventeen new messages in the group chat.

I snort. Then type out a reply.

```
                                    MITCH
            People who try to turn their
            boyfriends apparently
```

They reply almost instantly.

```
WREN
Fuck you, Mitchell.

LOLLY
No fuck Oscar.
When you're not grounded
anyway.
```

Don't love that Wren's picked up on Val's habit of calling me Mitchell when she's annoyed.

I look back to Oscar. 'Wren's grounded.'

'I'm gonna get killed. I'm actually going to be murdered.' He side-eyes their house.

Phelan is moving some long weapon cases into the shed with Magnus, who smiles and waves at us. I look up to

Wren's window. She's standing at it, flipping me off. I laugh and wave to her.

'Okay so,' I start, waiting until we have pulled out onto the main road to ask. 'What happened? What do you need advice on?'

'Right, okay.' He talks with his hands a lot, I notice. 'So, we had absolutely no intentions of like – ya know – last night.'

'Fucking?'

'Dude, that's so vulgar. Show a little respect.'

I roll my eyes. Damn, *this* is the guy her parents are worried about.

'Okay, so no intentions of taking *that* step. But we came pretty close, if you know what I mean.'

'Oscar, we both know *that* step can be so many different things. Especially for queer people. So coming close to that could also be fifty different things.'

'Okay…' He rolls his eyes all the way around in a circle. It's the most dramatic eye roll I've ever seen. 'Well, here's a hint. She gave me a love bite.'

'Got that part. Doesn't necessarily mean anything.'

'Okay, we were making out, she had her top off, there was some over clothes stuff. Is that what you wanna know?'

'That could definitely mean something.'

'Yeah, but then I stopped anything else happening. I kind of chickened out.'

'Okay, so do you not want to *make love* with her?' I wriggle my eyebrows as I say the last part.

Oscar hits my shoulder. 'Oh no, I want to have sex with her. That's what I need advice on. How do you do it?'

'Have sex? I dunno? You just do. Shit man, do ya want a demonstration?' I laugh, pulling the sun visor down.

He winks at me.

I grin. 'Seriously, I've only had sex with two people, and even then only Val has been allowed to do anything to me.

You're better off asking Lolly. But I can try to give you advice on what you wanna know.'

He looks at his hands and bites his lip. There is a moment of silence as I blend into the traffic lane. 'How do you like – let yourself do that? Like dysphoria wise?'

I think for a second. 'Do you have something in mind you wanna do with her?'

'I mean, yeah, but—'

'How do you think it would feel? How does thinking about it make you feel?'

'Amazing, excited, nervous, but like in a good way? But I'm worried I'll—'

'Are you worried it *would* make you dysphoric or that it *should*?'

He thinks about it for a second.

'No one can decide what should, or shouldn't make you dysphoric.'

He fiddles with the rips in his jeans. 'What if it *does*?'

'Then you can stop. And, babe… *talk* to Wren. She is literally also trans! She *gets* it.'

He laughs. 'I'm starting to understand why Lolly gets mad when you babe them.'

I raise an eyebrow.

'You only do it when you're calling someone out and know you're right.'

That's fair. I do that.

We pull into the drive-through before Oscar has realised what's going on.

'Have you eaten?' I ask as we pull into the queue.

He shakes his head. 'I don't really get hungry in the morning.'

'Oscar…' I look at my hands thinking about what I'm going to say.

While I don't buy into Radwa's theory, the not eating

thing is starting to make me slightly worried. How do you ask someone about that?

'I can never finish my chips, will you at least help me with that?'

He scratches the back of his neck and smiles. 'Sure, as long as I can get a small milkshake to dip them in.'

That's something at least. It's more than he was getting before, but—

'Fries in milkshake? You're such a weirdo.'

'Mitch, you wear socks to bed, so you'll forgive me for not taking your word on what constitutes weird. Besides, if you bully my food choices I *will* go on hunger strike so—'

I scoff, pulling the car forward in the drive-through. 'I mean, you don't really eat that much anyway.'

He shrugs.

He looks down thoughtfully, as if mustering up the urge to say something.

Then he does. 'That's because I'm in recovery.'

I turn to look at him, feeling my heart drop, even though I knew there must be something more going on there. 'Shit. I didn't know you were ill, sorry.'

'It's fine, it's nothing serious.' He waves me away. 'It's just – well – you know how I said I tried to fit into a really strict box after coming out?'

I nod, unable to avoid scanning him with my eyes, looking for some small indication that he's anything but fine.

'Well, turns out it's a bit of a tight fit for a guy like me. And there were only so many things I was able to control and so between that and gymnastics and – I kind-of-used-to have an eating disorder,' he says, far too quickly, scratching the back of his neck.

The words feel as though they suck all the breath from my lungs. That sounds pretty fucking serious. Those things can fucking kill you. And while I'm not an expert, I always thought eating disorders were kind of like self harm or addiction in that even if you stop the behaviour, the urge remains and so you're always in recovery.

I would say this but Oscar doesn't leave any room for questions. Instead, he starts assuring me that he's absolutely fine now because he eats three meals a day but just struggles a little with eating out, or takeaways, or snacking.

'It actually left me with the weirdest taste in snacks,' he quips. His laugh feels almost inappropriate, like the kind Lolly often has when they talk about their mum.

The odd thing is, it has a funny way of bringing conversations back to normal. 'That explains getting high and craving rice cakes,' I tease.

His face pulls into a small smile and even though a moment passes where neither of us are sure what to say I know everything between us is okay.

'Does Wren know?' I eventually ask.

He shakes his head. 'No. I'm trying to figure out how to tell her, so don't say anything, please.'

I raise my eyebrows. Wow. Okay then. Does that mean I'm the first one of us he told? Before he even told his girlfriend. I know we're *mates* and all but the idea creates a little lump in my throat. Worry – but it's more than that.

The air smells clean, like the whitening powder mum uses on my Tang Soo Do suit. Honour. I feel honoured.

'You definitely should do that if you're planning on getting any degree of naked with her,' I tell him with some concern, before I roll down the window to tell the worker our order.

He laughs, bringing his chest down to his knees and letting his forehead hit the dashboard with a dull thud. 'I really should.'

Val

> VAL
> I don't really know. Dad loves
> Mitch an embarrassing amount. He
> actually asks when he's staying
> over next.

Wren is still texting into our group chat about her sleepover with Oscar. Radwa has stopped looking at it and is playing games with Lolly in the living room across from me. Lolly keeps looking occasionally and butting in.

> LOLLY
> He literally calls him a bobo
> every single time he sees him

I laugh. He does that. It's sort of endearing though. If Dad doesn't give people nicknames, he just doesn't like them.

Lolly puts their phone down and goes back to their game.

Wren then decides to message me privately so we don't spam the rest of the pack.

> WREN
> So I'm sitting there, in his
> lap. In that black and purple
> bra, you know the one?

She sends a picture where she's wearing it under a tank top and the design is peeking out under her arm.

Oh, I know the one.

> WREN
> And I know I'm hot as shit, he
> knows it too, so his hands are
> like everywhere
> Like we're not having sex but
> we're pretty fucking close
> right?

```
And

Just when I think I can't be
dying anymore.

He stops to talk about things
going further and boundaries and
stuff.

Which omg I think I might love
this man.

But anyway

We talked about it, and we
decided we wanted to you know

Try taking things up a level

He even invited me to stay at
his next week

And now I'm grounded

Are you f u c k i n g
kidding me?

Jajsjsjswjwjsnajajshwjaajsn

We need to get me ungrounded by
next Friday. I need a game plan!
```

I can't help but smile when I read it. They're ridiculous.

But I also can't help but feel a sinking feeling in my stomach.

That's strange. That's new.

I look back at the picture she sent. She is holding iced coffee and her car keys in one hand, and the other is pushing up her sunglasses.

I remember this day. She was laughing at something Mitch had said. She looks so fucking gorgeous, as though her smile is the very thing that makes the sun shine.

I think about what he said about me liking her, and then I shake it away. I'm probably just nervous for her. Yeah. That's it.

Especially with all the theories Radwa's been coming up with. Even if they have no grounding, I just can't stop picturing Wren being hurt, thrown to the ground and crumpling like silk then— I shudder, tapping my shoulders in an effort to protect her from what I'm nearly certain is an insane conspiracy anyway.

Radwa's voice breaks my train of thought. 'Val can vouch for me! That thing was angry! It was black and blue!' she howls.

'What was?' I shake myself, looking up after typing a generic reply to Wren.

'My bruise! Lolly doesn't believe that that changes on estrogen.'

I nod. 'No, this thing was fucking massive.' I hold my hands up indicating the size.

'And you got it playing Mario Kart with Val and Mateo?'

'Things got intense.'

'She threw herself on the floor because she lost,' I tell them.

Radwa does about the same thing now, covering her face with a pillow and giggling. Lolly has a fond smile on their face.

I'm glad they've at least addressed what's going on. They seem so much more at ease around each other now.

Radwa

Lolly shakes their head at me. 'You're so competitive.'

Then they check their phone to reply to Wren.

'She's desperate to get ungrounded before Friday because she and Oscar have...' Val wiggles her eyebrows, '...plans.'

My heart drops to my stomach for a second. I still feel uneasy about the fact Wren knows nothing of my suspicions regarding Oscar. Especially if they're going to take their relationship further.

I know that my friends generally don't have the same hang ups about sex as I do, but after speaking to Wren about everything she went through, I hate to think of her having her trust violated like that again.

Nothing that I have managed to find on Emma's socials proves my theory definitively, either. It looks like Oscar and Emma were friends online, and both of them have periods where they just disappeared from social media for months. But Val said that doesn't mean anything, because any comments or messages are vague and at least friendly.

Lolly pulls a comical face. 'They need to calm down. I'm sure they can keep it together for a couple weeks.' They shrug. 'Like yeah, sex is nice, but settle the fuck down.'

'Nice!' Val howls. 'If I ever called it "nice" I think Mitch would cry.'

Lolly nods in agreement, putting a square of chocolate in their mouth. 'You'd bruise his fragile male ego,' they say with their mouth full.

I know I have no right to be annoyed right now, but the reminder Lolly has had that in a relationship kind of stings. This is exactly why I'm not sure we should start dating before they go to uni.

'Maybe their dad will loosen up if they get a good result tomorrow,' Lolly suggests.

Ew, another reminder. Our exam results come out tomorrow. Luckily for me, it doesn't determine whether or not I get in. I have another year left to mess up, but the outcome of this will definitely affect me and Lolly's conversation, and I can't promise I won't cry.

'You still coming over once you get yours?' I ask them.

'Of course!' they reply with a smile.

Their results also don't really matter this year either. They have an unconditional offer for Heriot-Watt, meaning they get in based on their grades last year alone. They give me a cheeky wink, and a thumbs up.

'You'll be fine,' they promise, and I try to internalise it.

Wren

Phelan and I sit in my room. He's still getting a kick out of this entire situation.

'Shut the fuck up.' I push him with my foot.

He holds his hands up. 'I would have defended you if you just said he came over this morning.'

Urgh. I roll my eyes and slam my head back into my pillow.

I can hear Magnus and Dad talking in their room.

'Darling, I'm not saying I don't understand your frustration, but I think you're taking it out on the wrong person. We *like* Oscar. Wren *likes* Oscar. And they were fine, they were just fooling around. Can you really say we never did anything like that?'

Ew.

Oh my God ew. Sometimes enhanced hearing is a fucking *curse*.

Magnus walks across their room and sits down on the bed next to Dad.

'She's my baby, Mags,' Dad says. 'And I couldn't protect her.'

Magnus sighs. 'We can't wrap her in bubble wrap forever, Arty.'

Dad tuts, then I hear him curse under his breath and Magnus walks over to their door and shuts it. The walls of their room are soundproofed for privacy. It's trickier with wolves but there's something about having silver in the lining that makes it work. I dunno.

What I do know is that their voices become inaudible when the door shuts.

I pick at my nail beds.

Eventually, the door opens, and Magnus comes out and knocks on my door frame, even though *my* door is sitting open.

'Hey, kiddo, could you come in here for a minute?' He nods towards Dad's room.

I stand up. When I walk in, Dad is sitting on his bed, looking at his hands as if he's the one that's in trouble. Magnus shuts the door behind us, telling me he just didn't want my brothers eavesdropping.

When Dad looks up, his eyes seem slightly red. It reminds me of when I first told him about Tyler. I could tell he was holding his breath when he cuddled me, then he came into his room, and when I saw him next his eyes were red like this.

He's a big crier, my dad. He does it when he gets frustrated more than anything. I once saw him get teary-eyed at a self-service checkout for pestering him to take his bags the first year we moved here.

Magnus was back home, and Mum and Ailsa had been sent out on a mission together for the first time since the war. He was worried about them, and about me, and about Phelan because he wasn't doing very well with anything when we first moved, and all of that came out in the middle of a Morrisons shopping trip.

I sit down next to him. 'I'm sorry,' I say as I do. 'I should've asked. I just knew you'd say no, and I don't think it's fair that Phelan can have Harley stay over but I can't have Oscar. I'm two and a half years older. But I should've told you that.'

Dad nods. 'I'm sorry too, kiddo. I'm sorry if...' He pauses, correcting himself. 'No, I'm sorry *that* I embarrassed you in front of Oscar. Magnus is right, he *is* a nice boy, and I like him a lot. And, with how you and he are, knowing there's a chance you're mates, I know you're gonna want to have your alone time with him.' He puts a hand on my knee and gives it a squeeze. 'I just ask you to be honest with me.'

I look up at him. 'Thanks Dad.' Then I pause. 'So, am I ungrounded?'

He looks at Magnus, then back to me, and nods, lips pulling into a tight but gentle smile.

I bite my lip, then decide to push my luck. 'So, on the basis of being honest with you... Oscar did ask if I wanted to stay over next weekend?' I pause, deciding not to tell him Kat will be out. 'At his flat?'

He inhales sharply, then looks up at Magnus. Magnus tilts his head to the side.

Dad looks back at me. 'Let us have a think about it.' Then he pats the bed and stands up. 'And let's see how things are looking tomorrow.'

I groan, putting my head in my hands. Dad rolls his eyes and walks away.

Magnus gives my shoulder a squeeze.

'Thank you,' I mouth to him, and he gives me a wink.

Chapter Twenty-Two

Mitch

I hear the post come early the next morning. A thick envelope hits the floor with a thud. Lolly and I are in the kitchen when it comes. I'm making tea and just pouring the milk in when the letterbox clatters.

Lolly walks over to go and get it, and then the door knocks and I hear them signing for a parcel, too. They come back with their results letter and a package addressed to me.

I put their cup down on the worktop so quickly that half the tea sloshes over the sides. I grab it from them, digging my nails into the cardboard and ripping it apart, not even bothering with scissors.

'Is that what I think it is?' they ask, lifting their tea up from the counter. Their hand gets wet so they shake it out.

A red ring box falls out of the packaging. I pick it up and open it.

Val is going to love this.

I turn it to show Lolly.

They beam. 'She's gonna cry, and so are Radwa and Mateo.'

I grin. Then I close my hand tight around the box. Imagining the look on Val's face when I propose, how her happy tears will feel against my cheeks when I kiss her. The picture makes my face flush as I turn to go up the stairs.

'Mum!' I shout, taking two steps at a time. 'Mum, look what came!'

Mum does cry when she sees it, placing her hand on her heart. 'I love it,' she says, then places both hands on my cheeks and kisses my forehead. 'When did you two get so grown up?' she asks, tearily.

Then she ruffles my hair and glances briefly at a picture of me and Mel hanging in the hallway as if to check she's seeing this. I can't help but wish she was.

Lolly

When Mitch comes down the stairs, I'm getting my shoes on. 'Could you give me a lift to Radwa's so we can open our letters together?'

Mitch nods, not looking up from his phone.

I lean over his shoulder to look at what he's staring so intently at.

He's looking at the menu page of a beauty salon, specifically the nails section. 'Do you know which ones of these varnishes are halal?'

Radwa can only use certain nail varnish because of how her *wudhu* works.

I shrug. 'I can find out if you give me a couple hours. Why?'

'Gonna get Val a nail appointment before I ask her so they're nice for the pictures, and I figured it would be nice to treat her and Radwa to a girls day.'

'Aw.' I shove into him affectionately. He is too sweet. 'I will find out if you give me a lift now,' I whine. 'The anticipation is killing me!'

Radwa

'I can't do it.' I'm pacing up and down when Lolly and Mitch arrive.

Val gives my shoulder a squeeze. 'Yes, you can. Just look on the count of three, ready?' She counts to three.

I push the envelope into her. 'I can't do it.'

Mitch sighs, putting his head in his hands. 'Radwa, we are all on the edge of our seats here. Come on.'

I sigh, doing an awkward sort of bouncing dance, looking like I need a wee.

Lolly holds their envelope up. Val passes mine back.

Ready? Lolly asks.

I nod.

Three, Lolly says.

Two, I reply.

One. I slide the papers out.

Wren

'An A in PE,' I read aloud to my parents.

Mum and Ailsa are calling us from their base camp. Magnus sits on the counter, arms around my Dad who stands between his legs.

'A in biology. B in French. B in Maths. B in Politics. C in English,' I finish.

Mum winks at me. 'That's my girl.'

Dad gives me a proud smile and comes over to give my shoulders a squeeze.

'So proud of you, kiddo,' he tells me.

Even Phelan congratulates me, and I do the same to him. He sat his first set of exams this year. He got ABCCCD but doesn't seem to care too much. The only thing he was determined to pass was Biology, which he got his A in.

I see the pack start to message their grades into our group

chat we have with Oscar. He got straight As. I tell my parents this and they look rather impressed. Lolly also got straight As and sent in a picture of Radwa smiling and holding her certificate. The chat is flowing rapidly.

> LOLLY
> She got AAABB and was acting like she failed at everything.
>
> RADWA
> Well I did fail maths … again … and the As are in art, Bengali and English sooo……
>
> LOLLY
> Who cares about maths?
>
> RADWA
> Does that mean you still owe me hot chocolate and video games for passing everything else? :3
>
> OSCAR
> Aren't you literally going to Edinburgh to do a maths degree?????
>
> LOLLY
> Well I did offer to help
>
> RADWA
> No you offered to cheat

I click back on Facetime with Mum and Ailsa.

'While everyone's here, what are your thoughts on me staying at Oscar's this weekend?'

Magnus gives Dad a look.

Dad sighs, then nods. 'Okay, kiddo, if you're sure you're ready.'

When Friday rolls around I am undeniably nervous.

I spend about three and a half excruciatingly embarrassing hours applying, removing, and reapplying my makeup after smudging it while crying because I managed to rip a tiny hole in the new underwear I bought for tonight. All the while keenly aware that my entire family are probably very able to guess exactly why I am so nervous considering this is the first time I've asked to stay at Oscar's.

After I finally finish my makeup – with four squirts of perfume, one on each wrist and behind each ear – I grab my phone to let him know that I'm coming for the keys.

There is an unread message sitting waiting for me from Radwa.

```
RADWA
Hey … Can we talk??
```

Wrinkles form in my forehead that look ridiculous when I catch them in the mirror.

```
                                          WREN
            Sure. I'm just about to be
            driving but I'll call you if you
            need me. Or just like reach out
            however.
```

I send the message and then pick up a kirby grip to pin my front two braids off of my face.

No sooner have I sent it than she is in my head.

You're not driving yet, are you? she asks, holding back whatever it is she wants to show me.

She must realise I'm not when the smell of setting spray starts to choke her because she continues.

I promised Val I wouldn't say anything, and I know it's probably nothing because he's Mitch's mate and all but—

I stop dead in my tracks as I'm cleaning up my stuff.

It's about Oscar, she continues, as if Mitch has any other male mates.

Then she goes on, and on, showing me all the 'evidence' she has gathered and I wish she fucking wouldn't because – aside from the fact that I know that there is no way in Hell she's right – it's actually pretty insulting.

First off, the idea that she thinks I'm so naïve and stupid that I would let something that major pass right under my nose with anyone is a slap in the face.

But more than that, the implication that the only reason someone would be interested in me is to get closer to the pack really fucking stings.

And the thing is, I'm used to people acting like even just hanging around me is an act of fucking charity, that anyone who dates me is a fucking martyr – my old friends in school did that well enough – but out of everyone I'd expect more from her.

She must hear this because she stops carefully. *Wren – I'm sorry but I – I didn't mean it like that I just—* she starts again, tentatively.

I shake my head, letting out an audible scoff which earns me a confused look from Phelan who is walking past with his morning coffee.

Forget it. My voice has more bite in my mind than even I'm expecting. *By the way, it's definitely not fucking him.*

And then I push her hard from my mind as if slamming a door.

By this point, Oscar has messaged me back to let me know he'll be up front when I arrive, so I dash downstairs for my bag, and after securing it on my bike, swing my leg over and kick the rest stop up, trying to shake off any additional unnecessary worries Radwa's words have to brought life.

I mean, I'm sure I've seen him eat. On our first date, we went to that ice cream shop.

Only, I don't actually remember him finishing it, or him eating at all. By the end of our date, it did look less full... but ice-cream melts right so what if...? And, I mean, he has been really interested in me and my friends and… But then, I am a pretty interesting person! I do all sorts of cool shit, why wouldn't he find that interesting?

My thoughts are still battling back and forth when I reach Oscar's flat.

And though I try to busy myself with making food, and tidying up so we can have a cute night – and just in case it does help me find any incriminating evidence – by the time Oscar gets home, my anxieties have bled through into my every action.

I burn my hand lighting the candles on the table. I drop half the food I made on the floor. I'm on my knees cleaning up when he comes in.

'Hey, darling.' He pauses, seeing me on the floor. 'What happened?'

As soon as I look at him I start crying. I can't help it, I just let out a sob. 'I tried to – candles – burnt finger – dinner – made mess – new underwear for tonight – tag – ripped – I—'

'Shh shh shh shh shh,' he soothes me, grabbing a glass of water, and bringing it down to my level. 'Here, drink this.'

I swallow most of the glass, my lungs burning with each deep gulp.

He sits down next to me, pulling the oven tray down with him and sitting it on a towel between us. The cheese on top was supposed to be crispy but that thing looks fucking charred. I put my head in my hands.

'I told you!' I whine. 'Tonight was supposed to be perfect and I ruined everything.'

'You didn't ruin everything.' He smiles softly and presses a kiss to my head. 'But I do think maybe we should leave tonight. I know I said virginity is a social construct, but I don't want to lose mine the same night that my girlfriend has been crying on the kitchen floor panicking over it.' He brushes my hair out of my face. 'That feels uncouth.'

'But Kat's away tonight,' I hiccup.

'Wren, I have known Kat for many years. If I have to tell her to piss off so I can have sex, I will.' He chuckles. 'Besides, she's not home 'til Sunday, and she has training like five times a week.'

'I'm sorry I spoiled everything. I just wanted to make it perfect.' I wipe my tears on my pinkies.

'I think that's the problem.' He smiles tightly.

I must pout without realising it.

Because he continues, 'Wren, it's never going to be perfect.' He laughs nervously, scratching the back of his neck. 'It's awkward, it's clunky and *I* don't know what I'm doing. But how much less stressed out did you feel earlier this week, when we were just making out in your bed? Things very easily could've gone further there. You said so yourself.'

I nod. They could've. They easily could've. But I wanted to plan it. I wanted to be in control.

Oscar can tell that, and I think what he's telling me is that, no matter what, neither of us will ever have total control of the situation. How's he the one teaching me about this?

'Trust me,' he grins. 'I *know* how scary letting go of total control can be, but I actually feel so much more in control when I'm not following a million rules I've created for myself.'

Then he turns around to grab a fork from the drawer behind him.

He stabs it into what's left of the blackened mess of lasagna.

'You're not going to—' I start, right as he takes a large mouthful which crunches as he chews.

God, the first time he's actually properly eaten in front of me and it's that atrocity. Disproves Radwa's theory, mind you, but I still don't understand what it is with him and food.

I cringe internally as he reaches for the glass of water that I hadn't quite finished and swallows hard.

'Well,' he starts, eyes watering slightly, 'it's definitely cooked all the way through.'

I scoff, giving his shoulder a gentle push.

He holds his hands up defensively but continues to grin at me. 'How about I clean up in here while you go and get yourself cleaned up and into pjs?' he asks, pointing down to my clothes which are clearly very stained with tomato sauce. 'Then we could order something in?'

I nod, letting him pull me to my feet and give me a quick kiss before I head through to the bathroom. I try not to wince as I hear him chip away at the charcoaled block of food with a spatula.

On my way back, I hear the kettle boiling. I feel my smile growing as I toss my clothes into my bag in his room and pick up his throw from his bed to wrap it around my shoulders. I'm about to join him in the kitchen when I notice the pile of blankets in the corner and am struck with a silly idea.

Oscar seems to find it profoundly funny when he eventually comes through to the living room. 'Did you make a blanket fort?' he asks, ducking under the cover to join me.

I nod rapidly, beam splitting my face. 'It's stupid I guess, but like I noticed that takeaways and that seem to make you kind of anxious, and I don't know if it's a money thing because you're dealing with that alone now, or if it's a food thing, but I know that when you're overwhelmed you like the dark and soft things and art – I got your sketchbook – so I figured that we could just chill – unless you want to talk about it we can do that too but—' I start, rapidly over-explaining myself.

But there doesn't seem to be a need, because he reaches forward to kiss me hard in a way that catches me off guard. It's not necessarily sexual, more... euphoric... like the joy of being seen by someone who loves you. I can feel his teeth scrape mine when he does it because we're both smiling.

Then he sits next to me. 'Thank you. I mean we *should* talk about it – but you've made it a lot easier for me, and that means a lot.'

I pull back from him to give him space to continue.

Then, he starts to explain.

Talking is really good for some things, like this. But others take less planning and more letting the moment take you.

Now that I'm finally able to calm down, I actually feel sort of bad for how I spoke to Radwa earlier. So, while we wait for food, and Oscar sits sketching, I pull out my phone to give her a message.

> WREN
> Sorry about earlier… If it makes you feel better I checked in with Oscar and I can't explain why because it's a personal thing but I promise there is nothing to worry about there.

I press send and pop my phone back down on the side, curling my legs underneath myself and settling back down to watch *Doctor Who*.

Oscar gives me a soft smile as I glance over at him, sweeping his hair from his face with his left hand. The smudge of oil pastels just under his pinky makes my heart flutter gently in my ribcage.

It's on Sunday, just before Kat's due home, that *it* finally happens.

We lie in Oscar's messy unmade bed, watching Netflix together.

His room always smells like oil paint and coffee.

'I wish I could name the stars,' I say, looking up at his skylight.

'I can.' He smiles and takes my hand, pointing to a constellation and tracing my finger down it. 'That's the dipper.'

'Did your fancy private school teach you that?' I ask.

He grins. I take my hand that was tracing the stars and follow similar patterns in the freckles that line his cheeks. He turns his head to kiss my palm.

I tilt my chin up towards him and then he reaches down to kiss me. I'm not sure which of us first turned the kiss into a deeper one but that's what it becomes. Oscar kisses me like my kisses are his only source of oxygen. It's something he needs to do to survive. I kiss him back with the same urgency.

Our bodies fall into a dance together. I want this. I need this. After a while, his hand comes to the waistband of my jeans.

'Yes,' I gasp before he can even ask.

He smiles underneath our kiss. Untying a button with one hand is always hard the first few times. I find myself laughing as he pulls away from the kiss to undo it. I move his hand out of the way and practically pull the button off getting them open.

He laughs, then he catches my eye. Holding my gaze, he looks up at me. Eyes wide. 'Can I touch you?' Desperation. Curiosity. Eagerness. His voice drips with all of it.

'Please,' is my reply.

I feel the gentle drag of his fingertips running down my hips, almost where I want him. Then he's there.

I guide his hand. Then I curse myself. He's a very quick learner. I pat his leg gently. He pulls back.

'I wanna help you out too,' I pant. My voice sounds absolutely ragged and I'm slightly embarrassed by it.

He doesn't seem to care. His eyes go wide and he nods quickly. 'I'd like that.'

He awkwardly wiggles and shifts into a better position, kicking the cover out of our way as we do. He laughs at me trying to free my leg from it.

Then I slide my hand under the waistband of his boxers. I run my fingers gently down the skin on his thigh, then catch his eye, wanting to check with him again before I actually do what I'm about to do. 'You sure this is okay?'

He nods quickly once more. 'Very sure.'

A flush creeps among his freckles when I finally touch him. He gasps and grabs my arm at the wrist.

'Want me to stop?' I ask.

'Fuck no.' He grins.

'Are you sure you're okay?' I ask, looking down at where his hand still holds my wrist in a vice-like grip.

He flushes again, letting go. 'Sorry, I was just shocked that it felt so *different*.'

'Good different?' I ask.

He nods, chasing my lips, trying to kiss me again. I start moving my hand again. He groans softly into my mouth. His free hand grips at my thigh.

I swear at that moment I would give this man anything he wanted from me as long as I could make him do that again. I press my lips to his gently, muffling the noises he makes slightly. We find a way to fall in time and move together.

His name leaves my lips in the form of a sigh.

I believe that everyone who's picked out a name for themselves, fashioned it from scratch, deserves to hear it moaned over and over again like a prayer. If they so desire.

Oscar is half awake as we cuddle together later. He clings to my back in a way that suggests to me that his first time meant more to him than he was willing to let on. I'm the little spoon, even though he is much shorter than I am.

He lifts his arm from underneath me quickly. I whine at the loss.

'I may not know a lot but I know I was supposed to go pee. I need to go pee and shower.'

I laugh at his urgency. It is still an hour till his housemates get home.

Maybe we have time to have a bath together. I suggest this to him.

'I need to take my binder off. My ribs kinda hurt.' He sighs, closing his eyes.

'Why didn't you say something?' I ask, turning over on my side to run my hand up and down his back.

'I didn't want to kill the mood!' He taps his fingers on the side of his neck.

'It wouldn't have,' I promise him, sitting up and pressing a kiss to his shoulder.

'It might have for me.' He grimaces.

That's fair. I wouldn't want to have tainted his memory of today. The way our bodies fit together like a jigsaw, the way we held each other, understood each other, with no judgement, just pure unadulterated love.

'So, that's a no on the bath together?' I ask, letting my hand fall down his back again.

'Not necessarily.' He smiles. 'Wren you were just—' He gestures to his bed, blinking.

I feel the warmth in my face reach my ears. 'I know what I was doing.'

'If you can see me like that, I think you can see me shirtless.' He shrugs. 'We could just make it extra bubbly.'

I agree gladly, with a smile.

He swings his legs around so he can get up. 'Fuck my abs,' he laughs. Then he tries to stand. 'Fuck my legs.'

He wobbles and I catch his arm. We look at each other and laugh hard.

When we eventually make it through to the bathroom, Oscar stands in front of the mirror staring at his reflection.

I come up behind him and kiss his neck.

'It's not changed just because we—'

'I know that!' He flushes again.

Then he looks over the little hickeys I left on his neck, his collarbones. There are some scattered on his soft stomach and the inside of his thighs that I'm sure he'll find later and text me about.

He's already frustrated that none of the ones he tried to give me actually left marks. Suddenly I'm very thankful my bite would only turn him on the days surrounding the full moon, if I was shifted or half-shifted.

His bath is probably too small to have two people in it. Especially when one is five-foot-nine. We laugh as we awkwardly try to slot our bodies together. It's kind of like earlier, trying to figure out how we fit around each other.

Eventually, we figure out how we fit and settle under a blanket of bubbles.

We lay there together for a moment in silence and I think about what it is to be understood so deeply by someone.

I've had a lot of sex, but I feel as though I've made love for the first time.

Chapter Twenty-Three

Lolly

'You know,' I chuckle, as Charlie pulls gently on the black silk tie he's helping me secure around my neck, 'when you ask the girl you're sort-of-but-not-really-maybe *talking* to on a date, it doesn't usually result in a funeral.'

He shakes his head, trying very clearly not to laugh at my bluntness as he backs up to inspect his work.

The suit I borrowed from Mitch is slightly too big for me. The sleeves hang over my knuckles, and I keep tripping over the ends of the trousers.

'Your son is too tall,' I scoff, hiking the trousers up so I can go downstairs without breaking my neck.

'You'll be fine when you put some boots on,' he says, finally cracking a smile. 'You know, I think it's nice what you pair are doing. Shows support. It goes a long way.'

It's then I realise making a joke to Mitch's parents about a young girl dying is probably unadvised. *Fuck.* Still, his dad doesn't seem to hold it against me.

I feel kind of awkward around death. I haven't been to very many funerals, except my great uncle's when I was younger. I saw the body and refused to sleep alone for months. That was on Dad's side of the family, so the funeral and Mass lasted about an hour and forty overall. I just remember getting in trouble from Mam for fidgeting when the priest was talking.

Are you just not allowed to move in a funeral? It's not like I was being loud or bouncing up and down in my seat. You just can't expect a seven-year-old to sit with their head bowed for like an hour, with a dead fucking body right across the room.

After that I've managed to avoid funerals like the plague until now. Mam kinda stopped going herself, and my grandparents weren't really the type to force a freshly traumatised child to confront death.

In conclusion, I'm really *really* chill about knowing how to react to them.

Radwa roped me into this one.

As promised, after she passed *most of* her exams, I took her out to get hot chocolate and discounted old video games. It was supposed to be cute, having the chance to hang out on our own, both knowing we had *something* going on between us.

But, at the bus stop, she saw the funeral notification.

Emma's family are finally able to grieve.

Wren told us that, after carrying out their investigations and ensuring their lycanthropy wouldn't be outed, the medical centre reported the discovery of her body to a local hospital – claiming, of course, that they had only just found it. I guess the hospital finally released her body to her family not long ago.

Going to her funeral makes some kind of sense; the invitation was extended to her school friends and, while we weren't exactly friendly, we knew people in common and she *was* really nice.

Radwa wants to go because she thinks it'll help give some insight as to who the rogue is.

She asked all of us to come, but Mitch and Val have too much trauma with this kind of thing after Mel. And Wren says if she has to attend another funeral before she turns twenty she'll gouge her own eyes out.

So, the two of us walk together, me picking up my trousers with my hands like a noble lady in a period drama would do with her skirt, as Radwa goes over what we already know.

I just, she continues, *I was looking at her Facebook again, and I find it kind of weird that she disappeared for like a year, and then her first notification when she got back was Oscar sending her a friend request. And there's the not eating thing, the water thing, the sensory stuff, being at multiple drop-off locations. Like, I know Mitch and Wren say it's not him, but they're his mates so they're biased.* Her brow furrows as she concentrates, arms flying wide as she punctuates her points with hand gestures. *And they won't even tell me how they know—*

I shrug, clicking the fidget cube in my trouser pocket, hoping it's subtle enough a fidget that it won't be deemed rude later today. 'Maybe it's personal.'

Honestly, I've been kind of thinking about some of the points she's made about Oscar, and while he does look suspicious, he seems to have an explanation for almost everything. Like with the sensory stuff; he is autistic. Besides, if he was the rogue, how is it possible he could be mates with two of our lot? It doesn't add up to me.

She sighs, letting her arms fall. 'I guess. But I feel like if he really is the rogue he'll be there today. And if he just knows her casually, he probably won't, right?'

'I guess that makes sense,' I concede, unsure she's quite thought of every possibility but uncertain how to tell her I think she could just be wrong.

Radwa

The funeral seems quite personal. I think the priest giving the sermon might be the one from Mitch's church – Emma's uncle – because he has to pause a few times to regain his composure. It's odd from a man so used to talking in front of people.

Despite the nagging suspicion chewing at me as I look around the room, I can't help but get lost in it all. Hearing stories about Emma's life, mixed with her favourite passages from the Bible. Funerals have a morbid way of making you think about death.

It makes me wonder, if I died tomorrow, how would they bury me? Would anyone know my favourite passages from the Qur'an? Would the people who did know do me the honour of burying me under my own name?

My parents are still my legal guardians even though Mateo and Karen have done more for me these past few years. But I'm not sure that they or the pack would know how I'd want to be buried. Maybe they'd talk to Aadilla and her family.

The ideas swirling around my head distract me so much that I almost miss the two blond heads bobbing by in the crowd of mourners until Lolly jumps into my head to point it out.

Oscar did show his face after all, and he brought Kat with him.

Do you think they're going to the wake? I ask Lolly, as we head out together, each taking a moment to thank the priest.

I don't know, but we shouldn't. We got our intel. Let's leave it there and regroup, they insist, buttoning their suit jacket back up and pulling their trousers higher up their waist. *They only say those things are for everyone, but they don't expect anyone other than close friends and family to go.*

But we could get more information— I start.

From who? They cut me off, side-stepping to toss some

coins in the donation box, which displays the emblem for some charity that deals with eating disorders. *It's not like we can interrogate her grieving parents.*

Just then, we come to the church doors, and our conversation pauses momentarily as we each take a moment to greet the grieving family.

Standing with her parents is a girl I recognise, about our age, with a soft round face, contoured with a darker orangey colour.

'Lolly?' she asks, looking up from the floor in a sort of disbelief, her heavy mascara smudged a little around her false eyelashes.

'Hi Aims, you holding up okay?' Their voice sounds gentle as they speak, stepping to the side to make way for those behind them.

I hear her asking if we're going to the wake and trying to squeeze in a quick catch up before giving them a hug and taking her place in line again.

When they turn back to me I struggle to contain my smile until we've turned the corner out of sight.

What? they ask, defensively. *Look, I know I have a history but —*

I think your history has given us a lead, I say, grinning now despite myself.

Absolutely not. They shake their head. *You saw how broken up she was.*

And she asked you to come to the wake. I insist.

She didn't mean it — they start to counter.

But, if anyone knows who was mad at Emma, it would be...? I return.

Lolly thinks for a moment, eyeing me carefully as they chew the skin on the inside of their cheek. Then they sigh.

As we arrive at the restaurant the wake is being held at, Oscar notices us through the crowd. He waves us over to sit with him. Lolly nods to the side, gesturing for me to take him up on the offer while they go and find Aimee.

I take a seat at the booth he's claimed in the corner with Kat, grabbing a bottle of water off the table on my way over.

'No food left?' I ask as I sit down, trying to seem friendly enough that the accusation doesn't ring through the air as I gesture to the empty space in front of him.

Kat scoffs, rolling her eyes. Here I thought we were supposed to be on good terms with her.

'Not hungry,' Oscar says gruffly by means of an answer. 'Besides, couldn't find a bin for my gum.'

'There's one.' Kat points, folding her arms, looking slightly annoyed.

Maybe it's not me? Maybe it's Oscar she has a problem with today?

Oscar shrugs her off.

'Is this what she would want?' Kat asks, raising her eyebrows.

Oscar sucks his teeth. 'Jesus, tell everyone why don't you?' he scoffs defensively, before spitting his gum in a napkin and putting it in the bin closest to us.

'Don't ask about it,' Kat whispers gently to me in the moment we're alone together before Oscar returns, once again foodless.

'How did you guys know Emma?' I try to steer the conversation away from whatever touchy topic they're both set on.

'School, same as you.' Kat shrugs, taking a sip from the water she picked up for herself.

Then she looks at Oscar expectantly.

He looks back and sighs. 'We were in the same hospital for a bit,' he says, trying to play it off as something that's not that big a deal.

'I was curious, because I was looking for her Facebook the other day to see if anything had been posted about what happened and I noticed you guys became friends after she'd been offline for like a year—' I start.

'I didn't know Facebook told you that kind of thing.' Oscar chuckles. 'That's some FBI agent kind of skill you've got there.'

'So did the hospital not allow phones? Or...' I trail off, trying to sound nonchalant, but I can tell I've failed when I see how he is looking at me, slightly startled at being pressed for information.

Kat reaches across the table cautiously to get my attention. When I look at her she is shaking her head – asking me not to press any further.

What gives her the right to tell me what to do, anyway? She has no idea why I'm asking. Does she think I have to listen to her because she *used* to date Lolly?

'No,' Oscar recovers himself. 'No phones, or anything with a camera, and no social media.'

'What kind of hospital makes you—'

'I don't really think you have to know,' Kat cuts in, infuriatingly.

But I do have to know, because I need to know that this supposed alibi actually holds up and it's not just a cover for—

'Okay,' a voice says from beside me.

I look up to see Lolly giving me a rather pointed glare.

'I've caught up with Aimee so we can go,' they say, picking up my jacket for me.

Kat looks up at them, crinkling her nose as if *she's* the one who has some kind of private means of communicating with them.

'I'm still catching up with Kat and Oscar,' I tell them, opening my bottle to take a drink while I scoot across the booth to make space for them.

'I think maybe Kat and Oscar want to be alone right now?' they try, nodding towards the exit. *Come on, I'll fill you in on what I got from Aimee.*

I put my open bottle down on the table in front of me.

'Thanks, Lol.' Kat smiles, as if they've just spoken about how awkward it is that I'm here, without so much as uttering a word. 'It's *really* good to see you again.'

'Nice to see you too.' I do my best impression of a sarcastic smile as I stand to get up, only when I do I accidentally elbow the bottle in front of me sending it spilling over Oscar.

'Shoot,' he curses, standing up, momentarily losing so much composure I almost think he's about to confirm my suspicions.

He flexes his hands like the sensation is uncomfortable, but then it stops there.

That's until he stands up. His white shirt is slightly see-through with water, the half-tank binder exposing his stomach.

He crosses his arms over his torso. 'Kat, this is tight, do you have—'

Oh. It's not about— He's just—

Kat instantly takes off the jumper she's wearing on top of her black dress and hands it to him. 'Put it on under your blazer and no one will even notice it's a little cropped.'

I was wrong.

'Thank you, lifesaver.' He squeezes her hand tightly then takes it from her. 'Nice seeing you guys! – Well, considering…' He waves before dipping behind the wall separating the lounge from the men's toilets.

After bidding a quick good-bye to Kat, and giving her a friendly hug, Lolly steers me through the crowd quietly to avoid any further water-related catastrophes.

Aimee told me that Oscar and Emma went to the same hospital for a while when she was off school, they tell me as we walk through the hallway towards the exit. *They were close there.*

What were they in hospital for? I ask following them, pulling my coat back on.

Lolly pauses as we reach the exit, gesturing towards a

436

bright blue donation box sporting the emblem of a charity that supports those recovering from eating disorders.

I exhale slowly. It does little to lift the weight of guilt that forms in the pit of my stomach.

I definitely owe Oscar an apology before we see him for Phelan's birthday tomorrow. I can't believe how pushy and obnoxious I must've seemed to him.

And worse, I upset Wren for no good reason. And I didn't listen to her or Mitch when they told me it wasn't him because they wouldn't tell me how they knew that... But of course, they wouldn't have told me this.

Lolly even said it was probably something personal but I – I was so sure I was right.

I mean, I've probably written off a million other leads because I was so fixated, so sure that it was him.

And more people are going to die. There's going to be more families experiencing days like today and I might've been able to stop that if I didn't get so caught up in my own ideas.

My eyes sting as the air hits them, and my lip starts to wobble.

Radwa. Lolly stops in their tracks. *Are you crying?*

No. I shrug them off. *I mean yeah, maybe.*

They stop, gesturing for me to follow them into the heritage garden so we can talk under the shade of the trees. *What's up?*

I've just been acting like such a... I struggle to find the word I'm looking for. *I've been so rude to everyone, and all my research has came to nothing and today was...* I trail off.

A lot? they ask, leaning back against the wall.

I nod. *I'm sorry for how I've acted today, I must've embarrassed you in front of Kat and—*

Lolly shakes their head, reaching inside their jacket pocket to fidget with something. I can hear their fingers tapping and clicking for a minute or so before they respond.

What was going on with you there? they ask. *I know you wanted information from Oscar, but Kat seemed to really rile you up and she wasn't really doing anything,* they think, starting to sound slightly cautious as they do, as if they're carefully trying not to upset me.

I lean forward to look at them, eyes widening. *She was trying to get under my skin. She was acting just like those girls who bullied me in school,* I scoff. *And the whole 'it* was *really nice to see you again'.*

The words are out before I realise they are. I see Lolly fight against a small smile threatening to carve their dimple out of their cheek.

We haven't quite spoken about all of that yet. I've not really given myself time to process things like I said I would.

Radwa, if you're jealous of Kat— they start.

I'm not jealous of Kat— I retort defensively.

Jealousy isn't a bad thing, they try again. *Your feelings are usually just an indication of something that you want or need that you're neglecting. But if we're going to have that talk I need you to genuinely be okay with all of my history – including the parts that are more prone to resurfacing.*

I look down at my nails. *Yeah, okay. Maybe it was* also *me getting in my head a bit.* I nod.

They sigh, tugging a tissue out of their jacket pocket. *It's okay. It happens.*

Back to the drawing board, I guess, I sniffle, taking it from them.

When I get home, I pull up a new chat window on my phone.

There are no messages between me and Oscar yet, and this feels like a bit of an awkward starting point, but here goes.

> RADWA
> Hi, I just wanted to apologise for today. I didn't realise how obnoxious I was being til Lolly pointed it out. It's not an excuse but I'm not great at reading tone and sometimes I can seem ruder than I'm trying to be :/

It doesn't take long before he replies.

> OSCAR
> Hey Radwa! It's okay don't worry about it. I'm the same! I was in a bit of a mood anyway or I probably would've explained better :/ Sorry you guys had to see me like that

Wow, if that's his rude I'd love to see his reaction to what my storms were like.

> RADWA
> Not at all! Hope you're feeling better now :3 See you tomorrow for Phelan's birthday!!

I go to close my phone but notice another notification come in on the top of the screen.

> KAT MCALISTER HAS SENT YOU A FRIEND REQUEST.

Oh, so she really has *no* problem with me.

Maybe Lolly's right. Everything about Kat that seems to annoy me is something that she had in her relationship with them. Maybe still has to an extent.

She's never been anything but nice to me, but she's had something I haven't, something I know I want regardless of any history they might have, and something I need to be open and honest about wanting.

Val

We all end up at Wren's house a day before the full moon. Her parents are out with Phelan, picking Harley up from the train station.

Mitch and Radwa are putting up some banners together for him. Lolly, Oscar and Conan have baked a cake together, and me and Wren are currently blowing up balloons.

'Mitch, your side needs to be higher!' Wren shouts over to him as he's about to stick the banner to the wall. He pushes it up higher. They give him a thumbs up.

Oscar squeezes by their seat to grab some more icing from the fridge. He puts his arms around them on the way back and kisses the side of their head.

Their eyes follow him as he walks away.

So the weekend went well? I ask them.

They give a proud smirk. *Maybe.* I hear their heart beating fast..

I can't decide how to feel for them. Part of me is so excited and wants to know everything, and the other part wants to bolt.

I settle for asking for details. In an attempt to ignore the sinking feeling in my stomach, my hand comes up to pick at a spot underneath my chin until it bleeds.

It's only a little, not even enough to make Mitch's heart race. But, annoyingly, the blood seems to have stained the design I had done on my nails. Oh well, they needed to be redone anyway.

Mitch actually recently told me he wanted to treat me and Radwa to a nail appointment. He said it was to celebrate her exam results. He's a bad liar. I say this because he also has arranged for us to go out the next day, just the two of us, to celebrate my finishing college.

I think he's going to propose.

This is not only because he blocks me out all the time just now, and Radwa and Lolly keep doing it as well. He also keeps looking at me right now and grinning, and Lolly will shove him like he has some ridiculous crush on me that I don't know about.

The idea makes me massively giddy. Before we even started dating I remember Mel joking about it. She said something about not knowing what side she would have to stand on. I thought about it for like a fortnight obsessively before I was even able to admit I had a crush on him. The idea makes my heart race in my chest and my cheeks burn hot. I fiddle with the bottom bar of my piercing between my teeth.

Even if I do end up having another mate, or feelings develop for... other people, we've been through so much together. He's my life partner. I can't imagine a universe where my future doesn't directly involve him.

Lolly

Wren's parents come home with Harley pretty soon after we finish baking the cake.

The boys go upstairs with his bags, after awkwardly tripping over each other on the way in. During the brief second they hover around the kitchen, Phelan's eyes seem to be glued to Harley, though Harley is behaving in the complete opposite way, refusing to even look at him.

There seems to be some kind of tension there. I'm not sure why, but they don't quite seem right today.

Art walks around checking out the decorations and telling us we did a good job. Magnus agrees and congratulates us on the lack of mess.

I scoop some icing out of the tub with my finger and put a blob on Conan's nose.

'Yeah.' I swing back on my chair. 'We did a pretty good job.'

He gets a mad burst of giggles. 'Lolly!'

'What!?' I exclaim. I put my hand to my face, getting the icing on my cheek.

'You're so silly!' he snickers.

Radwa leans forward with a tissue to help him clean up. Her beliefs around touching have never really extended to exclude little kids. She's actually pretty good with them even though she doesn't really speak to her brothers anymore.

I raise an eyebrow at Conan and nod towards Radwa, pointing at the icing when she isn't looking.

The manic giggles Conan releases seem to outweigh any annoyance Radwa might've felt when he smears a glob of strawberry icing on her face.

Magnus reaches over with a smile to pick him up. 'Did you do this all by yourself?' he asks.

Radwa chuckles, giving me a soft little look as she wipes her own cheek this time as Magnus carries him away.

'Hey,' I whisper.

'Hey,' she says.

Radwa

After some serious thinking last night following my outburst with Oscar and Kat – and some serious talking in circles that I'm sure made Val's ears bleed – I think I've decided what I want to do about the Lolly situation.

Like they kindly pointed out last night, I can't begrudge them their history, but I can question my own feelings of resentment towards their – otherwise lovely – ex-girlfriend.

It stems from my fear I can't give them what they've had

before. That's something I won't compromise on. I know that my worry over that has made me act a little bitterly.

But, as Val pointed out during our 2am chat, it's possible that they don't want what they've had before. I mean, there has to be a reason things didn't work with them and Kat – even though she was perfectly nice and they seem to be friends. Aiming for what they had before seems silly, because none of the girls from *before* have lasted as long as I have.

Maybe everyone I've talked to about this is right. What *Lolly* is willing to accept in a relationship should be *their* choice.

They were just saying the other day that *it* shouldn't be the be-all and end-all.

Could we—? I nod my head towards the door.

They straighten up. *Yeah. Yeah of course.*

We sit out on the front step of Wren's garden. Her husky decides to come with us and keeps dropping her toys in my lap.

I smile and scratch her behind the ears. They sit on the path picking at stones.

I think I'm ready for us to talk. I tell them.

They look up. *You sure?* they ask, raising an eyebrow. I can hear them thinking about our conversation regarding Kat.

I'm sure. I nod reassuringly.

They smile, looking down at the floor. Then their eyebrows furrow as they look to where a car, followed by a couple of motorbikes, has pulled up in the carpark. *It's gonna get kinda loud tonight.*

I shake my head. *Wait until after the moon tomorrow. Give it a couple days so we can rest. Then we'll talk, yeah?*

They nod. *Okay.*

Wren

Once the boys come back down the stairs, we decide to order food. I sit in Oscar's lap with the menu. I showed him it a couple of days ago so that he could prepare mentally.

Mitch gives him a smile and winks across the table. He flushes and winks back, only he doesn't manage to be quite as suave. I can't help but laugh.

I elbow him gently. He scowls. I do this whenever he's being obvious about his crush on Mitch. Lately I do it quite a lot. It's been especially bad since Oscar came out to his dad. Mitch being there really upgraded it from a joke to an actual crush. We'll laugh about it together later. I don't actually mind, I just like teasing him.

When the food comes, we sit together eating and playing card games. Phelan nudges Harley to show him a card he got, laughing at himself. Harley gives him a small nod, lips pulling into a tight smile. He's quiet today, and seems to be being blunt with Phelan, too, so I pull him aside to help me with the dishes afterwards.

What's going on? I ask, throwing him a towel while I stack the plates and run the tap. I don't feel weird asking. He wouldn't have come if it was a big fight.

Nothing. He rolls his eyes, pushing me out.

I flick his head. *People don't act like little pricks to their mates on their birthday over nothing. What is it?*

He flicks the towel over his shoulder. *You know? About us being mates?*

I plunge my hands into the water, lifting the sponge to the bowl. *I know about you being mates but not about how you know.*

He tenses his jaw. *Well, that part is why I'm mad.*

My hands slow in the water. *You're mad that you had to save him.*

No. He shakes his head. *That was always part of it. I'm mad at what I had to save him from.*

I pull my hands out of the water and motion for the towel. We sit down at the table together. *Okay, what do you mean by that?*

Harley looks away from me. *I shouldn't tell you. He'd be so angry.*

I reach my hand forward. *He's your mate, he can be angry at you and you'll still come back to each other. Wouldn't you rather he be a little pissed off and safe?*

He nods then starts slowly. *Do you know he gets bullied in school?*

Of course I do. It's half the reason he was moving school this year. I didn't realise how bad it had gotten until Dad and Magnus decided that that was the right thing to do. Maybe I was just too caught up in my own shit, the Tyler shit, to see it all – but I still knew it was happening.

What does that have to do with —

Harley looks up at me with a strange kind of pain in his eyes, willing me to see what he means.

Go on. I feel my heart hammering against my chest in a strange way.

It's like watching people fight. The wrong move is signposted nearly a hundred ways before the fighter feels the consequence. You can't do anything but watch the losing party walk into a blow.

Harley shakes his head and sighs. *I've lost so much already Wren, and he knows that better than anyone.*

His parents died in the war.

They were a really great couple and loved Phelan to death. Harley was out at the time on a patrol with Lycaon and Ash. He was only thirteen but a lot of the kids ended up doing shit they never should've had to. That's why Phelan was working in the infirmary when they brought them in. He had to block Harley out 'til he got home to keep him focused.

It was a turbulent time, and if he had found out like that, if his concentration slipped, all three of them might've been in danger. I still remember when he came home and came running up to him. He kept saying over and over, 'What's wrong Phe?', 'What happened?', 'Why are you blocking me out?' All Phelan could do for a minute was cry.

I look up at Harley's teary eyes.

He hates it here. Back home he was — we were never seen as strange or abnormal at all. He has never had to be anyone other than himself. But here, he shrugs, *they don't understand us. They don't like people like us and Phelan isn't the kind of person who can hide who he is. Sure, the physical shit heals. It doesn't leave a mark. But that doesn't mean he's okay. And the day before you guys left he tried to – he wanted to… He was gonna leave me, too. And I had to talk him down.*

Harley is crying when he stops. I stand up and wrap my arms around him. I can tell that he doesn't mean to make this about him. He's just hurt, and scared, like any teenage boy would be.

But he was supposed to be moving school – it was going to be different – I would've known if— I feel a lump forming in my throat stopping me from saying more.

Thing is, I *did* know. Deep down. Of course, I *knew*.

My brother has always been weird in his own way but until my mission dragged us here he'd never known what it was like to be an outcast. That transition was always going to be hard.

But it was hard for me too, so hard I think it blinded me. It's a fucked up thing to do but I guess I just took for granted that whatever he was going through I had it worse.

Thing is, even if more people were against me, even if there were ten transphobic comments for every one homophobic one… I'm better at brushing it off. Phelan takes things so much more to heart than I do, and I'm his sister. If he had told anyone it should've been me.

After all, he was the one who was there when I was finally ready to talk about Tyler. He is the one who has mercilessly scrutinised every guy that so much as got close to me since. And, while I have no proof of it, I'm willing to bet he was behind the black nail varnish covering every fresh piece of graffiti about the school after Tyler started spreading shit.

And I should have known the idea of moving to somewhere that might even be *worse* without me, without anyone else there to support him, would be tough… But I just got too caught up in everything with the pack to realise.

The idea that I wasn't there for him makes me feel sick to my stomach. But I have a real chance to help him now, or at least get him more help than his sixteen year old boyfriend can provide.

Suicide, or suicide attempts, are kind of a taboo thing with wolves. A lot of people see it as selfish, to just leave your mate like that. It's rare that people's mates are actually able to get to them when it happens. Most of the time the person will take themselves far enough away that no one could get to them on time.

I think it's sad. Maybe Phelan didn't really want to go. Maybe he just wanted help. Maybe he just wanted to be heard.

He's lucky to have survived that. I don't think he's the selfish one here. If anything I am, for not realising what was going on.

God, how many little signs have I missed?

How many conversations have we had about the psychology shit he's been wanting to do where he might've dropped hints? If it was when we were back home, I was *there*, I was right fucking *there*.

He could've spoke to me. Why didn't he feel like he could speak to me? Was I too hard on him when we were sparring? Did that push him over the edge? I was only teasing, I was only ever teasing I—

My lip starts to shake so I trap it between my lips, pressing my pinkies to my eyes to stop any tears from falling, trapping them in like a cork in a bottle. Across the table, Harley hasn't tried to stop his own from falling.

I reach across the table and take his hand.

I just keep wondering if there was something I could've done to—

It's nothing you've done or haven't done, I promise Harley. *He's just sick right now but he's not going anywhere. We are going to tell my Dad and Magnus about this, okay?* I ask.

I'm pretty glad I don't have to say that out loud because the lump in my throat is big and heavy enough that if I did try to speak I'm certain I'd lose all composure.

Just wait 'til after the moon tomorrow, and we'll tell them together, okay?

Chapter Twenty-Four

Val

My arms sting from how many times I've tapped them. Little red bumps have formed on each one.

This time has been bad, even for a moon. I knew it was going to be when the first two didn't work. After adding Oscar to my list of people to protect – given that he's my mate's boyfriend and my boyfriend's mate – I now have six taps which means I can't do them in multiples of three so even if the third one had went right I'd have to do a fourth.

Mitch slides into the seat next to me, handing me a tissue for the scab on my face that's started to bleed from me picking it. Oscar himself has just disappeared back to his flat. Wren told him that they have a family celebration tonight but asked that he come over tomorrow to help with their braids.

Wren's cousin Lycaon and his mate Ash arrive shortly after he leaves, with overnight bags and a present for Phelan. Lycaon's twists are tied up in a bun today, his laid-back smile replaced with a look of stern focus. Ash gives us a wave when he comes through the door but looks similarly concentrated. I don't think anything is going to be the same after the last moon.

Mitch stares up at them when they come in. I nudge him and he looks back to his phone.

Magnus makes the rest of us a big cooked lunch with fried eggs, fried mushrooms, hash browns, and sausages. He even made sure to get vegetarian options in for Radwa which was sweet.

He plates it all up and then sits down to talk with us. 'So.' He claps his hands together. 'Full moon tonight. Art is gonna be taking Conan, Harley and Phelan about sixty miles north—'

Phelan opens his mouth to protest.

Magnus gives him a stern look. 'Pup.'

'Hear me out,' he huffs. 'With Dad gone you don't have a healer. Let me and Harley take ourselves out the way, but by less, maybe ten or twenty miles instead. That way, if anyone is hurt we can run back before morning. I have a bad feeling, I can't explain it, I just do – I have a bad feeling.' His eyes are wide and panicked. He looks slightly deranged, his breathing elevated.

Harley puts a hand on his shoulder, concerned.

Art gives Magnus a look, sighs, and nods. 'Twenty miles,' he says. 'And lay low.'

Magnus nods, then clicks his fingers and points at Harley. 'Look after each other.'

Harley nods. He gives Phelan a reassuring look, as he glances sideways at him, biting his lip. This seems to ease whatever anxiety was infecting his behaviour last night and this morning because he leans into him, kissing his shoulder.

Magnus gives Harley a wink, then continues. 'Lycaon, Ash and I are going to be about five miles away at any given time. I'm going to follow the route you normally go down to see if I come across anything. You guys are gonna take a different one.'

Then he explains it. It crosses by the path where me and Mitch were turned.

Radwa gives me a look of concern. I shake my head and give Mitch's hand two squeezes. He squeezes back twice. It's one of our little signals to each other, to ask if the other is okay. Two squeezes means yes, then he squeezes two more times to check in. I tell him I am too.

'Lycaon and Ash, you're on the perimeter. Understood?'

I see as they switch from a family to an army again.

'Yes sir,' Lycaon replies to his uncle.

'We'll start from your clubhouse. Let's roll out.' Magnus whips his finger around a circle.

The five of us are left standing in Wren's kitchen together as her family make their way out: Magnus and Art have to get Conan ready, and the others just group off in their twos.

Lolly and Radwa wander towards the door together blushing softly as they blether. Radwa's fingers come to play with the ends of her scarf, rolling the thin fabric between her fingers. Lolly on the other hand is basically jumping about, throwing their hands in all directions, animated, as they talk.

I study them, each of their little actions and fidgets, storing them in my mind – just in case.

As I think, the thin thread holding the image together in my mind starts to fray and the shavings containing each and every violent possible outcome for this moon unravel themselves splintering across my mind: a missing poster with Lolly name that we all know just won't help; Radwa's eyes, cold, lifeless, locked on me in utter betrayal that I've survived what killed her.

Mitch's hand on the small of my back pulls me back into the moment. He looks at me with a gentle smile that makes his freckles dance across his face. I make a note to remember each and every one before my mind turns them to blood splatters.

'Wren asked if your arms are okay,' he says, nodding towards where she stands.

I nod quickly, not daring to look up and see her purple highlighter turn to bruises, her braids into ropes restraining her. Bashfully, I pull the shoulders of my cardigan up to cover where my arms are red, hoping that neither Wren nor Mitch notice six more gentle taps.

We eventually separate when Wren takes their bike to the clubhouse. Lycaon and Ash follow with theirs. Magnus and the boys get a lift with Art, while Mitch drives us.

The militantly close quarters we keep when driving down the road makes us feel like cars, struggling to follow a funeral hearse.

Mitch

I rub my eyes. When I open them, Val is leaning over me.

'Jesus fucking Christ!' I go to turn away from her.

She grabs my face. 'Don't!' she says urgently. She looks pale. 'Just look at me. Don't look over there.'

A strong metallic smell hits me. Someone is hurt.

I feel like I have a hangover after being so drunk I blacked out. Even for the morning after a full moon, I'm a lot more disorientated than normal.

It comes back in snippets.

I remember us running. We ran up the deer paths through the woods leading north.

Then I remember more. Flashes of the night come back to me. Snippets too small to make sense of on their own that I desperately try to string together.

The smell of fermented fruit as a wolf we've never seen before came close. Small and rust coloured. I knew we were connected from the moment I saw them walking, slow and stalking at first. Then they stood fierce, lips pulled back over their teeth, ears flat to their head.

Then it came to blows with Wren. She'd managed to scratch them, along their front leg by their paw, but they had hurt her too – and worse.

It's Wren's blood. *Wren* is hurt.

'Look at me.' Val's voice snaps me back.

I am trying to see Wren.

'They're fine. It's not deep enough to have hit anything but it looks bad. I panicked when I saw, and we don't need you doing the same.'

The smell of their blood is already starting to get to me. My throat feels like it's closing, like I can't breathe or speak.

'We need to get them to their brother!' she says, moving her body to block my attempts to see. 'We need you to be able to drive right now, so I need you not to panic for me, okay?'

I understand. There must be a lot of blood. Too much of it still makes me panic. 'Pass me my hoodie.'

The girls and Lolly get Wren into my car while I get dressed.

I try to manage my breathing as I drive us home. I try to name five things I can see, and smell, and taste and touch and hear. It's not easy when blood is the answer to most of them.

Val squeezes my leg. The feeling grounds me. *You're doing amazing. I'm so proud of you.*

Her own heartbeat is racing. I can tell she is panicking too. Her thoughts are stuck on naming something that is red.

My hair, I suggest.

Your hair. She smiles.

I squeeze her hand.

Wren

I forgot how much injuries that don't automatically heal suck. God, they burn. And losing blood feels even worse. I am so cold.

Shit.

My head can't really make sense of anything past the pain. It blacks out. Only it doesn't feel like a blackout. It feels white hot and burning. Someone at my side – Radwa, I think – nearly trips over something as we walk towards the house. Blearily forcing my eyes open, I can see that it's the wheel of a bike, carelessly thrown on its side.

I can hear Magnus pacing inside trying to get a hold of Dad.

Phelan is waiting for me at the gate with Harley. He looks serious, like he already knows what happened.

I squeeze my eyes shut. I don't want him to see me like this.

But when I do, an old memory of him wedges its way into my mind, fixing itself there like a tape I'm forced to watch. The night I realised I wanted to be an aconite.

We were really young, like four and seven. Mum came home from a mission hurt. It had looked terrifying. Even I was upset, but I was soothed pretty quickly – after Dad patched her up and she sat telling me stories about her travels. Phelan wasn't so easily won over. He had nightmares every night for months after. Nothing Dad or Magnus did could calm him until he saw that Mum was okay. He was terrified of coming to the dojo with us for years.

I can see that version of him so clearly in my mind right now – eyes wide, blinking rapidly. We were sitting together when she came in, on the couch in our pyjamas. The noise that his Spiderman action figure made as it clattered to the ground is imprinted in my memory indefinitely. His voice as he called out to her – Phelan didn't often speak out loud as a kid, he only knew like three words, so it shocked me even then.

I wrench my eyes open, forcing them to focus on a more recent memory of him

He looks nothing like that scared little boy now. His lips are pressed tightly together, his eyes narrowed and focused.

He leads me into the house and clears a space for me to lie down.

He's so strong nowadays. Maybe that's why I forget so often that both versions of my little brother still live in the man in front of me. And both versions are hurting in a way that I don't know if he's going to heal from anytime soon.

'Dad's on the way home with Conan right now. Magnus is on the phone to him,' he explains to the pack as he pulls our first aid kit from on top of the fridge.

It has sat there unused for months and is covered in dust.

He opens it and grabs a vial out, then a syringe, a needle and thread. 'Mitch, can you go get a drink of water and stay out of this room please? I can only help one person at a time.'

Phelan doesn't sound like a sixteen-year-old boy anymore. When did that happen? When did he age beyond his years? Where did he learn this calm, deliberate tone? Why did no one see what was going on with him?

He threads the needle then turns to look behind him. 'Mitch!' His voice is commanding.

I hear two sets of footsteps leaving the room.

My eyes feel heavy. They keep falling shut.

'I love you, Pup,' I hear myself saying. 'I love you so much and I never want anything bad to happen to you.'

He laughs. 'I'll write in your notes that you're delirious, then. You're about to hate me in a second. I need to stitch you up. Can you take off your jumper for me?' Then he turns behind himself to face the pack. 'Actually, can *everyone* give her a bit of privacy?'

I shake my head as I pull my zippy off. 'Nothing could make me hate you. I'm so glad you're alive. I'm so glad Harley is here.'

I hear him swallow. 'Okay, Wren, just try to relax, yeah?'

I don't really feel the stitches as they happen. All I know is that one minute Phelan is leaning over my back and the next he's loading a syringe.

"'Bout to stab you,' he warns me.

I laugh, then I feel it, then I don't feel much of anything.

When I wake up I can hear Oscar's voice.

Needily, I force my eyes open, willing them to focus on the scene around me to find where his voice is coming from. I catch little snippets between slow blinks.

The coffee table has been pushed back into the fireplace. There are muddy marks on the rug like someone has been pacing. Another slow blink shows it is topped with blood soaked towels, hastily unwrapped bandages, and a first aid box which has been thoroughly riffled through. Someone's hurt.

Moving my hands to my sides and attempting to push myself up is all the reminder that I need that *someone* is me.

Phelan launches himself up and to my side as soon as he sees me start to stir.

Hey. Are you sore? Do you need anything? he asks as he comes over, grasping my arm carefully to stop me from jostling myself too much.

Is Oscar here? I ask.

He fixes my pillow so I'm properly propped up, before sitting next to me. Once I'm sitting higher, I blink again, eyes adjusting more to the light.

Kitchen. He nods. *Are you okay? I was worried when you passed out.*

Just woozy, I assure him.

He does look worried. I can see that now I'm able to focus for more than a second at a time. There is mud on his face cut through with a tear track. His hair looks dishevelled. He's sitting right next to me, so close his hand brushes mine while picking at the chipped black varnish on his fingertips.

I look down, eyes fixed on the spots that are normally

covered with the wrist bands and rings which sit next to discarded blue gloves on the mantelpiece.

He clears his throat, pulling the long yellow sleeves of Harley's jumper over his knuckles. *No major damage to that scratch. Bled a shit ton, but didn't hit anything important.* He crosses his arms in an imitation of our Dad. *If you're woozy, do you—*

He is interrupted by Oscar who charges into the living room, eyes wide with concern.

Phelan jolts up to stand in front of me as Magnus follows him through.

'Are they – are you—?' Oscar breathes heavily as his eyes scan over me, taking it all in at once. The blood stained towels, the bandages and vials on the table. 'Holy moly… what happened here?'

Phelan makes towards the door as Magnus puts a hand on Oscar's shoulder to lead him out, but I can tell by the expression on his face that he has already seen too much. There won't be any way of explaining this without lying to his face, and if he is Mitch's mate, and maybe mine, then he will find out one way or another.

It's okay. I look up at Phelan, reaching a hand out to stop him from pacing forward. Then I look at Magnus. *I'm fine. I need to talk to him.*

Though I know it's true, this sentiment is definitely easier thought than done. We sit in tense silence until everyone else leaves.

'I got in a fight,' I eventually say, as he sits down beside me, taking both of my hands in his. He surveys me for a second as if he thinks I'm going mad.

Eventually he decides that if I am, he's willing to indulge me. 'With a wild animal?' he scoffs.

'Kind of.' I swallow thickly.

His eyebrows shoot up his forehead as he looks at me. 'With whatever's been killing people?'

I nod, unable to actually find the words to explain from here.

His mouth falls slack, he squeezes my hand more tightly. 'Well—' He starts to splutter. 'Are you okay? What was it? Did you see? What did you—'

I pause for a moment, studying his face. 'What do you think it was?'

The question seems to catch him off guard. Then he lets out a shaky laugh. 'Well there was a post on Facebook theorising that it was a werewolf, and last night was a full moon, so let me know if you start having an aversion to silver.'

Though he's joking, his breath is shaky. His knee bounces up and down seemingly of its own accord. He looks down at our laced together hands. It reminds me of when he first asked me out, sitting in his bedroom shrouded in darkness. Only now we're looking at each other in person in broad daylight. The summer evening sun splits the curtains and glistens off the gold frames in his glasses.

'Always have.' I laugh derisively.

His dark brown eyes steadily focus on me. Hot tears spill down my cheeks before I even recognise them brewing. Realistically, I know I owe him the truth, an explanation, but it's been so nice just to have this ... us ... him ... in this totally separate bubble.

I pull my hand back from between his to wipe my eyes.

'Wren?' He says my name so gently that it feels like a hug.

My lip starts to wobble so I catch it between my teeth. When I look into his eyes I feel as though his gaze bores into my soul.

He leans back a little. 'Are you—?' I'd think he was just going to ask if I was okay again if I didn't see that look that just darkened his expression.

'I don't hurt people!' I say defensively by means of an answer.

The way he sits back on his heels confirms his understanding of what I've said. The air around us smells like his dad's house, like clean linen sheets, whiskey and expensive cologne.

'I've *never* hurt anyone. Not anyone human anyway. The people who say it's instinctual are liars. Most of us never will – except rogues, like the one who turned Mitch and his pack.'

Oscar's eyes bulge out of his head as he looks up. 'Wait—'

'And we're trying to find them and get rid of them anyway. She's the one who I fought but I—'

'Wren.' His hand grips my arm strongly. He looks up at me through his fringe. 'I'm trying really hard to stay calm, but I need you to be quiet for a second.'

When I actually stop speaking to take him in properly I notice that his jaw is clenched. He presses the palms of his hands into his eyes and takes a deep breath.

I pause for a second, watching him.

Silence passes between us until I eventually say, 'I understand if this changes the way you feel about me.'

The words hurt me even as they come, more than the scratch across my back. As I stare at the cover in front of me, feeling the fibres damp where they sit catching tears just under my chin, I can picture everything we've been through lately. The sleepover, the blanket fort, the *Doctor Who* marathon, how amazingly he treated me finding me on the floor that evening—

'I know it's not what you signed up for and you probably want to run a million miles in the opposite direction—'

'I can't,' he whispers, leaning back and resting his head on the table, looking up at the ceiling. 'I can't leave. Not that I want to leave you – you're my girlfriend, and you're either very delusional from pain, or you're telling the truth and you're actually a werewolf sent by some higher order to fight a serial killer which – quite frankly – just makes me more concerned about your current condition. I mean assuming you are, are you not supposed to heal?' he asks, looking up.

'Like do you not have special healing powers like the stories – wait, no, that would explain why I can never give you hickies – wait, am I gonna be a werewolf? Because you give me a *lot* of hickies. Like *a lot* of hickies.'

I feel my face flush hot, eyeing the open door, as I hear Lycaon clear his throat in the other room.

'And say you are a werewolf, and you were born that way, does that mean that all your family are? Or is it like a once in a generation thing? Because I'm pretty sure your little brother shares his toys with the dog, and he wanted to bake with dog safe chocolate the other day too. I thought it was because he felt bad not being able to share them with Luna but—' He runs his hand through his hair, sitting up.

'And if Mitch and that were turned, does that mean they're all wolves? Wait, is that why you all go camping every month? Is the clubhouse a hide-out for that? And is that why you all have the same eyes? I thought it was just a fashion statement… Or that Mitch had issues with his eyes because of the scratch on his face. I know that his changed because they were green in the pictures in his room. So I thought maybe you all wore contacts in support or something. Wait, can scratches turn people too? And like when you wolf out does it hurt? Do you like become a full wolf or like—'

He continues firing a million questions at me without letting me get an answer in edgeways.

'And why can't I leave? Everytime I try to, I get this sick feeling in my throat like my heart is going to jump into my mouth and I can't go, I just—'

All of his words sort of blur together. The room spins and not just on account of the medication Phelan gave me earlier.

He's still going when there's a knock at the door.

Magnus smiles softly, sitting on the edge of the couch. When he sits down he claps a hand around my ankle, giving my leg a reassuring squeeze, before he interrupts Oscar.

'They're not delusional, but they are in pain.' His words seem to stop Oscar dead in his tracks.

He looks at me apologetically. I shake my head.

Magnus smiles a small warm smile. 'I think we have a lot in common,' he says to Oscar. 'For starters we were both born human. So maybe, while they rest, I can answer any *appropriate* questions you might have?'

Oscar's cheeks flush a warm pink colour between his freckles, but he nods a tiny little nod and Magnus gestures for him to follow into the kitchen while he makes tea. I drift off to the sound of him explaining how werewolf healing works.

By the time I wake up, Oscar has been filled in on most of the basics in Werewolf 101, and is sitting clearing space on the floor in front of him, sectioning kanekalon out into different colour groups with corresponding elastics sitting in piles in front of each one.

'Are you still planning on doing my hair?' I ask.

'Yes – no – I don't know. I will if you want. Sorting through things just helps me process my thoughts a bit better,' he admits, combing his fingers through a section. 'Magnus covered most of my questions when you were out but I'm still a little freaked out.'

I nod in a way that I hope seems understanding. Of course he's freaked out, that's only understandable. 'Well if it helps at all, you can't get turned by hickies if I use my human teeth – and it wasn't even the week of the full. I'm guessing you don't remember rampaging around the forest last night.' I offer him a hopeful smile as I put my hand out for the scissors to start taking out my braids for him.

He chuckles, eyes flitting up from the hair for just a second as he hands me them before looking back down at the floor. 'Would you believe that I was in my bedroom watching YouTube and doing art stuff?' he asks, tone inflected as if to imply that this would not be a shocking confession.

'No!' I laugh, bringing my hand to my chest in mock surprise.

He chuckles. 'I do have some questions I'd rather not ask your parents but we can go over all of that another time.'

I nod, undoing the first braid. 'In my room. It's soundproofed with silver.'

He grins. 'That *does* answer one of them.' Then he pauses looking up at me seriously as I bring the scissors to my hair again. 'I don't think your hair has grown *that* much in a month.'

'Shut up,' I laugh. 'You never know okay!'

Just then, Dad makes it home and rushes into the living room to check on what's happening with me, effectively derailing our earlier conversation. As it grows late, a bit of back and forth leads him to decide that *if* Oscar really feels as bad as he says he does about leaving, forcing him to would be a bad idea.

That's how I wake up to him shaking my shoulder at about three in the morning.

'Hey. I woke up and you were being sick in your sleep. I need you to wake up for me until it stops.' He pushes a bucket towards me.

I'm not sure if it's the pain or the meds but he's right. I hate being sick. No one likes it but I really hate it. I feel absolutely delirious but I lean over the bucket.

After it stops he grabs a wet cloth from the bathroom for me and helps me clean up.

'Thank you,' I groan.

He kisses my head gently. 'Well, I wasn't just gonna let you choke and die was I?'

My eyes feel wet. It takes me a moment to realise what just happened, then another to realise he has no idea what it means. I will explain it to him. I will, but for now…

'I love you,' I murmur, leaning into his shoulder. I did not plan to say it for the first time, smelling of sick with my hair half done and blood crusting a bandage to my back. But I do.

'I love you too,' he chuckles with a shaky exhale.

This is something I think I've known for a while, from how the scent of dog hair, oil paint, green tea and bubblegum fills the room every time we're together. That seems to be how love smells for him.

Radwa

Val and I leave Lolly and Mitch to sleep for the night after checking Wren is okay.

Val keeps tapping her arms on the way home, six times each side, over and over. She does this when she's nervous; when her thoughts are flooded with ways our little group might encounter any kind of harm. It's as if it's a magic spell that will protect us.

All she has to do is say some words and tap her arms and the wards come up. Only, the first time is never good enough for her.

'She's okay,' I promise, taking her hand. 'It's okay, we're all gonna be okay.'

Her hand comes up to play with the necklace Mitch bought her for their one-year anniversary.

Then she pats her chest frantically. Missing. It's missing.

I hear her breathing start to get fast. Visions of horrible, graphic things happening to him flood her brain.

All I can do is promise her that none of it will happen.

Chapter Twenty-Five

Lolly

'No, sweetheart, I promise I'm fine. I'm sitting on my step having tea with Lolly.' Mitch is covering one ear, holding the phone to the other.

It is the morning after we woke up to Wren hurt. Val has been panicking all night. Mitch looks tired.

To her credit, Val always calls instead of just thinking things when she's having intrusive thoughts because she doesn't want us to hear and think less of her. Not that we would, but I'm grateful she's learnt to – having five people panic in your head at once is *loud*.

Oscar comes out of Wren's front door. He stands with his back against the wall and takes a deep breath.

'Heard she told you,' I say.

He jumps around. 'Jesus Christ don't sneak up on me.'

I have to laugh. I've been sitting here so long my bum is going numb, I hardly snuck up.

He walks over into our garden holding a glass of water. 'Yeah, she did.' He nods.

'How you holding up?' I ask.

He wiggles his hand out in front of himself. 'So-so. Didn't really know what to say at first. I mean it's weird, don't get me wrong. But I just want her to be okay.'

That is not the reaction I was expecting. Fair play to him.

'Okay, I will see you then. Okay, bye, I love you.' Mitch shakes his head, hanging up the phone. 'Hey Oscar, sorry, Val isn't doing great. Her anxiety is through the roof after last night. I told her I'll help her look for her necklace tomorrow,' he says, turning to me. He and I are both working longer shifts today.

I give him a nudge. 'Well, a few days' time and she'll be wearing something you gave her everyday again anyway.'

Oscar looks at him quizzically.

Mitch claps his hand over his mouth. 'Oh shit you don't know! I'm proposing.'

I glance over at Oscar to see his reaction. Mitch might be completely oblivious but I've noticed how he acts around him.

If the news does upset Oscar he doesn't show it. He reaches out to pat his back. 'No way! Good luck man!'

Mitch taps his hand back. 'Thanks dude, I appreciate it.'

It's strange. Oscar looks genuinely happy, but the air feels a little thick and there is still something very restricted about how they're interacting.

'You'll be married before Lolly asks Radwa out.'

Wait, how the fuck did this turn back on me?

'I have tried.' I put my hands up to defend myself. 'And we are gonna be talking tomorrow, for your information. I'm meeting her at the clubhouse after work and we're going on a walk.' I take a sip of my tea. 'Besides, no fair comparing us. You don't have to worry about getting rejected by your mate.'

Radwa and I still haven't had our dramatic saving one another moment so I really don't know what to think there.

'You should be grateful you haven't had to,' Mitch says out loud to me. Then looks up at Oscar. 'Sorry, wolf telepathy thing. Lolly is just being salty. They and Radwa haven't had their big "mates" moment yet.'

Oscar's brow furrows. 'What do you mean by that?'

Oh shit. He doesn't know yet.

'Ask Wren,' I tell him, cutting off Mitch as he's starting to explain. 'Let her tell you.'

Wren

I'm half stirring awake when Oscar comes up to my room. God, I feel like shit.

Oscar helped me upstairs two hours ago when everyone else got up, promptly after telling my dad about me being sick in my sleep and receiving the most unexpected and awkward hug I've ever borne witness to. Honestly, he looked kind of like a deer caught in headlights.

Apparently, Magnus figured it was best to leave the whole *mates* thing to me. So he doesn't know that telling my dad that is basically telling him he's his son-in-law.

I wince, pushing myself up on my pillow, when he comes in.

'Hey. Mitch and Lolly are asking for you,' he whispers, coming to sit next to me. 'Please text Val – or you know the whole—' He wiggles his fingers in front of his forehead as if trying to imitate a telepathic wave coming from his mind.

This earns him a gentle smile, the sleepy kind that lends itself to a slow blink. I'm exhausted. Technically I'm fine now, I can walk to the toilet and upstairs and downstairs by myself. But Dad says I have to rest, which would have me climbing the walls if I wasn't so sleepy and dizzy with the blood loss.

'How are they?' I ask, reaching for my phone with a wince. I think Val is blocking us all out right now so it will probably be easier to message her online.

'She's worried about you I think. Good otherwise though.'

He blinks, looking down at his hands in his lap. 'Mitch is proposing to her soon. I dunno if you knew.'

I nod. I did. He told me not long ago. That must've hurt Oscar to hear a little. I know his crush on Mitch has only gotten worse the closer they've gotten. I tease him about it all the time, it's so funny. He always knew Mitch was straight, but this has got to sting a little.

'You okay?' I ask him, reaching over to touch his arm.

He nods quickly, running his fingers over mine. 'Lolly said something though, about them being mates. But not like mates mates, like a different kind of mates. They said to ask you what it meant.'

Honestly, I have no idea what to say in response. How much do I tell him? Where is the line between telling him the whole truth and freaking him out? There's no easy way to tell a guy you've been dating for a couple of months that your souls are tied together without sounding crazy, and that's not counting the fact that he might, you know, be turned into a werewolf on account of that.

I shift on the pillow. He puts a hand on my back and then moves the pillow behind me so I don't need to twist, so I start with a thank you.

'It's a wolf thing,' I continue. 'Like, you know how wolves mate for life? Well, a "mate" is like a soul mate. But it's not so singular and not exclusively romantic. Wolves have people, other wolves or just regular humans, that their souls are tied to, for life. It's like… fate. They're destined to cross paths, and are usually compelled to save each other.

'Some people will perform outlandish medical procedures they have no training in because the instinct to save each other is so strong. Some will be there for them in rough times. Val was there when Mitch's throat was slashed, and put pressure on it until he could get an ambulance, which is so tricky to get right, but she just knew exactly what to do, because they're mates.'

Oscar blinks slowly, looking down at the bed in front of him. When he turns to look at me his warm brown eyes are wide and his eyebrows have pulled together to form a crease in his forehead. 'I – I couldn't force myself to leave last night if I wanted to. And when you were sick, I was sleeping, sound asleep and then I heard my voice screaming at me in my head to wake up. Are – Am I – Are you—'

I put my hand in his. 'Mates. We're mates. Pretty sure at least. Felt that way when you told your—' I trail off, not wanting to upset him.

'Oh my God,' he whispers, looking down our fingers laced together. 'And – sorry, people have multiple mates?'

'Yeah, most people. Polyamory is so commonplace with werewolves because of it. I mean, Mum, Dad and Magnus are all like a triad, they're all paramours, and Ailsa—'

He looks at me, sitting up straight. 'Do you have more?'

I laugh awkwardly, reaching to move a braid out of my face. 'Well, not romantic or I'd have told you, but otherwise yeah, Val saved me when she first met me, so probably her. Telepathy is also much louder with her so it would make sense. I wouldn't be surprised if Mitch, Lolly or Radwa ended up being my mates as well though.'

Oscar thinks for a second, swinging his legs on the bed to sit next to me. 'I take it Mitch and Val are monogamous though.'

I shake my head. They're in a monogamous relationship but they're open to polyamory with regards to mates, they're just not actively seeking it. I tell him this.

'But they're getting married.'

I shrug. 'If Val says yes it'll be to celebrate their relationship together not close it. Wolves have multiple ceremonies for each mate.'

He tilts his head to the side, raising his eyebrows as if he hadn't considered this before.

He's quiet again for a moment. Then he says, 'You and

Mitch saved me before, you know.'

I nod and squeeze his hand. 'I know.' I pause. I think about telling him about him and Mitch too but decide to keep the moment just us for a second.

He pulls his hand back and then presses the tips of our fingers together so they are dancing off one another. 'So do you have any mates back home?' he asks, as his middle finger balances on mine. 'In your own pack?'

'Only a sibling bond with Phelan.' My lips curl into a tight smile.

Previously I would've said no. I would've believed I had no one. But then the last moon happened.

With healers it's pretty weird. They save everyone, so telling who they're compelled to save isn't always as clear. But there is no denying how freaked out Phelan was when Dad tried to make him leave on the moon. And his voice has always been quite loud in my head but I guess I've always just kind of taken how close we are for granted.

It's not unheard of for siblings to be mates. It's more common with dynamics like Lolly has with their sister, where all they have is each other, but I guess it kind of makes sense. I mean, he was the one that was there for me with all of the Tyler shit. Of course that only makes me feel worse about not following up on that weird instinct I had when we were down with our pack.

'Actually, on the topic of mates, I need to talk to my parents, Harley, and Phelan alone. Could you send them up and distract Conan for us?'

He looks at me concerned for a moment. 'Yeah, yeah of course. Is everything okay?'

I nod, then I shake my head feeling my eyes tear up. He kisses my temple gently. 'Wren?'

'No. It's not okay. But it will be,' I promise resolutely. 'It's gotta be.'

Telling Dad and Magnus isn't easy. I don't think it was

ever going to be.

Phelan knows what it is about from the second Harley closes the door after they walk in. His eyes flash over to me and Harley in a last ditch desperate plea before settling a betrayed expression as we explain what's happened.

Though the hardness in his look is chipped away when Harley starts talking about how the situation affected him. The whole time, Dad listens intently with a vacant look of fear in his eyes.

Then there's Magnus. I catch the exact moment he realises what's going on. I would say he looks like someone has just punched him in the gut, knocked the wind clean out of him, but I know exactly what that looks like and this expression is somehow worse.

Everyone wants better for their kids. I think that's only natural. So I can't imagine how painful it must be to watch them go through exactly what you did, and be almost completely helpless to stop it. I mean, sure, they can move his school, hell they can even move him back home as Magnus suggests, but they can't change the effect it's had on him, and the place it drove him to.

And while they resolve to talk to Cygnus about doing just that, I don't think this will be something we can simply sweep under the rug with a quick fix. It's not like a scratch – Phelan would be more than capable of dealing with that.

Nor do I think it's something a mate alone has the power to heal. Though when he's more open to it I would like to talk to him and understand how to see the warning signs, and what type of help he's likely to accept.

The thing is, mates act on instinct, usually fighters especially can only temporarily help until they can get to a healer. *This* requires a healer, or a psychologist, or someone more than his sixteen-year-old boyfriend and eighteen-year-old sister. It's a deep and dangerous wound that will never quite heal to be the same as it was before.

Val

'Wren text you,' Radwa says, as I duck behind the target we set to practise with our weapons after returning from Wren's base pack.

We're in the back garden of the clubhouse, shivering in our pyjamas, trying to find the necklace I lost. She stands over me, holding my phone up as a torch. I find myself almost wishing we could control our wolf eyes so I could activate some kind of dark vision right now.

'Is she okay?' I scramble to my feet, trousers wet with leaves and mulch.

The heavy denim replicates the tight, restricting feeling in my chest. When we woke up yesterday I was convinced that *I* had hurt someone from how potent the smell of blood was. Seeing Wren like that, it… really messed with me.

When I look up, I look past Radwa.

An image of Mel appears between the trees, one arm folded on her chest, hand sitting limply there as if she has any hope of stopping the blood darkening her shirt. The other hand is reaching for us like it was that night.

Sometimes, I think these pictures must be her way of haunting me, tormenting me for not saving her. My hand comes to my chest, looking for my necklace in an attempt to slow my heart – which has been racing since this morning.

The violent images that flood my mind in times like this are a stain, like tomato or turmeric on white cotton. There are a few tricks for getting it out, but they don't always work, and the harder I try to scrub them away the more they spread.

Images of Mel morph into fresher ones of Wren, still in the process of etching their way into my memory. Wrapped up in her blanket, covered in blood, skin pale and clammy.

A cool breeze brushes past us, stinging the exposed skin of my chest where I've picked enough for it to bleed.

'Everyone is fine,' Radwa promises me, then a rustle in the

trees behind us causes her to flinch so hard that the torch shakes. She turns on a tiny little squirrel which has just darted out from behind the trees. 'I feel as though this is maybe *slightly* more dangerous than *one night* without your necklace,' she says, gently. 'I just don't think it's a good idea for us to be here *alone* in the middle of the night. And Lolly and Mitch said they'd help tomorrow so—'

The memories of Wren swap out for visions of Mitch. More scars, bruises, spitting blood and tears.

I go to glare at Radwa. I know how stupid my little rituals seem. It's completely irrational from an outside perspective. I get that. But I resent any sort of reminder or implication that I'm just being *silly*.

Then, it's kind of hard to be mad at someone who agreed to come out of bed in the middle of the night in fleece pink pyjama bottoms and a hoodie to look for a necklace in near pitch darkness.

We were going to come earlier but it was raining so it was impossible to actually get here safely and my necklace would've just been stamped into the mud. So, we figured it was safe enough to come at night, considering that the rogue is currently injured.

Instead I let out a halfhearted grumble. 'We're not *entirely* alone,' I say, pointing at Tato who sniffs indignantly, shaking his head so hard his ears flap inside out.

Radwa lets out a mirthless noise, half sigh and half laugh. Then she lowers the torch. 'Look, there's only twelve hours until Mitch and Lolly will both have slept, woken up and gotten ready to come help us look. Why don't we just go home for now and play that game you liked?'

I smile gently, reaching out a hand so she can pull me up.

As we leave, I cast one final glance at the patch of woods I saw Mel in. Her face is gone once more.

Chapter Twenty Six

Mitch

Radwa is out in the garden of the clubhouse, training with her bow and arrow, when me and Lolly arrive the following day.

We are slightly late to arrive because we were waiting on Wren getting her bandages changed so she could come with us. Her and Oscar are still making their way slowly up from the carpark.

I did offer to help them carry anything they needed, but Wren said she was fine, and Lolly was stressing about the whole talking-to-Radwa thing so I decided to race them here as a distraction. They win, which is honestly enough to make me consider cutting back on smoking as I double over, spluttering for air.

They throw themself on the ground at Radwa's feet panting to catch their breath. 'I won!' They look up at her with a triumphant smile. Then they cough hard.

'I saw.' Radwa grins, lifting her quiver over her shoulder so she can carry it into the house. 'And it only cost you a lung.' Then her eyes sparkle. 'Wanna race me next?'

We both grimace at the idea which makes her laugh. Then

she turns to me and lets me know that Val is looking for her necklace upstairs so I decide to leave them to their *conversation*, giving Lolly a sly thumbs up as I pass.

Val looks stressed out when I get upstairs. Her eyes look heavy, and her hair isn't straightened for once.

'Hey,' I whisper delicately, opening my arms for her.

She walks into them and rests her head on my shoulder. I kiss her twice, inhaling the scent of her LUSH shampoo.

Then my nose wrinkles. The air around me reeks of body odour, Red Bull and something rotten.

'Do you smell that?' I ask, and as she goes to answer she is interrupted by a shout from downstairs.

It's Lolly. They shout for Radwa to watch out, and then Radwa screams.

It's a heart-wrenching, ear-splitting scream.

The sound seems to suspend the moment in slow motion. Val whirls around to look at me as the air fills with a new scent; one of iron, lavender and cheap vodka. I'm moving before I even realise what I'm doing. My feet carry me towards the chaos even though my mind is begging me to run in the exact fucking opposite direction.

The door frame catches my shoulder as I dive around it, racing down the old rickety steps. The sound as I clatter down each one is a desperate plea; not again, not again. I can't do this again. The bottom two are slightly broken and turn off at a corner so I launch myself over them, landing on all fours. My claws scratch against the floor as I scamper back upright.

I think part of me knows what's happening even before I open the door and close the gap between myself and my friends, but it really only registers when Lolly staggers back into me, their body colliding with mine. They knock me off balance, but I still manage to catch them half in my lap, half in my arms.

Radwa notches an arrow into the bow she has been

training with, aiming at a figure in the distance, then she pulls it back and releases it with a yell before dropping to her knees. She doesn't bother watching to see if it hits.

Val runs after her arrow.

Wren appears with Oscar and they follow.

'He tried to hit me,' Radwa starts, looking up at me, her eyes blazing silver with fury. 'And they pushed me out the way, but then he – and they – and –'

Words seem to fail her and she reaches out for Lolly, eyes scanning over them to take in the extent of their injuries, but her mind fills in all the blanks, projecting the image into my head like an emergency news broadcast.

It forces its way in, blaring over any other thought I might have.

A boy, our age. He'd been limping when he approached. Radwa was worried before she realised who it was because she took a step forward.

Then he looked up. His face was mottled and peeling like his skin was falling off of him. Blackened gangrenous cuts up his arms had still not yet healed from the moon, having not had the opportunity to feed.

The image is enough to make my stomach turn. The most disgusting part, the most truly terrifying, is when he grins – the horrible shit eating grin that I would know anywhere.

It was Tyler. Tyler is the rogue.

I think part of me already knew that. But it felt too easy. Branding him as an animal felt like giving him a free pass.

I look down. There's a deep gouge in Lolly's side. My hand has been automatically covering it, keeping pressure on it.

Their blood is smeared across my hand and spreads underneath my fingers. It's warm and fresh, and it's sticking to my skin. It smells metallic, yet also sweet, and sharp.

I gag. The smell is so strong I can taste it in my mouth. I cough again.

I can taste the blood on my lips as I cough.

'It's okay. You'll be okay. It doesn't even look that bad,' Val is sobbing. She is lying obviously. I put my hand over hers where it sits on my throat.

It's hard to breathe. I place my free hand on my neck to feel for blood that isn't there.

Radwa is saying something but I can't quite make out what it is. Every noise blurs into one, like the backing soundtrack in a movie. I know that I've started to panic.

Five things I can touch. There is blood on my hand. Lolly's blood is on my hand.

And smell. Lolly's blood.

I can smell Lolly's blood.

Oh God.

My best friend is bleeding out in my lap again.

I can't do this again.

But I can't run away.

I feel my mind slip from my body,

floating

higher and higher above the scene.

Come to me. Kill anyone who tries to stop you.

I'm half delirious when I hear it.

What?

My mind is slipping,
and then everything
goes blank and numb.

Radwa

'Mitch!' I shout after him as he leaves, pulling Lolly into my lap and covering their side with my hand. 'Mitch!'

I put my bow down and take off my jacket to wrap it around Lolly's shoulders. They are so cold.

They've always got cold hands. That's the first thing I thought when they pushed me. I usually complain. They've never been this cold.

I feel the heavy weight of sorrow pushing hard down on my throat. The tears fall before I realise they are. I don't want to admit they are because I don't want to admit what is happening.

They reach up to wipe them.

'Hey, don't cry for me.' They hiss with pain as they move. They close their eyes tight and put their hand out as if dizzy. 'I'm sure I'm already healing.'

'You're not gonna heal this time, Lol.' I hold them steady.

They smile. 'Nah, I'm sure I am.' They know they won't really, I can see it in their eyes. They look afraid, and the air smells like cheap alcohol. 'You just wanted an excuse to hold my hand again,' they tease. They're gripping mine so tightly their knuckles are turning white. Even that feels like a confession. We are only allowed to touch if it's life or death.

'You caught me,' I whisper.

I feel like I should know what to do. They cough again. Blood splatters on my skirt.

'Sorry,' they groan hoarsely.

I sigh exasperated. 'Lolly, it's a skirt, you're...' I don't finish the sentence.

'I do have to tell you something. Just in case, okay?' they say, lips pulling into a tight grimace.

'Don't, not now, please don't—' How is their heart not racing? I can hear my blood rushing in my ears right now, I feel like I'm going to explode.

'I'm not afraid to die *mo leannan*. I'm with you.' They cough. 'And if anyone is going to save me, it's you.' They pause. 'Because it's always been you, Radwa.' They cough again.

'Lolly—'

'I love you.' Their voice is shaky when they breathe in. 'I'm *in love* with you.' They cough again, and their eyes bubble up. Then they whisper in a voice so small it must belong to that version of them that curls up into a tiny ball to sleep, whose fluffy ears barely brush my shoulder on moons, 'Please stay with me.'

'Don't leave me then,' I whisper, holding their hand tight in mine and pressing it to my chest.

My eyes start to sting and a single tear falls. They untangle our hands to wipe it. Their chronically brave smile is plastered on their face.

Then an idea comes to me. I read somewhere that if someone's lung is collapsed you can help them breathe with— I tap my pockets. A pen.

I'm pulling it apart when they tap my arm.

'Radwa?' Their eyes flutter open, then slowly shut again. 'I'm so cold.'

'It's okay,' I whisper, more to myself than them. 'It's gonna be okay. And when all of this is over, you're taking me out on a date, because as much as I am in love with you too, saying it as you're bleeding out is rude and you will be making it up to me,' I tease, moving my jacket to the side and reaching for my arrows to make a small cut to relieve the pressure from their lung.

They don't laugh.

They don't even respond.

'Lolly?' I look up.

Their eyes have glazed over with a remarkably un-Lolly-like look.

Those eyes.

The ones that sparkled. That grabbed life by the reins. Sharp and cool like a Polaroid picture.

They look... empty.

'Lol?'

I want to hear that raspy cough which seems to have disappeared.

'Lolly!'

I shake them.

No response.

Silence has never sounded so loud.

There is no time to panic. Unscrewing the pen with one hand, I dump the contents out on the grass.

Then I take a deep breath.

Using the silver tip of my arrow, I make a small incision in the throat of the person I love most in the world, and then with a wet crunching noise I bury the end of the pen in it.

Wren

I told Oscar not to follow me when we heard Radwa scream.

And I told him not to get in Mitch's way when I saw how his eyes were glowing silver, how his claws protruded from his hands. I told him that Mitch wasn't there. That he was under orders.

Then again, I suppose there are better times to say, 'I told you so.'

Oscar's blood seeps through his t-shirt, blossoming into an ugly sort of flower that spreads across his chest.

He has fallen to his knees with the force at which he was hit.

Mitch has left. He was crying, eyes streaming, while the rest of his face seemed otherwise passive and relaxed. It was like our Mitch was in there, watching yet unable to fight what was happening.

Oscar puts his hand to his wound.

'Damn,' he says. 'I thought that would work.'

He had approached Mitch hoping he could break through Tyler's grasp on him, considering they're mates. I got where he was going but I told him not to.

He looks up at me. 'Am I gonna die?'

His eyes, normally a brown so dark that it blocks out all sunlight, are shining with amber and green. They are shining bronze.

'No,' I whisper, pulling him to his feet. 'Not on my watch.'

Even if ordered, Mitch couldn't kill Oscar. They're mates. That's one of the only times a wolf can resist an alpha's order with minimum effort.

'Am I—' He winces as he moves his arm. 'Am I going to become – ?'

I look at him. Lying would comfort him, saying 'probably not' or 'we don't know yet'. But he was scratched by a half-turned wolf mere days after the full moon, and his eyes have turned bronze already. So I don't say anything.

I send a distress signal to my pack who meet us at the clubhouse when we get there.

Harley is pacing the perimeter. Dad has taken to the woods with Magnus, Lycaon and Ash by the time we arrive to look for Mitch and Val. He left Conan with Mitch's parents, claiming he was called into the hospital.

Phelan is on his knees next to Radwa, who sounds frantic.

Then I hear why. I hear the weak and desperate fluttering of Lolly's heart.

'They stopped responding.' Radwa looks at me. Her cheeks are tear-stained, and she is covered in blood. 'They couldn't breathe, they – and I – and—'

'It's okay.' Phelan goes to rub her arm instinctively then pulls his hand back. He puts his ear down to Lolly's chest. 'They're breathing. Their heart rate is stable, it's just faint. You've done so well Radwa. You've given them the best chance possible.'

When he lifts his head I can see the pen sticking out of their throat. The shallow movement of their chest and the blood on Radwa's hands fills me in on all the blanks.

Lolly saved Radwa.

They are mates.

And now Lolly might die before they get the chance to talk about that.

I shake myself, remembering the urgency that brought me here: my mate.

'Bandages?' I ask Phelan.

He gestures to the bag next to him. I grab a couple along with: a bottle of water, a needle, thread, a lighter, and some antiseptic.

I take Oscar's hand and lead him through the clubhouse to a room upstairs to help him clean up.

We start with a cloth and some water. It looks less scary when the blood is cleared off. It's not as deep as I thought, but it's far from superficial and stops just before his heart.

Oscar scrunches his eyes shut when I put the antiseptic cream along the gash.

'Sorry.' I squeeze his hand.

He shakes his head. 'It's fine.'

Once I'm done he looks up at me. 'Does it need stitches?'

I smile awkwardly, holding the needle and thread. 'Sorry.'

His face greens. He groans.

'Can't promise it'll look the prettiest,' I start, holding the needle to the flame. 'But I know what I'm doing and it will help. It would probably be better if Phelan did it but he has his hands full.' I doubt Oscar would want Phelan to do this anyway.

Oscar looks like he's going to be sick. I grab a bucket from the corner of the room and empty papers out of it.

I put it next to him on the bed.

The red of his blood dyes the skin around my nails.

At one point his eyes begin to flutter and his head drops to the side.

'Hey, stay with me.' I stop what I'm doing and steady him with a hand on his shoulder.

An overwhelming feeling of queasiness hits me, followed by a stinging pain in my chest.

I've never had a weak stomach. That's weird.

I go back to what I was doing.

This room is brighter than I've ever noticed. It lets in way too much sunlight. Woah, someone needs to turn that down.

I walk over to the blind to pull it down, then come back to Oscar.

He is breathing hard. *Just let me pass out, honestly.*

I've never heard someone that loudly, freshly after being turned. I look up at him.

'What?' he asks, his eyebrows knit together. He wasn't even trying to speak.

'No, I will not!' I respond out loud.

What the hell? he thinks.

I explain how it works as I tie off the other end of the thread. 'I'm going to see if Phelan is done with Lolly. I'm good, but I'm not giving you painkillers that could knock you out good.'

He looks around. I pull off my hoodie and hand it to him. He smiles gratefully.

I can hear that he doesn't feel able to talk right now. He is sore, everything is bright and loud. His head is no longer just his own. He can speak, he'd just rather do anything but that right now.

Phelan is standing in the hall when I leave Oscar. He and

Harley have carried Lolly upstairs to lay them on a bed. Their heartbeat is quiet but consistent at least.

'Drugs?' he asks with a smile, holding up a vial and a syringe.

'Should I be worried?' Dad comes upstairs at that exact moment.

Phelan snorts, and then he knocks on Oscar's door.

Dad pulls me aside. 'We found your mate, the girl, Val.'

But not Mitch? I think.

He shakes his head. 'And she's refusing to come back without him. I was hoping you might have better luck, kiddo.'

I find Val sitting under a tree in the woods. It is thick and old and has a collection of orange stretchmarks and tattoos covering its greying body. I read over them.

EA + EL boldly proclaim their love for each other just below my eye level. I smile fondly.

C + N aren't brave enough to put their last initials.

M, M + V just want to tell everyone that they were here. My finger runs over the second M. It's rough, and more jagged than the first, carved over another now unreadable letter.

I look down at Val. Her eyes are wide and bloodshot.

'We tried to stop him,' I say by means of an apology. 'He attacked Oscar, and I wasn't strong enough to fight him.'

I feel guilty that my stupid scratch stopped me. Protecting your body is subconscious, though. You do it without thinking.

Val looks up. 'Is Oscar okay?' I nod, and she smiles a tiny forced smile. 'That's good. Mitch will be upset that he hurt him but at least he's okay.'

She is talking about Mitch as if he is waiting back at the clubhouse for us, even though she knows he's not.

'He turned him,' I say, sitting down next to her.

She presses her lips together, her mouth a thin line. 'That's gonna kill him.'

If Tyler doesn't. We both think it but we don't say it.

'Is Lolly okay?' she asks, changing the topic abruptly.

I shake my head. 'It's pretty touch and go. They're unconscious.'

Val nods, taking this in. 'Is Radwa okay?' she asks.

I look at her. Her hair frizzes out of the pleats she is wearing it in. Her eyes are teary, and she rocks gently back and forth to soothe herself. She keeps tapping her chest as if looking for her necklace, and settling to pick at her skin when she doesn't find it.

'Val, are you okay?'

She stops rocking, stops picking, and just looks at me. Her eyes are wide, as if she's surprised to be asked, as if she is used to just being an accessory in everyone else's story; there to check that they are okay. As if she was never supposed to have feelings of her own.

She shakes her head minutely. I take her hand in mine and give it a gentle squeeze. She squeezes back.

I swipe her hair out of her face. Her eyes are sparkling. I wipe her tears with the edge of my finger. Her face is hot, even though the air is getting cooler and she is wearing a cropped t-shirt and shorts.

'We are gonna figure this out,' I promise her. 'Phelan has bandaged up Lolly and Oscar. Radwa hasn't left Lolly's side. Me, you, and some of the others can go on a patrol if you like. I just need you to come back with me so I can get my bo staff, and we can get you some warmer clothes and food maybe.'

She looks around, aimlessly, then back at me. 'I want the knives I was training with.'

'Okay, we'll get you armed.' I nod. 'Just come with me.'

I manage to get her up, and as promised take her out on a search after making sure she's okay. We come back empty-handed. Getting her home from that trip is much harder.

She only comes back because Radwa begs her for support, and she can't say no to Radwa knowing what she's going through.

Lolly still hasn't woken up.

Oscar is starting to complain about how bright the lights are. Someone – probably me – will need to keep watch over him tonight, in case Tyler comes back for him. Since he's been freshly turned, his blood is worth its weight in gold right now. He falls asleep upstairs eventually.

Val, Radwa and I sit together halfway down the stairs, not really speaking except to check in on each other. It's going to be a long night.

Chapter Twenty-Seven

Mitch

I don't really remember passing out, but when I open my eyes I'm in a dark and dingy room. The walls are grey, with exposed brickwork. The floor is bare, cold concrete with drains in it.

My wrists are being held above me. I pull on one experimentally. It feels like scraping a fresh tattoo.

Silver.

Fuck.

The shackles clink off each other as I move.

The room smells awful. It reeks of blood, and BO, and warm Red Bull.

There's something else there though… fear. It smells like terror in here. Pure and utter panic. For me, that smells like blood, and sick, and that sweaty disinfectant smell hospitals have.

There is also the faintest scent of oranges. That doesn't surprise me. It was Mel's death that started all of this.

Guys? I call out mentally.

The last thing I remember is Lolly lying in my lap. I think – I might've seen Wren and Oscar since then?

I try to push my mind back. My head feels suffocated. I can't hear them at all.

'They're not going to respond. Even if they could, why would they want to?' Tyler says out loud.

They're my friends, I think, but I won't give him the satisfaction of asking what he means by his question.

He comes close to me and puts a finger under my chin. He holds my face as though we are about to kiss.

I don't blame the room for smelling like terror. Being alone with this man sends a shiver down my spine.

He tilts my head back so I'm looking at my hands. I cringe away from his touch instinctively.

My hands are bloody.

Lolly. They were bleeding out. I left Radwa to deal with that on her own.

'I guess we're really not that different after all – both the same type of monster,' he whispers in my ear, his voice a quiet hiss. He laughs. It vibrates off the back of his throat. He inhales, then sighs with a smile. 'Do you smell that, Mitch?'

I try to smell, but the various different scents of blood and panic in this room are overpowering.

This is where he takes them, it occurs to me. The missing people, the new wolves. Their blood, their terror, it's overwhelming. I feel a lump in my throat.

His hand holding my face falls away gently. A touch so soft it could be a lover. Then he slaps me.

'I asked you a question.' He holds my face tight in his hands. 'Do you know whose blood is on your hands?'

I close my eyes. Bubble gum, green tea, oil paint and dog hair. The smell hits me so strongly that I can imagine him, sitting drawing with oil pastels smudged down the side of his hand.

Oscar.

My eyes fly open in panic, betraying my silence. They feel wet. I don't remember doing it. I wish I could remember what happened.

Tyler leans forward, looking me in the eye, then he smiles. 'So you do know.' Then he continues. 'Here's the thing, Mitch. I didn't really even want to hurt Oscar. I don't have anything against the man. If he wants sloppy seconds, or, let's be honest, sloppy tenths or elevenths knowing that bitch, he's welcome to them. Even Lolly just got in the way.'

He scoffs, pulling away and taking a swig of Red Bull before he continues. 'The plan was always to get you or Val. Well, it was since I saw your eyes at your party, that's when I knew that I had to break you. I mean, you gave me no choice after that stunt you pulled in the woods, pulling the pack I created out from under my control. And teaming up with someone who was literally sent to kill me. Until then, I thought maybe we could come to some sort of understanding.'

He tuts, looking at the floor. 'Truthfully, I like it better this way,' he admits as he walks over and reaches above me, turning something.

I look up as something in the ceiling above me roars to life, igniting the room in warmth and light. There is an open hole in the middle, a furnace of sorts, surrounding a clear glass bucket, with a dark purple plant infusing inside and a tap at the bottom.

'This way,' Tyler continues, 'I can finally show you how much pain you caused me when you convinced Mel I wasn't good enough for her.'

He reaches up, pulling experimentally on my shackles. Pain sears through my arms as he does.

Then he pats my shoulder. 'I'll see you tomorrow, Mitch.'

Then he leaves, locking the door behind him.

I look up at my hands, searching for a way to escape, just in time to see the first drop of liquid fall. It scorches my skin as it runs down my face, dripping off the tip of my nose and catching my torso.

Hell hath no fury like an entitled man-child who's been rejected.

Seconds pass. Five, ten, maybe more, enough that I start to hope against hope his contraption is malfunctioning.

Then another drop falls, burning a path down my cheek, narrowly missing my eye.

The third one doesn't miss.

Chapter Twenty-Eight

Oscar

I guess I was expecting everything to be louder. To smell, taste, feel, and sound stronger. To look sharper.

But everything always has. I was ready for that.

I'm used to being overwhelmed. I'm used to feeling like I'm overreacting to everything around me. It's part of being autistic.

I've always been able to hear electricity in wires, candle flames crackling, and the noises most people think of as silence.

What I wasn't expecting was for the noises from *other people's* heads to be so loud.

I can hear them all constantly all the time.

Telepathy wasn't a surprise, but Wren says this is intense, even for a wolf. The way I see it, all my other senses have always been overwhelming, so in some cruel twist of fate whoever is up there said, 'why not this one?'

Wren takes me back to my flat in the morning. It's all getting too much. She has promised Val she will search the woods northwards today.

Lycaon, Magnus and Ash hang out in the car park outside. Occasionally, when I look out the window, Magnus will send me a thumbs-up. Apparently because I've just been turned I need an armed guard. I don't think they want me to recognise that using me as bait might be their best chance of catching him.

Kat, who is getting ready for another competition away next weekend, keeps poking her head in to check if I'm okay.

It's about lunch time when she comes to sit next to me. The mattress barely dips under her weight, she's extremely slight. 'Are you coming through to eat?' she asks, putting her hand on my shoulder.

I dread to think what she must assume is happening after Wren dropped me off with less than half the clothes I left with, then left her family to camp out downstairs.

She asked if we had broken up when Wren left. She was ready to go in with her guns blazing. It's nice to have someone be protective over me like that, someone who knows all the little things I'd be scared to tell anyone else. I love Heidi and Mum but I wouldn't tell them that me and Wren have been intimate together. Hell, I'd barely found the nerve to tell Kat but Wren promised it was okay to. She was worried we'd argued after that because she didn't want to see me trust someone like that only to be let down.

'Not hungry.' I pull the duvet tighter around me.

'What's happened?' Kat asks, wrapping her body around me so her chest is pressed against my back and her arms are around my stomach.

I wish I could tell her everything, or even anything at all.

We used to tell each other everything. She used to come and hide at mine when her parents were being dicks. We went to comps together, memorised each other's routines. I could still show you the last one she competed with me.

I don't see much wrong with telling her what I can. As long as I don't mention the lycanthropy part.

'You know Mitch?' I start to tell her.

'Lolly's straight friend?' She puts emphasis on the word straight.

She keeps teasing me about liking Mitch. It started as a joke when I first said he was hot, then it only got worse once he came to get me from Dad's. Kat said it was like every conversation we had somehow came back to him, until I guess it became obvious it wasn't exactly a joke anymore.

No. By the end of it I do actually have feelings for him.

'You can't mope forever,' Kat starts, rolling her eyes and tossing a curtain of silvery blonde hair over her shoulder. 'You already have a fucking bombshell of a girlfriend so—'

'He's missing.' I cut her off.

Her eyebrows knit together in the middle. 'Missing.'

'Yeah, Kat.' I roll over to look at the skylight. 'Missing. Gone. Royally fucked. So no, I don't want to bloody eat right now!'

Kat flinches.

I feel bad for shouting. She hates when people shout. The sound of her heart hammering only makes me feel worse.

She swallows, sitting up to remove herself from the situation. She knows I get snappy when I'm overloaded, and I don't expect her to sit around with me through it.

'That's why you need to eat something.' She squeezes my shoulder. 'You know how it gets if you stop cause you're stressed.'

She leaves a room temperature chicken and mayo sandwich sitting on the short bookshelf by the door.

I appreciate it but it smells fucking foul. The bread is white and the crusts are creased and squashed in the corners. It smells heavy and doughy. The mayo smells like warm eggs and the chicken stinks of death.

I close my eyes trying to listen for Mitch again. I can hear everyone every second of the day, but I can't hear him.

Thirty-six, thirty-seven, thirty-eight, thirty-nine, forty – wait, was that forty or thirty? Val starts counting again. She is counting how many steps it takes her to walk around the forest.

Radwa is praying, I try not to intrude but it is so loud.

I'm sure Lolly can hear it too. They are alive in there. I can hear that they are alive.

Wren is thinking about coming to check that I am okay.

I am not.

I can't hear Mitch. Every time I try to I get this blinding pain that feels as though it splits my face in two.

So I sit in the dark, underneath my covers, with no lights on, and put my earphones in, trying to concentrate on just one sound.

Eventually I fall asleep from the exhaustion of being so overwhelmed and only wake up when Wren comes in.

'Oscar?' she asks softly.

'Wren?' I turn to look for her with my head still under the cover.

She lifts it gently, sitting down on the edge of my bed.

She tucks herself under with me. It reminds me of the time we made a blanket fort together, one of the first times she stayed at mine. She had wanted to make this perfect night where we could have sex for the first time. She got herself so worked up about it that she had a panic attack on the kitchen floor. So we ordered food and made a blanket fort instead. We'd kissed a lot in that fort. Held each other. She cried, and I comforted her. Now I am crying and she is comforting me.

How can I help?

Too loud, her internal voice is too loud. Apparently that happens with mates. I indicate this to her by bringing my hands up to my head and scrunching my face up.

So she stops talking. Instead, she pulls over a big hoodie and my teddy bear.

It's from Build-a-Bear. I got it when I was nine. Kat had a

matching one and they both wore pink leotards. We got them after a competition down in Glasgow.

'Let's go for a nap,' she suggests in a whisper.

Then she passes me the hoodie. It is black with red writing and the Vans logo across the chest.

I run my finger over the bandage that sits on top of my chest.

I forgot to give it back.

You'd think I'd be mad at him for doing this to me, but I'm not. His eyes were glowing silver. They were streaming. His eyebrows were knitted together. Focused. Like he was fighting it somehow. Like this was him holding back on Tyler's command.

I wish I could talk to him. I wish I knew.

Mitch is on my mind when I fall asleep.

When I wake up I'm in someone else's body.

The room is dimly lit.

It smells horrendous.

I'm underground somewhere. I can tell by how the voices echo off the walls.

I feel a dull ache in my wrists. I look up to find them shackled to the ceiling. Only they are not mine. They belong to someone white, extremely pale, with light orange freckles and tattoos.

Someone enters the room.

He walks forward. 'Good morning, Mitchell. How are you today?' He grabs my face, fingers digging into a fresh wound down my cheek. It feels hot like a burn.

He turns me so I'm looking him in the eyes. I can barely see from one of them.

God, this is horrible.

'Did you enjoy your night? Cool machine huh?' Tyler opens his can of juice and walks in circles. 'I can make it stop. You just need to give it up. Accept me as your alpha.'

And leave them vulnerable? I think to myself. I know I can't let him take the reins.

I laugh at him derisively. I feel almost cocky.

I've handled much worse before, I think. I know it's true in this vision even though I personally haven't.

I hear Tyler put his can down. His footsteps approach.

I'll die before I let him hurt my friends. I think I'd die happy if they were safe.

His face enters my frame of vision.

'Oh, need I remind you?' He puts a finger under my chin, lifting my head so I'm looking up at my wrists, so I can see the blood smeared on my right hand, embedded under the fingernails of my left. 'You already have.'

I can smell it. Who it belongs to. It's mine, and not dream me, not Mitch. Mine; Oscar's.

I know at that moment Mitch thinks I am dead. He thinks he has killed me.

I try to scream for him, but as I do something forces me out of his head.

Wren is sitting over me when I wake up.

'Are you okay? You were having a—'

'I need Val.' I cut her off. 'Get Val.'

Val

Mitch's mum has been calling me all morning. So has my dad, and an unknown number that I reckon is probably a police officer of some kind.

Mitch's parents have already put out a call for information on his whereabouts. I know I should fill them in. But I can't do it. I can't bring myself to pick their calls up.

What would I even tell them? The last text I've received from Anna says, in bold letters:

> ANNA
> Hiya pet, Mitch n Lolly r not
> replying to my txts. R u all OK?
> Love you lots - Anna xxxxx

If I could hear him, hear anything at all, I'd have something more to tell her. I don't know how to even begin to tell her that Mitch is gone, and Lolly is as good as.

I'm about to throw my phone across the room again when Wren and Oscar come through the door.

'He's alive,' Oscar says as they come in. He sits down on the couch next to me. He grabs my hands. His eyes are wet and there are dark bags under them. 'Val, he's alive. He's with Tyler.'

Oscar's words hit me like a ton of bricks.

'How do you know?' I ask even though I knew that.

Logically, we all had to know that if he was alive he was with Tyler.

'Saw them.' Oscar's face is a grimace.

The fleeting relief I felt is replaced with panic as my mind draws up all kinds of images of what Tyler could be doing to him.

I tap my arms six times. Mitch, Me, Radwa, Lolly, Wren, Oscar. I don't know why it keeps up safe.

Wren crouches down to look at me with a gentle calmness, breathing slowly and meeting my eyes, watching for the moment my mind finds some clarity.

'Val.' She smiles. 'He's alive, that means that whatever else happens we can still save him.'

'Where is he?' I ask Oscar.

'Trying to get back in so I can see,' he promises. 'I don't think he's the one blocking me out, but he can't hear me there either.'

He shifts on the couch next to me. He looks like shit. Absolutely emotionally exhausted. I wonder if he's slept.

Mitch's jumper, it's slightly too long on his arms. The one I'm wearing is too long on me too. I hug it tight around me.

'Is he okay?' I feel the need to ask even though I know the answer.

I keep sniffling. Tears coat my cheeks. A beat passes where all I hear is my own shaky breath.

Then Oscar shakes his head. 'But he's holding on, and his cockiness is annoying the shit out of Tyler.'

I sniffle and let out a laugh. Sounds like Mitch.

'What's he doing to him?' I ask, even though I'm not sure I want to know. I feel like I owe it to him to know, to be able to be there with him.

'You really don't want to know that,' he groans, pressing the palms of his hands into his eyes as if to push the image out.

But not knowing somehow makes it worse. I can't stand to think about him alone with Tyler like that.

'Is he hurt?' I ask. I can feel my heartbeat rise.

'Val,' Wren warns. It's reproachful, as if to say that I shouldn't ask questions that I don't want answered.

But I do.

'Oscar?' I look at him.

He bites the dry skin around his nails as if he really doesn't want to tell me. 'Yes, he's hurt,' he eventually says.

Wren glares at him for telling me, and he shrugs apologetically.

'Is he fighting back?' I ask.

'Val.' Wren touches my arm gently.

'Can he fight back?' I push.

Oscar looks uncomfortable but I can't bring myself to care all that much.

Oh God, what if he can't? What if he's entirely at the mercy of that monster? What if—?

'Where is he hurt?'

My heart bangs in my ears.

'How did he hurt him, Oscar?'

I grab him.

'Is he going to be okay?'

Oscar looks up at me, scared, for a moment, and then his expression falls.

Oh God. He's not going to be okay, is he?

I have to keep him safe. I have to keep us all safe.

Tap. I tell myself. I try to shake it off by lightly tapping my arms. Six times. One for each other us.

Tap! How can I keep them safe? I ask myself. Since the first one clearly didn't work I try again just to pacify the thoughts.

TAP! The taps are harder this time. Bruises are forming and healing just as quickly under my hands. My skin feels tender. I know it's illogical, but how would I feel if I didn't do it and something did happen?

When I bring my hands to my shoulders again they meet Wren's, and she holds them. 'Val, you're making yourself panic, and you're hurting yourself.'

'Mitch has been kidnapped by a fucking serial killer, Wren. Amongst other things. Of course, I'm fucking panicking!' I basically shout in her face.

She takes a deep breath in and sits me down. 'Val, if you can calm down, I'll let Oscar explain what's going on, but I need you calm first.'

'I am calm!' I snap back. 'This is a rational response!'

Wren side-eyes me. Oscar asks me to name something red and I just about lose it at both of them.

'The writing,' I eventually spit out after snapping their heads off. 'On your jumper.' I point at Oscar.

Wren squeezes my shoulder gently. Radwa's Switch, which sits on the table, has orange stickers. The thread in Oscar's pride bracelet is yellow. His cargo pants are green. Wren's bracelet has a baby blue thread, and their jumper is purple.

I take a deep breath. 'Now tell me, please. I can handle it.'

I listen as Oscar explains the room, the pain in Mitch's face and around his wrists. I cringe to hear how Mitch remains cocky as ever in the face of all of it.

I want to tell him to stay quiet. I silently pray he can hear me begging him not to give Tyler any ammunition.

Wren

We convince Val that she has to be the one to tell Mitch's family what happened. Charlie and Anna look so confused when we appear at the door with Dad and Magnus in tow.

Dad helps a lot. Suggests we all have a cup of tea to talk.

Anna is stony like she's in utter disbelief.

Charlie is erratic and emotional. He cries and shouts. He keeps saying we all need to be out looking right now, himself included. He says he couldn't live with himself if something happened. It's his job to protect him, to look after his son.

Dad has to calm him down. He is shaking. I think it hits quite close to home right now with everything happening with Phelan.

He promises we will go out and look, we just need to get some things to get a scent to look for him.

Anna taps her nails against her mug. Her eyes seem entirely zoned out as if she's looking at nothing.

'Where's Lolly?' she eventually says. 'I want to see them.'

Magnus puts a hand on her shoulder. 'They're with Phelan. He's a healer. They're guarded by three of our best. Radwa is with them too. I can take you now if you want.'

Anna nods, making to go outside. Charlie follows her, clinging to Dad for support.

Val goes upstairs to look for some things with Mitch's scent as we get them into the car.

She takes a second, so I wave Dad off and tell him to take Mitch's parents and we'll meet them there. Oscar travels with them so Dad and Magnus can protect him from any attempts Tyler might make to get to him.

I climb Mitch's stairs one by one.

When I get to his room the first thing I notice is that we share a wall. Our beds are pressed back to back. His room is oddly neat, not the way I'd expect him to be.

He has several bookcases that appear to be overflowing, though, and collages of Polaroid pictures on the wall of him and the pack. Some of him and Melissa, too.

Val stands by his dresser, a jumper over her arm.

She holds a red box in her hands. It's open.

Her sobs are silent, but so strong that her entire body shakes. She has her left hand in her mouth, biting her finger to stay quiet.

I don't quite know what to say so I just wrap my arms around her while she sobs into my chest.

Radwa

I give Anna and Charlie some space with Lolly when they arrive. Val appears not long afterwards, having been given a ride back on Wren's bike.

She hands out articles of Mitch's clothing to people in Wren's pack. She has this strange look on her face.

When I come closer I see that her cheeks are red and puffy, tear-stained. She must've been crying not moments ago because they're still wet.

She takes a deep breath in when she opens the bag, then draws herself up to her full height. An icy curtain falls, and prideful hands grip tightly at a mask of calmness.

She looks terrifying.

I think what's scariest is I can hear her thoughts right now. They have stopped rushing. She has reached a level of clarity, of cold calculation, that could kill. And judging from where her thoughts are going, this time I think it will.

As she reaches forward to hand Lycaon a shirt, I see something glinting in the light on her left hand.

Val

They say the first twenty-four hours are the most important when someone goes missing. But they don't know my fiancé.

So we didn't find him tonight. That doesn't matter. We will tomorrow. We will.

I feel my teeth grind together as my jaw sets hard.

Radwa comes down the stairs and sits on the bottom step next to me. Oscar and Wren are out by the campfire with Wren's family and Mitch's parents.

She gestures to the ring. 'Where did you get that?'

I shrug. 'Found it in his drawer.'

I count my breaths, trying to stay calm. I feel ready to start crying again. There was a note in there too; a speech he'd been rehearsing, with bits crossed out, bits scribbled in. He had been planning it so precisely.

There had been so many moments scribbled down he wanted to talk about.

First kiss??
Christmas dance 6th year

I wondered what he wanted to say about that. I only remember skiving off the tail end to go and smoke a joint behind the science block. I don't smoke a lot but it did help me unwind that night. We laughed so hard I nearly peed, clutching my skirt up and falling into him as we walked home together.

Maybe that was it.

He's written down a joke about how we always make each other laugh, then lead into an anecdote about our first time. Which has then been scribbled out with a note to remind him not to say that in front of other people.

> → ~~our first time~~
> (don't say that in front of other people.)

He eventually decided less was more because those memories are scored out with a note that says:

> you'll stutter too much
> to say any of this

That's what made me cry. Throughout it all – his nerves, his careful planning of all the details, down to getting me and Radwa a nail appointment for pictures – his worst fear was not that I would say no.

No, the worst thing that Mitch could imagine in that moment was fucking up the moment somehow with his nervous energy. Good job babe, I mentally berate him. You really outdid yourself.

I look at Radwa. 'Did you know?'

She nods. 'We all did. Your dad too.'

God, Dad. I pick up my phone to give him a call.

He answers on the second ring. 'Valeria?'

When I hear his voice I start crying again. Then I tell him everything.

Chapter Twenty-Nine

Mitch

It's three days before I see Tyler again.
He comes in early in the morning as if excited
to see something, like a kid on Christmas.
'How are you feeling today?'
He looks at me.
There's something sadistic in his smile.
He comes closer and grabs at my face,
forcing my chin up to look at him.
I can feel tears welling in my eyes.
I won't cry.
This bastard isn't getting to see me cry.
He looks at them.
Studies them for a moment.
Then he throws the can of juice
he's holding against the wall.
He walks over to the table
and brushes everything off of it,

then kicks it over.
His tantrum doesn't intimidate me.
I feel myself start to smile;
he's losing.

Chapter Thirty

Mitch

Two more days pass.
Tyler tantrums
each time he sees me.
On the third day
something has changed.
I see the expression on his face
when he approaches me.
I pull back on the shackles.

'No.'

I hear my voice for the first time in days.

'You stay the fuck away from me.'

                                    The shackles rub up

and down my arms
as
I
twist
and
squirm
away
from

                                                him.

Chapter Thirty-One

Radwa

The steely way Val's eyes set on me lets me know I've messed up. She crosses her arms, pulling the soft red zippy she's wearing back onto her shoulder to cover her irritated skin.

'Right,' she scoffs, voice resigned, as she picks at the scabbed, bleeding skin on her chest where her bumblebee pendant usually sits. 'Because how could *I* possibly understand what it's like to have your mate bleeding out in your lap – choking on their own fucking blood?'

My jaw sets tense with the effort to hold my mouth shut.

I'm not saying that's the part she doesn't understand! I'm trying to say that no one tried to keep her from her mate's side when he was in that condition. Mateo would drive her up to the hospital every single day, waiting in the car park for hours at a time, just to placate Val's imminent need to be close to him.

Admittedly, I could've been nicer when I told Val that no, I didn't want to come on another pointless traipse around the woods trying to find a trail that has almost certainly been washed away by the last three nights' rain.

But she wasn't taking no for an answer, and the idea of leaving Lolly's side right now makes all my hair stand up on end.

My lack of response only angers Val further. 'Are you *really* doing this shit again *right now?*' She looks at me, utterly exhausted.

I know anything I do say now won't come out right. I care too much about our relationship to argue with her on this, and – while I know she's not wrong – too much righteous anger sits in my throat to let me admit that we could both be right.

My lips pull tighter and I bite my tongue 'til I taste blood.

'Radwa,' Val tries again, eyes wide. '*Seriously?*'

I grimace as she forces her way into my head. I push hard against her. Light flashes in my mind's eye, making my head throb.

'Are you blocking me out as well?' She laughs derisively, bloody fingernails coming away from her exposed scab.

I don't know how to tell her I have to. I *don't* want her in my head right now. Because she can't see how hopeless I feel.

Searching for Mitch with no evidence, no trail, no *anything*. I'm starting to wonder if we'll ever find him, and focusing my efforts on Lolly feels less dismal because – well, at least we know they're still alive.

That makes me sound horrible, doesn't it? I feel awful just thinking that, and I know if she heard that it would break her heart.

She doesn't though, because she's still looking at me expectantly.

Then she tuts and shakes her head, tugging a hand through her mop of silvery curls that she's not bothered straightening since the last moon. Dark hairs are creeping in at the roots.

'Fine.' She rolls her eyes, slapping her legs as she stands

up. 'I printed some posters; can you at least make yourself useful and ask Aadilla to put them up in the mosque?'

She closes the door behind herself, not giving me time to answer.

Val

I always found the flyers all over town for missing people sad. I know it's bad to say but I guess it just seems so… desperate. The longer they stay up the sadder it gets. Especially when the ink is clearly new, with no sign of being bleached by the sun, despite the date being months ago.

It doesn't stop me printing my own though.

Dad takes some to mass with him. Oscar, accompanied by three bodyguards at a time, asks his work to put some up. His flatmate Kat puts some up at her gym. This morning's fight with Radwa aside, we have all been trying to keep each other sane amidst the sea of anger and upset.

The most frustrating part is the reports from people thinking they're being helpful because his 'spirit came to them'. I'm not sure what the fuck that means but I'm damn sure if he came to any one it would be me, Lolly or Oscar. Or maybe his fucking parents, I don't know. It wouldn't be Becky in her corner shop down the street.

Besides, he's not dead. I know he's not, and I know that sounds like I'm in denial but Oscar can hear him. I know he's alive.

I decide to pop over to his church on Sunday, since it's the only day it's open outside of their summer camp. I'm not religious any more, but the one thing I did like about the church I was brought up in is that it was always open if you needed help. Protestants don't really do that.

I'm eyeing the rest of the desperately updated missing posters for people I know are likely dead or turned when the priest approaches me.

'Valeria,' he says with a smile. He's a nice man, with the kind of calm manner that makes you feel the need to hold your breath around him.

I hold the posters out to him wordlessly. I'm not really sure what to say.

He takes them from me and nods gently. He smiles sadly with a profound resignation. 'One of the only times he will accept a man of faith saying he'll pray for him, I imagine,' he says tightly. His voice sounds gruff.

'I told his favourite story at the service today. How Jesus fed the five thousand with fish and bread.' He folds his arms sitting back against the wall. It looks strange to see a priest lean. 'One of the children mentioned how he would bring extra fish he got from work for lunches and food drives.' He tuts. 'You have a good man there. I pray that's the last time his name will come up in a service for a long while. God willing he will be found safely. Have faith.' He squeezes my hand before turning to find a space in the pin board. When I turn to leave I swear I see the strangest wet sparkle in the old man's eyes.

When I get back in my car I see the rosary my *abuela* got me for my birthday one year hanging there. I've not prayed in years, I believe in myself more than I believe in any God. If God would let this happen then He's a sick fuck.

I stare at it blankly. The desperation to find Mitch that lives in me prickles like velour that's been brushed the wrong way.

I snatch the black beads down.

Radwa

After Val leaves, we have an emergency with Lolly. They almost don't pull through.

Phelan manages to get their heart going again and tells me

that he'll watch over them for an hour or so while I take some time to myself in case they need a healer on site.

So I sit downstairs going through my print-outs from Emma's social media and different pages of *Choosing Violence: Understanding Rogue Wolves and the Packs They Create* just to see if there's any hint I can find that would help us with Mitch, feeling bad for pushing against Val earlier.

I know she meant nothing by it, but her asking me to 'make myself useful' really stuck with me.

After all my research culminating in my suspicion of Oscar turned out to be wrong, I sort of got defeated. I let my friends down.

The infuriating thing is the evidence was all actually there in my notes.

Emma saved Aimee from being spiked at that party – the same party where Tyler spiked Wren. He was there at the other party where Mitch's journal was returned, and he *knew* Val studied art because we all went to school together. He probably found out about Lotta from Mitch's diary so it makes sense that I was the only one he couldn't track exactly. The way he looked at Mitch's eyes that night as well, like he recognised something, like he was daring him to try it. He stank, not because he didn't wash, but because he *couldn't*. He toyed with Lolly, purposefully goading them into a fight, just to see what would happen. And he had motive right from the very start: Mel, and how he thought she belonged to him. Like an object.

Moreover, he fits the exact personality type profiled by rogue-hunters for generations: egotistic, privileged, used to getting what he wants. My eyes burn with frustrated tears threatening to spill out. I hate how close I was to getting it.

Scanning over the pages of *Choosing Violence*, it's basically a checklist for this disgusting excuse for a man.

Then I get to chapter ten, 'The Rogue's Pack'. They turn a pack to use as a food supply, and so finding where they keep the victims is the most important thing to do after killing the rogue.

A paragraph stands out against the page.

In all but one of the case studies, both the primary den and the secondary location of the rogue wolf were found underground. This is widely believed to be due to rogues in the late stages of sickness becoming highly photosensitive.

I stare at it, burning the words into the page with my eyes, willing the text to tell me *where* I can find Mitch.

The door to the clubhouse clatters open and Wren appears. 'Sorry I'm late!' they call up the stairs. 'Val?'

I'm no longer crying when they see me. I think I've run out of tears the past few days.

They still know somehow. 'What now?' they ask.

I tell them.

I tell them about me and Val's fight, and how the information was right there. Then I tell them what happened with Lolly and how I'm not sure how long they have left. Phelan doesn't think there's much more their body can take before we're doing more harm than good. And I tell them I don't know what I'm supposed to think about that. Or say. Or do. Because if it was up to me I'd keep trying forever, but I'm not sure that's fair to them. I know Val would say to be persistent. It's what she's doing.

I'm telling Wren about it all when the door opens again.

Wren

Radwa's despair is palpable, suffocating, and it takes everything in me not to join her. I hate that she blames herself. If anyone *should* have known Tyler was the rogue, it was me. But I let him sneak past my defense undetected. I guess she *was* right about my naïvety.

When Val comes in, she unclips her knife holster and throws it on the floor. 'Fucking nothing! His scent leads nowhere. It just disappears!' she shouts, taking her jacket off as well.

The black beaded rosary that she's been wearing on her wrist since she visited Mitch's church this morning falls off with a clatter as she does. She races over to pick it up. Her hair falls into her face, half out her pleats.

'I tried looking,' Radwa says in a very small voice, then her lip wobbles. 'Lolly's gotten worse.'

Val's shoulders fall suddenly. She comes to hug her sister.

When she pulls back, Radwa looks at her. I see a strange emotion wash over her face.

She brushes Val's hair to the side. 'Val, what – what happened to your eyes?'

And sure enough, the girl in front of us stares back, unblinking, one eye the same silver it was this morning, the other a burning gold.

Oscar

My headache only gets worse the longer Mitch is missing. I keep trying to get back through. Picking at the corners of his psyche, trying to pull them up like a sticker to uncover what's happening.

I'm sitting upstairs in the clubhouse, listening to one of his playlists and leafing through the copy of *Dorian Gray* he gave me, when he gives me a glimpse again.

The first thing I notice is how much I hurt. I feel pained and defeated. My entire body aches. There is a pain deep inside me worse than anything I've ever felt. Mitch is used to it.

My skin crawls and I feel like I need to rip my way out of it. Like it's so contaminated that my only option is to destroy it entirely.

'You're a fucking coward,' Mitch shouts after Tyler.

He pulls at the shackles around his wrists, jangling them as he speaks. His skin sears all the way up his forearm. There is a fierce burn cutting through his bumblebee tattoo.

He sobs. I think about how determined he was not to let out so much as a gasp. What happened?

'You've always been nothing more than a fucking coward!' Spit and snot fly from his mouth as he speaks.

He holds his breath then takes in heavy gulps of air; he panics.

He thinks about Mel, about Wren, about himself and Val. He hates himself for giving in, for not fighting back enough.

I want to tell him it's okay to stop fighting. That he has done enough to protect them, to protect us. That we are coming.

He just needs to let us find him. To give us a hint.

Tyler gives a smirk. He tilts Mitch's head up. Mitch tries to turn his cheek away.

They make eye contact. 'Much better.' Tyler smiles, and then he leaves.

The door shuts behind him. I hear it lock.

Then I feel Mitch's legs buckle underneath him. His ears follow Tyler's footsteps up a set of stairs and to a hatch door.

He can hear animal noises above: forest animals. There's a river nearby. The sound is familiar to him. It feels like home. A place that was always safe, always dear to him, is close.

I grab his journal from the box next to me, pushing away the notebook I was using to write down each of the single letters that have been highlighted. Val said I could sit in their room. She brought his journal when we were trying to pick up a scent, but it was faded. He hadn't used it in a while and the pages had been sprayed with something unfamiliar.

Normally I wouldn't invade his privacy by looking through it, but I can't help but wonder if there's any clue to where he is in it. The code seems to just spell out his favourite quote which is sweet and makes so much sense for him but it doesn't seem to be helpful at all.

Photos of him with a horrendous black fringe spew out. Val is in some, her hair varying in length and colour across the years. His sister is in most of them.

There is one of them pressing their cheeks together, their eyes wide showing off the colour. Huh. I never knew what his eyes were like before he turned. God. They were breathtaking.

There's a scratch on the front of the picture, a line leading to the scenery behind them. An old grate in the ground. Like a doorway. Something or someone in me recognises it.

I turn it around to see if there are any hints.

The only thing that glaring back at me is the caption someone has given it. '**Pretty.**'

It's one of four that have been captioned, out of maybe thirty. I put it down next to the others.

What an odd note to make. It doesn't look like the writing I've been staring at in the book for hours.

I gather the four captioned pictures in my hand stacking them on top of each other to compare the writing.

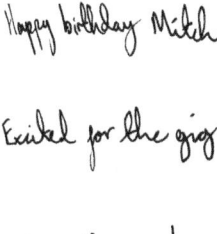

That's when I notice it. The letters each caption starts with spell out '**H. E. L. P.**'

I spread out the rest of the pictures on the bed. At least sixteen of them have the same building in the background. And all of them have purposeful scratches marking the same location.

Wren comes through the door quickly without knocking.

'Jesus!' I shout, coming back to and dropping the picture.

'It's Val,' they say. They're breathing heavily. Panicked. I think they're crying. 'Her eyes have changed.'

Mitch was the acting alpha for the pack. That meant one of his eyes was gold to represent his fate to challenge the rogue alpha and the other was silver to represent his obedience to him in the meantime.

If Val's eyes have changed it could mean two things: Mitch is dead, or Mitch has given up.

I think about my vision. Mitch was crying. Tyler has done something horrible to him, something which was enough to break his will, but also enough to give Val the strength to challenge him, to kill him.

I try to think about what he could do to make Mitch give up. Then I decide that I'd rather he was dead, for his sake.

'I think I know where he is,' I tell her. My voice shakes with the fear that it's too little too late.

Chapter Thirty-Two

Mitch

My skin feels raw.

Marks gouged into it,

imprinted on a body

that doesn't feel like mine anymore.

I've never felt this powerless in all my life.

He just keeps going,

until there is no part of my body

that does not belong to his game.

The urge to cry is gone now.
I want to, more than ever,
but now I can't feel anything but

numb.

                                        under my chin,

                              tucks a finger

               he's looking for when he

I don't know what change

forcing my tear stained face

                up into the light

                        of the fire but he seems to get it

                                because it finally, finally

        makes him leave.

                        me,

My legs buckle underneath

                    my wrists

        hanging from

leaving me

                                        once

                                                more.

The door opens and

                I feel a lump of tears enter my throat again.

            What more can he do to me?
            What more can he take from me?

But
the
breeze
doesn't
smell
like Tyler.

                It smells like hair dye, patchouli, and bleach.

'Mitch?'

                    Val.

I can hear her voice. I frantically look around.
'You're alive.' She runs over to me and pulls me back to my feet.

She explains that she ran into Tyler on his way out. She only just caught him with a knife to his shoulder. He's run off to lick his wounds. She didn't follow because she'd been too focused on finding me.

It sinks in somehow, but her words feel like white noise. I'm spinning with it all. I feel like I'm going to throw up.

'I'm gonna take you home, okay?'

I try to respond. But I can't open my mouth. I taste blood and bile. I feel as though he's taken my voice from me entirely.

She unclips the chain from the hook it hangs on, hissing as it burns her hands.

My legs shake when I try to move them and so she picks me up. I feel silly like I should be the one rescuing her. But I'm not afraid to admit that I bury my face into the crook of her neck and silently sob as she takes me back to the clubhouse. She gets to see me cry.

Everything that's happened in the past two weeks, that's happened just today, it all comes to the surface and comes out in floods. I wish I could forget.

I feel my brain slip away again as Val carries me back.

Chapter Thirty Three

Radwa

I wait back at the clubhouse for Oscar, Val and Wren to return with Mitch.

Lycaon waits with me, tapping his foot on the step. He is not impressed that they all left. He was out taking a call from back home when they did. I was the one to let him know.

I see four figures in the distance in front of us, and I run. I stop right before I get to Mitch. I have to fight myself not to wrap my arms around him.

'What the fuck, Wren?' Lycaon storms towards us.

She knows she's in trouble. She accepted that when she led two people with next to no training on a rescue mission against not just a rogue but a dangerous, callous man.

'Lycaon, he's our mate. The fuck did you want me to do?' she replies, holding her hands up.

'Wait for back-up! You put your other mates at risk.'

'Oh, suck a dick. They're fine.'

'You took a freshly turned werewolf, and your mate at that, straight into a rogue den, Wren!'

Honestly, he's right. She did put Val and Oscar at risk by

letting them go on this mission. But he's mad if he thinks there was ever going to be any stopping either of them going when they set their mind to it.

'Yeah,' Wren shrugs. 'Well, some of us are willing to take a fucking risk for our packs.'

Honestly, I think Oscar would've been more of a danger to himself and everyone else around him if he wasn't allowed to go. Even if they weren't relying on his telepathic connection to Mitch to find him, I think he would've fought tooth and nail to be part of the search party. There really is no stopping someone when their mate is at risk.

I think I understand that a lot better after the past week. It's like some feral instinct snaps in you.

Mitch stumbles forward from where he's stood behind her and hisses slightly as the heavy metal chain between his cuffs pulls on his wrist.

Lycaon's expression softens. 'Come over here and kneel by this stump.'

Val helps him get over and Lycaon takes out his axe.

'Hold still,' he instructs, seriously.

Mitch seems too exhausted to care when he swings the axe between his hands.

Mitch's hands and forearms are burnt, not in a simple band around his wrist but all the way up his hands and arms, as far up as the shackles could slide. As if he has been fighting against them. Long frantic burn lines jerk up and down them.

Lycaon looks at Wren as if they're going to be having words later, then ducks under Mitch's arm to help Val carry him inside.

Wren

When we get into the clubhouse, Phelan has already grabbed a first aid kit and started sanitising things. Radwa rushes ahead of us to help him clear a sterile place for Mitch.

Val and Lycaon take Mitch to the couch.

He sits there for a moment, staring. He's not saying anything and from the sounds of it he's not even thinking anything. A blistered scar runs down the centre of his face, dripping over to his eye which, once golden, is now a milky white.

His top half is bare, except for dirty, peeling tape around his chest and a tarnished cross hanging from his neck. His trousers are filthy, there's blood on them.

He is covered in fresh scratches: long jagged ones across his back, precise nicks on his stomach and arms telling of a calculated cruelty. His ribs are covered in black bruises, his face with lighter ones, and clusters of smaller ones on his hips and arms.

I think it must be a curse to be able to recognise each wound and predict what caused them. My eyes rest on the bruises on his torso and his hips. He catches me looking, then looks down as if scared to meet my glance.

I'm sorry, I think. *I should've realised what he was. I was closer to him than anyone. I'm sorry.*

Radwa comes to stand by my side and gives my shoulder a squeeze. I put my hand on hers. Her touch pulls me back into the moment.

'Mitch?' Phelan is asking when I zone back in.

Oscar glances at him, with concern.

'Can you speak?' Phelan asks.

Mitch looks like the question immobilises him. Oscar crouches down trying to get level with him. Mitch looks away. He can't meet his eyes either.

This doesn't seem to bother Oscar. 'Nod or shake. Anything physically stopping you speaking? Anything hurt?'

Mitch shakes his head.

'Do you feel like you can speak?'

Mitch shakes his head again.

'Okay. You don't have to speak. We're not gonna make

you speak, okay? Give him a second.' Oscar steps back. 'And some space. Give him some space.'

Val leaves, then comes back with some water and sits down at his side. She puts her arm on the couch so it wraps around him without holding him to her or overwhelming him.

Lycaon tells me he's gonna go and update Dad, Magnus, Ash and Harley who were out looking for us. We all wait for a moment.

It's Phelan who finally speaks. 'Can you nod and shake for me for some check-ins?'

Mitch lets out a breath and nods.

'Can you breathe without pain?'

Mitch shakes his head.

'Is the pain in your chest?'

He shakes his head and points to a black bruise across his ribs.

'Do you want some painkillers?'

He nods.

Phelan grabs a bag and starts rifling through. 'Any allergies?'

He nods, and Val answers for him.

'Can you swallow anything?'

He shakes his head. He smells like sick. I wonder if that's why.

'You've been sick right?' Phelan picks up on it.

Mitch nods.

'Are you gonna be sick again?'

Mitch nods.

'Why is he being sick?' Phelan asks more of himself than anyone else. 'Did he use aconite?'

Mitch shrugs.

'You didn't have your T. So is it a flare up making you sick?' Val asks.

Mitch nods.

Phelan nods and starts looking through his bag again. 'Aconite is a flower known as wolfsbane. It's poisonous in general but especially to us. Did you ingest anything like this?' He pulls up a picture on his phone.

Mitch's eyes go wide as he nods.

Phelan grabs a vial. 'Okay, that's fine. I can give you something to stop the sickness. This should work. I'll wait for your go-ahead on that, and I'll explain everything as I'm doing it, promise. Then I can give you painkillers that'll probably make you pass out. But we need to clean you up first so I can see what the damage is and assess some risks. Nothing seems to be haemorrhaging so my priority is cleaning up so we can bathe the burns and flush out any remaining aconite in the cuts. You won't heal normally if there's any in your bloodstream. If we clean you up and get the binding tape off we can figure out where the worst bruising is too. Do you think you can manage a shower? If Val helps you clean up?'

Mitch nods frantically as if he's begging to go for a shower, and for the first time, he makes eye contact with me. There are tears in his eyes.

Fuck. I get that choking feeling. Terror.

Val squeezes his hand gently. 'I'm gonna call your mum, let her know you're okay.'

It's going to take a long time before Mitch is okay again, isn't it?

Fuck.

Fuck Tyler.

Val leaves and Radwa follows her out, taking a momentary break to check on Lolly. Mitch curls in on himself in a ball on the couch.

Oscar sits on the edge by his head. He flinches slightly away from him.

'Sorry,' Oscar backs away a little, 'didn't mean to scare you.' He gives him a smile.

Mitch doesn't return it. His eyes dart away from Oscar the

second he looks at him. As if scared to meet his eyes. As if scared to see the change in them.

'Mitch,' I call softly. 'I'm gonna sit down on your other side, okay?'

He nods, sitting up to make space.

'Look at me,' I whisper, slotting myself in next to him, careful to keep our legs and arms from touching so as not to startle him.

He presses his lips together as if he's trying not to cry. He looks up.

'None of this was your fault, Mitch.' I put my hand between us, within his reach so he can take it if he wants to. 'Not what happened to Oscar, not what he did to you. No one blames you for not being able to fight him.' The words catch in my throat, and sting at my eyes.

Phelan looks over and gives me a look. The words are familiar.

Mitch's eyes well up and he swallows hard. He grips my hand for dear life. His nails are red and bloody, and his hands and arms are both scarred and dirty.

It's not your fault either, Phelan reminds me.

This is.

Mitch shakes his head. He looks me in the eye and shakes his head, then gives my hand a squeeze. I feel tears come to my eyes. Mitch is already crying.

'Do you want a hug?' I whisper.

In response, he lets his head fall on my shoulder and lets himself cry, harder than I've seen him cry before. His body shakes.

His hair is greasy against my cheek. He smells like blood, piss, sweat and something sour, like fear, like terror. I've never been happier to hug him.

I untangle my hand from his. 'Gonna hug you properly, okay?'

He nods. I wrap my arms around him tight, and he does the same.

He holds on. He cries so hard I'm scared he might fall apart in my arms, but he holds on.

Oscar

I watch as Mitch leans into Wren. I think about what I saw, how much it would've taken to break him like this. I back away from them carefully, giving him space.

His crying eventually quiets. He sits staring at his hands where they rest on Wren's shoulders. His bloodstained hands.

Then he looks around, panicked. His hand comes to touch his neck, just behind his ear, subconsciously settling over a small black semi-colon.

'They've not woke up yet,' Radwa tells him as she comes in.

He unfolds from the cuddle Wren had wrapped him in and drops his hands to his lap.

Val joins us. 'Their lung collapsed,' she adds to Radwa's point, putting a comforting hand on her knee. 'Radwa did some *ridiculously* quick thinking and managed to save them but they've been unconscious since.'

Radwa gives her a smile.

Then Val tells Mitch about my ability, how I can hear everyone more than most, how we found him, and how we know that they're still in there somewhere.

'We're doing everything we can,' Phelan promises him. 'And you can see them whenever you want. I just need to get you to clean up first so I can check your injuries out.'

Val crouches down to eye level with her fiancé. 'Your parents are gonna meet us here as soon as possible. Do you want to shower before you see them?'

He nods once more. Then follows Phelan to get the anti-sickness injection administered so he can shower safely.

Kat's out, so I take them back to my flat since it's closest. I pass them through the softest towel I can find, along with some joggers and a hoodie for Mitch to borrow.

I lean against the kitchen counter making tea while Ash and Phelan sit in the living room. Wren stayed back with her Dad because he wanted a word.

I hear the water start running.

And then I hear Mitch crying again.

Mitch doesn't cry quietly, he cries like he is falling apart. He chokes on his tears. It's so goddamn hard to listen to. It tugs at my heartstrings until they snap.

And it hurts because I can see him laughing, head thrown back, while we sat together on my bathroom floor that day he helped me take my stuff home from Dad's. I can see him looking at me softly, while we smoke together, his hand running through his hair, a smile on his lips.

I can imagine his smile.

It's so wide it splits his face in two, like a child in their first school picture. His full cheeks, his buck teeth.

His face was made for joy. He deserves nothing but joy, and yet here he is, sobbing as though he may never smile again.

Val

'Hey.' I crouch down by Mitch.

He has stripped as far as his boxers and is sitting on Oscar's bathroom floor, knees tucked up to his chest. Hyperventilating. His hands are balled into fists in his hair.

I gently cup mine around them and pry them open, before taking them in my own.

I don't know what to say from here. I have no fucking clue.

I feel like I used to when Mel first died. Powerless to help.

So I just sit there with him and let him cry, holding his

hands in mine so he doesn't hurt himself while he does. That's all I can do.

Eventually, he calms himself down a little, maybe just exhausted from the energy crying takes.

'I'm gonna get undressed so I can come in with you, is that okay?' I ask, pulling my hands from his.

He nods, still looking at the floor.

I unbuckle my knife holster and take it off carefully, then I pull off my skirt, my jacket, and then my jumper.

Mitch is still looking at the floor, tears in his eyes. He looks vacant. Like he's not quite there.

I turn the handle of the shower.

We sit in the bath, letting the shower come down on us, him between my legs, and my hands in his hair.

He still looks vacant, like he's not here in his mind. I can't hear anything from him.

Blood and dirt mix on the bath in front of him.

'Gonna wash your hair.' I tilt his head back so it's lying on my chest.

He holds his breath as the water hits his face, his heart is racing.

'I'm here,' I whisper, kissing the side of his head gently. 'You're safe.'

He screws his eyes shut as I wash his hair, breathing hard, tears running down his cheeks.

I remember our first shower together. It was actually before our first time, weirdly. We had dyed our hair together. He was wearing his binder, a skin-tone one that got wrecked with the dye.

'You're staring,' I had commented.

It was hard to tell if he turned red, his face was already covered in tracks of red dye. We were otherwise both naked.

'I – well you – I—'

'You're allowed to,' I laughed. It was a shy kind of laugh.

And then I pressed a kiss against his lips. A soft one, a slow one.

His hands held me close, resting on my lower back. My entire body seemed to be covered in goosebumps being this close to his, with this little on.

We knew things were changing between us.

I had washed his hair that night too. He had leaned into my hand as I did like a dog being patted. I had laughed at him hard, and he had been laughing too.

Now, I gently scratch his scalp as I wash his hair, but he doesn't move into it, and we don't laugh.

I wash his back. His cuts look more like they were intended to cause pain than cause damage.

He takes the sponge from me to do his front and along his legs. He scrubs so hard I think the new scars might fall off of him. The bruises scrubbed away like costume makeup.

He is red in the face, and his eyes look set, determined in their puffiness.

'Hey.' I place my hand on his. 'I think you got it.'

Then he starts to cry again. The water running down the drain is clear now, so I turn the shower off.

I grab the towel Oscar passed through for him and wrap it around his shoulders. He leans on my shoulder, sobbing. I kiss his head gently.

'Mitch,' I whisper, 'please tell me what happened.'

He presses his lips tightly together, holding back his sobs. He shakes his head hard.

'Okay.' I hold him. 'Okay, we don't have to talk right now.'

We sit there together. He sits naked on the floor. His hair is wet.

I take his towel and begin to rub at it to dry him off, brushing gently over every new mark.

I'm so glad we finally got him back but seeing what he had to endure before we saved him is brutal. Am I supposed to believe this was fate? This was some kind of plan or test that me and Oscar were destined to rescue him from? I don't know. I don't know what to believe anymore. And I don't know how Tyler is supposed to be punished for this.

But I don't think I care. Whoever is up there can shove whatever plan they have for him up their fucking arse – because I have a better one.

I bring my hand up to his face to wipe it from where it sticks to his burn marks. He catches it.

He stares at the ring sitting on my finger; the ring he bought me.

That got your attention, huh? I think.

He looks at me, confused.

I found it, I tell him. *In your drawer, with your speech.* I give him a little smile. *It was very sweet. And yes, I will. But we can talk about all that later, okay?*

He nods, then links his pinky around mine to promise me will. He gently strokes my face with his other hand, then tilts his head up. I can feel his tears against my cheeks when we kiss.

Chapter Thirty-Four

Radwa

Mitch's parents are there when he gets back with Ash, Phelan, Val, and Oscar.

I hear them talking to him for over an hour. His dad keeps telling him it's alright to talk about his feelings, to cry, to scream if he wants. He doesn't. He doesn't make a sound.

He's exhausted by the time they leave. They don't want to, but Wren's dad tells them he needs to stay here for his safety until we get rid of Tyler. They seem to realise they'd just be a liability.

I meet Mitch in the hallway on my way out of Lolly's room. I have to go and call their grandparents. No one has told them. Someone needs to get the message to their Dad too.

They wouldn't want their Mam to know. She would just make it about her, use it as a pity party. Lotta would probably want to visit but I don't know that inviting her, showing her into this house, telling her about this world would be my place.

If they don't wake up soon maybe I'll have to think about it, but that's not a decision I want to make now.

Mitch looks up when he sees me. His face is readable even if he's not saying anything

'They're not great, but they're stable again.' I look away for a moment. 'This morning they weren't great, but I called for Phelan and he got them sorted. It's a good sign they haven't dropped back since then.'

He gives me a smile and then sits down on the floor, nodding his head to the side for me to join him.

'You don't need to say anything, but once they're better, and Tyler is gone, we're gonna go on a run.' I tell him. 'You and me okay?'

He nods, swallowing hard.

I think I'm going to lose my voice if I scream as loudly as I need to right now.

I turn to Mitch. 'You know, Oscar thinks Lolly can hear us.'

He looks up.

I feel the corners of my mouth turn up, and my lips press together. 'Just thought you'd want to know.' Then I look at him again. I want to hug him.

I cross my arms over my chest giving myself a squeeze. He copies me. His smile is weary but he gives me a wink.

Mitch

When Radwa goes downstairs I make my way into Lolly's room.

They look so weird lying there. Not like Lolly. They're not smiling, or laughing, or cracking a joke. I don't think I realised how small they were until I saw them lying down. They'd probably punch me for that. Calling them short.

I sit on the edge of the bed next to them.

'Hey Lol,' I whisper.

My voice sounds hoarse. It barely makes a sound. I know everyone downstairs won't be able to hear me over the sound of each other's voices and thoughts.

'I'm back,' I tell them. 'Though I guess you didn't really know I was missing, right? Dammit, do you have to outdo me on everything?' I give their shoulder a nudge. 'I'm missing for a week only to find out you'd been passed out for just as long. We missed a lot. Val found the ring I bought her, and the little speech I had prepared. I wasn't there to tell her myself because I was with Tyler. He really did a number on me Lol. He hurt me, and—' My voice cracks and shakes but I keep telling them everything. 'He broke me Lol. And I – I really fucking need you. More than I've ever needed you before, because I need to talk to someone that's not gonna look at me like a kicked puppy. I need my best friend, so if you could please just open your eyes and wake the fuck up?' I laugh a little.

Then I look at them expectantly.

Silence.

They're plugged into a machine beside them. It beeps. Then it beeps again. I feel tears sliding down my cheeks for the millionth time today.

I reach down to kiss Lolly's forehead gently. 'Love you, Lol.'

I half expect them to open their eyes and sit up as my tears fall on them, like some dumb fucking movie. But they don't. Of course they don't. That only makes me cry harder.

Oscar

I find Mitch in Lolly's room in the clubhouse. I think he's been crying again. His face is too scarred and tear-stained to tell for sure.

'Hey.' I sit on the edge of Lolly's bed next to him. 'Are you feeling a bit better now? Well not better, but—'

He nods.

'The girls wanted me to tell you we're being put on lockdown together.'

Since Tyler needs the blood of freshly turned wolves, I've been under house arrest. Unable to go anywhere without Wren, Lycaon or Magnus' supervision. Mitch will be the same now that Tyler's been able to control him. We're going to be taken to mine since Tyler doesn't know where I live yet. I see his face tense, his teeth grind together.

'We don't need to talk about it. Or talk at all. So don't worry.'

I look at my hands in my lap. I feel sort of stupid. Anxious. I've never felt like that with him before, but I know he doesn't want to be around me right now.

He rolls his eyes and tuts loudly on hearing me think this then comes over to sit next to me, reaches for my hand and squeezes it.

'For the record, with the telepathy thing, I felt, or saw, a lot of what happened. And I get the gist of the rest of it. I mean I didn't see – I didn't see all of it. And it doesn't change how I think of you, other than the fact I now know you're insanely strong and your pain threshold is fucked. But I guess I just want you to know you don't need to feel like you have to explain it to me, but also you can talk without having to—'

He looks at me, face flushed, for a moment before pulling me into a hug.

He holds onto me tightly. He smells of my shampoo. I won't let go until he does. He rests his head in the crook of my neck and sighs. I put my hand in his hair and gently curl it around my fingers.

When he eventually lets go his eyes are wet.

He looks at me for a moment. I look at him.

I don't usually like people looking at my eyes like this. It's disconcerting. I don't really mind too much with him. Most of the pack I'm okay with.

His hair looks ruffled, and a strand is getting in the way of his stitches. I brush it from his face.

He grabs my face urgently as I do. 'Your eyes,' he whispers. His voice is a little hoarse.

I flutter my eyelashes dramatically. 'They're pretty, huh?'

'They were always pretty.'

Oh.

Okay then.

That's fine.

He flushes and looks down.

'I'm sorry,' he murmurs, leaning his head on my shoulder. 'I'm so fucking sorry Oscar. I just need you to know I'm sorry. I'm so sorry.'

He looks small. He's wearing clothes that don't fit him at all. My joggers finish somewhere on his shins. My hoodie is baggy on him.

I know he didn't mean to hurt me. I can feel it eating him up inside. He knows how much this will change the course of my life and it has left him at a loss for words.

'We're okay, Mitch. I promise.' I lean my head on top of his.

He smiles gently. 'See if you feel that way after the moon,' he whispers.

I groan just thinking about it. He opens his arms and pulls me into his chest for a hug. His arms are so strong. He gives these earth-shattering hugs.

I can hear him thinking about my eyes again, how perversely beautiful the evidence of me being turned is, and so I whisper into his embrace, '"Those who find ugly meaning in beautiful things are corrupt without being charming."'

'I'm just back, and you wanna talk about my faults?' His chest vibrates softly as he chuckles. 'You cracked the code then. Just figured it was a cool way of letting you know my favourite quote.'

I smile against him, feeling his cross necklace press into my shoulder as he tilts his chin slightly upward to rest his head on mine.

'I'm so glad you're okay,' I whisper into the crook of his neck. I feel a lump in my throat and swallow hard around it. 'Well, maybe not, but getting there and alive at least.'

He laughs again. God I've wanted to hear him laugh for weeks. It's deep, low, under his breath. It's understated.

Then he is silent for a minute. I can hear his heart hammering against his chest.

Then he kisses my head gently. 'I'm glad you're alive too. What Tyler did, all of it, it was—' He swallows. His heart is pounding. I sit up, holding his hand in mine. 'The idea that I had killed you... He told me to *kill* you.'

Wren thought he might've. She said it wouldn't work because we're mates. It's one of the only times a wolf can easily disobey their alpha.

'And I left Lolly and Radwa like that – I – and he – and even when – I...' His eyes are teary as he shrugs.

'Can't speak about it yet?' I finish for him.

He swallows and shakes his head, and then squeezes my hand tight.

Chapter Thirty-Five

Wren

I'm on guard duty with Val tonight. The adults from *my* pack are patrolling in the woods, worried Tyler might attack someone else.

I find Mitch and Oscar with their arms around each other in Lolly's room.

'I heard voices,' I say, walking in with Val and Radwa.

Mitch nods. 'Well, Radwa said they might hear me, and I dunno, I thought it might help, but they're either being an asshole or waiting to make a scene so…'

Radwa gives him a smile. Val laughs, sitting on his other side. She laces their fingers together. He winks at her when his fingers brush her ring.

We're quiet for a moment.

'Does anyone have any weed?' Mitch asks with a sniffly sort of laugh.

'You are on more than enough drugs right now!' Phelan shouts through from where he's lying in the spare room with Harley, resting his eyes for a moment.

Mitch groans. 'Tea then. Does anyone have any tea?'

Oscar gets up to make him some, and Mitch lays his head in Val's lap.

'Magnus dropped off board games to keep us entertained,' I scoff half-heartedly. As if we need entertainment right now. I think we could all sleep for a year.

'Well, I need something to keep me awake.' Val claps her hands together. 'What do we have?'

We position ourselves together in a circle in the hallway just outside of Lolly's room. Their door is open as if they are going to stand up and walk out of bed to join us. Their monitor beeps rhythmically next to them.

That has to count for something, right? Their heartbeat is regular again.

Radwa is half asleep but occasionally shakes herself awake every time it makes a slightly different noise than usual.

Mitch isn't saying much. He keeps looking off to the corner of the room, and then his thoughts go blank. We can't hear anything, and it's not that he's shutting us out. He's trying, he's really trying, just to act like nothing happened. Only it did.

Val pats his arm gently indicating it's his turn with the cards. He reads out the prompt we have to answer with ours, then goes back to staring at the corner.

I look at him to check in, and I see him catch it at the same moment I do.

There's a smell.

A strong one.

Of Red Bull, and Old Spice deodorant barely masking BO.

He looks at me.

I nod. It's him.

Get in Lolly's room. Now, I tell him and Oscar.

Radwa looks up.

I hand her her bow from next to me. *You stay with them.*

Keep guard, I tell her as if there is any chance of her leaving Lolly's side right now.

I put my hands on both of Phelan's shoulders. *Hide. I mean it, no matter what you hear. Hide. Right now.* I turn to Harley. *Both of you. And try to get Dad here.*

Dad is right. They're just kids. They have no part in this.

Val is already tying her knife holster to her leg. I pick up my staff, tucking it under my arm.

We stick close to the wall as we make our way downstairs. I can hear him rattling at the door. I stop myself just behind it, back flat to the wall, motioning for Val to go into the kitchen.

He bursts through with an almighty rattle of the frame, then turns behind him to make sure he's not being tailed. Stupid of him to not look ahead.

I don't really think before I act. I've always been like that. People think it's calculated, but I'm entirely driven by emotion.

All I know is that I can hear Mitch's heart racing. I can hear Oscar trying to comfort him. Radwa pulling an arrow out of her quiver. I act instinctually.

The bo staff sweeps in a circle. It comes up and over my shoulder in an arc to hit him over the skull as he turns back around. He puts both hands up to block it, exposing his vulnerable throat, his sunken chest.

Something darts underneath my arm from behind me. The silver knife glistens through the dark room, reflecting the dim lights that silhouette Tyler against the door. Spinning. Sparkling.

It scuffs past me.

In the reflection of the window beside the entrance, Val leans forward, her fingers reaching out, her hair splayed across her face from the momentum behind her shoulders and her arm.

It hits him square in the chest. There's no sound effect, no thud or squelch, to know he's been struck. His face is impassive, shadowy. I don't think it hits hard enough to pierce his heart... but the back end of my staff is drawn to it like a magnet. It swings up in a semicircle, underarm. It seems to move of its own accord, and instinct takes over.

Then I push the hilt, hard.

Tyler coughs and blood comes up.

His eyes are set on me, his cold, blue eyes, when his heartbeat stops. His legs collapse under him.

I expect him to fall straight back but he doesn't. He folds in on himself, then topples to the side.

The whole while his eyes are set on me. His lips part slightly, coated with bright red blood that sizzles as it drips onto the cold stone floor.

The silver knife in his heart boils it from the inside out.

I don't think I quite made the connection until now between the man who tortured Mitch, who killed Mel, the monster, the rapist... and the boy I was in love with, the boy I wrote every excuse in the book for, the boy I saw through rose-tinted glasses.

Don't get me wrong, he was a horrible, horrible man who deserved to die, who deserved a lot worse than the release death offered him, but I never expected to be the one behind it.

It's his eyes that get me. I thought they would close, but they don't. If anything they bulge open. And then they're set on me, as he lays there on the floor.

Before I have time to look at Val another figure comes through the door, but this one is safe. This one smells like hand sanitiser and Joop aftershave. He pulls me to his chest, holding the back of my head with one large hand.

'Mags!' he calls behind him. 'Need a hand in here.'

He holds me tightly in place as three more figures rush past me, as if he can protect me from everything going on around me, even though the threat is over.

It's over. My eyes feel wet, and it's not in sadness or in mourning, it's in… relief. It's over.

I feel my legs buckle under me. My dad pulls me tighter. I hear five sets of footsteps on the stairs.

'We've got this, kiddo.' Dad places a kiss on the top of my head. 'You girls go and look after each other now. We'll work on getting rid of this for you.'

When he lets me go I see Val next to me, with Radwa. Mitch is wrapped up in her embrace. She cradles his head in her arms, his face is hidden in her hair. She places two gentle kisses on his temple.

Standing in front of where Tyler was lying: Oscar, Lycaon, Ash, Phelan, Harley and Magnus are lined up, blocking him from my sight.

Val's eyes are wide, and… golden. Both of her eyes are golden.

Radwa looks pale.

My dad takes his place beside Magnus, who untangles Dad's sword from his rope dart and hands it to him. They all sort of spin as I turn to look at them.

'I – I can help,' I hear myself saying, even though I am screaming at myself that I *cannot* do that. I just *killed* someone.

Mitch swallows, straightening up. Then pulls back from Val.

'You have,' he promises, patting my arm, then taking a deep breath in and turning to look at the other men. He shouldn't have to do this either. He shakes his head. 'I want to.'

Val

I want to run. My hands are shaking when Radwa, Wren and I are ushered into Lolly's room.

I sit with my back against their bed, Radwa on one side of me, and Wren on the other.

Wren sits with a bucket between her legs. She looks green. I feel it.

Radwa hands her a hair bobble off of the floor to tie her braids back.

I can't really find the words to say anything.

I'm glad the guys are getting rid of – the… remnants.

I'd do it again, don't get me wrong. It's sort of thrilling knowing that he's gone, but killing someone is… something you don't prepare for.

Wren looks at me. Her eyes, like my own, flooded with liquid gold the moment Tyler's heart stopped beating. They still glow, glistening with tears, despite their tired expression. She leans her head on my shoulder, and I rub her back. She is still wearing padded armour over her hips, ribs and arms.

'Maybe we should take this off.' I tug at the strap. 'That can't be helping.'

She lifts her arm and I help her undo the buckle. Then throw the pads across the room.

I undo the straps of my knife holster.

The three of us sit together like that in silence for a moment, holding each other's hands, waiting, hoping that this is really the end of it all.

We fall asleep on each other like that, or we must because I wake up to a knock at the door.

The front door, downstairs.

I get up to answer it. Lifting a knife from the floor beside me.

The guys appear to have snuck back in after their detour because they are sleeping on the floor of the living room when I get down.

Mitch sits up hearing me, wiping sleep out of his eyes. 'Who is that?' he asks.

I shake my head.

He pushes himself up and comes to answer with me.

I position myself in front of him. *I* am the one who is armed.

When I open the door, a girl is standing there.

Her hair is greasy and matted to the point that the bright ginger now looks a murky brown colour. She looks gaunt. Her cheeks are lined with dull freckles. She has sunken eyes. One is green, and one is brown.

Heterochromia. Her brother used to have it too.

There is a deep black cut in her arm. It is gangrenous. Not healing at all.

It's impossible. I was at – I saw the – I hold onto the door frame for support.

'Mel?' Mitch asks behind me. I hear his voice falter.

'Where is he?'

∼

To Be Continued

Epilogue

Radwa

I wake up when Val closes the door behind her. I look around deliriously. I can't see anything. I pat around in the dark until I find a hoodie and put it on, pulling the hood up over my hair.

I can hear someone knocking at the door. I should go downstairs with Val. She shouldn't answer it alone, it's not safe.

I turn on the bedside table light so I can see the path to the door and make sure I don't stand on Wren or her sick bucket.

She is sound asleep on the floor. She doesn't even stir when the light goes on. Good, let her sleep. She needs it.

I'm about to step over her when I hear a noise coming from behind me.

'Radwa?' Lolly's voice is hoarse when they speak.

My eyes instantly wet.

Thank you so much for reading!

If you enjoyed *The Blood of The Covenant*, I would love it if you could **leave a rating or review** on Amazon, Goodreads, or social media.

Reviews for books by independent authors are incredibly helpful and important!

The final part of the duology, *The Water of The Womb*, is currently being worked on and will release in the future.

Join my mailing list to receive updates on the sequel as well as events, fan art submissions and more!

Check out my website at
https://ajnmbooks.squarespace.com/

About the Author

Andy J N McRae grew up in a small town in the Highlands of Scotland which he has spent most of his life describing as 'just North of Inverness'. He spent many happy childhood years, and less happy teenage years, reading and writing books that allowed him to escape such a place, only to finally do so at the age of eighteen when he went to Edinburgh to study English Literature. At this time a true love for queer gothic literature grew within him, which he eventually wrote his dissertation on. After spending four years there obtaining his degree, he decided – in a temporary lapse of judgement – to move back to the very same town he was raised in. He claims this is because the landscape inspires his writing but everyone knows it's because he is a dreadful granny's boy. He now happily resides there, writing fantastical stories based in the local housing estates – because after all, that is the landscape that inspires him most.

        facebook.com/ajnmbooks
        instagram.com/ajnmbooks
        tiktok.com/@ajnmauthor

Acknowledgments

Though I have already thanked them in the dedication, I think that some of my lovely 'mates' warrant a more personal show of gratitude.

So, in order of appearance:

Thank you to Hannah, Clara and my wonderful fiancé Luke – thank you for keeping me somewhat sane through high school.

Next, I'd like to thank Charlie and Beaux who had the misfortune of meeting me in my late teens while I was still getting to know myself. Thanks to both of you for bearing with me, and listening to me hyper fixate on my own little imaginary world for the past six years.

Then there are those who entered my life later and are still attempting to help me hold onto my remaining shreds of sanity. To Liam, Kai, and a little group of friends affectionately dubbed the 'PolyFAMorous Whores' by the name of our group chat, I love you all dearly.

I'd also like to thank my parents for fostering my love of reading through countless trips to the library as a child and my truly amazing grandparents whose stories will never get old. Particularly my grannies – Den and Brenda – whose houses I always seem to envision when creating my characters' homes after spending most of my childhood in them. And of course, there's my granda Gerry who always influences at least one character in every story I write because he's… well just that – a character.

Additionally, I'd like to thank my wonderful production team.

My editor Jasper Chatfield for his patience with my constant *shrugs* and his very thorough write ups.

The man behind my cover design is my dear friend Liam Urquhart – as mentioned previously – who managed to create a cover I love from a photograph, and rambled thoughts while I petted his cats.

Thank you to Newt and Lewy (aforementioned cats) for their moral support and *valuable* contributions.

Photography credits go to my fiancé Lukas Clydesdale who came into the kitchen to see me concocting the most foul-smelling fake blood, rolled his sleeves up and jumped on board.

I also had a fantastic team of sensitivity readers behind me, my friends Kai and Beaux has exclusive access in return for flagging any concerns. And then there were those professionally hired: Ash Hawthorne, Faith Inyang, Selin Balci and Siam Khandaker, who all showed remarkable tact when dealing with such sensitive topics.

Finally, I'd like to thank all the trans and queer trailblazers who pathed the way for me to release this novel. And to the trans youth reading this: I see you; I've felt your pain and I promise you we will get through this together.

Resources

If you or someone you love has been impacted by any of the heavier themes in *The Blood of The Covenant*, help is available.

Rape:

- Rape Crisis Scotland: 08088 010302 / https://www.rapecrisisscotland.org.uk/
- RASASH (Rape and Sexual Abuse Service Highland): Text line 07451 288080 / https://www.rasash.org.uk/

Self Harm/Suicidal Ideation:

- Mikeysline: https://www.mikeysline.co.uk/
- Suicide Bereavement UK: https://suicidebereavementuk.com/immediate-support-resources/

Queer-Specific Support:

- Mermaids: https://mermaidsuk.org.uk/
- Gendered Intelligence: https://genderedintelligence.co.uk/
- Switchboard: https://switchboard.lgbt/
- AKT: https://www.akt.org.uk/

Endometriosis UK: https://www.endometriosis-uk.org/
Neurodiverse Self Advocacy: https://ndsa.uk/content/
OCD Action: https://ocdaction.org.uk/
Better Help Online Therapy: https://www.betterhelp.com/

Also, Lolly isn't the only one passionate about getting people to learn more *Gàidhlig*. So, this is a friendly reminder that *Gàidhlig* is a *living* language worth learning and engaging with. Check out places like Learn Gaelic and *Soghal Mòr Ostaig* to learn or find local groups if you're in Scotland!

www.ingramcontent.com/pod-product-compliance
Ingram Content Group UK Ltd.
Pitfield, Milton Keynes, MK11 3LW, UK
UKHW032035260625
460128UK00001B/1